Leaflings

A Trilogy

Darren Shell

Fideli Publishing

ISBN: 978-1-60414-219-8

Fideli Publishing
Martinsville, IN, USA

Cover by Fideli Publishing
Cover Castle Art by Andy Simmons, USA ©2004

Leaflings

BOOK I

The Prophesy Rhymes Of Tal Kator

Other Works by the Author

Fiction

Lost Treasure

Graveyard Tour

Death Wish

Nonfiction

The History of Dale Hollow Lake

A Stone's Throw
(The History of the Game of Marbles
In Tennessee and Kentucky)

The Big Ones
(The World Record Smallmouth Bass
Of Dale Hollow Lake)

Video

Journey to Old Willow Grove
(A Historical look at Dale Hollow Lake)

Find out more:

www.FideliPublishing.com

www.DaleHollowGravedigger.com

The Prophesy Rhymes of Tal Kator

From the Book of Lore, the Dark Ages

Through forest and field,
Fen and glade,
A harsh and terrible
Sound is made.

Never a likely
Tale's been told,
In Leafling lore
From days of old.

There came a cry
From distant north,
And Devil Troll
Came raging forth.

He cast his spell
With poison rain,
And Tal Kator
Cried tears of pain.

And Quoth, said Troll,
"Nevermore!
Will Leafling toil
In Tal Kator!"

…and the Prophesy begins.

1

In the far reaches of the Deep Forest, lived a very large colony of Leaflings. It wasn't the very farthest depths of the woods, but it was far enough that most of the King's men and the wandering wizards never bothered to travel there. It was a fantastic glen, or valley, with the most placid small lake in the center. This body of water was fantastically beautiful, and for the peaceful village of Tal Kator, it was perfect.

The Leaflings of Tal Kator lived all around the confines of this sparkling lake that they named *Mirаré*... meaning mirror. There was a great waterfall that flowed into it that added vibrant sounds, and the beautiful swirling currents engulfed the Leaflings in very nutrient-rich and oxygen-filled water. It was a place of great beauty, with the woodland animals bouncing to and fro in their perfect little woodland setting. Its waters soothed body and soul for the Leaflings, and they all considered it the absolute Utopia of the world. And although many a wolf had trodden his way through this seemingly desolate section of forest, the existence of these special creatures has somehow remained a mystery for centuries beyond account.

It is no small wonder that the keen nose of a savvy wolf would not have discovered these vibrant little beings of the woods. But, the fact that they are not actually mammals could attest for that.

That's the trouble with these spiritual little creatures. They are not really animals...they are not really plants. They are somewhat of a combination. It seems impossible that such vibrant and strange life could exist in the Deep Forest, but for many centuries they lived happily without interaction with mankind.

In the very early tongues of man, they were called *Myrtos,* a Greek term meaning small green plant. Some of the descendents of these creatures actually became *Myrtle*, which is a long-known and loved ground cover that grows in many varieties in many places in the world. Most Myrtle varieties are very low-slung and vine-like. Their beautiful violet blooms enhance the stark winter floor of most woodland settings where other plants dare not delve. They have ivy-like characteristics that make them quite well suited for their protective nature of hugging the forest floor, with their network of net-like coverings. Myrtle's ancient ancestors, the Leaflings, were not much different in appearance.

The Leaflings so resembled their Myrtle cousins, that if they chose to simply stand still...they would be completely camouflaged and totally unnoticed. Their skin—or bark—was very rough looking and dark in color, but its texture was much softer to the touch than it appeared to the naked eye. Even though it looked very rough and crude, it smoothed out like hair when touched, and was actually quite pleasant to experience. Their limbs—or legs and arms—were exceptionally thin to view. They, too, looked vine-like and seemed as gangly as ivy. But despite their skinny appearance, these creatures were remarkably strong and durable. A full-grown man could step directly upon their eight-to-ten inch bodies, and they would simply bend to meet the weight.

The head of a Leafling is much the same as that of man. They have facial features that, at times, show quite vibrantly. And still other times, they could seem totally nonexistent. That's what makes them so hard to discern in the woods. You simply cannot see them if they choose to be unseen. All they really have to do is stand still and act…well…like a plant.

These wonderful creatures have numerous leafy coverings upon them, and some have much more than others. Some even go through a leafless state like that of trees, but it is rarely seen in the winter months. They seem to shed these leaf-like hairs in summer as a cooling mechanism. Even in their leafless state, the Leaflings are still impossible to see when they choose. They just look like little sticks.

Another very special characteristic of these creatures is located on their fingers and toes. Where modern man grows toenails and fingernails, the Leaflings grow long and slender root-like appendages. They are used in the gathering of food. You see, the Leaflings do not eat…at least not with their mouth. When they need nourishment, they simply pause and push their roots into any soft soil. Sometimes a wet pile of leaves serves as quite a meal. Now granted, this takes much longer than the time we humans take to eat, but for a long-lived and durable Leafling, the earthy nutrients are well worth the wait. And the fact that they don't eat, means one more trait of survival…they do not leave *droppings.* Where there's no poop, there must not be creatures, and that alone could attest for their long secrecy.

There have been times, over the years, that drought has become a troublesome battle for the Leaflings. They can tolerate a very long dry spell, and still live through it without much discomfort. The dryness does take its toll, though. For instance, they become much more brittle and much less tolerant of the footsteps of man. They tend to break, when dry. Also, their voices become almost nonexistent. Even when well lubricated, the voice of a Leafling is raspy and dry…like the rubbing of wood…the rustling of leaves. It is almost a loud whisper.

Their speech can be heard by those trained in the listening, but if one was not prepared to hear such noises, they would seem quite normal and woods-like. But, to the listening of the trained ear, the Leaflings have developed a language much like that of the very early English. Some of their words are of Latin decent, and some of Greek. Some other influences have changed their speech over the years, much like that of all walks of life. Language changes with the life around it, and the Leaflings have life all around them. Even the birds and animals played a part in their language.

Despite their developed language, the Leaflings live a fairly primitive sort of life. Their lifestyle resembles that of the Native American Indians. They can live from the land, and protect their own with the fierce anger of the toughest of warriors. They even carve their own tiny arrowheads and build their own arrows which they shoot from their own limbs like a sling. No bow and string…just their own limbs and the waxy vine-like twine of a root system at their fingertips. They can actually bend those roots and use their appendages as fingers, or stretch them out as tentacle-like whips with many uses. They can be ferocious little blokes when they want to be. They are like much-developed spiders, with limbs flailing and snapping back and forth with razor-like precision. Thankfully, they are quite calm and peace-loving creatures most of the time, which might be attributed to their lack of sexual differences. These Leafling creatures are both male… and female.

To reproduce, the Leafling parent simply leaves its root-like fingernails immersed in soil and waits. In a matter of a few days, tiny roots sprout from their fingers, and with a quick, intentional snap, they break off a piece of themselves…thus allowing a portion of themselves to root on its own and come to life. It is a very emotional time in the life of a Leafling. It is said to be quite painful, but very rewarding for a parent to fulfill its destiny…to bare the life of another. It is a choice made by the Leafling when the time is right, which is considerably different from the mammal world, where opportunity sometimes knocks at very inopportune and awkward times.

This reproductive nature seems to bring both the feminine qualities to the creature as well as masculine. It is said that this brings a greater and deeper understanding of living things than is accomplished through normal male/female conditions. They are normally *in tune* to the influences of the world that deal with the complexities of life. They are, in fact, quite peaceful creatures most of the time…and go way out of their way to avoid any sort of conflict. But Peace, my friends, isn't always peaceful, and it isn't always achieved through peaceful means. Peace…can sometimes only be upheld by force…by war…by some of the most unmerciful means imaginable. And, in the name of Peace…and because of the persistence of one disgusting old Troll, the floor of the Deep Forest was about to erupt.

2

The morning sun pierced the hazy morning sky and bounced from the surface of the Miraré. Young Kimbli and his Leafling parent, Tulas, sat peacefully on the shoreline with their toes pushed deeply into the muddy bank. They watched as tree swallows sailed overhead and elegantly soared over the lake surface, searching for tiny insects. Squirrels scampered from tree to tree, barking back and forth with one another, and bluebirds sang their morning song. The age-old branches of the great chestnut stretched out over the edge of The Great Falls, offering shade and shelter. In the distance, the chuckling voices of young Leaflings floated on the morning air, as they pounced and played merrily on the forest floor. Spring was in the air in Tal Kator, and life was as fresh as the morning dew.

Tulas looked down proudly at his young Leafling by his side. With a crooked smile, his mind danced back to the day when the little one was born. It seemed like only yesterday that he had pushed his hand deep into the soil and waited. Days passed as he silently and patiently sat as all vigilant Leafling parents must. He could easily remember the tingling sensation of new roots beginning to form, and could almost hear that dreaded, yet rewarding, snap of his arm breaking…creating life. Young Kimbli was the light of his life, and he loved him more than life itself.

Now, before this story goes any farther, one must consider how Leaflings were addressed by man. The Leaflings were referred to as males, (him, he, his, etc.) because they tend to look male. As has already been stated, they are not just male, but female as well. Many of their mannerisms are much more female than male, but overall, they appear male at first glance. Most have had trouble referring to them without gender references, so for a lack of a better way, most refer to them as male. Although at times, it isn't fitting at all.

For instance, the young Leaflings affectionately call their parents Ori. It is derived from the Latin term Oriri, meaning origin…or parent. The terms *Mom* and *Dad* do not fit, and Ori (to the Leaflings) is an address held in high regard. It is a playful and loving term, loved by one and all.

Kimbli was in his usual morning doldrums, impatiently waiting for his morning feeding to end so he could join his Leafling friends in their morning frolic. The young Leaflings, and sometimes old ones, love to play in the morning. They have many little games of fancy that nearly all contain swinging from tree limbs or swimming in the lake. One even consists of throwing one another into the air by using their long fingers to weave nets between themselves like firemen catching someone in a tarp. The Leaflings play with all their hearts, and few members of the forest could keep up when they chose to play along. Some of the young squirrels would play for awhile, but would shy away when the throwing got a little too close to the water. So, by now, young Kimbli had heard enough singing and playing to be well annoyed by the wait.

"Come on, Kimbli," yelled one of the youngsters. "Don't be such a stick-in-the-mud."

"Can I Ori, pleeeeeeease," he asked, with the sweetest sad-eyes he could conjure.

"Alright," said Tulas, "I suppose you've had enough. You may go." Tulas chuckled as Kimbli jerked his feet from the soil and scurried off. "Stay away from the old Apple Tree!" he shouted, in his raspy Leafling voice. Within seconds, the little one was five feet in the air and laughing out loud along with his friends. And, the floor of the Deep Forest was glad.

Tulas eventually pulled his feet from the soil and made his way across the clearing to the edge of the forest. He slowed his pace as he passed the old Apple tree. Some of the old Leaflings were enjoying a "good soaking" at the old Apple. The old Apple was a favorite destination among the old timers, and was quite popular as a local hang-out. Last year's apples had fallen and fermented upon the forest floor, and the old Leaflings loved the fermented soil like mankind loves the effects of a fine barrel of ale or wine. They were having a right-jolly old time as Tulas approached.

"A bit early to be hitting the fruit, Ducah," smarted Tulas to one of the barkies. The term *barky* was used by younger Leaflings to poke fun at the older crowd. "You barkies can always be found near here."

"My purpose," suggested Ducah, with a drunken smile, "is purely medicinal, and nothing more! Me old boughs hurt me so, you know!"

"Yes, yes, of course," said Tulas, "how could I be so judgmental? Do accept my humble apologies, dear friend." Tulas smiled his crafty smile and raised a knowing eyebrow. "Carry on, my friends.....as you were!"

The old blokes continued their conversations, laughing to and fro as Tulas strolled past, chuckling to himself. Today was a good day. The young ones were frolicking playfully and the barkies were happy doing what they do best, and Tulas was just glad to be a part of it. Tal

Kator had all the comforts of a warm civilization, and all the serenity of the most remote and natural portions of the wood, and life seemed to float along with the sweetest of harmonies. Life was pure and simple here…just as life is supposed to be.

Tulas reached his destination and waited patiently on the rock overhang, just outside a small cave. He watched as a number of young ones hung from the old Chestnut and slung others into the vibrant waters of the Miraré. They laughed and played as if there was no tomorrow. Today, he wished he could play along, but knew that Azir would be ready for his teachings.

Tulas was a faithful student of the elder Leafling by the name of Azir. Azir was the oldest and wisest of all the Leaflings and carried a weight of knowledge that seemed to burden him beyond his years. Knowledge can be a great and terrible weight to carry. Some of the happiest creatures one could ever meet in this world are just plum stupid. That sounds harsh, but sometimes, ignorance is bliss. Sometimes, the wiser one becomes, the more worried one becomes…and vise-versa. Sometimes knowledge and destiny become too entwined, and Azir was a very knowledgeable individual.

Today was to be just another day of lessons and spiritual work for Tulas. He attended a meeting several days a week to learn the teachings of Leafling lore. Leaflings rarely ever documented anything on paper or stone. They chose, like many civilizations, to simply relay, from one to another, the important occurrences of a very old civilization. They learned…from word of mouth…from old-to-young…and that seemed to be enough. It was history from folklore…and folklore from history, and it served this community well for generations.

"Come, Tulas," came the coarse voice of old Azir, "we have much to cover today." Tulas stepped beneath the rock ledge and found Azir in his usual meditating position of setting with all fours pushed into the soil and eyes closed. Azir had parented Leaflings more then once, and had lived long enough to re-grow his hands to full potential. It was rare for a Leafling to parent more than once, and certainly, most that had, did not live long enough to fully recover use of their limbs. Azir was well preserved for his age and carried himself well as the wise and respected individual that he had become. He had taken it upon himself to educate the colony and had also made great strides in broadening the language spoken here in Tal Kator. His teachings of Faith warmed the hearts of all the Leaflings, and he was as loved as he was respected. He had come to love Tulas as his own young and hoped that he would someday take over his position as Elder of the colony. Tulas was very much like Azir in his spirituality, and the two had an uncommonly close relationship as friends.

"You look tired today, Azir," spoke Tulas with a concerned glance. "Would you like to carry out our lesson here?"

"The Shard will strengthen me," Azir replied. "I will feel better when we arrive."

"Alright, my barky friend," smiled Tulas, "have it your way. To the Shard we go! I could use a sip from the falls myself. It should be an excellent walk on this fine day. The little ones are making waves as we speak."

Tulas extended a supportive arm to Azir, and the two slowly made their way along the stony path from Azir's abode to the shelter beneath The Great Falls. The jagged rocks along the path were worn beautifully smooth by the countless touchings of Leafling hands, and the greenery of trees and plants seemed to creep only close enough to offer their beauty to passers-by. The two paused at a long row of daffodils and admired the rich yellow blooms dripping with morning dew in the bright morning sun. "We are fortunate," said Azir, quietly, "to live near such beauty…and take the time to see it."

"I will accept that as my first lesson of the day." Tulas smiled as he spoke and continued his trek down the path. It wasn't long before the path ended at the base of the rock bluff that overlooked the Miraré and supported the falling water of The Great Falls. As Tulas suspected, the young ones were dangling hand from hand from the Old Chestnut and slinging one another out into the lake with a splash. Their chuckling voices seemed to please Azir, and he called out to them, "I see you are giving the Old Chestnut a workout this morning. Don't be too hard on the old rascal, he needs his rest."

The young ones hardly slowed down long enough to hear the old Leafling's words, and it appeared that the Old Chestnut enjoyed the attention of having the little ones crawling and hugging all about him. Even if the old tree could talk, it's doubtful he would have any objections.

Their path continued along the water's edge. It narrowed considerably where the bluff met the water, and the two hugged closely to the rock wall. The path meandered along the bluff and up to the waters of the Great Falls. The water was crisp and clear and very cool to the touch. The two paused at a bench ledge and sat there soaking up the tiny drops of mist in the air. "There is no greater place in the world than right here," exclaimed Tulas, eyes closed with enjoyment. "This water soothes the soul. It rejuvenates me."

"It rejuvenates us all, Tulas," said Azir. "The water, the soil, the stones of this cave…they are the life source of the Leaflings. We are as much a part of this place as it is a part of us. Our beautiful home is our life." Azir often spoke his spiritual thoughts aloud, and Tulas sometimes shunned them as just a little too deep for him. "Yeah, yeah," joked Tulas, "and the sun and the moon and the stars…I think you've been over at the Old Apple with the rest of the barkies."

Azir shook his head and wondered what the youth of this world was coming to. "Come along, Tulas," he barked with a frown, "there are many lessons I must try to pound into your head. Your Ori's head was hard as an oak, and I don't believe the branch has fallen far from the tree." Tulas smiled at the old one's insults and helped him on into the cavern behind the falls.

Part of the lake extended back into the cavern behind the falls. The reflection of the morning sun from the lake surface helped to light up the stone room that the two Leaflings had entered. It was a very large room with many passageways extending into the deep darkness of the cave. The two instinctively made their way to the center of the cave and stopped at the foot of a large stalagmite protruding from the ground. The top of the stalagmite had been cut flat, and upon it sat a beautiful, sparkling, purple stone. Both Leaflings dropped to their knees and bowed their heads in prayer, and both recited, in unison, a portion of an age-old rhyme known as *The Lay of the Amethyst Stone*. Their raspy voices echoed through the cool darkness of the cave, and they opened their hearts and minds as they spoke.

From fiery night it fell
As if from burning Hell.
It scorched into the ground
To places still unfound.
And from disaster came
Life without a name.

They pulled their roots from land
And walked on foot and hand.
And raised by human fist
Came the Shard of Amethyst.

Azir began a very low and deep rumble of a chant. Tulas joined in harmony. The faint light from the pool's reflection was piercing the Amethyst Stone and reflecting vibrant, pale-purple light inside the cave. In the purple darkness, the two meditated and absorbed the radiant energy of the Shard. At last, Azir spoke aloud, "Long live the Literati'," and Tulas then spoke the same.

After a few moments of silence, they raised their heads and stood. Azir slowly walked to the edge of the water inside the cave and seated himself with his feet and toes extended out into the cool water. "Tell me, Tulas," called Azir, "what you remember of the Literati' scholars. And tell me," he said, "…as you would tell Kimbli."

Tulas joined his ancient friend at the edge of the pool. His heart swelled at the mention of his young one, and he smiled the same crooked smile as he had earlier in the day with Kimbli. "I have been working with Kimbli for many days, and he has absorbed his lessons well. Shall I start from the beginning, Azir?"

"From whence we came," he replied. The old Leafling bowed his head and listened closely as his old roots soaked up the refreshing waters of the Miraré.

Tulas cleared his raspy throat and prepared for his speech. Since the Leaflings rarely put words on paper or stone, the precise reciting of historical events was treated with deep regard, and Tulas took every effort to relay his teachings with the utmost perfection.

At last, he spoke. "Long before the awakening of the Leaflings, the Literati' scholars studied the ways of the world, and wrote volumes of spiritual lore and wisdom from the days of old."

He paused and searched his mind for the proper words. He finally collected himself and spoke again. "Our creed states *from disaster came…life without a name*…and from disaster, we did in fact come. There is a very rare condition that occurs in this world. From the far reaches of outer space, meteors…balls of fiery burning mass…enter the Earth's atmosphere. It was during one of these rare times that one particular meteor plummeted deeply into the Earth's crust. Its fiery mass pushed itself hundreds of feet into the soil, melting its way through rock and clay. It came to rest deep below what is now the Miraré. Its scorching core produced steaming gases that belched and sizzled their way to the surface, causing large tunnel-like passageways that culminated in the cavern behind the falls.

The meteor had enormous power…huge radiant energy. The forest floor that lay disrupted and scorched in jumbled and turbulent piles began to re-grow. Life forms that once existed….now evolved. The Deep Forest became rich with life…and our *roots pulled from land... and walked on foot and hand.* Our colony became known as Tal Kator. *Tal* is derived from the Greek term *Telesma,* meaning *a religious rite, or charm. Kator* is derived from the Greek term *Kata-strephein,* meaning *disaster,* or *catastrophe.* Our name literally means *Life Created from Disaster.* The Leaflings…had awakened."

Old Azir smiled quietly as he absorbed Tulas' words. He was proud of how Tulas had accepted his teachings, and enjoyed the listening of the tales of old.

"The Literati'," continued Tulas, "sensed the immediate changes in the old forest. Being in tune with nature and the spirit of the forest, these spiritual and scholarly people of the church came forth and raised the first-born Leaflings…or *Myrtos*, as they were called. It is from the loving gift of these ancient scholars and holy people that we speak and live with the very true harmonies of the forest. Although we worship the life-giving properties of the fiery meteor, we worship the Literati' for their generous gift of the parental raising given to our ancestors. It is the Literati' that took us under their wing and raised us as their own. It was they who showed us the true spirit of the forest…the true love of life…the path of enlightened living. To them, we owe our existence."

"Well done, Tulas," suggested Azir, "you have listened well. There is much more to tell, but we shall get to that." The old Leafling paused for a moment and dangled his toes. "We must cover more of the Amethyst Stone today. Let's see…let me collect my thoughts. Are you in frame of mind to listen?"

"Most certainly," replied Tulas, "as long as you shall speak." And there they sat…young Leafling and mentor, student and teacher…friends reciting history and learning life. And in the pale-purple darkness of this ancient cave, two Leaflings were glad.

Azir again spoke, “The Literati’ began to fear that mankind would discover the Leaflings…and more importantly, the Amethyst Stone. There is much more to the Amethyst Stone than just…”

At that very moment, a hush fell over the outside forest floor. The Leaflings had a way of *shushing* one another when danger arose. It was much like when birds sense something out of place and fly. When one flies, they all do. When Leaflings sense danger, they quietly make a hushing sound, and the closest Leafling then does the same. In this way, a wave of wind-like precaution flowed through the colony and looked like nothing more than a cool breeze drifting over the forest floor. When danger passed, life would carry on as it had before the incident. It was simple, yet very effective.

“It’s probably just that band of stupid crows again, Azir,” spoke Tulas, with a frown. Crows were a common nuisance with the Leaflings, and the Leaflings tried to evade them whenever possible. They really weren’t too much of a problem for an older Leafling, but they could be very dangerous to a young one. The problem with crows is that they are stupid. They have virtually no language of their own, other than a few *caws* and *cackles,* but no real distinguishable verbal skills at all. Most of the creatures of the forest have some sort of communication between them. The Leaflings had learned to communicate with many of those creatures, and had quite a relationship with most. Crows, however, were just stupid. They had a love of anything new or shiny. Their nests were full of completely useless items found on their journeys over the countryside. They just collected things or toyed with them on the forest floor, much like a cat plays with its prey. So, when crows came into contact with a Leafling, they might grab it with their sharp beak and toss it into the air…just to see what will happen. If it makes noise, so much the better. And if it fights back a little…great! A properly delivered bite of a crow could snap a Leafling in two, so all Leaflings did their best to avoid them. Now, most adult Leaflings can overpower a crow if given the need, but some danger still impends, and Leaflings generally hushed and tried their best to look like a tree limb until any nearby crows moved on.

"Quiet!" exclaimed Azir at a whisper. "Listen closely."

There was utter quiet outside the falls for quite some time. Then, a startling squawk of a bird was heard. Shortly thereafter, a huge splash interrupted the peaceful surface of the Miraré, and Tulas and Azir raced for the entrance of the cave. As they peered from behind the falls, they saw a large black bird flopping in a panic in the center of the lake. "Stupid crow," said Tulas, with a scowl.

"No!" exclaimed Azir. "That's no crow! Summon the guards! Save him!" With a questioning look of surprise, Tulas raced from the cave and out into the light along the shores of the Miraré. "Help me!" he shouted, as he swam out into the lake. Numerous Leaflings piled in after him, creating a vine-like lifeline of hand-to-hand Leaflings. Tulas grasped the wing of the frantic bird, and with one swift pull, the line of Leaflings tugged the animal from the water in seconds. A wave of others swept the bird into the safety of the cave and stared in disbelief at the gaping wound in its chest. The bird coughed and gagged and held his wings to his bleeding breast.

Outside, the Leafling guards surrounded the entrance of the cave, with small spears shining in the sun. Many of the Leaflings from inside the cave raced outside to help the Leafling guards, and a barricade of green and brown little bodies reinforced the cave entrance. Inside the cave, another row of Leaflings was standing ready for any infiltration. Behind those, deep in the darkness of the cave, a grinding and clacking sound of wooden gears could be heard. File after file of Leaflings brought piles of wooden spears from deep within the cave. Meanwhile, a bloody and battered black bird was whaling uncontrollably.

In the far distance outside of the cave, a bewildered individual stood in amazement at what he had just witnessed. A leather slingshot fell from his hand as he stepped forward into the view of the cave. At that precise moment, twenty razor-sharp spears entered the ground at his feet as a warning.

Despite the fiery anger burning in his heart, he backed away in retreat. With a hateful growl, he carefully walked away, mumbling to himself, and wondering what in the world had just happened.

One day earlier…

The last few rays of daylight were disappearing over the mountains as a very large figure lit the kindling beneath his evening fire. The flickering fire pushed its orange glare against the bluff wall of the home of Tolokah, the Troll. He was well-known in the Deep Forest for his hateful and deceitful ways, and he was more commonly called Terrere', which is a Latin term meaning *terrible.* So, *Tolokah the Terrible* could be—and was—a very fitting name for the wretched individual that lived beneath this stone bluff in the distant edges of the forest.

Now, it is hardly fitting to tell of some of his rotten actions without first telling of the reason for his awful nature. Trolls, by most measurable means, are all disgusting and mean creatures. They are a product of a very simple, yet perplexing, trouble. It seems that the very core of every troll problem begins in troll-perpetuation—meaning trolls became extinct for a reason. It was a very calculated and long-foreknown plight that the trolls were forced to face. Quite simply, there were very, very few female trolls, and even those that did exist, would rarely bear a female offspring. So every troll male not only did without the comforts of female companionship but also continually connived and planned to gain himself a female. They all were constantly fighting for the love (and reproduction rights) of a female troll. This single problem could be studied by every psychologist in the country for years. Every action affects the next and strong repercussions followed every troll movement.

For instance, every whim of every female troll would be fought for, and if she did not receive it from one male, another would be standing in line begging for her hand. No marriages lasted, and of course, females were expected—and forced—to bear young to perpetuate the species. Often times, females would have eight or ten young male offspring with one male, and switch spouses to try to give birth to a female. It was a life-long feverish attempt to procreate life…and it caused deep aggression with all walks of troll life. There was simply no love or affection, what-so-ever. There was only a perpetual attempt to save troll-kind, and hate and loneliness and despair followed every troll.

Males would tarry off into the forest to live their lonely lives, and females battled the age-old question of what male could give her the most during her long and pregnant life. It was a life none should be forced to endure, and yet it happened. Great battles were fought over females, and many male trolls simply would rather die fighting for the hand of a female than face a life alone. It was truly a horrid existence for most trolls. Eventually, these very large and immensely strong beings that once could have been the leading race of the world…. left the face of the earth forever—but not before causing great havoc. Their bitterness ate at the very core of their souls for so long, that these creatures hated and battled everything in their path. Unfortunately for the rest of the world, they were also fairly intelligent beings…and intelligence and anger can be devastating to behold.

* * *

The very name, Tolokah, would strike fear in the hearts of many. Even in the cities of man, that name could put fright in the heartiest of warriors. Thankfully, Tolokah had little business in the cities of man. He loathed the sight of humans but did tolerate their being when he needed something from their far-more-civilized communities and lavishly-built homes and businesses. Even their politics and religion intrigued him, but his jealousy of man's perfect lives disallowed all but a little communication with them. He would stoop to their level when he needed something, and toss them aside if they should push themselves upon him. He had killed more men than he could remember, and cared not to try. They were barely worth his effort to kill…and he made no bones about. *Give me what I want…and you might live.*

By this time of evening, Tolokah had his feet propped up, and he was leaning back against the stone wall of his bluff. By his side sat a very large stone jug. He had numerous ones just like it, stacked safely along the base of the bluff wall. Inside these many jugs was a concoction he had made himself. It was known as troll-wine, but it was really more of a very strong fruit whiskey. Nearly all trolls love their wine, and Tolokah was no exception to the rule. His nights were spent delving deeply into his jugs of wine and desperately trying to find a way to capture the heart of the one and only female he had ever known (besides his own mother).

The female of Tolokah's dreams (and at least one hundred other male trolls) was and older woman by the name of Meilan. Despite the fact that she was a troll, she was quite beautiful. Troll women did not generally look as troll-ish as their male counterparts. Most were better than seven feet tall, and they carried their strong, but slender build with a very sensuous heir. Their attitudes were equally rotten to those of the males, but their looks were quite different. They were very much like hot, Neanderthal chicks…with an attitude.

Other than their remarkably strong arms, they looked quite human, and Meilan was the perfect specimen. She had very long, flowing black hair that hung well below her well-defined breasts, and her shapely hips gave every male a reason to fight for her hand. She had already given birth to six young males, but none had blemished her appearance in any way. She was still very desirable, despite the scarceness of other females. And, like clockwork, every twelve months she would give birth…with whomever male she chose.

Tolokah sat as he always did…angry almost to the point of tears and drunk as an in-port sailor. Although most would never have guessed it, he was really a deep individual. He would hum little songs he had written for Meilan, although he never believed she would ever hear them. No one ever saw the complexity in Tolokah's make up. As with most individuals from all walks of life, those tender sides rarely show themselves, and the rough and tumble ways shine because of their ease-of-display. Tolokah could have been a great individual, but his bitterness never failed to dominate. Still, there were times when old Terrere' wasn't so terrible. When the wine was flowing, and he truly longed for Meilan, some of the sweetest poetry flowed from his tongue. One of his lovely verses follows:

Cast upon the air,
Flows flawless brunette hair
And wafts its scent divine
Upon this skin of mine…

On skin of mine.

I would build for thee
Halls of tranquility.
and tend your every whim
To steal you neigh from him.

Neigh from him.

I would place you high above...
on pedestal made of love.
And move mountains made of sand,
Just to gain your hand.

To gain your hand.

These words are just a piece of many, many strands of long-winded and heart-felt words he had written for her. Each night, he would hum and sing, curse and growl, and drink himself into oblivion. It's a sad tale, and without a doubt, poor Tolokah had reason for his bitter anger. But reason does not make his deeds right… it only makes them more understandable. His deeds were not only sorrowful…but also detestable.

Such was his plight.

And as the last few embers of his fire dwindled down to ash, Tolokah drifted into sleep. As he tossed in drunken slumber, he mumbled a few crude words… "Some day soon, my dear…my pretty." And that was all for the night.

* * *

Tolokah woke as usual…his mouth was dry and his head hurt. He had no appetite, but knew that by noon he would be quite hungry and ready to start the whole process once more.

He picked up his leather sling from the stone beside him and slowly meandered his way through the forest, looking for something edible to shoot.

Tolokah was a deadly shot with his sling. He could toss a rock with absolute precision, and kill nearly any small animal with one blow. Rabbit was one of his favorites, but he would settle for anything that wiggled when squeezed. Birds were a delicacy when they could be found, but most scattered far before his bulky feet could plow through the forest floor. He wasn't exactly light on his feet, and hunting was a day-long challenge for him. Thankfully for him, he was a great aim, and that made up for his lack of quiet stalking. He was still a formidable hunter.

After a few failed attempts at a barking squirrel, Tolokah continued his search farther south than usual. He could see a few crows flying in the far distance. He could really enjoy a finely-cooked crow from his fireplace. Despite the old adage, crow wasn't all that bad to eat, and Tolokah could almost smell the warming meat on his roasting stick. "Yeah," he said, "south we go."

After a few miles of southward travel, Tolokah came upon three black birds high up in the tall branches of a Sycamore tree. They appeared to be more interested in something below them, and they chattered back and forth between themselves in a way that allowed Tolokah to creep far too closely. His eye was fixed upon one particular bird that was considerably closer than the rest. The bird's gaze was focused solely on the other two and the movement below them near a beautiful small lake.

As the bird continued to focus below himself, Tolokah placed a very sharp and weighty stone into his leather sling. Ordinarily, these birds would have taken flight at the quiet sound of the swirling strands of leather spinning below them, but their interest was held elsewhere. Tolokah took careful aim as he wound up his shot. Faster and faster his stone swirled. As the old black bird refocused on the happenings below,

Tolokah released his grip of one of his strands of leather…releasing the stone with remarkable speed.

Within a second, the bird fell backward from its perch and flailed uncontrollably downward into the pool of water. Its companions jumped in startled dismay and flew cautiously overhead and watched their leader plunder into the cold clear water. As they circled in frantic dismay, they watched as an unbelievable occurrence unfolded before their eyes.

The floor of the forest swept toward the lake with a wave of motion. A raspy call of some sort echoed through the valley. Within seconds, the leader of this band of secretive birds was swept into a waterfall by this wave of greenery and disappeared from sight. Almost simultaneously, Tolokah stepped forth to view the same occurrence. Spears flew through the air, and a deafening hush spread over the forest…and a very suspicious troll quietly crept away. And as two black birds flew solemnly overhead, the greenery below them came to a screeching halt…and the forest floor became deadly quiet.

4

Within the confines of Great Falls Cave, the groups of Leafling fighters were beginning to disband. Quite some time had passed, and Azir was growing impatient with the incessant questions and constant prodding for information from the Leafling guards. "Leave us," commanded Azir, "I will call you if needed. Tulas...send word to the sentinels...man their posts until further notice. Keep all young ones within the confines of the Miraré. I should like to be alone with the bird...at least until we can make certain of its intentions."

Tulas reluctantly did as he was told and waited patiently outside the entrance to the cave for further instructions. Tulas was both head of the sentinel guard and spiritual leader for most of the younger Leafling children. The older Leaflings, of course, preferred to speak with Azir when possible. But as time passed, old Azir was less and less available for lessons, and more commonly than not, chose to let Tulas take the reins. Despite some odd comments from many older Leaflings, young Tulas was becoming a stronghold in the community and did his best to conduct himself in an appropriate manner. He was approaching the spiritual age of five years. Adulthood in Leaflings happens at about two years of age. Those two year-olds are much like the teenagers of man's prodigy.

Tulas' son, Kimbli, was just approaching these tender teen-age equivalent years. He was well-beyond his first year, and had moved much further along in his studies than most his age. He was a product of a loving parent...as most truly strong students are, and conducted himself in a knowledgeable and confident way. He was the well-behaved, well-educated, and well-spoiled youth of Tulas the Knight. He was well-loved, but also held in a jealous regard by some of the Leafling youngsters. They all admired his strong and intelligent demeanor, yet fantasized about the lofty position that he would someday hold. Someday, he would be the Leafling equivalent to a prince. He would be heir to the throne of Tal Kator, and everyone here knew it.

After a few hours of Azir consoling this bird, it finally calmed down some and Azir was able to discern a few odd ramblings from it. Most of its speech was a series of gurgling sounds and sharp whistles, and it took Azir quite a while to make any sense of what the bird was trying to say. Azir could communicate with most birds quite fluently, but this bird's speech was different from that of any of the large birds he had come in contact with in his long life. Finally, Azir spoke, "You appear to us as a crow."

The bird appeared disgusted with the term *crow*, and even made a nasty coughing sound followed by a crudely spoken word, "Alck! Crow! Alck!"

"Alright," said Azir, "then what are you?"

The old bird made several attempts to speak in his own language before he gave up and rolled his tongue with a raspy growl, "Rrrrrraven!"

"Now, we are getting somewhere, my friend," said Azir, that precious piece of information soaking in. "You are safe here until you heal. I assume you are a tower raven." The bird gave a bobbing head nod.

But soon, the raven gave Azir a strange look of confusion. He looked down at his bloody breast and then back at Azir. Slowly Azir was beginning to understand why the bird was still so frightened. Aside from his wound, the raven evidently felt as if the Leaflings had been the ones who had shot him from his perch. He had no idea what had happened to him when he fell from the sky…only that he hurt badly, and hundreds of tiny creatures whisked him away into a cave.

Over the next several minutes, Azir spoke to the raven and listened intently for anything he could make out in the old bird's speech. Unfortunately, the bird was quite traumatized, and his wounds had taken much of the bird's energy. As the day wore on, the bird's wounds were tended, and Azir left the bird to get some rest within the safety of the cave. He ventured out onto the rock ledge with Tulas and some of the other guards. "How is he?" asked Tulas as Azir took a seat along the rocky ledge.

"I can make out very little of what he has said," said Azir. "He thought that we were who shot him from his perch. You can imagine how frightened he must have been."

"Now what?" asked Tulas. "What do we do with him now?"

"First, he must rest," spoke Azir, "but, I now need time to think. I do not feel good about this. Something is dreadfully out of place." The old Leafling paused a moment and then spoke again, "See to it that the nurses have what they need. The sentinels must man their positions until further notice. Change the guard every ten hours, and keep in close contact with them all. Do not bother me unless under attack. I will need time."

He then walked back into the cave with his arms by his side and his shoulders hanging with a great weight of impending worry. Tulas did not ask any more of his mentor. Azir would let him know when the time was right, and he could tell that Azir was deeply troubled. "For all our sakes," spoke Tulas to a fellow guard, "I hope he finds his answers…and soon."

* * *

After a few hours rest, the old raven opened his eyes and focused on his surroundings. After a startling first glance, he came to his senses and settled back into his bedding. A young Leafling nurse placed his hand upon the raven's wings and smiled. The raven looked down at his bandages and felt a twinge of pain shoot through his breast. Although his wounds were dreadful to view, he felt much better than he expected. In fact, he was healing considerably faster than he had ever before. The Leafling nurse spoke a few words of comfort and left the raven to himself. This old raven had never intended to be in such a predicament.

The bird's name in raven and in English was Glock. He was a fairly aged bird but carried his years well and had attained a high status in his flock. His mind was sorting through many thoughts as he took in all the sights and sounds of this cave. He scoured every detail he could and plugged it into his memory, half-expecting these strange creatures to turn on him at any moment. Ravens were not very trusting in their nature and rarely accepted anything for what it seemed. They had several run-ins with numerous creatures over the years, and it left them with a natural distaste for any beings other than their own. And any reference to crows sent them into rage.

Meanwhile, Azir paced the halls of a dimly-lit room. The flickering yellow light of a few candles shone upon the stone walls deep within the confines of the passageways of the cave. The rough and bark-like fingers of Azir traced numerous inscriptions carved deeply into stone slabs on the walls of the room, and his face strained with the thoughts of an individual that carried a great weight.

Azir was worried. He racked his memory through and through but simply could not remember some of the very early teachings of his youth. Somewhere within the countless etchings on this wall was what he wanted to remember. Deciphering the old carvings of the slabs was difficult for most students...and no one in the Leafling colony truly knew the key to the scrolls on these walls except Azir. He could remember some of the etchings from their translations from when he was young, but many were only a foggy memory.

He had been patiently taught by his Ori elder and learned the ways of the Leaflings through the same channels by which he was teaching Tulas. He had spent many years teaching several of the Leaflings of the colony, but those years had robbed him of much of the intense study he had planned for himself since his early days. He now racked his mind, trying to recall the many teachings of his youth.

Azir could now picture the purple light reflecting in the eyes of Tulas' parent, and his heart melted with anguish. Tumo was to be the elder when Azir was ready to back away from his teachings. Tumo was chosen by Azir from the moment of his birth...and Azir spent countless hours lovingly singing to him and teaching and guiding him through the processes of learning the ways of the Leaflings. Tumo was almost his own sapling ... taking the place of his own two saplings that fell ... fighting to save the colony during the Great Flood.

Tumo had been special to Azir. He had given up his own two young ones in that horrible storm...and Tumo was to replace them both in the Hall of Scrolls when Azir died...being the adopted youth of one who lost his own.

But, tragedy fell again for Azir. Despite his loyal religion—and despite his constant giving and perpetual desire to carry the Leaflings into the future, Azir faced yet another loss.

Tumo fell sick in the blight of the Cold Winter, and after days of agonizing pain and torture, the chosen one died. Tumo's limbs lie twisted and dry as Azir laid his body into his grave and pushed the soil of the Miraré in around him. Azir would have given his own life many times over to save this young life…this chosen one…this product of thousands of hours of faithful teaching. He would have grafted himself unto Tumo with every once of his being…but it was not to be. And in this dark candle-lit cavern, Azir fell to his knees in remembrance and cried.

He looked at the elaborate carvings in stone slabs on the walls as tears fell from his nose. He wept as he cried aloud, "I am not sure I can do this. It was not supposed to happen this way. Where are my young.... my little ones? I am old, even beyond my years. I have lived so very, very long. Why is it that I must live to see the last days of my own family....WHY? Send me strength, my fathers…send me strength… help me…oh Great Literati', help me." And in the dark depths of the ancient cave … the old Leafling mourned.

* * *

After hours of thought, Azir returned from the depths of the cave and spoke again with the raven. Something unnatural had happened to this raven. He did not speak like the birds of the forest. Something had changed the bird's vocabulary, and Azir could not make much of its strange ramblings. He finally gave up and went outside to find Tulas.

As he suspected, Tulas was still manning his post as he was told and watching the community closely. He addressed Tulas quietly, "I have spoken to the raven and do not understand his speech. What I make out does not make sense."

Tulas raised an eyebrow.

"Don't laugh," spoke Azir with a smile. "He says that he is the messenger of monkeys."

Tulas laughed out loud. "Now we're in trouble, Azir," he said, still chuckling, "The monkeys are coming to get us!"

Azir managed a bit of a smile, and spoke again. "I'm still very concerned—nothing good ever came from a troll. I think he will return."

"Then we shall put him in his place," said Tulas. "We have warded off many predators over the years, and we shall do so again. He should be no match for our defenses."

"Never underestimate an opponent, Tulas," said Azir. "It will lead to disaster every time." After a moment of thought, he spoke again, "Where are Kimbli and the other young ones?"

"They are with Mesigh at the base of the old Chestnut…probably still grumbling about not being able to swing and swim on this sunny day!"

"I guess we can let them play some," said Azir. "I don't think we are in immediate danger, but keep a very close eye…I feel very uneasy with this entire ordeal." He motioned for Tulas to speak with Mesigh and gave him a rewarding smile. "Thank you for all you do, Tulas. You are dear to me."

"And you to me, my friend," spoke Tulas, and some of the tension of a very strange day was relieved…and in the late afternoon sun, Azir the Old continued to search his memory for answers.

5

Far beyond the outskirts of the forest, and high above the forest floor, there was a very tall stone tower. Its long and spiraling staircase ascended many stories above a castle-like building on the very edge of a township of man by the name of Cobblestone. This little city had been a settlement for ages beyond account. Its lovely streets were worthy of the town's name, and the clip-clop of hooves often echoed through the cobblestone streets. The large stone tower of this quaint abbey sat comfortably on the street corner near the edge of the city, and its window boxes almost always contained the most beautiful blossoms currently in bloom. The monks kept a very tidy household, and their gardens were the talk of the town. Few places in this ancient time were so lavishly decorated with natural flora.

The abbey was most certainly the oldest building in the city, and it housed the only library of sorts within miles. The old books that adorned the shelves of this building were age-old, leather-bound hard covers, and many of them were also hand-written. The old monks of the abbey had wonderful penmanship, and managed to make time to recopy some of the old manuscripts of yesteryear whenever inclement weather disallowed a day in the garden. A monk's work is never done, and idle hands are the devil's work…or so some say.

Today, as a thunderhead rumbled through the town of Cobblestone, so too did a large troll. His rough demeanor hardly fit in here at this pleasant little town that housed a quaint and subtle monastery. His presence was known immediately as the footsteps of Tolokah plodded through the rock-laden streets. Shutters of windows quickly slammed home, and a hush fell throughout the streets and alleyways of Cobblestone.

Tolokah knew little of this monastery and cared even less, but he needed information, and he would not leave without it. He eventually found his way to the abbey steps and climbed them two-fold with his large strides. He spoke as little as possible with the young doorman that addressed him after he opened the large green doors of the monastery. The voice of the young monk was simply too sweet for Tolokah's ears. "Er…Umm…Good day Mr. Tro….I mean Sir. How can I help you today?"

The door man was Jon. He was a young and vibrant student of the monk faith, and his eager ears and eyes constantly searched for more to learn. He was quite intelligent and spent a large portion of each day pouring through the many books of lore on the shelves here at the monastery. He was well-known as a tender-heart, and he was most certainly a well loved young man from near to far. He had a comfortable, all-knowing smile that warmed the heart and soul of all who had come to know him. His parents had died young, and the lad had come to love his quiet life here at the abbey. He was well suited for his intern here at the monastery, and the town of Cobblestone had come to love him. "The gospel according to Jon" was a loving play-on-words of the townspeople of this spiritual and warm community. He smiled as he addressed this formidable troll.

"I have not come," growled Tolokah, "to banter with the likes of some youth. I should like to speak to an elder."

Tolokah's fair words were certainly not spoken cordially. He could speak elegantly and frightfully at the same time. His fearful frown and snarling lip led Jon to realize that he was not dealing with a reasonable individual. His elders should be notified as soon as possible.

"One moment, Sir," he said as pleasantly and quickly as possible. "I shall fetch an elder." He smiled as he turned and did his best to not show the utter detest he felt for the enormous troll in the doorway. He scampered away to the tall stone stairwell nearby.

He extended his arm up to a small white string that stretched way up into the stairwell. His hand grasped the string and gave it a tug. At the very end of the line was a small brass bell. As it chimed aloud, the eyes of a very old man raised from his book. With a raised voice, the old monk spoke, "Yes, Jon."

"Father," called Jon, "you have a very pressing visitor."

The monk at the end of the string…and at the top of the stairwell… was none other than Father Mathias. He was the "eldest" elder, and the very mentioning of his name commanded respect. It was said that he was now in his late eighties, but looked to be of much less years. Nearly all of his living days had been spent in or around this stone building, and he cared for it as if it were a member of the family.

The clip-clop of Father Mathias' soft leather sandals echoed through the stone tower as he slowly eased down the long and spiraling staircase to the foyer. The light of the mid morning sun shone through the stained-glass windows and shrouded the deep brown cloak of the monk in tiny rainbows of light. The light danced in sparkles on the surface of a beautiful ring on Father Mathias' finger. Winding vines and flowers were deeply carved around a single stone in the center, and the monk's thumb spun it gently around his finger as he descended the stairwell.

Jon met his mentor near the bottom of the stairs and offered a supportive arm. He then led Father Mathias to the foyer and left the room and disappeared into the labyrinth of rooms of the abbey…just as all good interns should when company presented themselves to an elder. Father Mathias stepped forward and spoke, "Master Troll, what is it that we of the abbey may do for you?"

"Enough with the niceties, old man," spoke the troll, "I've come for information." The enormous body of the troll towered over Father Mathias. The stench of Tolokah's uncleanly body filling the air was very fitting of the name *Terrere'*.

"My acquaintances usually address me as Father, kind troll," spoke Father Mathias, with an obvious display of distaste. "Surely, you could find it within yourself to do so."

Tolokah gave Father Mathias a smug smile as he stepped up to his face. He grabbed the old monk by the nap of his deep brown cloak and growled a nasty sentence, "My acquaintances usually address me as *please, please don't kill me.*" The troll breathed heavily into the old monk's face as he held it near his own and snarled into it. "What I need…FATHER," spoke Tolokah, with a very aggressive growl of intolerance, "is information. I have run across some very strange little leafy creatures in the forest. Now, we can play games if you like…but I'm sure you won't want your spine snapped." With that, the troll began to raise his other hand to Father Mathias' neck. As the old monk's eyes widened, the troll smiled with satisfaction.

"Only if you want your skull pierced, Master Troll," spoke the very young and very angry voice of Jon from across the room. In his hands, was a very large and drawn crossbow. The sight of the bow and the eye of Jon were both accurately aimed at the old troll's ear. The feathers on the arrow quivered with Jon's deep breath, and his finger twitched at the trigger with exhilaration. "You have three seconds," continued Jon.

Tolokah reluctantly released his grip on Father Mathias. With a growl of distaste, he stared at Jon, wrinkling his lip in anger.

Father Mathias spoke, "We know nothing of leafy creatures…or trolls for that matter. You may find your way to the door and only return when you have found respect and manners."

"We shall meet again…Father!" growled Tolokah. "Sleep well 'til then…and you, dwarf monk," he said to Jon with a scowl, "…will not always carry that cumbersome crossbow. I look forward to then." With a disgusting smile and an evil glare, Terrere' the terrible walked through the large wooden doors of the abbey and into the streets of Cobblestone.

Jon rushed to his mentor's side and offered comfort. "Are you alright, Father?"

"I am fine, Jon," spoke Father Mathias. "I need to think, my son. Please help me to my room."

As two monks navigated the high and winding stairs of the abbey tower, one angry troll stomped his way from this village of man to the only other place he could go for answers. He would make his way to the very last place in the world he wanted to go. He must see Anté. And that could prove fatal. The thoughts of Anté were all-knowing. The words of Anté were all final.

But, despite the pangs of fear in his heart…there was still a burning desire for answers…still something coaxing him forward. There was something in this matter that he must see to. He felt absolutely drawn to this intriguing and unfolding story of leafy creatures in the woods. And—he felt strongly enough about it to face Anté, and Anté would not be welcoming Tolokah with open arms.

Tolokah propped his aching feet up onto a nearby rock and opened a fresh jug of wine. The popping sound of the cork echoed from the stone bluff and out into the chill night air. It was a calm night, and Tolokah's fire crackled its warm glow into the dark forest. As his feet warmed, he tipped his jug and began to form a plan.

It was long ago when Tolokah first engaged in business with Anté. He dreaded Antés hurtful glare when he arrived at Stone Castle, and he wondered if Anté would allow him to enter. He never wanted to be in contact with Anté at all, but a number of fellow trolls had been contracted to remove one of the stone garden walls behind the old castle, and Tolokah elected to help only for pay and nothing more. He expected to be done with the process in a day or two and move on, but one job led to another until Tolokah was deeply under the thumb of Anté. Anté owed him a good bit of money, and he continued to hold it over Tolokah's head to get him to do his next nasty job. His jobs eventually entailed little more than that of a hired thug, collecting bills and promises from other forest peoples. And finally, with a large sum of money still owed to Tolokah from Anté, Tolokah confiscated his last large "collection" from the village of man and never returned to Anté. Even though the amount of the collection was close to what Anté owed him, Anté was furious with the insult and vowed to repay the insult one day, ten-fold. Anté was more than intelligent enough—and quite capable of doing so…it was just a matter of time.

Tolokah was just certain there would be something in this story for him. It was just too good a secret. There would be something in it for him; he just wasn't sure what it was, yet.

His stomach growled as he took another large chug from his jug of wine. "He will accept me…this is good information," he said under his breath. And, as the wine flowed, he looked forward to his day tomorrow and began to hum a little tune. It was another of his verses for Meilan, and his mind and heart were soon completely engulfed in thoughts of her.

"To the ends of this earth we know
Is the least of where I shall go.
I will wait there for thee,
And forever guarantee
Devotion no more divine
Than that of the love of mine.

My Meilan, my Meilan!"

The humming and singing continued until it was completely indiscernible…and the drunken old troll drifted off to sleep.

By now, two days had passed in the cave behind the Great Falls. What was once a nearly dead raven, was now a strong-willed and semi-healthy bird. His wounds were well on their way to being healed, and the old bird was amazed at his own progress. He could not communicate well with these leafy creatures, but he sensed that they must be friends, or they would have killed him by now…and how they managed to heal his large wounds so quickly, he would never know.

He practiced a few flaps of his wings for flight but realized it was too soon for that. It did feel good for the raven to move some and begin to regain his strength. He wondered how and when they would ever let him leave from this very secretive … and apparently *sacred* location. He was resting comfortably when Azir walked in.

"Raven," he spoke aloud, "it is time we talk." The old Leafling sat down beside the raven and placed his hand on the bird's shoulder and smiled. He thought for a moment and then began to recite the many early teachings of Leafling speech. Azir had finally decided that teachers must teach…and leaders must lead…and Azir the Old…was about to do both.

* * *

Outside the confines of the cave, some of the aspects of Leafling life were getting closer to normal. Although the sentinels were still at post, and the guards stood vigilant, the young ones were allowed to play and some of the others scurried through their daily rituals. Even under the close watch during this fearful time, the colony of Tal Kator was still a very peaceful and beautiful place. Some of the old barkies were allowed to "take a walk" to you know where, and the playful splashing of swimming youngsters could again be heard.

Young Kimbli and his best friend, Kikah were strolling along the banks of the Miraré and skipping stones. Kikah spoke up, "I'm tired of being kept up near the cave. Why don't we slip over to the Apple and talk with Ducah…anything to liven things up a bit."

"Your Ori would fall leafless if we were caught near the old Apple," suggested Kimbli.

"Yeah…" replied Kikah, "…let's go, shall we?" Within minutes, the two were tiptoeing down the winding path to the old Apple and chuckling to themselves. These two could find fun in the simplest places. It didn't take much to keep these youngsters happy. One day, they sat in the bushes and tossed an occasional acorn at Ducah setting under the old Apple whenever he dozed off. The old Leafling would startle himself awake and look at the sky, wondering if it might be falling. They were good youngsters…just a little on the ornery side.

The two strolled on down the winding path away from the Miraré.

Kimbli strolled up to Ducah, who was fast asleep with his feet pushed into the soil. He tapped him lightly on the back and plopped down beside him.

Ducah jumped as he awakened and both young Leaflings laughed aloud. "Ducah, my friend," said Kimbli, "you've been here so long; you're growing moss on your back side."

Ducah was not amused by the young one's playful antics. "Nonsense," grumbled the Leafling, "I've merely taken a short nap… and besides, do your Oris know you are here? I somehow doubt it."

"The sentinels gave us leave this morning. We were sick of the same ol'-same ol'. We thought we might get you to tell us that old story of you and Azir and that wild shrew. We do love that story."

Both young ones knew that old Ducah loved the sound of his own voice and could talk for hours about nothing but himself and be quite content. He had been known to keep talking even after his listeners had slipped off to get away.

Ducah immediately began his story in his rough and tumble sort of way just as the young ones had expected. He also took no note of the two pranksters gently slipping their roots beneath the leaves with a quiet chuckle. They began their usual little quotes of "do tell" and "you don't say"…and old Ducah was in the height of his glory.

The old Leafling talked and talked and after about an hour, the two quietly pulled their roots from beneath the leaves and slipped away from the old bloke. As they crept back up the trail, they could still hear Ducah's voice in the distance ranting of yesteryear and the pesky shrew that just could not outsmart him.

"You just have to love old Ducah," said Kimbli. "I've been trying to picture the shrew that couldn't outsmart him!" The two laughed out loud and continued giggling their way up the path toward the lake.

"Have you noticed," asked Kikah, "how concerned Azir is over that old crow?"

Kimbli nodded his head and answered, "Yeah, Ori says it is a raven, whatever that is. I didn't know there was a difference. It doesn't seem much smarter than a crow, but Azir is taking great pains to communicate with him. I guess I don't understand why the group is so worried about this whole ordeal. The troll left and the crow…raven…is healing quickly. Looks to me as if things are on the up-and-up."

"I don't know either," replied Kikah, "but we'd better get our limbs on up the trail and closer to the lake before they catch us this far from the colony. Let's go, nut head!"

"Nut head? You're the nut head! Your Ori has bark like a hickory."

"Oh yeah, your Ori has termites!"

"Oh yeah," and the arguments continued as if these two were bitter enemies about to strike blows, while all the time they were merely battling wits and loving the camaraderie. The playful twosome always had fun. And life, as far as they were concerned, was back to normal.

The heavy footsteps of Tolokah crushed their way through the rarely trodden path to Stone Castle. It had been an all-day walk for him to the far edge of the forest, and he was more than ready to arrive, but was in no particular hurry to meet up with Anté. He could see the frightening old castle looming ahead of him in the distance. The coming darkness only added to its uninviting appearance.

As he stepped closer to the large open doors of the ancient castle, he paused and looked at its magnificent architecture. Although many of the age old stones were crumbling in decay, the domed windows still housed their stained glass, and the green copper roof still remained in near perfect repair. Vines of ivy clung to the precipice of nearly every story of the building, and it completely covered the wrought iron gate that once hung proudly on its hinges in better days. It was once a proud and noble building, but now it felt foreboding and eerie with its old wooden doors hanging crooked on their rusty and broken hinges. Even the fearless heart of Tolokah the troll sank as his footsteps entered the main doors and looked to the halls within.

Tolokah desperately wanted to be quiet, but found his footsteps echoing through the stone walls with utter clarity. He made his way down a long corridor toward a dim light near the end. He felt the darkness close in around him, and the stench of dusty mold filled his nostrils. Each footstep was harder to make than the last. As he stepped from the corridor and into the dim light of a large chamber, a loud and terrible voice clamored through the air and pierced his heart like a dagger.

"Why have you come?" it shouted.

The enormously strong arms of this formidable troll shook with fear as he tried to speak. He did his best to sound strong, but the words did not come. "I…have…"

"SILENCE!" shouted the voice of Anté. "Come forth and speak with the strength of one worthy of being named Terrere'. There is nothing more disgusting than the whimpered words of a coward. Are you a troll or a whipped pup?"

The frightening voice was coming from the center of the room behind a very large and long table that stretched from one end of the room to the other. The entire surface of the table was laden with dust covered books. There were ancient leather-bound hard backs and loose hand-written pages yellowed with great age. There were notes and maps, as well as a number of sketched drawings scattered across the table.

At the center of the table, resting comfortably in the velvety seat of a huge throne was none other than Anté. He needed no other name…no other reference at all. He was known far and wide by the name Anté; meaning *before,* or *ancient*…and he filled those shoes well. His old and decrepit body was very tall and thin, and his deep green robe could have covered him many times over. His long gray whiskers hung well beyond his chest; combed and braided to perfection. His bald head sat firmly upon his slender neck, and it was nearly lost in the shadows of the hood of his robe. His deep dark eyes glistened with the eerie glare of the lake surface on a moonlit night. And if his appearance was not frightful enough, his voice could shake the very foundations of the most fearless of souls.

Some felt that Anté was a wizard. Still others felt that he was more of a warlock, practicing witchcraft deep within the halls of Stone Castle. But man or beast, Anté was a formidable soul with a contempt for nearly all walks of life. He had lived a very long life, and studied the lore of man…religion and politics, history and folklore. He had read every word of every book in this vast library, and understood all that was within them. He was old beyond old…wise beyond wise… and evil beyond evil…and it was obvious. With a harsh and disgusted growl, he shouted again, “Come forth and speak, coward!”

By now, the anger in Tolokah’s heart was beginning to overpower his fear. His eyes regained their hateful glare, and he stepped forward as he was commanded. At last, he spoke, “I have come, Anté, for information. I have some to share.”

“So the thief comes to the home of the victim and wants to barter information,” spoke Anté with detest. “How very troll-like…why should I not slay you now?”

Tolokah chuckled aloud, “You are quite old and fragile to be slaying, I might suggest!”

Within a split second, the once fragile and frail looking old man before Tolokah rose from his seat and whipped his sword just inches above the troll’s head and embedded it into the table before him. “I think not, Master Troll.”

Tolokah stood in total amazement as Anté cast a menacing scowl and sat back down, leaving the sword still embedded in the table before him.

Anté raised both hands in the air in gesture to show Tolokah the room in which they stood. The walls were covered with row after row of shelves that housed thousands more books like the ones on the table in front of them. Cobwebs and dust covered everything there, and some of the dusty surfaces sparkled in the pale candle light. "What information could you possibly offer me, Tolokah the Terrible?"

Tolokah spoke with a sly whisper, "Only the location of a village of tiny leafy creatures."

Anté gave Tolokah a long and questioning stare. The wheels were turning in his head, and he was not about to give up any information before he had time to think this through.

At last, Anté stood from his throne and looked Tolokah deeply in the eye. His dark eyes were menacing, but intrigued, and he spoke with great hesitation. "What kind of leafy creatures?"

"I thought maybe you could tell me that," replied Tolokah. "I found them while shooting crows. I suspect it might have been more than a mere crow, for I got only close enough to receive numerous little spears in the ground before me."

"Where is this place?" asked Anté, still glaring an evil smile.

"Now, what kind of bargain would I possibly have if I gave up my information so quickly?" asked Tolokah with a knowing smile.

"I must consult my books," said Anté. "I have heard of such creatures, but I need time to study. Leave me and return tomorrow. I shall have an answer for you…if I choose."

"I have no intention of walking home, Anté," spoke Tolokah. "I walked a great distance to give you this information. I have no intention of leaving."

"And I," laughed Anté, "have no intention of caring! Leave at once, before I pull this sword from the table!"

Tolokah wrinkled his nose with a growl and slowly turned and walked down the hall, out the main doors and into the night. He stopped just outside of the vine covered gates and found a large oak tree to rest against. His eyes stared at the dark castle walls as his mind raced with ideas.

"Wish I had a good jug of wine," he grumbled as he thought of the possibilities of what old Anté might have in store for him. He pictured handsome rewards of jewels or gold, but never in his wildest imagination would he have dreamed of what was in store for him the following day. His life was about to change.

* * *

In the cool and dusty library of Stone Castle, an evil mind was busy at work on an elaborate plan. Anté gently spun a beautiful ring around his finger. The light of the candelabra flickered upon its leafy surface and small stone. His quiet chuckle echoed through the cool damp halls, "A puppet troll for me…must be my birthday…and I've been a *very* good boy…ha, ha, ha, ha!"

Father Mathias stepped onto the balcony of the tower in the abbey. He scattered a handful of seeds to a couple of black birds on the ledge. The ravens jumped to the floor of the balcony and began their meal. Father Mathias shook his head in disappointment.

"Where ever is Glock?" he asked to himself. He wished deeply that he had taken more time to communicate with some of the younger ravens as well as Glock. Perhaps he had spent too much time with Glock and not enough with the others. At this point, it mattered little. Glock was gone, and the young ravens at his side were of no use to him other than running simple written messages locally. Glock was a special bird...and Father Mathias missed him dearly.

Father Mathias navigated the stairs to the hall below. Young Jon soon met him and led him to the dining hall. As he became seated in his head position at the end of the table, he spoke quietly to Jon, "I should like to call a meeting this morning, Jon. Could I trouble you to send word to the Fathers, my son?"

"Certainly", replied Jon in his usual overzealous manner. "I shall report back to you as soon as possible…if I may, Father."

"That will be fine, Jon," he replied with a smile. "Let us make it for 10 a.m., if possible."

Jon nodded and raced off to deliver messages to the other monk Fathers. Father Mathias ate his breakfast and hardly noticed what he was eating. His mind was awash with numerous theories and an impending worry. He wondered what, if anything, he should do. Maybe the other Fathers would have some counsel.

Soon, ten o'clock rolled around, and Father Mathias found himself looking in the eyes of eight old monks…all pondering the reason for this meeting. Father Mathias rang a small bell to gain the attention of the Fathers. All turned and gave Mathias their full attention.

He cleared his throat and began to speak, "I have called you all hither to discuss an impending worry. I fear…that Tal Kator may be in danger."

Quiet murmurs rumbled around the room, and Mathias spoke again, "As many of you know, I often send the ravens to view the Leafling colony. More importantly, I send Glock. Glock and I have developed repose…a crude language between us. There are few words, but we can communicate well enough to serve the needs of the trip to Tal Kator. Three days ago, I sent Glock and two others to view the Leafling colony. Glock did not return. I cannot communicate well enough with the young ravens to determine what happened. They flap their wings and fall to the ground…and I fear that is what happened to Glock."

The men around the large table looked at one another with confused glances. One finally spoke, "What may this have to do with Tal Kator? Something could have happened anywhere along the way."

"That question, Father Finley," spoke Mathias, "leads me to my next and most disturbing piece of information. I was paid a visit yesterday from a troll. Not just any troll…Tolokah."

A roar of dismay filled the hall, and Mathias continued so speak, "He came in search of information … and mentioned small, leafy creatures in the forest."

"Father Mathias," spoke Father Finley, "you know the defenses of Tal Kator as well as the rest of us. The troll will never breach the entrance, and if so…."

"It is not the troll I fear, Father Finley," implied Mathias, "I fear he may have help. Tolokah is menace enough unto himself, but he has been known to cohort with the likes of Anté."

A groan of distaste arose from the crowd of men, and they all began to see the possibilities that Father Mathias was trying to convey. After a moment of thought, Mathias spoke again, "I think we all know what Anté is capable of doing…even without the help of a troll. I dread the possible outcome. The good world may never be rid of him."

"I suggest, my friends," continued Mathias, "that you all take this afternoon to think this over. I should like to reconvene tonight. Let us make a decision…for the good of us all…and follow through with a plan. Are we all in agreement?"

The motion carried, and a forlorn group of monks made their way to their quarters…with quite a load in their mind.

10

Tolokah dusted the morning frost from his leather sleeves. With a shiver, he stood and walked through the vine-covered iron gate of Stone Castle. He was quite angered by his uncomfortable night's rest but was still very intrigued by what might lie in store for him this morning.

He entered the open front doors of the castle and made his way down the hall to the room he had entered the night before. He hardly knew what to expect with old Anté, but he was willing and ready to receive what Anté had to say. He entered the old library room and found Anté nearly asleep with his head in his hands atop a very old and worn book. Its leather-bound cover was weathered and cracked with age. Its yellowed pages appeared to be hand-written, and the center of the book was discolored by the constant turning of pages by searching hands. This book was heavily studied by more than just Anté.

Anté woke as if from a dream and addressed Tolokah as he walked closer. With a very dry and very quiet voice, Anté spoke, "I have discovered much more than I ever imagined. Sit, Tolokah, and hear what I have to say."

Tolokah pulled up a chair and anxiously awaited the information he had been waiting for so impatiently. He was ready to soak up what ever Anté had to say.

"I have reason," spoke Anté in amazement, "that the Prophesy Rhymes are coming to pass!"

He paused and allowed the old troll to absorb the information he had been given. Anté was certain that this troll would have no knowledge of this well-known and heavily studied book. He knew that Tolokah would have no knowledge of the Literati' and their ancient writings. Their tireless work would be lost on the old troll without much instruction.

"I see," he continued, "that you know not of the Literati' and their life-long work of writings. That is unfortunate. The Literati' were brilliant men—scholars with foresight. Their writings have inspired many kings and warriors. It is all here…in the *Book of Lore*."

Anté held his hands open above the book before him and again paused and allowed the troll to catch up. By now, Tolokah's eyes were wide with anticipation, and his knees began to tremble with excitement. Anté took note…and was pleased.

Anté spoke again, "I have prepared a copy of these writings for your review…at no charge…with no strings…for fear of hindering prophesy. I care not to delve deeper. I wish to neither help nor hinder what is above my knowledge. I care not to go further, Tolokah—into the labyrinth of twisted foretelling that I have read tonight. Recent occurrences have caused me to believe that you may be the chosen one."

By now, Tolokah was beside himself. He sat tediously on the edge of his seat, wide-eyed and trembling. He could barely contain himself.

"Tell me more…go on!"

Anté took one of the papers he had prepared for Tolokah and read it aloud.

"This, Tolokah, is from a portion of the *Book of Lore*, known as *The Prophesy Rhymes of Tal Kator.* The first is an accountment written by one of the elder Literati' known as Tolk. His early writings have inspired many...and this is one of his first...concerning the creation of Tal Kator during the Meteor Shower of the Dark Ages. It reads as follows:"

Here follows the account of Tolk:

"The Awakening"

From fear and despair they came
In fiery night of flame.

From smoldering soil and steam,
As if from hazy dream,

They raised their roots from land
And walked on foot and hand,

And like nothing 'ere before
Rose the Leaflings of Tal Kator.

"By now," spoke Anté, "you must assume that the Leaflings are what you have encountered. And if so, these next pages will cause you to believe that maybe you, Tolokah, are in line for the Prophesy!"

Tolokah's head could explode. *Prophesy!* Tolokah, the Terrible, was aptly named! *Tell me more,* he thought excitedly. *Tell me everything!*

"Take these pages, Tolokah. Take them. Use them well, chosen one, to your advantage. Fulfill your destiny! Go forth and take what is yours by Prophesy! Live like the King *AND QUEEN* you have been chosen to become! Take what is rightfully yours!"

With that, Anté bent forward and handed Tolokah three additional pieces of parchment. Along with the *Accountment of Tolk*, he received three other very important pieces of writing … and, the troll was moved beyond words.

"Read them aloud, Tolokah," spoke Anté, "and give me your thoughts. I don't think I am mistaken."

Tolokah pulled the first piece of parchment and stared in disbelief as he read the words penned across it. They read as follows:

Troll sat alone
On his bitter throne
Full of anger and despair,

Full of troll wine…
And leg of wild swine…
And a resentment that few could bear.

With a drunken nod,
He asked of the Gods,
"Why is it that I should suffer?

While the vermin of man
And wild beasts can
Mate with a feminine other?"

With a solemn yearning
And desire burning
And thoughts of her in his head,

He would build her a throne
in halls of stone,
And with a jewel for her hand…they would wed.

“My God!” exclaimed Tolokah, “….Meilan.”

He continued to stare at the parchment. “And what of a *jewel*?” he asked, looking to Anté for answers.

“I have studied,” spoke Anté, “…the Leafling Lore for years…and never dreamed of finding them. It is said that there is an enormous purple jewel within the confines of that cave…one worthy of great praise…one worthy of a female troll! This alone, could be enough to consider in this prophesy. But read the next piece of paper and give me your thoughts.”

Tolokah delicately unfolded another piece of parchment and again stared in disbelief. “I cannot believe this.”

Through forest and field,
Fen and glade,
A harsh and terrible
Sound is made.

Never a likely
Tale's been told,
In Leafling lore
From days of old.

There came a cry
From distant north,
And Devil Troll
Came raging forth.

He cast his spell
With poison rain,
And Tal Kator
Cried tears of pain.

And Quoth, said Troll,
"Nevermore!
Will Leafling toil
In Tal Kator!"

"You think this could be me?" Tolokah simply could not take in all this information at once. "Poison rain?" he asked. "I don't…I don't know what to say."

"I shall help you decipher some of this," said Anté with a helpful nod. "I know more of the Leaflings than you. Perhaps I can help. You also mentioned an odd crow yesterday. If you read that last parchment, perhaps it could make sense as well." Tolokah unfolded his last paper and again stared in utter disbelief.

Beware to they…
That see the raven fall,
For few shall live to see the day
When trolls leave Leafling walls.

"How may I ever repay you, Anté," spoke Tolokah, "I could never have found this information without you. Don't you want to know the location?"

"I care not for the location, Tolokah," he said. "This is your prophesy, and not mine. I shall not hinder it. A wizard will not mess with prophesy. Only harm will come of it. If this prophesy is fulfilled, you will be able to repay me many times over…but I shall not intervene. I shall not. Prophesy is prophesy, with or without this wizard."

After many hours of consultation, an overwhelmed troll scampered from the halls of Stone Castle. As he watched the troll tarry off into the forest, Anté the Old reveled in his own brilliance. Quietly he spoke, "Go ahead, Master Troll, fulfill your destiny…and fulfill mine!"

And the hollow halls of Stone Castle were once again filled with hideous laughter.

11

A light sprinkle of rain began to fall on the rock-laden streets of Cobblestone. A distant rumble of harsh thunder rolled through the evening sky, and the foreboding worry of weather was mirrored by the rumble of angry voices deep within the walls of Cobblestone Abbey. As the young monk, Jon, listened carefully at the doors of the council hall, loud arguing voices filled his head, and his inquisitive ears wondered what in the world could cause such a ruckus. The rumbling voices within the hall could not quite be made out by Jon, and he longed to know…and help…the situation. Patiently, he waited.

Behind the doors of council hall, Father Mathias and eight monks argued furiously about the impending danger at Tal Kator.

With a pound of his fist, Father Finley raised his voice, "The weight of the world is not ours to carry! We have pressing issues here at home. I do not feel that nine old monks can battle Tolokah the Terrible…

much less the evils that can be conjured by Anté. We cannot battle the resources of the old wizard. His voice is strong…and is heard both near and far. Not with the forces of man could we do this…and I do not think that any of you are willing to trust mankind with the weight of the Shard … not before … and not since."

"Anté," spoke Mathias, "is no wizard. He is—one of us."

"THAT VILE SOUL IS NO MONK," shouted Finley, "HE IS NO DESCENDANT! His words are poison! Have you heard that retched voice, Father Mathias? Have you felt them delve your inner soul? Have you stood by…trying to maintain your thoughts…while the words of that deceitful soul make sense of madness! Few can endure those conniving words, Mathias…and I ponder if any of our strong souls can hold out. I care not to try. I vote we allow life to take its course."

"And I, Father Finley," spoke Mathias loudly, "vote that you remember the vows of our forefathers…the vows that created the ring on your finger."

"My ancestors," growled Finley, "would not jeopardize the wellness of the abbey…all on a whim of worry. My vote is cast…and I shall not change it."

Murmurs rolled through the room as a very important group of men pondered the possible fate of another group of Leafy individuals that housed a very important item…one capable of changing some of mankind's fate…forever.

* * *

After a number of hours had unfolded, Father Mathias raised his voice in anger and stood from his seat. His final words were just that… final. He cleared his throat to gain the attention of the arguing monks, and then spoke.

"There is too much unrest in this group to allow action. I call this meeting adjourned…and the monk descendants of the great Literati' will stand cowardly and watch...and quite possibly wish we had gone forth. The majority has spoken. Mind your oaths, FAIR Fathers ... keep this secret ... we are adjourned."

Father Mathias slammed his chair back against the wall, and for the first time in his life, he stomped away from a hall of amazed monks and made his way for the abbey tower. The large doors of the council room slammed forward, nearly toppling young Jon as he awaited orders just outside. He could tell that Father Mathias was in no mood for questioning, so he simply followed behind at a safe distance, listening for any hint of what Mathias may wish. Mathias stopped short at the base of the stairs and looked Jon square in the eye.

Jon nearly collapsed in fear...expecting the Father to shout aloud. "Father!" he whispered. "What is it?"

Father Mathias was still shaking with anger. He calmed himself enough to speak, "Listen closely." He again looked Jon square in the eye and calmly asked, "Of all the abbey monks, who is it you trust most?"

Jon did not hesitate. He immediately answered, "You Father... without question....you. What can I do?"

"Meet me in my quarters in one hour. Bring food...but more importantly...bring a very important book from the archive. Do you know of *The Book of Lore*?"

Jon nodded and spoke, "I copied it for Father Haley, last year."

"Bring it with you, my son. You must be absolutely silent about this, do you understand?" Jon gave Mathias a worried nod in agreement.

Father Mathias spoke one last sentence, "...and...and one more thing, Jon. Bring your Bible. We may both need it before the night is out."

And somehow, one way or another, during a long and troublesome argument, the oaths of nine monks were broken...and rain fell in the streets of Cobblestone...and through the treetops of the Deep Forest.

12

If it wasn't for the shear volume of troll wine, Tolokah would not have slept a wink. He managed to doze momentarily in between the loud claps of thunder, but it wasn't the weather that was keeping him awake. He was still nearly beside himself with excited anticipation. Finally, life was going to go the way of Tolokah the troll. After years of unfair and misfortunate occurrences, the tide was finally about to turn for this old troll…and of course, there was the very plausible possibility of obtaining his most valuable desire … Meilan.

He hummed and sang and let his mind wander to their inevitable future together. Soon, she would be his. After all, how could she resist Tolokah with his hall of stone and vibrant jeweled stone for her? Yes, sir…the time had come for Tolokah the troll…no…Terrere'! Terrere' the Terrible!

With the consoling aid and instruction of Anté and his vast knowledge of ancient lore, Tolokah was indeed ready to take prophesy by the horns. He was ready to take Tal Kator by storm, and all the preparations lay scattered below his stone bluff, just a few miles away from the peaceful home of the colony of Leaflings and the falls of the Miraré. Raw excitement and troll wine pulsated through his veins and his enormous body quivered with anticipation. The time was near! Over and over he read the pages of prophesy, and they gave him cold chills. *Devil Troll came raging forth!* He chuckled to himself as he continued to read that line, and he chanted "Nevermore" all through the night.

With a drunken slur in his voice, he spoke to Meilan as he fell off to sleep. "Just a few more nights…my lovely…my princess…your handsome prince is coming, my dear." He grumbled another phrase or two. "NEVERMORE! Ha! Ha! Nevermore, nevermore."

* * *

Meanwhile, miles across the Deep Forest, two monks high in the abbey tower were in deep counsel. Jon's young ears had heard more about life this evening than ever before, and his mind was becoming a little confused with all the deep concepts written long ago by the hands of their very own predecessors.

Father Mathias was deeply troubled about bringing young Jon into the equation. By oath, only the nine elders may discuss official business within the walls of the abbey, and by no means, was anyone EVER to discuss what was being shared with the young lad tonight. Jon was clearly too young to truly understand the importance of what had been written so long ago, but he listened closely, none-the-less, to his friend and mentor, Father Mathias. He would go to the ends of the earth for the old man, and looked to do what ever it was that the monk had up his sleeve.

They covered the coming of the Leaflings, as well as the importance of their secrecy. They discussed Tolokah, and Anté, and of the Amethyst Stone. Many of the writings of Tolk were discussed, as well.

Jon stood frightened, yet determined before Mathias, ready and willing to follow through with the old monk's plan. Jon bowed to Mathias and spoke a few quiet words. "I will do what my strength allows, Father. You have my word…and my allegiance. Goodbye, Father."

As the two knelt in prayer high in the abbey tower, thunder rolled through the night sky, and rain did its best to cleanse the hearts of monks of all ages.

* * *

In the few hours before the morning sunrise, Jon tucked a hand-penned map into his chest pocket and made his way through the wooded trails of the Deep Forest. He knew very little of the forest and only used the shelter of darkness to help him ease away from the abbey unseen. Soon, the morning sun would give him light to follow Father Mathias' map and help him navigate the forest floor. He had never been where he was going, and he was not sure of what to do upon arrival, but onward he sloshed through the darkness and rain, hoping it would make sense when he got there.

13

Kimbli and Kikah had volunteered again this early morning to gather worms for the healing raven in the cave. By now, the raven was recovering nicely and had taken up some exercise as part of his therapy. The little Leaflings happily gathered worms for the bird and strangely…always found some down near the old Apple.

"That's where the larger worms hide," commented young Kikah to old Ducah…who seemed to understand the importance of worm gathering near the tree. He would sometimes help in the task, if it allowed an early access to his favorite spot.

The worms were quite a challenge for little Leaflings. Many were as large as the youngsters themselves, and they looked as if they were men wrestling pythons in the Amazon. The worms were a bit slimy, but the two could usually wrestle one apiece back to the cave, and they tended to wait for two very close together, so that one did not have to wrangle one while the other hunted for his catch. It was a good task for energy-filled youngsters early in the morning, while many other Leaflings enjoyed a little longer rest. So after a short pause near the old Apple, the two little ones continued to hunt the dewy morning grass for slimy signs of worm trails.

Just as the two were about to pounce on two very succulent worms, the worms quickly tugged their heads beneath the surface, and shortly thereafter the two could feel the ground shake in the distance.

Something didn't seem right in the forest. There was no sound of birds…no bouncing squirrels…no morning calm that they had become accustomed to hearing. Something was wrong.

Soon, breaking sticks and branches could be heard, and a strong thump of raging footsteps rushed past them to the far right…maybe thirty yards. A tall dark shadow gloomed over the forest floor and a hideous grumbling laughter echoed through the crisp morning air. Whatever was passing by was taking no pains to be quiet, and the raging noise thundered through the otherwise quiet forest. The two stood stone still and gazed frightfully at the passing danger.

Ahead in the distance, the raspy calls of Leafling sentinels filled the air. Spears were carted quickly from the cave, and the ratcheting chatter of wooden gears sounded within the cavern. Armies manned their posts, and a deafening hush fell across the Miraré.

Tolokah the troll slowed his pace and approached the colony with a huge smile and an obvious air of excitement. He held his arms unfurled and slowly approached a very surprised and frightened group of almost unknown leafy creatures. The normal hush of the Leafling colony was not of any use here. This assailant knew exactly where he was going and made no bones about it. He knew of these Leafling "people" and stepped forward to address them as if he had known them for decades. Tolokah was where he needed to be, and he knew it beyond question. He stepped forward with a smile and raised his voice as dozens of sharp spears surrounded his enormous body.

"MY FRIENDS!" shouted Tolokah.

Tolokah was certain that with an address like that, someone of importance would come forward to answer his call. He stood smiling and chuckling to himself as he cast his gaze over numerous Leaflings lying in wait near the confines of the Miraré. He could catch a slight glimpse of hundreds of shining little spears surrounding his giant shadow in the morning sun. Again, he addressed his audience. "MY FRIENDS! COME FORTH … LET US SPEAK!"

The forest floor rippled with waves, and the greenery was getting much closer…to Tolokah's approval. The vast majority of Leaflings came forth to hear words spoken from foreign lips for the first time in their history. They came in absolute curiosity…to hear spoken words of another species. They came forth in awe of what they saw. They came forth to hear enticing words from the very last individual that they should have come forth to trust. They came forth…to die.

Again, Tolokah spoke, "MY FRIENDS, COME CLOSE!" With a conniving smile, he said, "I have brought for you a gift. I shall forgive you for your distasteful welcoming upon my last visit…I have prepared this for you in forgiveness of my previous treatment. I offer it to you freely."

The old troll was carrying a very large leather flask. It was fairly triangular in shape…culminating in a tiny little tube near the end. He offered it for view to the Leaflings. "This, my friends, is what I have brought."

The Leafling colony crept closer to gain a better view of what the old troll held dangling from a leather strap…heavily laden with weight. As he held it out for view, his knowing smile became a hideous chuckle. He turned his enormous body to the far left with calm and collected aim.

And then…with absolute hatred in his heart…he squeezed the leather bag with all his might. His other hand pinched the small outlet of the leather bag with deadly precision. A fine spray of deep red liquid filled the air above the Leaflings. As the droplets of red rain fell to the earth from Tolokah's bag, Leaflings began to fall to the ground in utterly uncontrollable convulsions. In quivering dismay, Leaflings cried and moaned in absolute pain. A deep burning sensation had taken hold of their flailing limbs and of their conscious mind, and they began to shake as their limbs absorbed a very, very potent poisonous liquid. Their strong, yet very absorbent limbs, seized in crippling shock. Their minds swam in drunken dismay. Gallons of troll wine had been sprayed upon them…and their tender roots absorbed every ounce… and there was absolutely nothing that they could do about it. Most died immediately…but some lingered to die minutes later.

One particular Leafling lay twitching uncontrollably in the dew-covered soil. "Why?" asked the fading voice of Tulas. "Why have you done this? We are a peaceful colony. Why?"

"Why, you ask, my sentinel friend?" said Tolokah, with a smile, "…because I can!" And with those words, Tolokah the Terrible stomped the heal of his boot firmly into the mud of the Miraré shore…with the body of Tulas the Knight pressed beneath. As he lifted his muddy boot from the soil, Tolokah shook his foot in full view in front of the others as if he was shaking gum from his shoe. Fear entered the hearts of those poor Leaflings doomed to die. It was not bad enough for them to simply die, writhing in pain. They were forced to watch helplessly as their leader was squashed into the ground, as their last few fading moments of life escaped their grasp.

Many watched in horror at the painful deaths of their close friends, writhing in pain along the shores of the Miraré. They struggled toward the water's edge to try to cleanse their bodies of the painful red liquid.

Tolokah the Terrible effortlessly stepped forward to gain his prize, deep within the confines of the cavern. Two or three feeble spears bounced from his thick leather vest as he pressed on.

He reached the entrance of the cave and stuck the end of his wine flask beyond the edge of the falls and sprayed. A few spears left the cave and stuck into the arm of Tolokah. With a groan of pain, he jerked the tiny spears from his arm and sprayed again. He then stepped fearlessly into the cave. As his eyes adjusted to the dim purple light, he could see numerous Leaflings wallowing on the floor of the cavern…rolling and moaning in pain.

"Who's next?" he shouted aloud.

Tolokah's words were unanswered. He waited patiently for a reply and moved forward toward the Amethyst Stone. As his steps came closer to the Stone, a gust of air moved through the darkness of the cave and a dark figure flew near Tolokah. The sharp claw of Glock the raven pierced the right eye of the troll, as he swatted in vain at the bird. With a cry of pain and anger, Tolokah cursed aloud and held his hand against his eye.

He stepped closer to the Stone…trying to gain proper sight in the darkness. His blurred vision hindered his progress, but Tolokah still pressed on. His goal was now in sight. No simple bird was going to hinder him now. His prize lay directly before him on the raised stone pillar. The hint of morning sun through the falls was reflecting in the purple stone as he extended his arm to pick it up.

At that exact moment, a tiny click was heard in the deep darkness of one of the tunnels. In a split second, Tolokah felt a harsh thrust of pain as an enormous spear entered his chest. The huge arrow from a giant mechanical crossbow had pierced the heart of Terrere' the terrible, and he fell backward into the darkness of the cave as blood spewed from his gaping wound. He tried to raise himself, but fell back, coughing blood from his throat. Tolokah's fingers twitched uncontrollably as he tried to maintain focus.

One lone Leafling raced forth from the dark tunnel. Old Azir gazed at the blood-soaked troll lying motionless on the floor of the cave. The old mechanical crossbow had fulfilled its purpose, after years of setting dusty in the dark tunnel of the cave.

At that moment, another shocking occurrence plagued the halls of the Miraré cavern. As the last few moments of Tolokah's life ticked down, a large dark figure stepped into the cavern from outside. The footsteps of Anté approached the dying troll. His dark eyes smiled down upon Tolokah with an evil chuckle. "Fool of a troll!" laughed Anté. "Prophesy! Ha! There is no prophesy, you pathetic rogue. The only thing predictable in Tal Kator is you, fool troll. Dangle the mousy in front of the cat and watch it scamper along. Tolk was not the only Literati' scholar. I, too, have written a line or two of verse, and the ink had not even dried on your fine prophesy! Farewell, fool."

Ante pulled a long dagger from the sheath at his side and raised it high into the air. With a fierce downward thrust, he rammed it deeply into Tolokah's chest near the gaping wound of the spear. "NEVERMORE!" he shouted with a laugh.

Tolokah's chest heaved in agony. For the last time, his mind again wandered to his beautiful Meilan. A solitary tear fell from the cold cheek of the dying troll. He would never touch her soft skin…never feel her long brunette hair…and his lips would never meet those of hers. His life long dreams of a life of happiness with her would not come to pass. And, in the purple darkness of the Miraré cave, a long and dedicated infatuation of Meilan, the troll, came to an end. As his last breath exhaled from his body, and his mind drifted off to her, he sang his last two words, "My Meilan," and Tolokah Terrere' the Terrible died.

Azir stared in frightened disbelief. He picked up a spear from the pile in the floor and stood guard before the rock pillar of the Shard of Amethyst. "Oh, please, Azir," spoke Anté with a scowl. "Put down your tiny spear. I shall be doing you a favor. The old troll would have taken your home and your Shard. And, for your long years of *friendship,* I shall let you keep your home, and you can live here…for a while."

With one swift kick, Anté leveled Azir to the ground and against the rock wall. He picked the Shard from its mantle. From beneath his cloak, Anté pulled a large clasp on a golden necklace. It had been prepared many years ago by Anté in preparation of this very moment.

He dropped the stone into its clasp and slipped it back into place inside his cloak. He felt the warm energy of the Shard radiating into his chest as it hung from its chain, and he smiled with a deep satisfaction.

"You should have given it to me years ago, Azir," spoke Anté. "I would have been much easier on you…give my best to the family!"

With that, Anté strolled from beneath the falls and into the cool morning air, leaving poor Azir to suffer along side his fellow Leaflings.

Anté took a deep breath. The smell of troll wine still lingered among the dead and dying Leaflings around the Miraré. He was so smug and satisfied with himself, that he did not notice the young monk and raven in the edge of the woods. With absolute satisfaction, Anté raised his hands to the sky with a huge smile and said, "THE SHARD IS MINE!"

"Not for long," spoke a quiet voice in the trees. The silence of Tal Kator was broken only by the quiet wisp of a crossbow. The shaft of a speeding arrow left the bow of young Jon the monk. With Antés arms still raised high to the sky, the arrow pierced the deep green cloak covering the chest of Anté.

As fate would have it, the shaft of the arrow centered the Shard of Amethyst still hanging from its chain from the neck of Anté. As its sharp point touched the surface of the Shard, the stone shattered into thousands of tiny dust-like particles that pushed themselves into the chest of Anté. His body jolted backward with extreme force, and landed amid a pile of dead Leaflings. His mangled chest pumped blood across the ground and down the banks into the waters of the Miraré. Within seconds, the once-brilliant mind of one of the most intelligent descendants of the Literati' scholars lie dead in one of the most disgusting and heart-breaking disasters to ever be witnessed in the woods of the Deep Forest…and Tal Kator…cried tears of pain.

14

Even before Anté had left the cave; Azir had already begun dragging Leaflings into the waters of the Miraré. As quickly as his old boughs could carry him, he pulled and tugged Leaflings from the cavern into the water.

As he raced outside, he noticed the body of Anté lying in a pile. The waters of the Miraré were stained with the red tints of troll wine and Literati' blood. Still, Azir dragged Leaflings into the water. His limbs ached with exhaustion.

When he came to the body of Tulas, he collapsed into the soil in sorrow. "Tulas," he cried, "my God, Tulas!"

He pulled Tulas from the muddy soil and held him closely. His body fell limply in his grasp. "My God, Tulas, not you…not you, too, Tulas…not you…precious Lord, not you."

Azir could move no more. His body gave out, and his mind was grieved beyond words. He had given up every loved one he had ever gotten close to, and this was the last straw. Perhaps it was exhaustion. Perhaps it was his agonizing loss…but Azir fell over as he held Tulas tightly in his arms…and his world went black.

At that same moment, young Jon began doing the same as Azir… tossing Leafling after Leafling into the fresh waters of the Miraré. He raced the shores of the lake, gathering Leaflings with every stride. He gently placed Azir and Tulas along the shore, partially submerged, and continued his vigilance.

Glock the raven scoured the countryside in search of others. It wasn't long before he found two young Leaflings racing toward the lake. He sailed down to meet them and beckoned them to follow by leading them on. When they met Jon at the pool, they stood stone still, having never been in contact with man other than in mere passing in the forest, where both would simply stand camouflaged and quiet, waiting for them to pass.

Jon shouted commands immediately, and given the gravity of the situation, both began to help out, having little choice to do otherwise.

As they dragged their limp Leafling friends to the shoreline of the Miraré, they frantically called for their Oris and searched the seemingly endless piles of dead Leaflings. Despite their desperate calls, neither received a reply.

Amid the rubble, Kimbli finally came upon the bodies of Tulas and Azir. As tears fell from his Leafling eyes, he lifted the head of his Ori and called to him. "Ori…Ori…please wake!"

After what seemed to be hours, but only consisted of minutes, the head of Tulas the Knight raised slightly. In poisoned dismay and confusion, he spoke the name "Kimbli".

"Ori…Ori…don't leave me…please! Please don't leave me." Kimbli's voice was desperate. "Please stay with me!"

The voice of Tulas was very weak. "Where…is Azir?" His raspy voice was barely understandable.

"Ori!" spoke Kimbli through the tears, "Azir…he…he…lies next to you."

Tulas was drifting in and out of consciousness. Again, he tried to speak, "Is…is…he…alive?"

"I don't know, Ori…I don't know. Please stay with me, Ori. Please!" Kimbli's head lowered to Tulas and he held him in absolute fear of losing him forever. Tears poured from his eyes as he begged to Tulas. "You cannot leave me. I love you so much."

The weak voice of Tulas the Knight somehow raised above the whimpering cries of his own young. He spoke with the utmost earnest and drew from the sources of his deepest magnitude. The poor Leafling fought every ailing pain in his body. "You must…save Azir."

Kimbli turned his attention to Azir, lying limply in the Miraré mud. He splashed water on his face, and called his name aloud. The old one woke with a start, and slowly took in his surroundings. When he fully came to consciousness, he immediately rose and turned his attention to Tulas. "You must stay with us…do not give up…do not give up!"

The old Leafling took matters into his own hands and made a tough decision. He looked to Kimbli for help, who was knelt down beside them in tears.

"Kimbli," spoke Azir, "you must listen closely. In a moment, you will see something you have never seen before. Be strong. You must do as I say…for the love of Tulas…and me…you must be strong."

Kimbli was in an absolute state of shock. The fear in his eyes even overshadowed the sorrow in his heart. He looked to Azir for instruction.

Azir gave one more glance to Kimbli and said, "Be strong…you must."

Azir picked up the nearly lifeless hand of his beloved student, Tulas. He held it close to his face. As tears fell from his eyes, he murmured the words, “Forgive me”.

Azir took the arm of Tulas with a firm grip. With all his might, he pressed his fingers into the bark of Tulas’ arm…and ripped the bark from it. As Kimbli stared in horror, Azir turned his attention to his own arm…and did the same. A cry of pain from Azir shook Kimbli to the core.

By now, Kimbli was crying in absolute shock. He found himself fighting desperately to maintain consciousness, staring at the gaping wounds in the arms of his Ori and Azir.

“KIMBLI!” shouted Azir, “FOCUS!”

Azir ignored the bitter pain in his arm and wiped away tears. He picked up the torn arm of Tulas and pressed it firmly against his own, and pressed tightly. He could feel the poison flowing from Tulas and into himself. As Azir began to lose consciousness, he spoke to Kimbli, “Grab our arms…GRAB THEM! You must not let go…no matter what, Kimbli…do not let go…hold tightly. It will take us days…hold tightly…” In a matter of minutes, Azir’s mind again slipped into oblivion.

Every living Leafling in the colony was summoned to help pull Tal Kator out of this madness. Some of the affected Leaflings were beginning to come to from their poisoning. Many suffered permanent damage, and most did not revive from the ordeal at all. The entire area was a massive display of devastation and death. Leafling bodies lay everywhere and the bodies of a troll and man lie stiffened in the daytime sun.

Young Kikah was forced to bury his only true relative…his Ori. The stench of death abounded and Tal Kator reeked of sorrow and pain. In all essence, Tal Kator, itself, had died. And with the help of what few beings were left alive, two young Leaflings aged into adulthood, and began the long and heart-breaking chore of burying the dead in a place that was once so full of life.

15

Father Mathias sat calmly on a wooden pew on the stone balcony of the abbey tower. More than two days had passed since Jon slipped away from the abbey, and Mathias found his eyes searching the edge of the forest, hoping his young counterpart would soon emerge from the leafy canopy. His heart was heavy with the turmoil within the abbey between the once-friendly monks that resided there. His attempt at keeping peace in the forest… and in Cobblestone…had failed miserably. It seemed that in an attempt to save Tal Kator…and quite possibly Cobblestone…the old monk had only created anger and havoc, and it did not sit well with him. He was a very spiritual man with an open conscience, but this situation filled his heart with pangs of guilt, and it weighed heavily on his mind. There was no peace in this peace-keeping venture…at least none that could be seen in these early stages by this old and solemn monk.

Mathias sat depressed and forlorn on the balcony, as the streets of Cobblestone bustled with energy in this warm sunny morning. Tree swallows circled in flight near the tower, almost as if trying to cheer up the old monk. Hummingbirds sped along, pausing long enough to delve the flowery outcroppings of the abbey tower, but their playful antics did little this morning to cheer the soul of Mathias the Elder Monk of Cobblestone Abbey.

Mathias began to doubt his decision to include Jon in this ordeal. Jon had not heard of Antés dealings with the Leaflings until that late-night meeting with Mathias in the abbey tower. Jon had been amazed by the stories Mathias had relayed to him. Never in his wildest dreams had he imagined the power of the Amethyst Stone. Its radiant power not only gave strength to the Leaflings, but it was also the very life source that allowed the Leaflings to exist. Quite simply, without that stone, there would be no Leaflings…no life…in Tal Kator. The "life from disaster" would cease to exist.

Anté had longed for the power of the Stone his entire life, and had planned, for decades, ways around the safeguards put in place by the Literati' so many years ago. Although he was a direct descendant of those early fathers, some of the secrets and lore of that spiritual spot were kept quiet…even among the elders.

Tolk had written numerous volumes of his account of the early Leafling civilization, but much of the ancient lore of what the other Literati' knew went to the grave with the old Monks that lived it. Much was now lost and even old Mathias built much of his belief in Leafling lore around the nightly tales woven by entertaining monks of all ages. There was certainly uncertainty in the folklore of old, and Mathias had done his best to sort fact from fiction.

"Why," asked Jon, that night in the tower, "would Anté want the Stone?"

Father Mathias remembered closing his eyes in dread and speaking. "Imagine if that stone could bring life to the Leaflings…to non-animated plants…think of what power it could posses in the hands of Man. The all-knowing power of Anté could take over the world. In theory, he might just live forever…and rule with an iron fist and a natural hatred of his dealings with man. The possibilities are endless. I do not know what Anté is capable of…but no man should live forever…no man should know all. I fear for the lives of the Leaflings…and of men."

Mathias began thinking of alternate plans of how to deal with Anté should the opportunity present itself. Anté was a formidable foe without help. With the help of the Stone…and possibly a giant Troll… there would be Hell to pay in Cobblestone. Anté had dealt with the villagers of Cobblestone for decades…and never forgot his dealings with the elders of the abbey. He was cast out of the abbey before he had reached his thirtieth birthday, due to his deceitful nature and conjuring ways. He brought turmoil and discomfort to the halls of the abbey, and regardless of his lineage, was pushed from the abbey and forced into the streets of Cobblestone.

But Anté was not welcomed in the streets of Cobblestone either. His shady dealings with the townsfolk had gained him a reputation of a shyster…and he no longer had the blessing or protection of the church. He was shunned and belittled, and soon found himself living at the abandoned abbey of his ancient forefathers called Stone Castle.

Most called it fate. A monk returning to an age-old castle somehow fit to everyone's fancy. All avoided his frightful abode, and it allowed Anté countless hours of quiet solitude in which to study. All of the ancient books of the old abbey still lined the shelves of a once-elaborate library. Antés eyes had devoured every page, and he still longed for more learning. He was a bitter student of life…and carried a resentful, yet resourceful air about him. He became a product of his surroundings, and his surroundings became a product of him. This perpetual motion pushed Anté into a pathetic downward spiral; and it eventually left him in bitter dismay with a natural distaste for most of mankind.

His shady deals continued, and most avoided his fearful glare if at all possible. And as old age crept up on Anté, he began to connive ways to gain the Amethyst Stone to perpetuate his control over man…and maybe…attain eternal life. He planned to take the stone by force… somehow…some way. It would just take him a while to put the pieces in place.

Father Mathias' mind was in deep thought when a pair of flapping wings brought him back into the present. With a start, Mathias focused his eyes on the shiny black body of Glock. With the tilt of his head Glock spoke, "Glock bak".

Mathias raced to the precipice edge where Glock stood, waiting for his handful of food. He picked the old bird from the wall and held him close. "I have missed you, my friend," he spoke, as his eyes swelled in tears. "I am glad you are back."

"Glock bak…Glock bak," the old bird chanted as he danced around over the surface of the rock wall.

"Where have you been?" spoke Mathias, "What has happened… Where…." Mathias stopped short as he noticed a yellowed note attached to the leg of the old bird. Mathias knew immediately that if there was a note attached to the leg of this particular bird, that the news would either be truly good…or horrendously bad. He drew the bird forth and plucked the parchment from his leg.

He took a deep breath, hoping for good news, and slowly opened the tiny note from the raven's leg. To Mathias' dismay, the note read:

I have failed you Father
The Shard and most of the Leaflings are lost
Terrere' and Anté are dead
All is lost
Jon

Tears fell on the ancient stone of the abbey tower. Father Mathias held his head in his hands and prayed for the lives of all that died. Even the troll received the blessings of the old monk's prayer. He gently spun the ring on his finger and looked at it longingly as if for advice. For the first time in the old monk's life, he was at a complete loss. He had no thoughts to convey…he had no offerings of hope…only dismay filled his heart, and on the highest tower in the village of Cobblestone, Father Mathias, the eldest elder among monks … descendant of the Literati' of old…wept.

16

Day two after the massacre at Tal Kator was no less depressing than the first. There were still several Leaflings to bury and the two enormous bodies of Tolokah and Anté. Jon had unknowingly brought a small folding camp shovel in his bag of gear. It helped immensely in the burial of the tiny Leaflings, but the two larger bodies would require much more attention.

Jon had prepared a large pile of wood to be used as a bonfire. He had built a makeshift gurney to drag the troll and Anté to the fireplace. After two hours of prying and tugging, both bodies lay at rest atop an elevated structure of wood and debris.

With a very heavy heart, Jon tapped his pieces of flint toward the tiny pile of dried grass at the base of the structure. Small puffs of smoke began to rise, and eventually, the entire rack was ablaze. Jon said a few words for the deceased and turned from the burning bodies of Tolokah and Anté. He turned away and pressed on to help with the burial of the last few Leaflings. Dark smoke rose from Tal Kator for the first time since the coming of the meteor…so many ages before.

By now, Jon had come to know some of the Leaflings by name, and the Leaflings accepted his humble generosity with open arms. Their relationship would have been even more special in better days, but, by and large, the first Leafling relations with mankind since the dark ages went as smoothly as the conditions would allow. With death and despair rearing its ugly head in every corner of Tal Kator, Jon and the Leaflings got along as well as could be expected. Although, they could easily communicate, there was a bland sorrow that nearly disconnected every living creature near the colony. Most plodded along in a state of shock and disbelief…doing what they must to survive and move on with what was left of their bleak looking lives. Tal Kator was a ghost town of survivors, and all knew that their future was uncertain at the very best. With two days of pain and despair during the burials, still none had found time to truly mourn for those closest to them.

As the last crumbles of dirt were scattered over the last Leafling body, Kikah stood and walked away from most of the burials. Though his limbs could barely move, he made his way to the distant shore of the Miraré and collapsed at the foot of a lone grave. Tears gushed from his young eyes and onto the grave of his Ori. Exhaustion had taken its toll on the young one, and his loss was as much as he could bear. He looked to the soil beside this lone grave and nearly dug a hole of his own. As he stared in total dismay, his best friend Kimbli stepped to his side and placed his hand on his shoulder and spoke, "Let us go set by the pool and do our best to nourish ourselves. Come, my friend."

Kikah did not move. Quietly, he spoke, "What is the use, Kimbli? Starving may be a quicker death. We will perish without the Stone… you know this. I care not."

"You must care, my friend. Your Ori did not raise a quitter. Your Ori would be proud of what you have done…and how you have helped the colony. You must care, Kikah. I need your help. I cannot care for the others alone. All that is left is a few old ones…and the sick and wounded. Please care Kikah. Please care…and help me."

Kimbli sat beside his friend and consoled him as best he could. Kikah sobbed uncontrollably for quite some time before allowing himself to leave the grave of his Ori. His hand passed over the soft soil of the grave, and somehow, through the tears, he quietly spoke, "I care, Ori…I care."

He raised himself up from soil and gave Kimbli an understanding nod. "I will try…let us rest by the water, and maybe I can gather my senses. I do care Kimbli…I just feel hopeless."

The two wandered to the water's edge and sat down. They pushed their roots into the soil and did their best to relax. At last Kikah spoke, "Tell me of Tulas and Azir."

"Jon helped me bind their arms. I had no idea what was happening when Azir pulled the bark from their limbs. I've never seen anything like that in my life. Jon has helped me come to terms with it. He says they have grafted many plants at the abbey in Cobblestone. He had never seen anything like what Azir had done, but he understood immediately what he was trying to do. I guess I see what Azir was trying to accomplish…it was just very, very disturbing. Hopefully, Azir's body is strong enough to save Ori. He had to absorb much of Ori's poison in order to provide some of his own healthy fluids. It was very selfless of him…I know he loves him dearly, but it is frightening for me to watch them lying motionless in the cave together. I miss them both so very much."

Kikah looked at Kimbli with swelling eyes. "I know, my friend…I know."

It wasn't long before the heavy steps of Jon walked toward the two Leaflings on the shore. He spoke as he approached, "I need to talk with all of the survivors. I must see the elder of the monks. I have done what I can, but my time is short. Can you come to the cave?"

Both Leaflings nodded and walked to the entrance of what was once the resting place of the Shard of Amethyst. It now held the resting bodies of two very important Leaflings within its halls, and no purple glare sparkled there anymore.

As the two entered, Ducah gave Kimbli a shake of his head to show that there had been no noticeable improvement in the two bound Leaflings. With a nod of understanding, Kimbli called to the other Leaflings within the confines of the cave. They had all gathered for the speech of Jon, and Kimbli counted heads as he came to rest at the feet of Azir and Tulas. "I believe we are all here."

"Amid your sorrow," spoke Jon, as he addressed the crowd, "you can all be proud. Your ancestors would be proud, as well. You have persevered with the gritty determination of no beings I have ever seen before. You have pressed forward with strength and prowess. I commend you. But it is time I see my Elder. It was he that sent me to your aid. I fear I came to late…but I hope you can accept what I have done as the best and only option we knew to undertake. There is much more to this story than most of you know, but rest assured that we care deeply for Tal Kator…or my Elder would not have sent me. I have no intention of leaving you in your time of need, but I must seek counsel. He may not have gotten word…and if he sees the dark smoke of the cremation, he will worry all the more. I must go…and now. I have done what I can, and I will return if possible. I make no promises…I only give my word that I will do all within my power for you. I will send word with Glock, if possible. I wish you luck…and strength. Farewell."

Jon bowed and then left the darkness of the Miraré cave, and the few remaining Leaflings of Tal Kator felt as if their last ray of hope had just diminished.

Kimbli's head hung with despair. "Now what?" he asked, still staring at the ground beneath him.

"Now," spoke Kikah, "we care. You shall look after these two while I take this old barky into the caverns of this cave." He looked upon Ducah with a knowing smile, and Ducah returned a questioning glance.

"You know where we are going…you moss-covered old barky. You are old enough to know…you just might not remember. Drag your butt up. We have work to do."

Kikah gave Kimbli an encouraging smile. "I'll bring him back when I'm done with him." With that, an old barky and a clever little young-un tarried off into the darkness of the Miraré caverns…and they were on a mission.

"The last thing I need," commented Ducah, "is some cocky sapling dragging me around in the dark. I suggest we go back."

"You're not getting off that easy, barky," spoke Kikah. "There is no one left that is old enough to know what you should remember. It might not come to you right away, but I intend to drag it out of you, if it is the last thing I do."

Ducah grumbled a few obscenities under his voice as they walked down the dark path, deeper into the cave. "How do you know where you're going, you little sap?"

"Do not think that I spent my entire young life idle. Exploration was one of my best attributes! I once overheard Azir deep within these walls…talking to himself…and chanting something about scrolls. Now, I know nothing of scrolls, but I am certain that scrolls must contain information of some sort … something important … or they would not have been written in the first place…now would they?"

"I don't know," spoke Ducah, still pondering the words of the young lad. "How should I know of scrolls?"

"I think," chided Kikah, "that if you search your memory…you old, decrepit barky…that you just might find more than you expect."

"I should hardly think so…little sap," he said, "there is little that I have witnessed in my long days that I do not remember…and I do not think that some young sap will merely drag me into some dark cav…"

Ducah stopped mid-sentence as his feet stepped beyond a threshold he had not crossed since his early youth. He stared in wild wonder at what his old mind had completely forgotten. This age-old cavern laid much the same as when his very own Ori had brought him here in his early days of his youth. His mind caved in as if an avalanche had come crashing down in his head. He stood bewildered in the doorway of a dark and musty cavern, as his mind traveled through time to when his Ori had given him instruction…given him advice…given him the very few words necessary to place hope in every living Leafling in Tal Kator…he just didn't know it at the time. With a very slow and questioning air, he asked, "What is it that you need to know?"

"Let us," Kikah said loudly, "shed a little light on the subject!" To Ducah's surprise, Kikah had brought with him the same flint that Jon had used in the fire outside. What Ducah thought was a walking stick, in fact, turned out to be a make-shift torch of tightly wrapped dry grass.

After a few strikes of the flint, the torch ignited quickly. The two stood in amazement as the light of the torch increased…and the walls of the stone room brightened with the increasing light of its flames. Before the two…on the ancient walls of this spectacular chamber…were many stone tablets. Each was etched and tinted with elaborate carvings. Both Leaflings stood in awe at the eerie tablets upon the walls. Nothing written upon them could be understood by either Leafling. There were fantastic scrolling letters penned across each, and the flickering light of the torch reflected dimly over them. As the two stared in wonder…the ancient teachings of Ducah the Old were beginning to turn some old and rusty wheels within his mind…and maybe, just maybe…there was still hope within the hopeless walls of Tal Kator.

17

Father Mathias was again sitting near the ledge of the abbey tower. The evening sun was just setting over the forest beyond the town of Cobblestone. As usual, his eyes paced the edge of the forest for his young friend Jon. As the forest cast its dusky hues over the abbey yard, a dark figure emerged from the forest and made its way over the yard. Mathias could tell that it was Jon. He exhaled with a sigh of relief, and patiently waited for Jon's footsteps to ascend the stairs.

It wasn't long before the clip-clop of Jon's sandals could be heard in the stairwell. When Jon reached the top, Mathias was waiting for him with the door open. As Jon stepped closer, Father Mathias pulled him into a close hug. "I am so glad you have made it! I have been worried sick."

"I am fine, Father," he said with a faint smile. "But, the Leaflings are not. Tolokah was killed by the Leaflings."

After a moment of silence, he stared at the floor as he said, "I took the life of Anté…and in doing so … shattered the Shard into oblivion. I had no idea the Shard was within his cloak on a necklace. I had no idea, Father. I didn't know."

He paused as his eyes watered, and he shook his head in disappointment. "I fear I have cost the lives of the Leaflings. I have failed you, Father. I have failed."

Father Mathias placed both hands upon the shoulders of the young monk. "What you have done," spoke Mathias, "is what no one else would. You have quite possibly saved the world of man from the evils of Anté. I, too, fear that it may cost the Leaflings their lives…but you did what you must…and there is no shame in that, my son."

"And there is more," spoke Mathias. "You have rid this world of one of the Amethyst Rings. Someday you shall have mine…but, today, there is one less soul responsible for their proper use. One less soul must carry that weight. That is a comforting thought."

"And what of the Leaflings?" asked Jon, "How will they survive?"

"I don't believe they will, Jon. There is nothing more we can do. We cannot recreate the Stone, and if we continue to travel to Tal Kator, mankind will eventually find them, and unfortunately, without the Stone they will not be around long enough for someone to find. It is a cross they must bear."

"May I send them a message with Glock?" he asked. "I feel they should know I cannot return."

"I do not wish to jeopardize Glock with another trip into the forest. The Leaflings will have to endure on their own. If they are to survive, they will have to find a way on their own. The Literati' can no longer help them in their perils. We must now look out for our own…and they theirs."

"But they will look to us for guidance. How can we let them down? How can I let them know our dilemma? I must send Glock." The young monk's words were desperate.

"I will not take any more chances with Glock," spoke Mathias. "He is far too valuable to us. He will not go. The Literati' fathers have their rings…and Anté is out of the picture. Together, Jon, we have helped the monks of the abbey … and quite possibly the people of Cobblestone."

"And what," asked Jon, with a distrusting glance, "do the people of Cobblestone have to do with the Amethyst rings?"

"Jon," said Mathias, in a quiet voice, "do not get upset. The people of Cobblestone look to us for spiritual guidance…they look to us for leadership. The Amethyst Stones in each ring help to give us strength. Those of us who wear the rings receive the radiant benefits of the stone…much like the Leaflings. For the Leaflings, the Amethyst Stone was a life source. For us, these tiny stones help to extend our lives… thus, allowing us to rule and guide the fair peoples of the world for decades longer than we ordinarily would live. With these rings, we carry the weight of the future…and it is our cross to bear."

"So we live longer," spoke Jon with dismay, "and the Leaflings disappear from the world forever." The young monk shook his head with distaste. He turned from Mathias and quietly asked, "May I be excused, Father? I am in need of rest."

Jon felt many things swirling within his heart…and not the least of which was the overwhelming feeling of betrayal. There was no Leafling love in these futuristic Literati' fathers. There was only the desire to maintain their rule over man…for as long as their old bodies would last. It was their love of the Amethyst rings that spurred so much interest in Leafling lore. Perhaps, they too longed for the Stone of the Leaflings. Jon was certain that their concern over Anté may have been spurred by their interest in his ring. It was much larger than some of the rings worn by some of the monks of the abbey, which might lead one to believe that part of Antés strength and great age may have been enhanced by his ownership in his stone; not to mention the fact he was so drawn to the enormous Amethyst Stone of the Leafling colony.

If one stone so tiny could have lengthened one's life, imagine what one the size of the stone of the Leaflings could have done for one individual. Much of what was once hazy in the mind of Jon had now become clear as crystal…or Amethyst, and the fury in his heart was growing by the minute.

Jon had lived long enough to know that when his heart was heavy and his mind was angry, that he must sleep on his decisions. He made his way to the confines of his keep for just that purpose. It had been days since he had the time for more than just a short nap with the Leaflings. He needed sleep…if his mind would allow it. Stones and trolls, Leaflings and Literati'…all clouded his mind as he tried to doze off. Sleep did not come easy for the young monk with a lot of life on his mind.

Shortly after midnight, Jon's open eyes were still furious with anger. He had not slept but a few odd minutes. He stared quietly at the ceiling as he plotted his next moves. With one quick jolt from his bed, he grabbed the same pack from the day before and stormed from his room. As far as he was concerned, the Leafling colony would know of the Literati's ways…one way or another.

18

"Mirare' Scrolls," said old Ducah, pulling words from his far memory. "I don't know what they mean, but that is what they are called…Miraré Scrolls."

"Told ya, barky," said Kikah with a smile, "think you're soooo smart. I knew I could pull something from that waste-land of a memory of yours."

"I think," said Ducah, "I shall thump your head. It wouldn't hurt you saps to have a little respect…a little common grace for the old. Why, when I was your age…"

"Stop, stop," said Kikah, laughing. "Stop talking."

Ducah shook his head in disgust, yet trying not to laugh at the young one's vibrant insults. "You really are a vile young creature, you know."

Kikah chuckled out loud and said, "Flattery...my friend...will get you nowhere. And besides, if I had guessed what these scrolls were called, I might have guessed Miraré myself. Surely there is more to it than that."

"I'm certain there is, if I could just get you to shut up long enough for me to think a little," spoke Ducah.

"So sorry, outstanding one," spoke Kikah with a smile. "Please carry on."

Ducah paced the walls of the room, looking at the slabs for answers. The flickering light from the torch was burning down to its last few inches of grass.

Ducah finally spoke. "Let's take this first one out into the light. Grab that side." The two struggled to lift the stone from its shelf. It was remarkably heavy, but the two managed to cart it out the opening in the cave wall and down the corridor to the large cavern near the entrance. As they entered the main chamber of the cave, they met Kimbli and several other Leaflings waiting for their return. They looked in surprise at the large stone tablet and its strange letters.

Kimbli spoke up, "What is this...and from where has it come?"

Kikah answered, "There are several of these in a cavern down the corridor. Ducah says they are Miraré scrolls, but we do not know what they say...or what they are for. We have brought one from there to view in the light. Have you ever seen them?"

None of the Leaflings answered. It appeared that none knew anything about the slabs, and all looked to Ducah for answers. They stood the stone along the wall in the light shining from the entrance of the cave. The strange and beautiful letters chiseled into the stone were foreign to the Leaflings, and all stared, trying to decipher the meaning of them.

As the large group of Leaflings stared at the stone, an unexpected and rough voice entered the air. It was that of old Azir. "You have brought the wrong one, my friends. You should have brought the last one…not the first."

All stared in disbelief at their old mentor. The elder Leafling of Tal Kator had spoken for the first time since the horrible occurrences a few days before. His voice was weak, but the old one's words were heard with the greatest of enthusiasm by the Leafling tribe. They raced to his side and questioned him about his well-being.

"How are you, my friend," asked Kimbli with a tearful smile.

"Never mind me," he said, "you need to know of what you have found. Even without seeing all of the stone you have brought, I can tell that it is the first of the collection of stones from the Hall. It is the beginning of *The Lay the Amethyst Stone,* written by our elders of long ago.

Kimbli spoke up and asked, "Shall we bring it closer…for you to read?"

Azir managed a small chuckle. His sleepy eyes rolled and tried to refocus. The old Leafling closed his eyes and spoke from memory:

"From fear and despair they came
In fiery night of flame.

From smoldering soil and steam,
As if from hazy dream,

They raised their roots from land
And walked on foot and hand,

And like nothing 'ere before
Rose the Leaflings of Tal Kator.

"It was written by Ralfalla, the earliest of writing Leaflings. There is much more, my friends, but I have not the energy to recall them.

Our time is short...bring forth the last slab of scroll for translation. Be quick. My time runs short." After his words fell into the silence of the cave, Azir dozed back into deep sleep.

"What are we waiting for, friends?" spoke Kikah. "Kimbli...come with me...Ducah...watch Azir and Tulas and wait for our return!"

With that, the two Leaflings carted an age-old tablet back into the dark confines of the cavern. When they crossed the threshold of the ancient stone room, Kimbli gazed in wonder. "My word! I had no idea this was here. So this is the Hall of Scrolls. Ori once spoke of it, but I had no idea it was this fantastic. This is beautiful."

"No time for stargazing, young Prince," said Kikah. "We have a stone to carry." The two gently placed the stone slab back on its perch and proceeded to the farther depths of the room.

At the far end of the row of slabs, Kikah stopped and smiled at Kimbli. "This, my friend, is what we came for."

In the near darkness of the stone room, the two fumbled with the slab as they brought it from its dusty shelf. They wrestled its heavy weight out of the chamber and back up the shaft to the main entrance. There was a hush of excitement as the two stumbled into the front chamber of the cave. All of the present Leaflings gazed at the stone with great anticipation, yet none could discern anything in the elaborate scrolls within the slab. As the Leaflings gathered around the stone, Kimbli approached the two bound Leaflings lying silent in the dim light of the edge of the cavern.

"Azir," he said, in a quiet whisper. "We have returned with the slab...can you help us?"

Azir's groggy eyes struggled to focus, and then drifted back off into the depths of his mind. He struggled to come back...but had great trouble in doing so. Kimbli again spoke.

"We cannot make out the writing of the scrolls. Can you help us, Azir?"

Azir again raised his head, and looked toward the stone. Its strange and winding words were quite familiar to him. They were deeply carved into the surface of the stone, and though they were not recognizable to many who viewed them, they were still beautiful to behold.

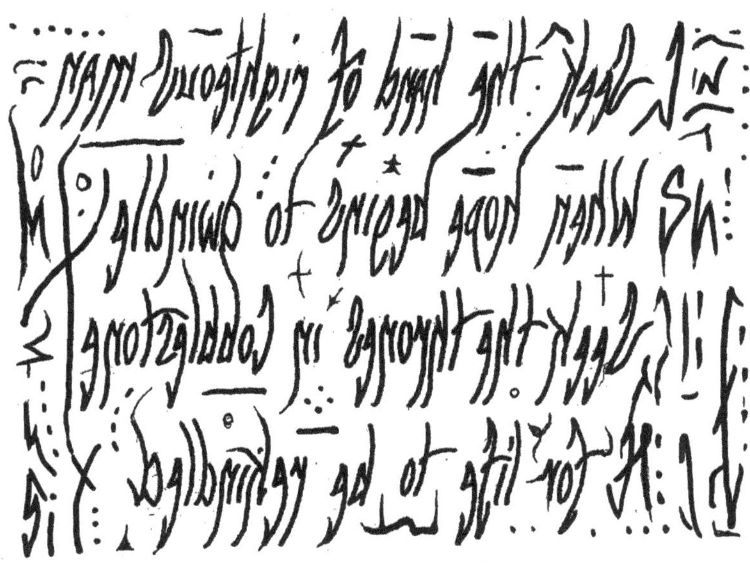

As his mind wandered in and out of consciousness, he said three simple words that made more sense to Kimbli than any he had ever spoken. His tender and falling words rang in the damp air of the cave. "Miraré…think Miraré."

Kikah gave Kimbli a questioning glance. "I am afraid I don't understand."

"You will, my friend," spoke Kimbli. "Help me take this stone out into the sunlight." The two again picked up the heavy slab and carted it out into the bright light of day. "Watch closely," spoke Kimbli, "and learn the true meaning of Miraré."

Kimbli instructed Kikah to help flip the stone over upside down. They edged their way over to the shoreline of the Miraré. As the two Leafling friends waded out into the shallow shore of the Miraré…and the gentle waves finally ceased to ripple over its surface…the mirror reflection of the Miraré surface showed a vibrant and clear reflection of the stone slab in their hands. At last, it made sense to Kikah and the rest of the Leaflings. The fantastic reflection in the Miraré was very apparent:

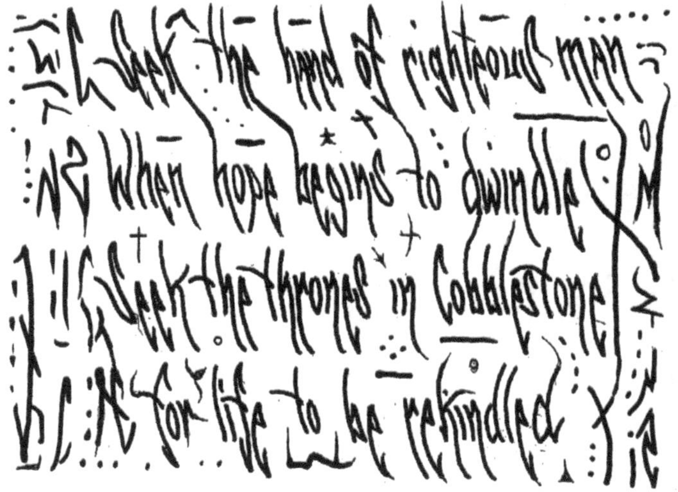

"Well," spoke Kikah, "just look at that…amazing!" As all stared in wonder, Kikah read aloud the words chiseled into this ancient stone. "Seek the hand of righteous man…when hope begins to dwindle…seek the thrones in Cobblestone…for life to be rekindled."

Kikah and Kimbli eased back to shore and laid down the heavy slab. Finally, Kikah spoke. "So we must seek the help of the Monk descendents of the Literati'."

Kimbli gave Kikah a disappointing glance. "I don't think so, Kikah. I think there is much more to it than that. We must speak to Azir."

Kikah was now troubled by Kimbli's look of worry. The two carried the old slab back into the cave and gently set it down along the wall. Kimbli approached Azir and Tulas once again, and spoke quietly, "We are back, Azir…can you hear me?"

Azir raised his head and wearily spoke, "Do you understand the words in the stone?"

"They are very vague, Azir, can you tell us what they mean?"

Azir summoned every ounce of his strength and began a very important speech. His dry voice spoke, "In the beginning…when the Literati' adopted us and reared us like their own…there was great trust among us all. Every Leafling and every Literati' had great repose. The relationship between us was very special."

Azir coughed and collected himself. It was apparent that he was in a great deal of pain. He winced as he spoke, "Once…there were two Amethyst Stones…two. They were brought forth from the very depths of this cave by the Literati'…from deep within the earth where the meteor came to rest. They were the heart of the meteor. The Literati'… in return for the labor of our raising, and for bringing the stones forth… took one of the stones and carved it into ten smaller stones. They then set the stones into beautiful rings…and those stones continued to emit strength and a tremendous healing power."

The old Leafling paused again, clearing his throat. "The Literati' came to worship them…almost beyond anything else on earth. Soon, their fear of losing them overshadowed their lives here in Tal Kator. That is when they chose to move themselves to the community of Cobblestone. We have had no contact with them since then…so many ages and ages ago. The elder Leaflings chose to keep the other stones secret…for fear of the young ones holding contempt for the Literati' of old. The Literati' of old were true at heart…and did much for the Leaflings…at least in the beginning. They deserve praise from us… they deserve respect. We owe our lives to the early Literati'. Without them, we would not exist."

Kimbli bowed his head and spoke to Azir, “We no longer have the Amethyst Stone, Azir…it is destroyed. It shattered when Anté died. We know not what to do.”

Azir let his head rest back on its pillow. He gave a sigh of remorse. “That is why we are not healing. That is why we do not strengthen. I fear we are doomed. We will not last long without the stone, my young ones.”

Finally, Kikah could take no more. His fiery demeanor rarely kept quiet…even when necessary. His words chopped through the air, “So let me get this straight…because of man, we all live…and because of man…we shall now die! The greed of man took one of our stones…and corrupted a troll to take the other. Now, we set poised to die…because of these GREAT Literati’? Will they not come to our aid? Will they not undo their wrong of taking our stone of life?”

“I do not know what fate the hand of man will deal,” spoke Azir quietly. “And we have little time to tarry at wait. We must make a decision...and make it soon. Will we wither and die in this cave…or take a stand with the descendents of the Literati’?”

Kikah stood tall and proud. With a fierce determination in his eyes, he spoke aloud, “I say we take back what is ours! In the name of my Ori…and the names of all who have died…I shall reclaim the stones for Tal Kator…or die in the trying!”

A tear fell from his cheek as he spoke of his Ori. Kimbli stood tall beside him and spoke, “You shall have my spear…and every ounce of strength in my body … FOR TAL KATOR!”

“FOR TAL KATOR!” shouted a chorus of Leaflings. “FOR TAL KATOR!”

And in the darkness of a once-illuminated cave, peace and anguish left the hearts of many…and anger and desperation raged in their souls…for Tal Kator.

“FOR TAL KATOR!”

19

The raspy hush of a dozen Leafling guards spread through the dark forest as heavy footsteps thrashed into the community of Tal Kator. As he reached the near edge of the clearing, the voice of Jon rattled the Leafling guards. "Leafling guards! It is Jon. I need to speak with the colony. May I come forth?"

The guards immediately recognized the voice of Jon and welcomed him to the cave. The cave was quiet in the early pre-dawn hours. He soon found the eager eyes of Kimbli. "I need to speak with you…about the monks of the abbey."

Kimbli gave Jon an understanding glance. "Tell me what you can, Jon, we need to talk."

"I fear that the monks will not come forward to help you. They do not know I am here…and would disallow it if they knew of it. I know that they will not come forward…and there is little help I can offer…I am sorry."

"You know, of course," said Kimbli, "that we must have the remaining stones to survive. We cannot live without them. Without the Amethyst Stone…and with Antés stone no longer in existence, we need the remaining nine to live. We MUST have them."

"The monks will not relinquish the stones to you, Kimbli. They will fight to the death. I know them well…they will fight."

"Then fight we must," spoke Kimbli. "We have no choice. We must have the stones. Thank you for coming to talk with us. You have been a good friend, Jon. We can ask no more of you. You have done well. But we, Jon…we must fight."

Jon shook his head in sorrow. "I wish things were different…I should like to get to know the Leaflings of Tal Kator much better. I must leave now, before the elders find me gone. I must go…do take care, Kimbli. I wish you the best of luck. May there be no more bloodshed for either side."

"Let us hope for the best," spoke Kimbli. "May we meet someday on better terms."

With a nod and a smile, Jon turned and left the cave. Within seconds, he scampered beyond the Miraré and into the darkness of the forest.

Kimbli sat down and put his head in his hands. It was time to put a plan together. If Jon was correct, the Leaflings were in for quite a battle, and Kimbli was ready to give them one. As the first rays of morning sun entered the cave, Kimbli called a meeting of the colony. Thirty fiery Leaflings came forth with spears in hand.

"Alright, friends," spoke Kimbli. "Let's talk strategy."

20

Jon was now in a jam. The men that helped in his raising…those that he cared for deeply…were in possible danger. If he went to Mathias with news of a possible attack, he would immediately suspect that he had made a trip back to talk with the Leaflings. He knew deep in his heart, that the only elder that would even consider giving up his ring would be Mathias. And even he was very unlikely to give up such a token that would lengthen his life.

It seemed that Jon was in a predicament where no one involved would be happy with any news from him. These old men were not willing to give up something that could allow them a longer life…and yet, their life stood in immediate danger.

"How good is that ring to a dead man?" he wondered. Jon finally took a piece of advice that Father Mathias gave him years ago. Mathias had said, "When faced with making a decision where no one involved will be pleased…please yourself."

Jon elected to do just that. Although his heart was heavy with worry, he chose to please himself. He simply plodded along in his daily rituals, letting life run its course. He would let the Leaflings and monks battle how they may. As far as Jon was concerned, the battle was theirs to fight…and to victor would go the spoils. The Leaflings and monks would have to cross their own bridges. Jon felt he had went above and beyond the call of duty for both sides of this story, and he had no intention of being a casualty of some war with no real victors. He would play along and give hope where he could, and offer consolation where needed.

As Jon finished his last duties of the day, he prepared himself for a well-deserved night's sleep. He said a prayer for all of those involved in this horrendous tragedy. He prayed that all could be left unharmed in this frightful story with no rational ending…this story without a peaceful solution. And as night fell on the abbey in Cobblestone, sleep fell deeply on young Jon for the first time in many very long nights.

* * *

Meanwhile, the strong wooden doors and stone walls of the abbey were being infiltrated. Despite the thick doors and the deep and heavy stone walls, thirty Leaflings slid easily beneath the doors and entered every room within the rock-solid walls of the abbey. Their vigilant eyes viewed every hand of every sleeping monk and scoured all flat surfaces within each room. They were on a hunt…and their prey would not be hidden from them.

Within minutes, eight of the nine stones had been found, and every elder within the rooms of the abbey were being stalked with a fiery temper. The Leaflings had little remorse for the sleeping monks, but held fast to their oaths to Kimbli and Kikah to give every possible avenue of escape to those willing to cooperate…those willing to relinquish their Amethyst rings in good faith…those willing to not lose their lives over something that may, or may not, lengthen it. They chose to give all a chance to accept their terms…or face the consequences. Despite the dead quiet within the walls of the abbey, very much was happening…and happening fast.

A raspy voice scratched through the silence of the bedroom of Father Finley. "Awaken, monk!" shouted a Leafling guard. As Father Finley's eyes focused near the voice at the foot of the bed, he jumped with a start. He immediately sat up in disbelief. The old monk could hardly believe his eyes…*a real Leafling here in the abbey!*

"How did you get in here?" he whipered with a hint of fear in his voice.

"We have come to ask you to relinquish your ring…so that we Leaflings may continue to live as your ancestors wished. We no longer have the Amethyst Stone…and we need the rings of the Literati' Fathers to maintain life as we know it. We ask you to please consider allowing us to take the ring…and visit us regularly if you wish to bask in the glory of our lives and the radiance of the stones. We welcome you back to Tal Kator to rejoice with us and be at one with nature once again. Please let us take your ring to Tal Kator."

"You may take my ring when you wrestle it from my cold dead finger!" shouted Finley, with an evil glare.

"As you wish, Father," spoke the Leafling. Within a split second, the connecting fingers of two Leaflings surrounded the neck of Father Finley. Two more restrained his hands. And, within a matter of five minutes, Father Finley…descendent of the Literati' of old…lie dead in his bed. The Leaflings gathered together and chanted a prayer for the dead. "Rest in peace," they spoke in unison.

Throughout the abbey, identical situations were occurring with each monk. None, so far, had offered their ring to the Leaflings, and with eight down and one to go, Kikah went to the only place left he felt he could…and still keep a clear conscience. He made his way downstairs to the tiny quarters of the young monks. It did not take him long to find the quarters of whom he sought.

Kikah now stood at the foot of the bed of young Jon. His eyes lie firmly on the face of the young monk sleeping soundly. He finally stepped upon the wool bedspread and spoke, "Awaken…friend Jon." His voice grew louder with his temper. "AWAKEN JON!"

Jon eyes tried to focus in the dark of the room. He was deep into the very restful and intense sleep of the first few hours of nightfall. His confusion was obvious to Kikah, and he showed Jon all the respect that one could under such harsh conditions.

"It is time you wake!" said Kikah.

By now, Jon was wide eyed and frightened by the sight of Kikah and two other Leaflings within the walls of Cobblestone Abbey. His excited energy shook him to full attention…and he stared in wonder at Kikah.

Kikah again spoke, "You and I have a trip to make, my friend. If you care for your elder priest as much as you have said, then you will talk him into relinquishing his ring…and save his life. Take us to him."

Three tiny spears were now pointed at Jon, and he realized that Kikah's words were not a request. He rose and began an agonizing journey to Father Mathias' keep. The long and winding stairs to Mathias' room seemed endless. As he reached the top of the spiral stairwell, he was surprised to find the door to Father Mathias' room wide open. As he stepped near, he could tell that Mathias had been bound by Leafling hands, and all were apparently waiting for Jon's arrival.

As he approached Mathias' bedside, Jon spoke, "They want me to speak to you. If you do not give them the last ring, they will kill you. Please…please Father, give them the ring. Live here with me…you are dear to me…please."

"You know of what you ask," spoke Mathias. "What you do not know, Jon, is that the monks of the abbey think I am eighty-four years old. I am over one hundred. Whether they take the ring, or take my life, either way…I am dead."

"You must give them the ring, Father," spoke Jon with tears of anguish. "GIVE THEM THE RING…for God's sake…and mine… give them the ring."

Jon approached the old monk's bedside. He grasped Father Mathias by the shoulders and begged, "GIVE THEM THE RING, NOW!"

Mathias looked Jon in the eye with sorrow and distaste. He did understand his peril…and that of the Leaflings…but it didn't make matters any easier.

"I do not think I can do it, Jon."

Jon choked back more tears, "This time, Father…this time…trust in me. I will not let you down. Please, Father…I beg of you."

Father Mathias looked at Jon with the most sullen of glances. He bowed his head and took a deep breath. With a quiet shake of his head, he gently released the grip of his fist. He allowed the Leafling by his side to tug the ring from his finger. With a quick snap and a bounce from the bed, Leaflings from all sides of the room scampered away.

Kimbli and Kikah stood motionless on the foot of the bed. Kimbli spoke, "I am truly sorry for this. We are all in dire straights. You are both welcome in Tal Kator as long as you live. We truly wish you the very best…we are sorry."

As tears of joy fell from many Leafling eyes, Mathias the monk sat motionless in bed, with tears of loss falling from his.

When Jon was certain that the Leaflings had long since made their way into the forest, he finally spoke to Mathias. "I have not forsaken you, Father. I did what I must to save your life."

"It doesn't matter now, Jon. The weight of this monastery now lies solely upon your shoulders. I will be gone soon, and you must carry on. We have dead to bury. We have an explanation to make to the world. How will we explain this to Cobblestone? They will not understand about little creatures in the woods coming forth and taking lives. We will be a laughing stock. And, worst of all, Jon, I don't think I shall be around long enough to help you."

"Now Father," said Jon, with a wry smile, "I asked you to trust me, didn't I? I would not ask if I could not have backed my word."

Jon continued his crafty smile to Mathias, and Mathias finally spoke, "I do not understand."

"Well, my Father," spoke Jon, "I have something for you. I just couldn't let some of the pretty things of old Uncle Anté burn. I thought you might like this." Jon reached into his pocket and removed something in his tight grip. With cupped hands, he dropped a shiny, vine-covered ring into Mathias' hands. "I didn't think it would be of any use to old Anté, anyway." Mathias stared in disbelief at the ring in his hand.

"And another thing," spoke Jon, "...could it be possible that our monk brethren may have left in the night for some far away sabbatical? If so, I have some digging to do tonight!"

"Jon, my son," spoke Mathias, "I shall never doubt you again!"

21

A host of thirty Leaflings scampered through the forest. As they reached the borders of Tal Kator, the first rays of morning sun were reflecting from the Miraré. The group was welcomed with the first displays of joy that Tal Kator had seen in many days. Kimbli and Kikah smiled with satisfaction as they stepped into the cave. Only a few hours had passed, but they felt they had been gone ages. Both young Leaflings had returned victorious with a crowd of proud Leaflings by their side. They all appeared to be returning from war…and in all reality … they were. They felt the thrill of victory…and the emptiness that accompanies the taking of another life. They had all aged many years in the last few days…but the peace of Tal Kator was returning.

Nine golden rings hung from a vine of ivy, as Kimbli and Kikah entered the cave. The tiny Amethyst stones glimmered in what little morning light the cave had to offer. The two could easily see Tulas and Azir still bound and lying side by side on their bedding. As the two approached, Azir raised his head. "My little ones…you have returned!"

Kimbli looked at Azir with a smile. He stretched his hand out to Azir and spoke, "We have returned victorious." The vine of Literati' rings dangled from his fist.

"Hang them," spoke Azir, "in honor…around his neck." He motioned toward the almost lifeless body of Tulas. "He is in great need."

As he hung the vine of rings around the neck of Tulas, a gasp of air entered his lungs and the warm and vibrant energy of the stones was emitted almost immediately. "Now," spoke Azir, "we must wait."

After a few moments of silence, Kimbli and Kikah stepped from the sleeping duo before them and out into the early morning sun. "Feels good, doesn't it?" spoke Kikah.

"If you are talking about the warm spring sun," said Kimbli, "then I most definitely agree. I have missed feeling sunshine…and splashing in the Miraré."

The two walked the confines of the Miraré and touched base with the Leafling guards that had stayed behind during the Cobblestone ordeal. Some joking camaraderie began to take the place of constant worry and remorse.

The healing process in Tal Kator had begun…and life had begun to grow again where hope and despair had prospered. Slowly, the joy in Tal Kator returned. Days passed…then a week.

"Ori," called Kimbli, "you look well today."

"If I could just shed myself of this old barky, I could get on with life!"

Azir shook his head as usual at the incessant and chiding ramblings of today's youth. "I think I am about ready to rid myself of this parasite, as well. And besides, I saved this life…I might just take it back!" Azir constantly batted at Tulas with a playful joust. A battle of words would always ensue, as the two bantered back and forth. Few in any walk of life could deliver slams and shots at one another and still walk away truest of friends. Unfortunately, walking away was not quite possible yet.

Kimbli walked out into the light of day and joined his friend, Kikah, at the base of the old Chestnut. "Mesigh would often teach me here," spoke Kikah. "My Ori would sometimes join in the chain and toss us all into the water from this high limb."

Kikah pointed to the boughs of the huge tree above. As Kimbli sat and listened to the solemn words of Kikah, he sat comfortably at the base of the tree and let his friend vent his sorrow.

"I think," said Kikah, "that I shall carve a letter in this old tree. I think a large letter 'L' would look nice. You know, for the old Literati'. My heart has lightened little, Kimbli. It was not fair for the monks to die…or us, for that matter. It is all about death…suffering. I wish there had been a better way."

Kikah paused and looked into the distance. "You know, Kimbli, I thought that somehow … regaining the stones would take away some of the pain. I thought that revenge would somehow help heal that vacancy in my heart. There is a hole…an emptiness…that pounds through me with giant waves. I feel it every hour of every day. No revenge…no victory…could ever fill it. I just don't know, Kimbli. How do I fill such a void? How does one rinse the heart of loss? How do I feel whole again?"

"I don't know, Kikah," spoke Kimbli. "I wish I could guide you to an easier path. But, there is no easy path for those that have witnessed such destruction, or have felt such loss. But, we have persevered…we have fought a hard battle. We should move on and live life as best we can. Fill the void with positive things, Kikah…fill the void with life…not death."

"I know…and I will," spoke Kikah, "But, an 'L' would look nice here, don't you think?"

"I suppose so," said Kimbli with a chuckle and a smile. "Carve away, my friend. Fill the void!" And in the quiet and serene setting beneath the old chestnut, one Leafling began filling his void and this peaceful valley seemed a lot more like Tal Kator.

* * *

A couple of hundred yards away, two Leaflings were battling wits. "Say," said Azir.

"What is it now, barky?" asked Tulas.

"Barky?" spoke Azir. "You'll think barky. You can thank your lucky stars I haven't pulled off all your bark, instead of that little patch on your arm! What I was going to ask was; do you know what is worse than being bound up with a Leafling?" Azir began untying the wrappings of their arms as he spoke.

"I guess not," Tulas replied.

"This!" said Azir. With a quick and deliberate tug, he yanked their arms apart. Tulas screamed at the top of his lungs and winced in pain. Although Azir fought the same pain, he managed to laugh at Tulas' surprise. "Told ya it was worse!"

"Free at last!" exclaimed Tulas, grasping at his arm in pain. "…and good riddance."

One year later…

Kimbli walked the shores of the Miraré as tiny waves rippled over its surface. Harmonizing chuckles of young Leaflings filled the air as they slung one another into the waters of the Miraré. Squirrels were again scampering through the forest and swallows darted over the lake surface. Tal Kator was again full of life.

Soon, Kimbli found his best friend, Kikah, setting beneath the chestnut, soaking in the lakeshore. Beside him, tiny little roots wiggled in the muddy shoreline. Kikah looked down proudly on the baby Leafling at his side. As he approached, Kimbli spoke aloud, "And, how is young Mesigh this morning?"

The tiny Leafling looked up to him and smiled. "We are absolutely fabulous today, my friend," spoke Kikah. "Where is the rest of your ragged group?"

"Ori and Azir are in their studies…probably where I should be. But, I certainly hated to miss such a fantastic morning of swimming. How about a dip…old timer?" Kimbli asked.

"I think I will watch today," said Kikah, "Mesigh and I are having fun here in the mud. But go right ahead there barky."

"I believe I will, Master Kikah. Watch closely Mesigh…you may have to learn from me!"

Kimbli ran up the bank and grabbed hold of the long line of Leaflings dangling from the limbs. Within seconds, he flew over the lake surface and landed with a splash.

"Ahhhh…that was fantastic!" he said, shaking water from his leaves. "Maybe once more, then off to my studies."

He again climbed the hill and began throwing little ones into the air…forgetting his studies for the day.

While they swam and played in the sunny waters of the Miraré, Tulas and old Azir walked up to the chestnut.

Azir spoke aloud, "The weather is too nice to study today. We thought a short walk could do us some good. It is wonderful to see Tal Kator in such great spirits. May the heart-break of last year never return!"

"NEVERMORE!" shouted Kimbli. "Nevermore."

Leaflings

Book Two

The Prophesy Rhymes Of Tolk's Tomb

From the Book of Lore, the Dark Ages:

~ The Missing Page ~

Look to those…with hearts unsold,
to renew the Faith of young and old.

When King forsakes Father for lust and greed,
Cobblestone hearts will again be freed.

Find written answers in dismal doom,
in sullen, dark dungeon of Tolk's lonely Tomb.

Seek for the chosen…born of King,
soon the bearer of righteous ring.

There will be proof for those unswayed…
for the forest will awaken…and come to his aid.

…and the Prophesy begins.

1

The streets of Cobblestone were damp with the morning dew. It was a dreary late summer day, and the skies were drab with the rainy gray clouds that seemed to loom over the city with an impending sorrow. Shutters were closed, even with the warm and humid conditions, in anticipation of an impending shower. The thirsty plants and flowers in the yards and window boxes welcomed the drops of rain, but for the town of Cobblestone, the dreary weather mirrored the heavy hearts of its civilians. Recent years had shown a change in the quaint little town. What was once a vibrant and warm dwelling of man, had slowly dwindled into a more subtle and forlorn community of a people who questioned their leadership…even their faith. It was still as lovely as ever—there just seemed to be a change in the air.

More than a decade had passed since the leaving of eight of the most influential members of the old abbey in Cobblestone. No one knew where they had chosen to travel, and even more questioned their leaving altogether. People missed these inspirational men in their lives and wondered if the young ones would ever properly fill their shoes. Could this abbey ever truly recover from such an upheaval? The elders were sorely missed, and many townspeople began to shirk what was once a rock-solid family tradition of attending sermons with the monk elders. It wasn't really a full church service, but more of a sermon and a short counsel thereafter. There was once a time that the town filled its pews; yet now, the attendance had dwindled considerably.

To make things worse, King Lawrence rarely ever showed his face these days. There were times, though, that he would make an appearance. He would come forth to deliver the inevitable increase in taxes, which had become an almost monthly occurrence. He would sometimes come into the merry places of town in search of...well...entertainment. Few now remembered his father's warm ways of walking the streets for a morning stroll. The king's father, and sometimes mother, would walk a slow and intentional path through the city streets. They would pause and speak with the townspeople. They would take pleasure in the refreshing morning air and enjoy the healthful walk. They would listen to the voices of those they governed. It was a good system that worked for years. But, unfortunately, that was decades ago, and the most recent of kings was now in his late fifties and still very unwed with no children. He had no siblings, no Uncles, no apparent tie to family other than the line after line of portraits down the main halls of his castle.

Cobblestone's king would have been lonely if it weren't for all the people in his life. They were not family, or for that matter, even true friends. They were the King's People and little more. But, by most measurable means, the king was quite happy being king. In fact, he loved it. He could throw horrid tantrums...could curse and rant and rave...could throw down detestable commands...all for his spoiled arrogance. His every wish, good and bad, was fulfilled. Perhaps that's kingship.

During the last decade, the town had slowly and subtly undergone a change. Since the elders of the abbey had left so abruptly, many townspeople harbored a fear in their hearts. Why didn't anyone mention this foreign sabbatical prior to their leaving? Where were the beloved men of God that most had come to trust? Many began to succumb to the neigh-saying and less righteous thoughts of those who were in the employ of the king.

Now, most would admit that the king had been a very successful king. He had conquered all that he had set out to take. He had provided a fantastic army to preserve and protect his citizens. He had employed many walks of life…trolls for extra strength in protection…dwarves for their fantastic metal works…even local men and women for their honed talents in various ways. In all essence, he had been a very strong and valiant leader, worthy and just. He had been regal and domineering. He even looked "kingly". He was the prodigy of many years of royalty. Despite his brilliant and cordial, kingly ways, he had slipped into a less-than-perfect social life and was quite a pampered and egotistical sort. He looked first and foremost to himself..."Old number one". "All for one…and all for me!" And "Me" liked things the way they were.

On this particular day, as with many days, Earl, the right-hand servant of the king, walked the streets of Cobblestone knocking on doors and doing the uncomfortable job of extracting taxes from the local folks and doing his best to make *pleasant* of the unpleasantries.

Each reluctant knock on the door was a blow to Earl's heart. He had a strong love for his king, yet felt the pain of facing every civilian on their own turf…as every king should. The king should understand the complexities of his own hierarchy, and yet feel the voice of the people he governs.

Earl was a strong and heart-felt fellow, good to his fellow man, and respectful to his king. He was worthy of high praise; he just rarely received it. He was the common man's man…warm and simple. He was Good Earl, as most knew him, and Earl did his best to live up to his name.

Earl lifted his hand to the old wooden door of the home of an old friend, Bartholomew Smith. As he rapped gently on the door, old Smitty, as they called him, reluctantly stepped to the door and opened it. "Good morning, Good Earl," he said quietly, not to awaken his household, "It is good to see you, friend."

Smitty did mean the words he spoke, but felt the usual awkward pang in his stomach that came from both hunger and Earl's knowing smile. He welcomed Earl inside.

"I cannot linger this morning, Smitty. I am on my usual dreaded mission. You know you are behind on your taxes, still." As he spoke, he too felt the pang in his stomach and delivered his speech as soft and gentle as possible. It is never easy asking for blood from a turnip.

Poor Smitty seemed to cower under the large and stately figure in his doorway and looked to him through sullen eyes. "I have not worked since my accident in the field…" he said, as he glanced down at his bandaged leg.

"I know." spoke Earl, with an understanding nod. "I will come back another day…but you mustn't tarry long. The king grows impatient." As he spoke, he reached into his pocket and retrieved two small coins. One he dropped into the colorful pouch of the king's; the other he dropped into the old man's hand. "Claven needs a hand in the kitchen down at the tavern…" He tipped his hat and smiled at Smitty and stepped from the doorway into the alley.

"Bless you, Good Earl," he said with swelling eyes. "Bless you." And he closed the door after him.

After a number of knocks on doors, Earl eventually meandered into a small portion of town known as Flagstone Row. It was a long row of connected housing usually occupied by those a little more fortunate than Earl's old friend, Smitty.

The row of buildings were not lavish but still had some nice touches like window boxes and small fountains. It was a pleasant little setting, well-known to Earl. It was his childhood home. He still knew many of its residents and visited now and then. As he turned a corner and began his purpose, a voice called out to him.

"You need not knock on my door, Good Earl," shouted the voice of a middle-aged man dressed in clean leather attire, "for I stand attentive to such graces as a visit from the king's puppet. I see you are still in the employ of Lucky Larry."

"Draw your sword, peasant!" Earl shouted. "Lest I behead you for treason to the king!"

"Unless your swordsmanship has improved, Great Earl of Flagstone…might I draw a mop…or perhaps a walking stick?" the voice chided.

Earl stepped to arm's distance of the man speaking and stared into his face with a scowl. Within seconds, the scowls of both men turned to smiles culminating in hearty laughs. With a forceful handshake, Earl said "Dominick! It is good to see you. How have you been, my nearly headless friend?"

"I have been away at work aboard the *Sea Dragon,* in the Bay of Greenwale. I dare say I shall never eat another crab in all my days!" spoke Dominick, chuckling.

"….away PIRATING, I'd rather believe," joked Earl.

After a bit of small talk and joke-filled bantering, Dom, as he was known in these streets, invited Earl in for a cup of tea. They discussed the comings and goings of Cobblestone and the many facets of crab fishing in the bay. Dom had been gone for nearly two years, and he mentioned the slight difference in the air.

"The streets do not seem as enchanting as I remember," he stated, "and far fewer fair maidens, as well." He smiled and gazed out the window at the quiet streets.

"Ah," laughed Earl, "there are still many fair maidens within our fine walls. We have penned them up in preparation of your arrival! We will set them free once you've gone, and things are much safer."

"Touché, my friend" smiled Dom.

The two continued their talk for another few minutes until Earl finally stood and prepared to leave. Dom again spoke, "It really has been good to see you, my friend. I intend to stay in your fair city for the better part of autumn. Should you or our fair king need my service, I am at your immediate disposal. You know where to find me."

"Certainly," laughed Earl, with a wry smile, "you will be somewhere near the pent up maidens! Until next time…keep your mop handy!" And, as the two friends parted ways, it was good to know that there were still a few hearty laughs left in Cobblestone.

2

The walls of Cobblestone Abbey were warm against the back of a young monk's cloak. Brother Jon sat quietly on the stone wall of the garden with quill pen in hand. He would pause now and again to rest his tired grip of the pen and gaze out over the many roses and late summer flowers currently in bloom. The back garden of the abbey was Jon's favorite place to do his scribing and copying of the old books of the abbey's vast library. He had copied many volumes himself and had watched attentively, in his youth, while many other volumes were lovingly copied by the hands of the monks of the abbey in much the same way as Jon was now. It was considered an honor to re-scribe a book of importance, and to do so in the beautiful garden setting of the abbey was a very rewarding and peaceful pastime for Jon. He always initialed his books with a small printing of his name on the back cover...*Jon.*

Today, the overcast weather provided a cool spot for Jon's work. He was about midway through his copying of one of the most important books of the time. The writings of Tolk were all immensely important works, but his *Book of Lore* was consulted by virtually everyone from the churches and schools to the king himself. It was a work of both history and prophesy. It was regarded as a gospel of a great prophet, and it was renowned far and wide. Tolk's writing was always of a rhyming and rhythmic sort, and within his words, great stories were told…and eerie prophesies foreshadowed. Within this book, some of the prophesies of Tal Kator were entwined. Although the Leaflings were mentioned numerous times within that portion of the book, most people merely overlooked the Leaflings as some long-ago figment. Nearly every other word in this large volume was hung upon, studied, and lived by. It was a treasured piece of literature.

Jon had copied this book before. Father Haley had requested one in Jon's handwriting years ago, not long before his untimely death. A pang of guilt rumbled in Jon's stomach. His mind flashed back to the night he buried Father Haley and the rest of the "Eight Missing Fathers". He had never worked harder in his life than that night. There were still signs of his once bloody and swollen blisters on his hands to this day, a decade later. He could remember the cool, clammy soil like it was yesterday and could feel the pain in his back. His heart had never been the same after that gut-wrenching ordeal. He questioned his actions of that night over and over and never fully gained confidence that what he did was right. He had saved the abbey a barrage of questions, and moreover, he saved a lynching of the Leaflings.

So much death, he thought. *Who is to know what was right?* But, right or wrong, his actions that night had profoundly changed the abbey, as well as the city of Cobblestone. It seemed everyone now needed proof of everything from unimportant daily chores to the very scripture the monks worshipped.

Evidence, thought Jon. *Everyone needs proof...proof unattainable.*

One of the few things that lightened Jon's heart was a visit the small cemetery he had created for the eight monks. It was only a small clearing with unmarked fieldstones as headstones and one larger one with four simple words carved into its face.

It simply read: *Here Lie Great Men.*

Although ten years had now passed, a tear still rolled down Jon's nose and fell onto his page. It really wasn't his fault. The men had had the opportunity to live but chose to fight instead.

But none of that mattered to Jon; he still felt sorrow and guilt over the ordeal and carried it with him daily. He hoped to someday make amends to the abbey for what had befallen it...he just had no idea how to do it. So everyday he plodded along, doing his best to keep his chin up, serving the abbey to the best of his ability and caring for his mentor...Father Mathias.

Mathias, who was now astonishingly old, was still able to carefully navigate the spiral stairwell. He still made his presence known throughout the abbey. His knowledgeable smile and kind words were the strongholds of the abbey. Yet in these days, faith was aging like the beloved old monk himself. He was still loved, and very much respected; yet people just didn't seem to seek his counsel as often as years ago. The abbey was far less visited now.

Father Mathias slowly approached as Jon sat comfortably on the garden wall. He finally spoke to the lad in front of him, "Your hands are never idle, my good son."

Jon was humbled when the old monk spoke to him as son. Even though that sort of thing was quite common among members of the monk faith, Jon took great pride in it and always made certain his address to Mathias was always in the form of "Father".

"Idle hands, Father," said Jon, "are the hands of the Devil." He gave Mathias a warm smile and motioned to the wall beside him. "Father," he continued, "I am copying Tolk again. It is such a shame that some of these pages have fallen out and lost. I should love to see them and copy the book in full."

Father Mathias gave a solemn look. "I'm afraid those pages were not lost…" he said with a sigh, "…they were removed." He looked to Jon for his response and received Jon's astonished gasp. "The good kingship has seen fit to save us that blessing. It has been said by royalty for years beyond account that those pages plagued the city with undue worry. The kings and queens of old had them removed."

"How does one remove history?" asked Jon, astonished.

"I feel you have forgotten some of my teachings," spoke Mathias. Jon let his head fall with disappointment. It was obvious that the lad was delving into his memory deeply as possible. Bits and pieces of his studies of Tolk began to re-enter his mind.

"Tolk..." stammered Jon, "was in the employ of one of the old kings." Jon's head tilted side to side and appeared to be allowing thoughts to bounce around a bit. "... uhmmm ... he was scribe for some time. Yes! He was scribe for the king! He was the king's personal scribe before he went off into the forest to study and write. But how does this relate to history...to my question?"

Mathias' shoulders seemed to sag with the weight of Jon's question. "I have delayed telling you many things, Jon...for fear of weakening your faith."

"I shall never lose faith, Father. I have your words...your example... your love." He gave Mathias a concerned glance. "I shall wait patiently for you to tell of what and when...in what ever manner you wish."

Mathias took a deep breath and released it with a worrisome tone of voice. "Since the good Lord has provided us with such a cool and cloudy afternoon, here in such a blessed place, I suppose it is time."

Jon laid down his pen and stared in wonder at the old man before him. He looked to Mathias and said, "When the student is ready, the teacher will appear. I shall wait patiently, Father."

"You need not wait, my son. I will tell of it. You should know. Do not lose faith. Do not lose heart. You are all I have. I will need you in the end." As he spoke, a tear slid from his eye, much like that of Jon a moment or two earlier. "You know of our king?"

"Of course, Father, he has been a strong leader...a force for Cobblestone."

"Yes...yes he has," spoke Mathias cautiously. "But not all of his actions are so stately. He has provided proof unto the people. He states his plans and follows through. He professed to the conquering of the thieves and thugs of the Farfold Marshes...and did so. People can count on the foretellings of that nature. They seek a much sooner faith and receive it through him. He has been a great warrior and savior in their eyes. The kings of old did the same. There is great valor in such, and I do not condemn it. But it has been said among the Literati of old that every precaution has been taken to ensure that those same kingly conditions present themselves in the future. Any foretellings otherwise in Tolk's work would be *removed.* Any *prophesies* told otherwise would be omitted. Quite simply, anything that did not suit the king and queen during those early days of Tolk was simply removed."

"What did the other pages contain, Father?"

"It has been rumored that the Literati of old had read them. They were part of a much larger work of Tolk. They were his *own* manuscripts. It has been said that all of Tolk's works were to be buried with him in his tomb to be kept safe until they were needed. They were referred to as the *Scribes of Tolk* and were said to have great power to he who found them…he who studied them…used their gift of prophesy for good."

"So…" spoke Jon, with an obvious look of disbelief, "our copy of *The Book of Lore* has been *censored* by the royal family…to suit them." Mathias nodded. "What were those pages about, Father?"

"Few now know. I suppose they were about something the royal family did not want the rest of the world to know. It is said that the king's copy of the book is still intact."

"Can you not go see it, Father?" But even as he spoke the words, Jon knew the answer. The king was not about to allow anyone to view anything that could jeopardize the kingship. Mathias was certain of that long before this conversation had taken place.

"I worry about what the king will do when I pass," spoke Mathias solemnly. Jon continued to watch Mathias as the old man searched his mind and clinched his hands nervously. "The king once paid me a visit. He and a few of his men requested a tour of the abbey and asked to examine the place on their own. I did not allow it. This did not set well with the king…for kings expect full cooperation. In a rage, he left and commented that someday, somehow, he would come back."

"What would be his reasoning for searching our abbey? What would he seek here?"

"I fear," spoke Mathias, "that he may have been in search of Tolk's tomb…to find the last copy of the *Scribes.* None of the modern monks have ever found it, although many have tried. In the fifth quatrain of the fifth chapter, Tolk states that *In my earthly days, few will know my worth. In my death, I shall be the foundation of the Church.* Some say these lines suggest his remains could be buried beneath the Abbey…its foundation. Some say the lines only reflect his impact on the church, or abbey. I have had no luck finding anything that could constitute as a tomb, not even a grave. I have many theories and have studied many writings but have had no luck finding answers. All monks want to be the one who finds the Scribes…the one who brings Faith back to Cobblestone. I think the king would like to be the one who finds it, but I have no intention of letting that rat soul of a king pilfer our halls."

"Father!" spoke Jon in amazement. "He is our king! You mustn't say such things…if someone heard? He is KING!"

"You know little of the real king, my son. It is my fault. I have withheld too many things from you. You are worthy of much better. I am sorry."

"Father, you worry me," said Jon. "You mustn't have fear of my losing faith. I am your humble servant…your friend. I will be by your side until the very end. No stone in my path shall be too large to overturn…not if you are with me."

"Then you shall hear it all, my good son," said Mathias with a sigh of relief. "Forgive me for not telling you sooner."

Jon listened in total silence as Mathias searched his mind for the proper words. It was a relief for the old monk to finally be telling Jon, and yet, the telling was breaking his heart.

He continued. "Have you not noticed that our fair king has no queen? He is up in age and appears to have little intention of gaining one. I suspect he will take a wife soon, if only to keep the bloodline, and more importantly, the king line. But he has been no pillar in our society, no example for the young ones. He has many fair women in wait for him. There are those ladies, who by little choice of their own, await his call. He has kept them for years…tucked neatly away in the castle, out of view. There is a constant rotation of women in and out of the castle. It is deplorable."

"But the king," questioned Jon, "…his *preferences* should not discount his leadership…his strength in battle. He has been a valiant king."

Mathias paused and appeared to be struggling, fighting some urge to speak. At last, he looked long and hard into Jon's eyes, drew a deep breath, and continued, "Twenty-six years ago…a woman…a gentle and kind and beautiful woman stepped into the halls of this abbey. She looked for counsel. She looked for faith. Her spirit was broken. She had given up hope. She turned to this abbey for help. Her name…was Marie, and her eyes were the most hauntingly beautiful pools I had ever seen. She was young and so very vibrant…yet full of sorrow and despair. Along with Sister Margaret from the orphanage, we took her in, hoping to soothe the sorrow in her heart."

Mathias paused and took another deep breath. Jon still had no idea where this story was going and appeared to hang upon every word. Mathias continued, stammering, "She…had been…hmmm…in the *employ* … of the king."

"Oh, Father, how could she?" cried Jon in dismay, "…not such a kind woman, so tender, so loving?"

"One does not simply say *no* to the king," said Mathias bitterly. "That would be treason. She would be hanged before noon…*hanged*!" As these words slowly sank into Jon's mind, Mathias began again.

"When she came here…she was…" Mathias fought every word and drew them from deep inside, "she was…was…with child." He wiped his hand over his eyes, and tears filled his palm. "She had so many questions that we could not answer. Sister Margaret counseled her daily and provided a warm place for her to stay. Marie helped in the orphanage and gardened with the sisters. She eventually regained her self-esteem and became a wonderful and spiritual woman…all the while, carrying the unborn son of the king. She was such a pleasure to be around…so pleasant…so beautiful…so wonderful. All who knew her, loved her and cherished her kindness."

By now, Mathias was bent over his knees with his head facing his clinched fists…speaking…almost praying…and crying. Tears fell onto his hands as he continued to speak as his body shook gently.

As his trembling hands quivered and shook, his voice gently filled the garden with anguish, "Her screaming voice filled the air…the day… the day the newborn son of the king entered this world. The wonderful son of the king was born…and lived! But she…the tender woman we had come to love…did not…."

"But what of this woman?" asked Jon desperately.

"Jon…" sobbed Mathias, "….she was your mother."

3

The parched streets of Cobblestone were baking Jon with the radiant heat from the hot afternoon sun. He stomped down one street, then another, as sweat poured from his brow. His turns had taken him nowhere, other than through a maze of twists and turns in the Cobblestone backstreets. A leather-clad fellow watched attentively from the side street as the angry young monk stomped by, again and again. Dominick wondered what could cause a monk to react in such a way. He had always thought of those men as quiet, refined individuals that rarely left the confines of the abbey. Jon stomped on, and Dom went about his day.

Along with the fury in Jon's head, many, many thoughts ricocheted from within. *Scribes of Tolk*...my father, the king...my Mother. *Your Mother and Father died when you were young...blah! Lies! Died? How disgusting! Father...oh my Father...he lives! Ha! He lives...yet cares not for me.*

Despite the many dreadful thoughts in his mind, Jon's heart was beginning to come to terms. And not long after his heart came to terms…his mind began to place things in order. *What of these rhymes of Tolk? Foundation…of the church?*

After many hours of sweltering heat, Jon succumbed to a tall glass of lemonade and rested quietly upon the same stone on which he had sat earlier in the day. His temper was cooling along with his body. He was now somewhat more collected, and the craftiness of his mind was beginning to size up the situation. *If I could find the Scribes…set the record straight…bring Faith back to the people of Cobblestone…*

Those would all be worthy endeavors, but all were way in the distance, far from Jon's ability as a monk of this abbey. He was still a young monk and seemed so very youthful in comparison to Father Mathias. Mathias was older than anyone in Cobblestone but carried himself so lightly and lively. He was an example to all.

Although Jon was still fighting some anger inside, he was also feeling awkward about the way he had let his rage consume him. So, by now, along with his anger, he was now feeling a little foolish and embarrassed.

He glanced high up at the tower beside him. It seemed to reach the heavens with its large stone coverings jutting into the sky. Jon knew in his heart that it was time for counsel with his friend and mentor. Mathias would no doubt be waiting in his room at the top of the stairs and expecting Jon to come forward when he was ready. Mathias always had words of wisdom for him; and their bond grew with time.

Jon's sandals slapped against the rock surface of the steps of the spiral staircase of the abbey tower. The evening sun was piercing the panes of the stained glass windows of the tower, and it filled the air with warm and colorful light. It was a strange and pleasant light; and it never failed to tingle Jon's spine as he used the stairs. To Jon, it truly seemed like a stairway to the heavens, and he cherished the feel of the whole tower.

Jon approached the old wooden door of Father Mathias' quarters and gently rapped upon it. The elderly voice of Mathias could be heard through the door.

"Come in, my son. I have been waiting."

"I am sorry, Father," spoke Jon, timidly. "I was angry, but I did not lose faith."

"Come forward, my son. You owe me no apology. You have every right to be angry, both with me and the world." Mathias motioned Jon to take a seat beside him and offered a warm smile. "I need to show you what little I have learned in my search for the elusive Tomb of Tolk."

Jon was surprised that Mathias had already known what he had been pondering during his angry walk through Cobblestone. He smiled at the knowledge of Mathias and listened closely to the old man's words.

Mathias pulled from his side table an old and worn leather-bound book. It was his personal Bible, and it had all the signs of a heavily-used document of an elderly man. Its tattered cover and yellowed pages seemed warm and inviting.

Jon had always admired that old Bible and hoped to someday own it when the inevitable time came when he would need it most…when its current owner no longer needed it. As Mathias leafed though the pages, Jon watched quietly and respectfully.

"You remember this old book, do you not?" he asked.

"Of course, Father, it once was Father Genivah's … the Elder before you."

"I thought you might remember it," said Mathias, with a warm and understanding grin of appreciation. "It has served me well." Mathias caressed his hands over the book's cover. "I hold it everyday, even when I am not reading it. It is a great comfort to me. It is part of me. I want you to have it when I am gone." Mathias paused and smiled lovingly at Jon. "You will also receive my ring…" Mathias paused and looked down at the Amethyst ring on his finger, and then looked again to Jon, "…thus, making you the youngest High Elder in the history of Cobblestone Abbey."

Mathias again paused and watched Jon's responses. Jon knew that he would someday be an Elder of the abbey, but the office of High Elder had somehow evaded his imagination. He had known he would inherit Mathias' ring; yet the repercussions for doing so had not entered his mind. The weight of the situation was sinking in on him. This was quite a responsibility for such a young man. Jon was less than thirty years old; and yet, he would now fill the shoes of men who had never served the office younger than at least fifty years of age. It was a time in the abbey's history that would be shunned by much of society and watched closely by even those who believed he could somehow fill those shoes. The job alone would be quite a task for a young lad, but the political repercussions that could follow would be another obstacle altogether. He would be in constant view of the people of Cobblestone, and his actions would be picked apart by many of the most knowledgeable minds in the city. He would be under much scrutiny. Mathias understood the weight that the lad would carry and took all precautions to ensure as smooth a transition as possible.

"Although nearly every monk to cross our threshold has longed to be the one to find the *Scribes*, I believe it will be you that finds them." Mathias spoke with a strange and elusive tone, and Jon's astonished eyes looked on. "I believe this not just because you are true of heart… and strong of courage…and worthy beyond that of many men. I believe this because I feel that you…you, Jon of Cobblestone…will *need it* most."

"I do not know if I possess such strength, Father. I wish to fill your shoes as best I can. I long to save the Faith of Cobblestone…but I do not know if the strength is within me."

"Perhaps Faith is all that you need, Jon. Perhaps some of what you need is in here." Mathias handed Jon his Bible and spoke again, "There is more in here than just gospel. There are notes of mine…notes of

Genivah's...and room for your comments as well. Even if you do not solve this ancient mystery, place your thoughts within for he who will someday come. It is all we can do."

As Jon took the Book from Mathias' hands, Mathias spoke again, "Copy all of what is written in notations. Gather all of what the Book has to offer and return it. I shall miss it sorely. There are bits and pieces throughout it. Some are loose notes, and some are scribblings within the bindings. Copy them to your Bible and return it... until you can keep it for your own."

Jon grasped the Bible as a tear slid down his nose. He finally pushed words past the lump in his throat. "I've much to do and much to think about." He smiled at Mathias and bowed. "I shall have it back to you tomorrow."

As Jon descended the stairwell, the weight of the world followed. But even as his emotions swelled, his determination seemed to grind forward with equal strength. Jon of Cobblestone was inspired.

The morning sun shone warmly on the front steps of Cobblestone Abbey. A tall figure stood at the door and looked reluctantly at the giant knocker hanging in the center. *Go ahead,* he thought, *you can do this.*

The loud knock on the door rattled through the abbey and echoed down the halls. The noise shook Jon fully awake. He lay face down on his writing desk in a pool of slobber.

One of the younger monks had already made his way to the door, and Jon listened attentively while wiping his face and hands. He could faintly overhear the voices in the corridor and prepared himself as best he could to meet the visitor as promptly as possible.

The voice of Brother Michael soon entered Jon's room. "Brother Jon, we have a visitor who would like to speak to an Elder. Father Howard is in the rose garden. Shall I fetch Father Mathias?"

"No, no," commented Jon, "I shall see him."

It wasn't long before Jon found himself face to chest with a tall and agile-looking man in his mid to late forties. After a quiet smile, Jon spoke, "I am Jon. How may we of the abbey help you?"

"Well Sir…or Brother Jon…I am sorry, I do not know the proper addresses of the abbey."

Jon gave an understanding smile and said, "Either will suffice, my friend. Please continue."

"My name is Dominick Sebastian. I was once a native of Cobblestone but have spent the last years in the Bay of Greenwale. I have sailed and have worked the mule trains in the lower farthings, hauling the ship's cargos to and from many of the seaports. This life has hardened me, and I have returned to seek enlightenment … to seek a more rewarding life for myself. I have come in search of work and shelter and the chance to learn from the learned."

Jon was surprised by the words of this soft-spoken fellow and could easily tell by the man's sun-dried face that he had indeed been onboard a ship of some sort. His words seemed to resonate for young Jon. Jon was always willing and ready to help strangers…especially those with interesting stories and a worldly feel about them. He admired those people willing to tarry off into the vast world and experience what it has to offer. He had no intention of ever doing so himself but found the stories to be enlightening and entertaining. And, he also just liked to help those truly in search of help, not just those looking for handouts. There was a significant difference in the two for Jon. He could always find work for idle hands and truly enjoyed helping those that were willing to help themselves. He had a set answer lined up for people such as the one in the foyer.

"My friend Dominick, there is great Faith and much work in the abbey. If you choose to stay with us, you will not find one without the other."

"Then I should feel quite at home. I care not for idle hands." He held out his palms. Each was covered in thick calluses and darkened with worn-in grime. "I look for work and enlightenment. I would also love to learn more of this beautiful abbey."

"Then welcome to Cobblestone Abbey, Dominick Sebastian. May you find what you seek."

Jon called for Brother Michael. As Michael entered the room, Jon spoke, "Brother Michael, could you show Mr. Sebastian to the guest quarters downstairs. See to it he has all that he needs."

He again looked to Dominick. "I am afraid you have missed the morning meal, but we keep a number of breads and cheeses and vegetables available in the dining hall throughout the day. We will have an evening meal just before nightfall. I would like to meet with you this afternoon to discuss your duties…if that is acceptable."

"I shall look forward to it, Brother Jon. You have been very kind. I will not disappoint you."

Dominick left with Michael and disappeared into the labyrinth of halls that filled the lower spaces beneath the abbey.

Jon again turned his attention to the old Bible of Mathias. After thumbing through the pages, he found that he had nearly finished his copying of the hand-written notes within. He settled into his chair and spent an hour finishing the job he had begun the night before. Although many of the notations in the old Bible made little sense to him, some of them clicked, and he marked those pages to speak with Mathias about.

By now, Jon's rumbling stomach was reminding him that he had slept through breakfast. He tucked both books under one arm and made his way to the dining hall for a bite of bread and cheese. As he entered the hall, he was surprised to find Dominick there sampling the fresh apples and a break of bread.

Dominick spoke up, "I hope it is not disrespectful of me to take advantage of the dining hall so soon. The sweet smell of your bread was quite enticing. The cheese is far better than any I have ever eaten. I would love to see how it is made."

"You are most welcome, Dominick. There are many recipes to enjoy here in the abbey. I hope your stay will be long enough to taste them all."

Dominick smiled and said, "If they are anything like the cheese and bread, then I may never leave!"

Jon gave an understanding chuckle and turned to leave the room. As he did, Dominick spoke again, "I have little to do until this afternoon. I wonder if there is something I could be doing until then that would justify my breakfast?"

Jon thought a moment and gave a reply, "The library is down the long corridor on the left. Brother Joseph has been dusting the shelves. Speak with him and help where you may. I will find you after while."

Dominick nodded thankfully and made his way toward the library with a handful of bread and cheeses.

Jon began his ascent up the stairwell of the tower. Once again, his gentle knock was answered by Mathias. "Come in, my son."

"I have brought your Bible, Father," spoke Jon. He gently wiped his hand across its face as if to clean it of his fingerprints. "It has a warm feel to it."

"No Bible should be clean and new," spoke Mathias. "The more it is read, the warm hues reflect its long and useful life."

"I do not understand many of the notations within it," spoke Jon. "Some appear to be a code of some kind."

"They are not really codes," explained Mathias. "They are written references to the *Book of Lore*. They refer to what chapter and rhyme to read. Some refer to the quatrains and some to the simple rhymes early in the book. I have entered many notes over the years as I have read and pondered the book in search of the tomb. There were times when I only wrote a sentence or two of a whole rhyme. Some just seemed to *feel* right. I can't explain it. The Fifth Quatrain, I feel very strongly about...*In my death, I shall be the foundation of the church.* But, alas, I have found no tomb in our foundation. You should study what you will. I may lead you astray, for I have been unsuccessful."

"I will study, Father, but now, it is time to get some work done. I have spent plenty of time on this today. I will give you my thoughts as I study. Tomorrow is another day." With a tender smile, Jon turned and skipped down the steps to begin his day.

5

Jon entered the library in search of Dominick. As he suspected, Brother Joseph had instructed Dominick to dust the many shelves of books on the walls of the library. It seemed like an endless job, but it still must be done. The more helpers, the merrier.

As Jon approached, he noticed how gently Dominick handled the old and fragile books. He was admiring a very old copy of a manuscript once written by one of the early kings entitled *The Fall of the House of Romb.* The book chronicled the king's strategic maneuvers to take over the domain of his rival, King Romb, of the nearby seaport realm of Blue Haven. The book was a famous work, but few commoners had ever actually held a copy in their own hands. Dominick was in awe as he held the book carefully and leafed through its many pages, stopping here and there to read certain passages.

Jon watched as Dominick admired the book closely. Jon finally spoke, "I see you know a good book when you see one."

"I had no idea a copy still existed," spoke Dominick with an astonished look. "And there are hundreds of other books like this in this place. I would not know where to start studying."

"You will start here," said Jon as he pointed to a long row of Bibles on one shelf. "Then you will be expected to know the *Book of Lore*. That could keep you busy the rest of your life."

"I have only been here part of one day, and I have tasted the best breads of my life. I have held some of the greatest literary works known to man." Dominick smiled excitedly. "I cannot wait to see what tomorrow brings!"

"It will bring the scrubbing of the floor in the lower halls. It is what the younger ones refer to as the dungeon. It is not a pleasant task, but you will find it tolerable."

"Shall I continue my work in the library today or start that task now?"

"Work with Brother Joseph this afternoon. I will come for you after the evening meal. Do as Brother Joseph commands. He will not lead you astray. You will have worked up a hearty appetite by then." Jon nodded to Joseph and left the men to work at their task.

Jon spent the majority of his day in the rose garden. Most of the young monks had little interest in it, and since the leaving of the eight Elders, the rose garden had nearly overgrown itself before Jon took up the charge of its keep. He didn't mind the task, and it seemed to fall into the same category as some of the other tasks around the abbey. Eventually, someone took over certain tasks because it suited them more than some others. Although work is work, some tasks are just performed better by some individuals, and many actually enjoy a sense of pride with the tasks undone by others. It was a delicate balance here in the abbey, and the monk brothers tried to carry out their daily chores without constant instruction by an Elder. It was a good system, and it kept the work flowing smoothly.

After the evening meal, Jon found Dominick in the kitchen helping with the clean up of dinner. He was pleasantly surprised with the way Dominick seemed to fit right in with the monks. He wondered if the fellow might actually stay and become one of the monks of the abbey. He liked Dom's work ethic and his inquisitive nature. He was sure the fellow would have many questions for him tonight after his day of work in the abbey library. Although Jon had many things on his mind, he felt compelled to talk with Dominick and make sure he was comfortable with his stay so far.

"How was your day?" asked Jon, as he looked at Dom's sudsy dishwater hands. Although the monks had no indoor plumbing, they did keep a large caldron in the kitchen that they kept filled with water and lye. Their hand-crafted stoneware bowls were stacked on both sides of the pot, and Dom had a bewildered look as he sized up the task of washing them.

"It was a good day. It will be all the better when this stack of bowls dwindles." He chuckled as he washed and said, "Will there be anything else that needs tending tonight?"

"No, no," replied Jon, "You have earned your keep today. You may retire when you finish, if you wish. I will be in the garden for a short while if you like conversation before bed."

Dom smiled and continued his washing, and Jon found his way to the garden wall. He seemed to find this place quite often. Despite the hard stone seat of the garden wall, it was a pleasant place, and Jon enjoyed its peaceful tranquility even in the darkness of evening. As he pondered about the king and Tolk and the city of Cobblestone, Dom entered the garden and settle into the wall beside him.

"You mentioned great Faith and much work this morning when I arrived. You must add *reward* to that list. I have gotten more for my day's work than any payment I have ever received. Thank you for allowing my stay. It is an almost magical place…full of history and energy. It feels like every stone in this giant building has a story to tell, and its old boards creak with voices of old."

"Well said, my friend," spoke Jon with pride. "I find it to be the most inspiring building I have ever stepped into. It is warm in winter and cool in summer, and so very inviting to those who enter its halls. I find Faith here…or perhaps Faith has found me. It is my home…my castle."

"Tell me more of your castle," suggested Dom. "I want to know more of this wonderful old building."

"Ah," spoke Jon, "Cobblestone Abbey. I will tell you what I know of it. The abbey was never really a church but rather more of a place of study for the Literati'. As time passed, it became more of a monastery."

Jon paused and assessed his new friend. "Do you know of the Literati'?" he asked.

"Not really, I don't suppose. That was a very long time ago."

"The Literati'," began Jon, "were a group of men who studied the world. Originally, the Literati' studied art and literature, even astrology here in these halls. All of which gained them the wisdom they desired and provided the backbone for their society—their religion. Eventually, the people of Cobblestone began to use its halls for worship and sought counsel of the monk descendents of the Literati'."

Jon paused and searched his memory. "They created their society in the far section of the forest in a castle much like this one. In those early days, Stone Castle was once their dwelling, but for some reason, they uprooted and moved themselves to Cobblestone and built this abbey. Some of the early monks descended from those Literati'. Of course, now, we monks do not take spouses, and therefore do not have descendents. The Elders teach the younger monks and they, in turn, become Elders someday themselves. We still call ourselves descendents; yet we are of no blood relation."

Dominick listened closely as Jon continued. "There was a time when there were always ten Elders. After the passing of an Elder, the remaining Elders would elect a new one from the younger monks of the abbey. All that changed when one Elder left the abbey. He was Anté, and he lived in the old castle I just spoke of. Then about ten years ago, we lost eight more. They left in the night…never to return. Now there is only Mathias…and he is quite old."

"Who then will lead the monks when the old master passes?" asked Dominick.

"Mathias has chosen me to fill his shoes. I do not relish the thought. There will be much unrest within the remainder of the other monks. I am not the oldest, but Mathias has chosen me. It will not be an easy transition."

"Do not discount yourself," said Dom reassuringly. "These men hold you in high regard."

"I hope it is so," said Jon. "I shall need all the help I can get if Mathias should pass. He has been the only father I have ever known. He is dear to me."

"Let us hope that it will be a long while before that happens," said Dom, offering reassurance. "But as for tonight, I think I have learned enough. I shall need my rest for the dungeon floor tomorrow."

The two exchanged pleasantries; and Dom made his way to his quarters. Jon sat quietly on the garden wall, pondering the rhymes and notations Mathias had penned in his old Bible. His busy day had left him quite tired, but his mind still rattled with thoughts. In his head, he could almost see large volumes of Tolk's work stacked in a dusty dark tomb. The rhyming hints in his writing only added to the mystery. He kept reflecting on the rhymes Father Mathias had extracted over the years. *In my life, few will know my worth…in my death, I will be the foundation of the church.* Could these really be hints to the location of his tomb?

Jon racked his mind to remember the many pages of the *Book of Lore* that he had copied. Even though he had copied the book in full twice, nothing seemed to come to mind. After several minutes of deep thought, Jon finally meandered his way to his quarters.

As his head snuggled into his pillow, he thought *High Elder...that will be a strange day indeed.* And the future High Elder of Cobblestone Abbey drifted off to sleep.

Jon woke early and began thumbing through his notes from Mathias. He had borrowed one of the copies of the *Book of Lore* from the library. By now, he had looked up the correlating rhymes of Tolk with those of Mathias' code numbers. Some made sense for him, and others seemed to have no connection whatsoever. For no apparent reason, he was drawn to some of the rhymes more than others. One of the first ones contained the word *tomb*, but sounded more spiritual to him. It read:

Shielded from the blissful sun,
Keeps dark the dusty gloom.
But those who seek the righteous light,
Find it beyond the tomb.
The hand of God will show the way
To those who will believe.
With Cross at hand, enter and
Joyous one will be.

Jon felt as though this rhyme was more of a spiritual reference than a clue, but he still read it a number of times to make sure. His mind still came back to *foundation of the church.* That one seemed to echo in his head all day. He was confident that this one was part of the equation somehow. He just did not know how it fit in. There were many other references to stones and Crosses and several made mention of something called *The Hall of Enlightenment.* Jon knew nothing of this hall, if there was such a thing in the abbey. Most rooms of the abbey were named more by necessity than creativity…dining hall, library, and so on. Unless it was the main gathering hall, then Jon had no clue where this one could be. He decided to let these ideas bounce around awhile and start his day.

Before Jon could enter the dining hall, Dom met him at the entry. "Reporting for duty, Sir," joked Dom in his spirited voice. "To the dungeon I shall go."

Jon shook his head and smiled. "I suppose I could postpone my breakfast long enough to get you started."

The two navigated the winding stairwell to the lower halls. The basement of this old building housed a large fireplace mostly used in winter months to help heat the abbey. There were a number of sleeping rooms scattered down one wall, and long shelves housed numerous bushels of potatoes and apples and the like. Large crocks contained ground corn and wheat, and baskets held bundles of dried spices and fruits. Despite its tidy appearance, the lower halls did need a good scrubbing. Jon found the buckets and mops for Dom and helped him get started.

Dom noticed that Jon seemed distracted. Although he said nothing out of line, Dom couldn't help noticing how Jon's eyes wandered over the stone walls as if he was seeking something. Dom didn't question him but took mental note of this strange behavior. Besides, he had plenty of work to occupy his mind.

Jon left Dom to his chores and climbed the stairs to the dining hall. Even though his stomach was rumbling with hunger, he slowed his pace and simply searched the walls and doors for anything that might strike a chord with the thoughts in his mind. The abbey seemed even more alive to him today. Much like Dom, he could almost hear the voices of history in the stones and boards of the old building. He listened closely as if the walls could reveal clues. The building was warm with character, but Jon's trail was cold. He saw nothing of importance.

Before entering the dining hall, Jon stepped into the large open meeting hall of the abbey. It was lined with rows of pews, and candelabras sat on many shelves and tables throughout the room. A few small vases of freshly-cut flowers provided a splash of color to the plain grey walls. His mind pondered whether the room had ever been called the Hall of Enlightenment. It was an inspiring room to view, but there were no real tell-tale signs of it ever being named anything of the like.

Jon gathered himself a plateful of fruit and sweet breads. He was about to fill another plate for Mathias, when he noticed Mathias sitting at the end of one of the long dining tables. He walked over and sat along side of him and greeted him with his usual smiling address, "Good morning, Father. I was about to bring a plate to you."

"No need," replied Mathias, "it is a pretty morning. I could use a little walk."

After a few minor discussions about the daily plans, Jon questioned the old monk about the abbey. "I have been thinking long and hard about Tolk. Do you suppose our meeting hall could be this Hall of Enlightenment?"

"It is unlikely," replied Mathias. "One of the Elders in Father Genivah's time had the entire room stripped of paint and searched for secret doors or writings of any sort. Nothing was ever found. Even the pulpit was dismantled and reassembled…all for nothing."

"Why do you think it is here in the abbey?" questioned Jon. "Might there be an actual tomb somewhere?"

"It has always been said that he was buried in the church. Many have searched the town over for other sites that could possibly be his tomb. All have fallen short...or kept their finding of the *Scribes* to themselves."

Jon scratched his head and asked another question. "Anté was one of the most intelligent of all the monk descendents. Do you suppose he could have found the *Scribes?*"

"I suppose it is possible, but I do not think he cared about the Faith of Cobblestone or whether it dried up and blew away. He only cared for himself. He might have tried to find it in his thirst for knowledge but not for spiritual reasons. And if he had found the Tomb, he most certainly would not have shared any of the information. He would have hoarded it until his death."

Jon's eyes widened. "The book could still be at Stone Castle! You have told me of the vast library. Anté may have kept it there; and no one has even looked for it!"

"Alas," spoke Mathias, disappointedly. "It is not. A year after Antés death, I sent Glock to search the old castle. He narrowly escaped with his life. A group of rogue trolls took up residence in the old castle and burned the entire library of books for heat. He said that every item of furniture had been broken and burned a piece at a time. Even the curtains had not escaped the trolls' need for fire. The fireplace was filled with a treasure of useless ash. I wish I had sent him much sooner. The result may have been different."

Jon sat quietly, trying to soak up all he had heard. After a moment, he said, "So we must hope he did not find the Book. Perhaps there is still hope."

"There is always hope, my son, but keep in mind...the greatest minds of Cobblestone have not solved this simple mystery. If Anté did not or could not find it, then it may never be found."

Jon shook his head. "Then, I guess I am back to *the foundation of the church.* I will think on it some more and come back to you. I have much work today, but I will see you again tonight or tomorrow. Thank you for your time, Father. I don't know what I would do without you."

Mathias gave Jon a gentle smile and motioned for him to carry on with his business. As Jon walked away, the same old thoughts crossed the old monk's mind. *What will you do, Jon of Cobblestone, without me...without me here to defend you from the king? What will happen when I am gone? The king will not risk taking on the church with me at the helm...but what of young Jon? Lawrence will make a mockery of the abbey, if there is no longer a tie to the old church. How ever will Jon cope?*

So, as a group of young monks carried out their daily tasks, one old monk worried over their well-being...and wondered what the future might hold for Cobblestone Abbey.

As the next few days unfolded, young Jon of Cobblestone sorted through many things in his head. He still had not fully regained his composure over learning that the king was his father. Even though he had never mentioned it to anyone other than Mathias, he still felt awkward about the whole thing. There were times when he thought he could almost see his mother in his mind. It was not possible, of course, but given the circumstances, anything could have presented itself inside this young monk's mind.

But more than anything else, Jon thought mostly about the *Scribes of Tolk*. He found himself mentally sifting through the many notations from Mathias' Bible. Even though he had memorized nearly every line of notes, still nothing really made sense to him. It was quite frustrating to him, but he tried not to beat himself up too badly. After all, it was a very old mystery, and it was quite unlikely anyone else had solved this ancient puzzle. So, he reassured himself by reflecting upon it in that way and comforted himself with Mathias' words…*it may never be found.*

Jon's day ticked along as usual. He saw the comings and goings of guests in the abbey and guided the other monks to the chores at hand. He oversaw Brother Michael's work on the front stairwell of the abbey. He prepared the vineyard for the late-summer harvest and took time to wash the windows of the dining hall. The ever-constant workload never seemed to lessen for him; and yet, he didn't seem to mind. He loved his work here in the abbey and never delayed in the completion of any task. This was his rightful home; and it suited him perfectly. The other monks seemed to enjoy his companionship and felt satisfied that his constant overseeing was in good faith with the best interests of the abbey always in check. Despite his tender age, he was becoming quite an Elder already.

As Jon was carting in some firewood to the abbey kitchen, Dominick peered through the open door. "I thought I might find you here. I see you, too, do not believe in idle hands." After a few words of pleasant small talk, Dom asked if he might make a stroll into town to visit his family and friends. Jon's reply was kind and truthful.

"You may come and go as your heart sees fit. You have more than earned your keep here in the abbey. You have come here to learn…not just learn how to clean. One must find time to study and enjoy life a little." Jon gave a reassuring wave of his hand. "The door is open for you, my friend."

Dom gave an understanding nod and made his way for the door. He lifted the old latch of the heavy front door of the abbey and disappeared into the night.

Jon was pleased with the good nature of this wayfaring sailor friend. He hoped to spend some time with him soon and pry some stories from the fellow's past. Jon had always wanted to see the ocean, or better yet…one of its large bays, like that of Greenwale. Yet, somehow, he doubted that his life would ever take a turn in that direction. The Bay was far beyond the Deep Forest, and even the old forest was farther than Jon had ever expected to travel. His dealings with the Leaflings years ago had taken him farther into the forest than he had ever wanted. He was quite happy being Jon…just Jon of Cobblestone Abbey.

By now, the evening meal was being cleaned up, and Brother Michael was doing his usual cleaning of the dining area and kitchen. Michael was a good friend of Jon and understood the importance of the upcoming and inevitable troubles that would surface with the new Elder being charged. Michael was quite happy being a loyal servant and enjoyed his time here in the abbey, regardless of what Elder was at the helm. He was a happy soul, and many townspeople had come to love him as they had Jon in his early youth. Michael was highly respected and went about his daily life in a slow and sorted way. Each day, one could count on Michael being in the same location at the same time. He was a creature of habit and liked his days planned well in advance. He was a very sweet young man, plain and simple.

Jon approached Michael and asked, "Have you ever studied any of Tolk's work?"

"Of course, I have found it almost as enlightening as the Bible itself...and easier to understand, at least for me. I am a simple sort."

"Have you ever pondered the old question of the whereabouts of his tomb?"

Michael replied in his usual demeanor, "I have no use for the dead or their belongings. I respect them all the same but need no confirmation to appease my heart. I am happy with my simple self, as most monks should be."

Michael had a point. Simplicity had always been a strength for most monks. The old adage of "keep it simple" probably came from an old monk proverb. This old abbey seemed to enjoy the quiet life of Cobblestone, and Brother Jon tried to continue to tell himself that. But for some people, it is difficult to steer one's self to mediocrity. There just isn't any fun in it; and no one ever saved the world from their easy chair. Despite Jon's simple life, he was nowhere near simple, and this task seemed to provoke his every move. He was more than willing to take this challenge head on.

"I am sorry, Brother Michael," said Jon. "I think I know you well enough to have guessed your mind. I did not mean to pry."

"It is fine, my friend. I will be by your side when you save Cobblestone. I believe in you…completely." Michael's heart was on his sleeve, and it showed like a brilliant sunset.

Jon placed his hand on Michael's shoulder. "I could not receive any higher praise. You are a friend, indeed. Thank you from the bottom of my heart."

Jon was now quite tired and allowed Michael to finish his work in the kitchen. He spoke with several other monks on his way to his quarters. He was beginning to feel more at peace with his place in the order of things within the abbey. He felt more certain of himself after his conversation with Michael. There was an understanding that seemed to strengthen Jon's determination. At least one of the monks had faith in him. One good Brother had expressed himself. There was at least some support within the ranks, and Jon felt the release of at least some of the tension related to the turmoil of the ongoing mystery of the Tomb of Tolk. Thankfully, someone in the abbey was willing to stand along side him and testify…even if nothing ever came of it.

So Jon made his way to his quarters and let the comings and goings of his day settle away. As he fell into bed, another series of Tolk rhymes entered his head…

I will be
amid the thrones
of Deity
in hall of stone.

Hall of stone, he thought, as he burrowed into his pillow. *Might be the dining hall...maybe he tried to eat some of Brother Michael's biscuits.* He chuckled to himself and drifted off to sleep.

* * *

Far across the town of Cobblestone, Dominick Sebastian settled into a seat at the old tavern. It only took a moment for his acquaintance to speak. "So what is your news?"

"It appears..." said Dom, as he sipped on a tall mug of ale, "...that all is going according to plan."

Jon awoke with a start. His heart was beating fast, and it was difficult for him to catch his breath. What had been a restful night had become a worrisome dream. Three words pounded in his mind: *hall of stone.* As thoughts bounced around in his head, a plan began to take shape. He simply had to do something about this mystery. It was consuming him little by little. It was not long before he found his way to the keep of Mathias. "Father," he called, "I have thoughts to share."

To Jon's surprise, a young orderly came to the door. "Our Father is not feeling well. Perhaps you could come back."

"COME BACK!" exclaimed Jon. "Why was I not notified of his condition? Who has done this? Who is in charge?" he shouted.

"Do not hold them responsible," commanded Mathias from his bed. "They have only done what I have asked."

"And you have chosen for me to be kept in the dark?" questioned Jon. "I WILL NOT HAVE IT!"

"Calm yourself, my son," spoke Mathias from inside the room. "I only suggested that you be left asleep until your waking. You would have been notified." Even as he spoke, Mathias panted heavily and appeared to be struggling with a deep pain in his chest. "If conditions had worsened, I would most certainly have called for you."

"I am sorry," spoke Jon, "You know I worry over you. I do not take kindly to being kept in the dark."

The old monk readjusted himself in the bed and spoke again, "I grow tired. Let us speak of your thoughts, and then I should like some rest."

Jon settled into the chair beside the bed and began to speak. "It is my understanding that the Literati' originally lived beyond Tal Kator in Stone Castle. You have said that you do not feel the *Scribes* are in the old library there because of the burning done by the trolls. And, there is no proof that Anté ever found them and took them there. Is this correct?"

"Yes, Jon," spoke Mathias with a tired tone in his voice. "We have been over this."

"My question is," continued Jon, "would the tomb of Tolk not be there…in Stone Castle?"

A look of surprise flickered over Mathias' face. "It most certainly could be. I never even gave that a thought; and yet, it is an obvious possibility. I can't believe I never considered that. It is older than the abbey…and much more mysterious. You may have stumbled onto something."

Although Mathias was intrigued with Jon's new idea, it was obvious he was exhausted and still in considerable pain. Jon tapped his mentor on the arm reassuringly and spoke, "I will let you rest, Father. Think on this awhile and I will return later when you have had time to sleep. I will check on you in a few hours. Call if you need anything."

As Jon left the room, he immediately began thinking about the location of Stone Castle. He was sure he could find Tal Kator with little effort, but Stone Castle was another story. It was somewhere beyond Tal Kator near the edge of the Deep Forest. He had heard that the old road to the bay came near it, but the road took a much longer and winding path through the woods. But directions were something to worry about later. Right now, he needed to think about the Castle and focus on the clues from the old Bible. So as his day unfolded, Jon carried his Bible along with him and paused now and again to re-read portions and ponder their meaning.

During his evening meal, Jon had borrowed a copy of an old hand-drawn map of the Deep Forest and brought it outside into the garden to view. Since there were few landmarks in the old woods, the map of the Deep Forest showed little more than large patches of green. It did have a large rock building marked and listed as Stone Castle, and it appeared to be considerably farther beyond Tal Kator than he expected. Since Tal Kator was not on the map, Jon could only guess at the distances of his locations.

As Jon was about to give up on the map, the voice of Dominick startled him, "Now, what would a monk like yourself need with a map?" Dom smiled as he sat down beside Jon and gave him a pat on the back.

"Oh," replied Jon, "old maps and castles intrigue me. Even though I would never move from Cobblestone Abbey, I would love to see some of the fair sights beyond the forest. I don't think I could ever find my way though. I am not a worldly monk, and my monk brothers have gone nowhere beyond the confines of the city."

"In return for your kind hospitality," spoke Dom, "I would happily show you the sights from here to beyond the Bay of Greenwale. We could sail into the gulf if you wish."

"No boats for me, thank you, but I could use a guide to Stone Castle if you would be so obliged."

"Why in the bloody world would you wish to see that foul stone ruin? It has been pilfered and riddled of every ounce of its glory. It is not a pleasant place." Dominick paused and looked at Jon questioningly.

"I feel drawn to it for some reason," spoke Jon. "I feel as if I should see it once...just to say I have been there. I want to see its craftsmanship."

"Then," said Dom, "...to the castle we go. It will take us a day on the old road. I will be ready for travel when you wish."

"I must ask Father Mathias before I make any plans." Jon gave Dom a worried glance. "He is not well today. I hope that rest has helped him."

"Well, my friend," said Dom, "then it is good night for me. I look forward to the old pillow. Sleep well."

Jon was pleasantly surprised to find help from Dominick. It seemed as though everything had come together, as if by fate. He felt good about the possibilities of finding the tomb somewhere in Stone Castle. His gut feelings were starting to make sense, and he was glad to possibly have a companion that might even help. He felt comfortable with Dom, and he was certain that he could be trusted. But if Jon had one particularly bad trait, it was his naivety. He entrusted all until proven guilty. He was raised in the abbey where all was at it appeared. There was no deception. There were no untruths. He wore his heart on his sleeve, and it showed to all who viewed it. Most would have trusted no one with any information in a situation like this, but Jon felt a need to talk. He felt compelled to share the weight of his heart and take counsel with someone willing to listen. Dominick just happened to be that person. And despite the conditions, Dom just happened to be at the right place at the right time.

Jon planned to talk to Mathias about the whole concept of his journey tomorrow. Mathias could get a good night's rest and give him advice then. But, by now, it was quite late, and Jon's mind had once again filled his day completely. It seemed like he had just gotten out of bed, and it was now late into the night. So, with a much lighter heart, Jon of Cobblestone found his pillow and drifted off to sleep.

Jon sat up in bed, wide-eyed and awake. He had slept hard again this past night and had awakened with much the same insight and enthusiasm as the day before. He again dreamt of castles and stones and Crosses. This morning, he had a vision in his head, and he racked his brain to remember the details of his dream that caused this mental picture. He felt a deep certainty in his heart that this particular image was quite important. He closed his eyes and tried to get a good view of his dream.

Jon pictured himself in a cool and musty stone room with arched doorways and echoing halls. As he entered one of the stone archways, he viewed a long and narrow hallway. The full length of the right hand wall was spaced with tall windows that arched like the door he had entered. Directly across from each arched window, on the opposite wall, were lavishly painted coats-of-arms. Each contained swords and shields and iron helmets. Colorful flowering vines wrapped themselves around each of these elaborate crest-like paintings, and tall stone vases sat on each side of them all. In the middle of each of these paintings was a carved stone cross with words etched into them.

In his dream, he could not make out the inscribed words of the Crosses, but was certain that they must have been some sort of names placed there in remembrance. The rest of the room had other fantastic artwork upon the walls and ceiling, and a bench was located at each window. He felt the drabness and solemnity of a place long forgotten.

That was all he could remember.

Once again, the slap of Jon's sandals could be heard ascending the stairs to Father Mathias' keep. He knocked and entered after the sound of Mathias' voice. "Come in, Jon."

"How are you Father?"

"I am alright," replied Mathias, "the pain comes and goes, but I am alright."

"I have come again to talk of Stone Castle. I wish to go there…to see it for myself." Jon gave a reassuring smile to Mathias. "I think I will find what I seek in Stone Castle."

"If you feel that strongly," said Mathias, "then I feel you should go. How will you find it? You have never navigated the winding roads beyond Cobblestone."

"I may have a guide. I wanted to ask you about that also." Jon rubbed his hands together and spoke again. "The fellow that has been staying here has offered to take me. I believe he can be trusted. I think he will help. I thought I might only tell him what I must…at least until we get there. If we find no tomb, then there will be nothing to tell. If we are lucky enough to find it, then I guess I will tell him the story and hope that I have not misjudged him."

"Trust your heart, my son," spoke Mathias. "It will not lie to you. I believe there is more to Jon of Cobblestone than a just a young monk of the abbey. I believe that you will fulfill your task. I believe you will renew the Faith of Cobblestone. You have my prayers, Jon. Let your conscience guide you on your journey. Trust only who you must. Take great care. For you are all I have. Your Brothers will need you soon. May God be with you on this journey. I will not rest easy until your return."

"We will leave in the night," said Jon. "I do not know when we will return." The two friends talked a while and then Jon left the room. He was hesitant to leave his mentor. He could tell that Mathias was still in pain, and he worried about his care during his journey. He would make certain that Brother Michael would stop in and check on him often.

After a quick search of the grounds, Jon found Dom trimming the hedge near the back garden. As Jon approached, Dom gave his usual morning greetings. It did not take long to orchestrate a plan to leave in the night. They felt that they could cover the old road even in the night, and with any luck, be back home by late the next evening. Dom would leave this evening and gather some traveling supplies. They would meet in the garden a couple of hours after midnight, having had a few hours sleep to begin the long journey.

With excited smiles, the two parted ways and continued on with their daily chores. Jon arranged his plans with the other monks and packed a small bag of fruit and bread and a few minor items to help on the trip.

After an agonizingly long day, Jon tucked himself into bed and waited impatiently for sleep to come. Eventually it did, but the castles and rhymes let him sleep little. No doubt he was ready, if for no other reason than to simply make the dreams stop. He would look forward to a dreamless night of calm sleep, but there would be no rest for Jon of Cobblestone tomorrow; he just didn't know it yet.

10

ominick was patiently waiting in the garden when Jon arrived from his restless few hours of sleep. He spoke as Jon stepped close. "Judging by your sleepy eyes, we might have left at nightfall and taken a short nap somewhere down the road."

"It might have been better time spent," spoke Jon with a yawn. "I hardly slept a wink."

"Then let us be off. I think today is going to be a good day. I can feel it. It is not often I can exchange tales with someone. I look forward to the trip."

With a nod of agreement, Jon led Dom to the front of the abbey and out into the road. As they stepped onto the old cobblestones of their path, their footsteps echoed through the streets. Jon had never traveled the road out of Cobblestone. He came to the realization that the only time he had ever left town were his trips to Tal Kator, and that was years ago. So this trip today was intimidating for the young monk, but

Jon was more than ready to carry out his plan. Despite his lack of sleep, he was alert and focused on his journey.

The Old Road had more hills and valleys than Jon expected, and he soon realized how out of shape his young body was. Dom occasionally slowed his pace and waited for Jon's tired feet to catch up. Even with Jon's slow pace, the two were making progress down the road. Dominick suspected that by sunup they would have covered half of the trip.

Since the Old Road meandered its way along the forest's edge, the darkness of the trees shadowed the men, even in the hazy light of early morning. At the top of one of the highest hills they had climbed, Dom stopped and sat down on a bench like outcropping of rock. "Sit," he said to Jon. "This might be a great place to watch the sun rise. I think it is time for an apple also."

Jon happily accepted Dom's offer to sit awhile. Although the young man was eager for the journey, his feet were hurting by now, and his limbs were getting sore. It was a good time for a break.

The two sat comfortably, eating their apples and watching the sun peek over the distant mountains. It was a beautiful sight as the sun burned through the hazy fog of early morning and shed light on the sparkling dew-covered valleys before them. Dom was engrossed in the sunrise and seemed to take great pleasure from the sun climbing into the pale-orange sky. From what he knew of his companion beside him, he fully expected Jon to be equally moved by the morning sunrise. But to his surprise, Jon sat staring into the morning sky almost oblivious to the beauty that surrounded him. Finally Dom spoke up.

"I had expected some conversation on this trip. I know little of the perils of monks, but if I didn't know better, I would suspect that Jon of Cobblestone could have something on his mind."

Jon gave a half-hearted smile. "I do have something weighing on my mind quite heavily. I really should not tell anyone…and yet…I wish I could just talk about it. My mind does not rest from it."

Jon sat a moment longer pondering the repercussions of telling his secret. He liked Dominick and wanted him to share in his hunt but worried about including a near stranger in his story. He desperately needed a companion that understood his dilemma. After weighing his options, he elected to talk.

"What I am trying to do could have some strange repercussions. It could change Cobblestone."

Dominick glanced questioningly at Jon. "Is that what this trip is about?"

"It is. I am searching for the Scribes in Tolk's Tomb. Don't laugh. Many have tried and failed. I do not know what strength is in me, but I feel I must search. It is time for Cobblestone to regain its faith. I hope to be the one to instill it."

Dom still had a strange look of confusion on his face. He knew nothing of the *Scribes* and was completely lost in this discussion. "I'm sorry, but I don't understand."

"Let me start over," said Jon. "The Tomb of Tolk is rumored to contain his entire written work. Many volumes of prophesy are said to lie in his tomb to be found by the one who is to renew Faith in Cobblestone. If these wondrous old works were found and brought to the public, maybe faith could again be found in Cobblestone."

Dominick looked down at the ground, searching for the right words. Finally he spoke, "One monk, be he ever so mighty, and together with all the scribes in the world, will never overthrow the king."

Jon sat in complete disbelief. He looked at Dominick with questioning eyes and finally spoke, "I don't want to overthrow the king! Where did you get an idea like that?"

Both men sat looking at one another and doing their best to understand one another's point of view. Dominick avoided the question and asked, "If you do not want to overthrow the king, then how do you intend to take over Cobblestone?"

"I don't want to take over anything," said Jon, still amazed. "All I want is to bring Faith back into Cobblestone. I want truth and happiness to fill the streets again as they once did…back before our many monk Fathers left."

Jon continued to state his case. "The king has been a stronghold for Cobblestone. He has been a strong leader. I have no desire to replace him. I only want the chance to show Cobblestone that there is still hope in life, still a place for worship, still room for love and happiness."

Dominick could easily tell that Jon meant every word of his story. It was obvious that he had no dominant desires to conquer or rule. He felt certain that Jon of Cobblestone was as true as his word.

Unfortunately, Dom also felt truly awful about it. He took a deep breath and spoke, "I have been lead astray, my friend. I fear I may have hindered your chances of success."

Dominick's head sank as he struggled for words. He spoke as if the ground was listening. "The king feels threatened by the abbey, and is watching every move it makes. He is on some quest for some icon. I suppose yours is one and the same. He will stop at nothing to gain it…although I do not know for what reason."

Dominick paused and shook his head slightly and continued, "I did not come to the abbey for enlightenment. I came as a spy. But I want you to know that I have found it. I have found enlightenment, and I thank you for allowing me to share your world, if only for a short time."

Jon eyed Dom disapprovingly. "You came as a spy in the employ of the king? And what did you expect to find?"

"I was instructed to search the abbey for possible hidden rooms and to watch for any strange behavior. Your current behavior, Jon…is strange."

Dom spoke reluctantly and had trouble looking Jon in the eye. "Our knows where we are going to Stone Castle."

Jon held his hand to his head and pondered his next move. "We seem an unlikely pair, Dominick Sebastian. Neither should trust the other. I have taken you on a journey without giving you knowledge of my purpose. And you have entered my world as a spy. And here we sit, chatting idly like old friends. What path do we take now?"

"Tell me," said Dom, "I have never asked for your word. Can you tell me in trust that you have no desire for the throne?"

"That I can," replied Jon fervently. "You have my word."

Dom's solution was simple enough. "Then I say we go treasure hunting…for the Faith of Cobblestone."

"Will you help me, Dom?"

"You have *my* word."

Two unlikely friends stepped forward on the Old Road with renewed enthusiasm. And for the first time…the two had a similar goal.

11

The long and winding road to Stone Castle was no longer quiet of words from the mouth of Jon of Cobblestone. His pent up thoughts from the last few days came flowing forth, and Dominick gained much knowledge and understanding from the young monk by his side. Dom could now see why Jon had felt so inspired to search for the tomb and seek faith for Cobblestone. His heart was true, and Dom felt excited to be on the quest by Jon's side. It was a fantastic tale. Even if they found no tomb, Dominick Sebastian felt more alive with faith than ever before. He now studied Jon's moves and listened closely to the monk's words, and he was amazed how this lad pressed forward with eager determination. Dom was becoming certain that this simple man might just be the one to find the elusive Tomb of Tolk, and he was elated to be right here to help.

Jon had mentioned all the rhymes he had studied from Mathias' Bible and gave his thoughts as to what he thought they might find in the Castle. During their walk, both shared ideas and discussed what to do if and when they did find their treasure.

By now, it was mid-day, and the men were nearing their destination. They shared some dried meat from their packs and broke some bread as they walked.

Soon, the two found themselves at a rusty and dilapidated old iron gate. It hung partially on its hinges, and its fencing was covered in long and twisted vinery. Tall stones that were once elaborate carvings stood in crumbling decay on both sides of the old gate, and ancient stone planters sat broken in the untrimmed weeds. At the end of an overgrown foot path, just in front of the men, was the tall and looming outline of Stone Castle.

Even in the mid-day sun, the old castle looked ominous and dark. Pieces of the building's crumbling precipice lie scattered in the yard and gaping holes were showing in the roof where immaculate brass had once sheltered the rooms within. Although some of the stained-glass windows still remained in place, most were scattered about the path to the castle as if they had been broken from inside, possibly to gain a view of oncoming visitors. Nothing about the place was welcoming, and both men looked to one another wondering what dangers could possibly be lurking within.

Dominick chuckled out loud, "Who wants to go in the creepy castle first?" Jon returned the chuckle and took a deep breath. As he stepped forward to the building, he scanned the broken windows and crumbling ledges for peering eyes. He could imagine grumbling trolls burning books in the library and wondered what other woodland creatures could be lurking inside the shadowy halls. Both men summoned their courage and walked to the front entrance.

As the men climbed the front steps of the castle, they could see that the doors were ajar and probably had been for many years. Their hinges were rusted and broken. Much of their old wood had rotted away. Their footsteps seemed to echo deep into the building, and the men could smell mold and mildew and the faint scent of smoke from some long ago fire. Jon called into the darkness, “Hello!”

They received no reply, even after a number of attempts. Although parts of the castle were quite dark, there were places lit from the daytime sun through the large domed windows.

As the two men walked farther into the halls of the castle, the great age of the place amazed them both. Despite the complete lack of any contents in the building, they could almost feel the history in the large rooms and high ceilings. No doubt there had been decades of lavish gatherings here—grand parties and meetings of all sorts. As creepy as the ancient walls seemed to them, they could tell that this was once a special place.

As they continued, their footsteps still chopped through the dank air.

Jon scanned the walls and floors around them. He studied every outcropping and carved fixture. He quietly murmured, “I wish I knew what to look for.”

“How about the way out?” joked Dom, trying to ease their nerves.

Jon continued to think out loud as he walked, “I keep thinking *foundation of the church*. Let’s look for a lower room…maybe a stairwell.”

“Yeah,” joked Dom, “down where there’s NO light at all!” Even as he spoke, Dom began searching the walls and corners for some sort of torch, but found nothing at all. The trolls had burned everything they could find, so there were no torches or wood left to burn anywhere in the building.

Farther into the building, the men noticed a brighter room. They could tell that the light must be coming from a room with large windows or maybe crumbled walls. They decided to search where light allowed, and then try to delve deeper after a more thorough search.

As they walked from room to room, Jon pondered the many people and *things* that had walked here before him. He wondered if anyone had had rhymes and riddles running through their mind as well. If one was not in search of a tomb, would one overlook it in the architecture? Could Tolk's Tomb have been here for years and no one have known it? There just seemed to be so much to see in the nothingness of this dark old castle. Amid the stale darkness, a light filtered into a room ahead of them.

As they approached this lightened room, Jon noticed the large arched doorway leading into it. A cold chill ran up his spine, and he stopped in his tracks. His view was exactly as his dream about the hall of stone. As he stared in surprise, he said, "I think we are getting close."

As the men made a few steps into the room, their eyes adjusted to the light and they stared in wonder. A long row of ten large domed windows ran down the right-hand wall. The light of the sun was shining brightly through them and onto the opposite wall. Down that wall, just like in Jon's dream, were the ten painted coats-of-arms.

Both men stood breathless as they stared at the colorful walls with the winding painted ivy and plants. Vibrant flowers were adorned in lavish paint here and there, and murals of brilliant scenes were scattered down the walls.

"Looks like the trolls didn't get everything," said Dom as he stared. "At least the paint survived."

The men took a few more steps and gazed at the ceiling where they entered. To their astonishment, an enormous mural of God was painted brilliantly on the ceiling with his hands reaching down both walls. It was absolutely breathtaking for the men to stand and view what had been created so many years ago.

Jon slowly backed his way to one of the small benches by the window. His mind raced with many thoughts and he scratched his chin in wonder at the beauty within this dungeon of a building. As the thoughts in his mind began to culminate, he looked at Dom with a smile of excitement and exasperation. A tear of joy ran down his nose, and he said, "Dominick Sebastian…welcome to The Hall of Enlightenment!"

12

"It is all here...every word," said Jon. In a matter of seconds, he had pieced together dozens of clues from many of the rhymes that had been racing through his head. It all made sense to him now. He stood and began to pace as he spoke aloud.

"*I will be amid the thrones of Deity in hall of stone*. Here is our Deity," he said as he waved his hand to show the wall of crests. "There are ten of these, Dom. There were ten amethyst rings...worn by the ten Literati Fathers. These are their family crests."

By now, Jon was talking as if he was in a trance...speaking as he paced... thoughts entering his head in waves.

"Look at the names, Dom!" he said with excitement and joy.

He paced down the wall reading names from the carved crosses that each contained. He paused at the end of the wall when he read the name sculpted into the stone cross. His finger traced its letters as he read the name aloud. "TOLK." His head fell backward and he stared at the ceiling above him. The giant hand of God was painted directly above him. He turned to Dom and spoke, "The hand of God will show the way." He then recited another verse,

"Shielded from the blissful sun,
Keeps dark the dusty gloom.
But those who seek the righteous light,
Find it beyond the tomb.
The hand of God will show the way
To those who will believe.
With Cross at hand, enter and
Joyous one will be."

Jon closed his eyes and thought for a moment. Dominick watched in total amazement as this young monk strung together long rhymes and made sense out of very vague riddles. He was amazed at how Jon seemed to pull so much from within. It was truly something to behold, and Dom stood silent and watched.

Jon again paced the floor with his hand on his chin in deep thought. At last, he raised his head with a smile. He walked to the small bench by the window and gazed at the crest in front of him. The family crest of Tolk, the greatest of writing Literati', was in front of him. And there was more. With his eyes closed, he took in deep breaths as the rays of the bright sun warmed his back.

Jon slid from the stone bench and onto his knees on the floor. He bowed his head and silently began to pray as Dominick stared in wonder.

He lifted his head when he was finished and sat back down on the bench. He let his head roll back on his shoulders, and he took another deep breath.

Dominick finally broke the silence, "Are you alright?"

“I am fine,” he said, smiling. “I am just savoring this moment… taking my time. This might be the greatest thing I ever do. I want to prepare myself for the next twenty seconds of our lives.”

“I don’t understand, Jon,” spoke Dominick, “the next twenty seconds?”

“Look at the shields…those crests. *Shielded from the blissful sun, keeps dark the dusty gloom.*”

“Prepare yourself, my friend,” he said, still smiling. “We are about to enter the Tomb of Tolk.”

13

Dominick, who was still standing with his jaw nearly on the floor, had been lost in amazement since he had walked in the door. Now, he stood in total disbelief that he was actually in the place that housed the Tomb of Tolk and with someone who had so simply unscrambled years of scattered little riddles of rhyme. "How do you know it is here?"

"Oh, its here," said Jon. "It is the foundation of the church…the foundation of this once spiritual building."

Jon stood and walked over to the crest of Tolk. His fingers touched the letters of the name carved into the three-dimensional stone cross carving. He smiled at Dom as he grasped the cross firmly and recited the words, "*with cross in hand, enter and, joyous one will be*."

As he spoke, he turned the cross with all his might. The creaking grind of an old steel bolt could be heard dragging over stone. When the cross came to a stop, the heavy stone door slowly hinged forward into the room. Dust and dirt crumbled from around it, and it creaked loudly on its hinges. The rays of sunshine from the window shone down into a long and narrow stone staircase.

By design, the outside light illuminated the stairwell and filtered into the room beneath. Even in the depths of this ancient building, when the dust cleared, there was enough light to see.

Dominick was too surprised to speak, and Jon did not give him the chance. Jon stepped through the opening without hesitation and began his descent into the chamber below. Dominick felt as if he was in a dream. This young monk before him was leading him into dark labyrinths of chambers and reciting scripture like a Prophet, and Dom was beginning to believe that Jon just might be one. "Lead on my friend," he said to himself.

Jon entered the lower chamber before Dom. And once Dom's shadow left the stairwell and entered the room, the light from outside filtered in and reflected from the walls. Both men stood like stone for a

moment as they took in their surroundings. In a matter of seconds, their eyes adjusted to the light, and they saw before them a large stone casket against the wall. On the wall behind the casket was a large stone cross. On each side of that were two partially spent candle lamps. On the very top of the casket was a full-sized carved statue of the man inside.

Jon immediately dropped to his knees near the casket and placed his hands on the sides. He murmured a prayer to himself and knelt quietly for quite some time.

While Jon prayed, Dominick scanned the room. To his amazement, beside the casket was a stone platform of a table that had a number of large leather-bound books stacked neatly on top. It almost took his breath to see the objects for which they came.

Those books were still here after all those years of waiting in the dark for some unknown individual to find. Here they waited to again feel the light of the sun shining through the open door.

Jon stood and stepped to the side of the stone platform. He gently slid the top book from its stack and wiped the dust from the cover. The inscription read *Scribes of Tolk, Book One.* Although he had a desire to view everything in the pile, he felt a burning need to read that missing page of the *Book of Lore*.

He slid another from the pile and wiped away the dust. He then found *Books Two* and *Three.*

The fourth and final book in the pile was *The Book of Lore.* Jon excitedly opened the bindings of the book and quickly thumbed through the many pages he knew so well. He stared at the page he had longed to see…the one he had longed to copy for years.

The page read:

Look to those…with hearts unsold,
to renew the Faith of young and old.

When King forsakes Father for lust and greed,
Cobblestone hearts will again be freed.

Find written answers in dismal doom,
in sullen, dark dungeon of Tolk's lonely Tomb.

Seek for the chosen... born of King,
soon the bearer of righteous ring.

There will be proof for those unswayed...
for the forest will awaken... and come to his aid.

As Dominick read along with Jon, he was taken back by what he read. He looked at Jon as if he were a ghost. With a pale look he said, "You are to inherit the righteous ring…" His eyes widened. "…are you…born of king?"

Jon looked Dominick in the eye and slowly nodded his head.

"This really *IS* you!" exclaimed Dominick. "It is you that will renew the Faith. We must rush to Cobblestone!"

"We must," said Jon, with a look of contentment.

The two bundled the four books in a large leather strap and climbed the steps to the hall above. By now, the sun had lowered slightly in the sky and the room was somewhat dimmer than before. The two pushed the heavy stone door back into place and turned the cross handle to its closed position.

With books in hand, the men left the *Hall of Enlightenment* with one final gaze of appreciation. They did not wish to leave the beauty of the Hall and made their departure respectfully.

As they stepped out the open front doors of the castle, Dominick looked to Jon and said, "This is the find of a lifetime!"

At that very moment, a loud and gruff voice shouted, "Yes, yes it is...Jon of Cobblestone."

Both men were shaken by the startling voice. To their dismay and disbelief, before them stood two very large trolls...and the king! With a smug smile and a detestable laugh, the king spoke again, "Thank you men. You have done well for me. I will kindly take those, my friends."

The two trolls stepped forward, and Jon looked frantically for a place to run. But within a split second, the strong arms of the trolls had both of the men by the throat. The trolls snarled into each man's face as the king laughed and said, "Now, now, men. I would hate to see the abbey lose even more of its faithful members. It is simple. Hand me the books, and I will call off my friends."

By now, the troll had wrestled the books from Jon and extended them to the king. The king nodded to the two trolls, and they released their grip on the men.

Jon choked and shouted, "Why must you do this? I have done nothing to you. Those books could bring Faith back into Cobblestone! Let them rest in the abbey. Let us study them...share them."

"You, fool monk," spoke the king, "will be found guilty of treason if you so much as squeak a word of this. Remember dear Mathias, high in his tower. We wouldn't want anything to happen to the poor old fellow."

"You are no king," yelled Dominick, who had been quiet up until now. "You have no idea who you are dealing with. Someday you will regret your actions of today."

"Ah, friend Dominick!" spoke the king. "I see the ocean has taught you no manners. Another outburst from you, and my friends will snap your every limb...one at a time."

With that, the king and his bodyguards mounted horses hidden in the woods. Before the trio galloped away, the king shouted one last reminder, "Remember Mathias." And the sound of hideous laughter rumbled with the stomping hooves in the afternoon air.

Dominick fell to his knees in sorrow. "I am so sorry…so very, very sorry. I had no idea. I swear."

"Stand, Brother Dominick," commanded Jon. "We have much to do and much ground to cover. We can beat them to Cobblestone. The old road is much farther than the path through the forest. I have never navigated this end of the forest, but we have no choice. Come."

The young monk seemed to grow in stature, and he began to emit the strength of one destined to accomplish great things. The two immediately ran into the forest with all the might they could muster.

By Jon's reckoning, he felt they should travel westward toward the sun. After more than two hours of hard running, both men collapsed into the forest floor and rested there panting and trying to drink from their flasks of water.

When both had collected themselves, Jon spoke up. "You must travel on from here. You must find Mathias and the others. Stop the king in front of the abbey and have Mathias address him while the eyes of Cobblestone watch. I will come with all the might I can muster."

"But, where are you going?" cried Dominick. But it was too late. Jon was already many steps away and shouted over his shoulder. "Travel west. You will be there before nightfall. You must not fail!"

And, as exhaustion set in, desperation filled the hearts of two very determined men, and the floor of the Deep Forest thrashed with running feet.

* * *

Dominick's heart was pounding as his teeth tore at his last apple in his pouch. He chewed between deep breaths and wiped sweat from his brow with the back of his hand. He was worried that he might not make it to Cobblestone. He hoped that his directional calculations were correct; but mostly, he hoped his body could stand the trip. His feet were bleeding from the blisters inside his boots, and his body bled in many other places from snagging briars and limbs.

Still, he pressed on.

At last, as the sun was still visible in the sky, Dom could see the outline of Cobblestone Abbey in the late afternoon sky. Even though his legs burned with pain, he managed to keep one foot in front of the other long enough to reach the edge of the forest behind the abbey. As he burst from the edge of the forest, Brother Michael was standing in the edge of the rose garden and was startled by the thrashing noise stumbling through the forest. He watched in surprise as Dominick crashed into a pile of sweat and blood before him in the grassy lawn.

"My God, Dominick, what is wrong?" he cried.

"Get Mathias!" he gasped. "Get him now!"

14

The king and his hired thug trolls had long since slowed their pace and let their horses walk. The sun was nearing the distant mountains as the clopping hooves of the horses tapped on the cobblestone streets. The king had planned to wear his same smug smile and hold up the *Scribes* as he walked his horse through town. He sent his trolls ahead to raise the townspeople and make them aware of the king's coming—thus proving again how the king had provided for—and protected—the people of Cobblestone. It would be another jewel in his crown.

But as the king entered the edge of the city, something seemed strange. It seemed just a little more crowded than he expected. It appeared that most of the townspeople had gathered in and around the abbey. As the king was passing, Father Mathias stepped from within the abbey and called his name.

"King Lawrence!" shouted Mathias. "I would like a word with you here in front of all of Cobblestone."

The king showed that all-knowing and smug smile that the townsfolk had come to know all too well. "No trouble at all," he said, "that is precisely what I had intended. I have a special package beneath my arm that should prove once and for all that **I**...am King for a reason."

"People of Cobblestone," shouted Mathias, "let it be known that the king holds in his hands *The Scribes of Tolk*...the true written artifacts of Tolk, himself."

A gasp rushed through the crowd as people murmured amongst themselves. Not everyone knew of the *Scribes,* but all could tell that they were of the utmost importance just by the reaction from the crowd.

Mathias continued, "He did not get them through fair measure. He has taken them from the rightful finder."

"Nonsense!" shouted the king, "I found them myself near the far edge of the forest in an undisclosed location. My bodyguards will testify."

"You lie!" shouted a voice from behind Mathias. Dominick stepped from behind the old monk and walked forward. "You lie! I can testify to that."

The king was amazed to see Dominick. "I left on horseback before you. How did you arrive here before me?"

"It doesn't matter how I arrived; what matters is that Jon of Cobblestone found those *Scribes*, and he deserves the credit for it."

"Jon of Cobblestone," yelled the king, "deserves to hang for treason! He has been planning to overthrow the kingship. I should like to see that coward now!"

Mathias was now again speaking and had stepped part way down the steps of the abbey. "Jon has planned no such thing, and he is NO coward. When he returns, he will recite Tolk for you, fair king." Mathias seemed to growl his words, and his temper was rising.

"If he is no coward…" said the king deceitfully, "then where is this noted scholar? I would love a word with him."

"I AM HERE!" shouted a stone-cold voice from the edge of the forest. Limbs parted as Jon stepped from within the leaves. A rumble of voices swept through the streets as Jon stepped forward to meet the king. "I am here, my king," snarled Jon, wiping sweat and grime from his brow.

"Very good, very good…" spoke the king. "Shall we hang you here or at the castle?"

"Do what you will with me, my FAIR king," said Jon, "but the people of Cobblestone will hear the words of Tolk that have been kept from them for so many years. I have read the words, those beneath your arm, and now the people shall hear them."

Jon raised his voice and shouted to the people in the streets. He walked as he spoke, and the townspeople heard every word.

"Look to those…with hearts unsold,
to renew the Faith of young and old.

When King forsakes Father for lust and greed,
Cobblestone hearts will again be freed.

Find written answers in dismal doom,
in sullen, dark dungeon of Tolk's lonely Tomb.

Seek for the chosen…born of King,
soon the bearer of righteous ring.

There will be proof for those unswayed…
for the forest will awaken…and come to his aid."

Jon now turned his attention back to the king and shouted to him high on his horse. "It is I you fear, my KING. I will free the Cobblestone hearts!"

The king furiously jumped from his horse and stomped closer to Jon. With his hand on the hilt of his sword, he shouted, "I fear NO MAN!"

"Is it not I you fear, my king?" asked Jon. "Is it not I that has concerned you with thoughts of conspiracy? For it is we of the abbey with hearts unsold. It is we that shall renew the Faith to young and old."

"And what do you, dwarf monk, know of Tolk?" shouted the king.

"It is I—I have been to the Tomb of Tolk," spoke Jon aloud. "It is I…soon to bear the Righteous Ring."

"It seems you have overlooked a line," spoke the king with his renowned smug smile. "Who among us is born of king? I see no princes among us!"

"Tell me, MY KING," shouted Jon. "Look into my eyes and tell me you do not recognize them. Tell me, has it been so long that you do not remember the enduring eyes of one named Marie? Has is been so long that you no longer see what once was special to you?"

As Jon's words entered the air, the king was taken back. His eyes widened and he stepped backward into his horse. He blinked his eyes and tried to refocus, but he still stood in amazement, trying to regain his composure.

Jon again turned his attention to the townspeople and spoke, "People of Cobblestone, you have sought faith in our king, and he has provided. He has been a strong force for Cobblestone. He has protected our borders and provided strength and prowess to our communities. But I ask you…do we need such immediate confirmation in our spirituality? Must we have proof of all that the good Lord has provided us? Must we have immediate redemption for all we do? Some of you have asked me *Where is the God we worship*? I say to you, LOOK AROUND! Look at the skies and tell me there is no God. Look to the bountiful nature that surrounds us. Look to the friend beside you, and tell me God is not within us. Is there not life and love pulsing through our veins?"

Jon paused and looked around. Even the king was held captive by his words. The people of Cobblestone were mesmerized by all that was being said, and even those that did not understand all that was happening were in awe of the energy evoked by this young monk.

Jon again raised his voice, "You have asked me for proof. You have asked me to show you the way. You have asked me what I know of Tolk. I have delivered to you ALL of what is in the missing page of the *Book of Lore*. It is I, born of king, soon the bearer of Righteous Ring…and there will be proof for those unswayed…for the forest will awaken and come to my aid!"

Jon climbed the steps of Cobblestone Abbey and took the hand of Father Mathias. They raised their hands high to the sky together as Jon shouted, "People of Cobblestone … I give you … THE FOREST!"

A deafening wave of rustling noise swept through the city streets.

Rush…rush…rush, echoed the noise.

From over the roof tops and around buildings came a sea of greenery, rustling and chanting in unison.

Rush…rush…rush.

The townspeople were engulfed in a pool of green leaves as they stood bewildered and frightened.

Rush…rush…rush.

The streets of Cobblestone shook with the pounding of tiny little spears, all rapping in unison, louder and louder.

Rush…rush…rush.

Jon and Mathias stood immovable as their bodies turned green with a rustling clamor of tiny little creatures.

Rush…RUSH…RUSH !

And then, dead silence…

The Leaflings had come.

15

"Do not be afraid!" shouted Jon. "The Leaflings have come to my aid, to our aid, just as the Literati' fathers came to theirs so many years ago. The Leaflings have come as a show of support to the people of Cobblestone. They respectfully ask that the *Scribes* be handed over."

The king looked around and saw thousands of tiny flint spears pointed in his direction. The townspeople gazed about themselves and wondered what the Leaflings had in store for them all.

To the complete surprise of the king, one of the Leaflings flung himself up onto the back of the king's horse. He was at the king's eye level, and with a shaking of his spear, he spoke, "We do not wish to use force. I had hoped that our first meeting would be rather different."

The king was now in awe of all that had happened. He stood speechless as he looked at the Leafling facing him. His mind was awash with emotions he had never felt. He no longer felt threatened by conspiracy within the ranks of the abbey. He no longer felt the contempt that filled his heart only a few moments ago. The anger and smug emotions that had swelled within him had subsided, and he felt humbled by what he had just witnessed.

As he stared into the eyes of the son he never knew, his heart was coming to terms, and even without the influence of the Leaflings, the King had decided that Jon must have been chosen…destined, perhaps, for this task. He gently extended the bundle of books toward Jon and spoke, "I would like a copy. And it appears that we will need to talk soon…my son." The king's words seemed to drift into silence.

As Jon took the books from the king's hands, a roar of applause came from the crowd. The king gave a nod of approval, since he really had little choice in the matter, and mounted his horse. He and his trolls made their way toward the castle and left the crowd of townspeople and Leaflings behind. The crowd parted and allowed the king to pass.

Jon now turned his attention to the Leaflings and spoke, "Kimbli… Kikah…I owe you a debt of gratitude. I don't know how to repay you."

"You owe no such thing," spoke Kimbli in his raspy Leafling voice. "You came to our aid when we were in dire need. You came when no one else would. It was time we returned the favor."

"Well, I thank you just the same," said Jon.

"If our services are no longer needed," spoke Kimbli, "then we will make our way back to the Miraré. You are welcome in Tal Kator anytime."

"I am not sure you will be able to pry the little ones away," commented Jon with a chuckle. The younger Leaflings had begun toying with the children of the crowd. Leaflings hung from the arms of many of the kids, and laughter seemed to lighten the mood of the whole crowd. With a quick call by Kimbli, the Leaflings scurried away into the woods as quickly as they came. Jon called out to them, "And you are welcome here!"

Jon then turned his attention to the crowd. He then called out to them, "People of Cobblestone, you have witnessed many things today. You are welcome in the abbey. Come when you wish. Study, worship, and take counsel. Join us when you wish. But, tonight we need rest. We will leave you now, but thank you for your support. REJOICE!"

As the last hues of daylight dwindled away, the setting sun let its last rays touch a much happier Cobblestone, and those of the abbey knelt in joyous prayer.

16

The morning dew still covered the grass as Dominick knelt, pulling weeds from the rows of the herbs growing in the garden. He still had trouble knowing weed from plant, but managed the job well enough that Brother Michael no longer scolded him. As he tugged at the weeds, his mind reflected on the last two weeks.

If someone would have told him two weeks ago, in his little flat on Flagstone Row, that he would take part in such an exciting story, he would have certainly called them crazy and dismissed the idea immediately. It was an amazing week for this ex-sailor, and his feet still ached with bloody blisters from his run through the forest. He had no idea how he had endured that torturous flight from Stone Castle and still lived. Over a week afterward, pulling weeds was about the only job he was feeling up to fulfilling.

As Dom stood for a stretch, a voice called from over his shoulder. "It seems that the Pirates gain all the glory in this town."

"Good Earl," laughed Dominick, "you have caught me unarmed. My mop is still in the kitchen!"

"I have not come to joust today, my friend," said Earl. "I have accompanied the king on his visit here. Is what they say true? Is Jon really his son? Did Leaflings really fill the streets? I miss *all* the action."

"If I had not stood and watched it all first hand," commented Dom, "then I would not have believed a word of it. Those little Leaflings can be quite frightening when they wish. And yet, they were so very pleasant and soft-spoken. I should really like to visit them and be around them some."

"And what of Stone Castle?" asked Earl.

"The building is still full of beauty, even in its condition," said Dom. "You would not believe the artwork inside. I have passed that castle a dozen times and never realized what it contained. There is a mural of God painted on the ceiling in the *Hall of Enlightenment*. It is frighteningly realistic…and breathtaking to view. We must go there to see it."

"Don't worry," spoke Earl, "the king has plans for it, and I am certain that I will see plenty of it."

Dominick gave Earl a questioning glance.

"The king plans to restore the building and use it as an outpost. It will be a stronghold for the outskirts of Cobblestone. It will be a stately watchtower manned by the king's people. He intends to restore it back to its glory of generations ago. It is to be functional, and yet spiritual. He has given it much thought. He is quite the changed man."

"Changed man or not, that will be no small task," said Dom. "I should hope he has planned for someone worthy of an enormous undertaking. The castle is in ruins."

"That is why I have come. The king respectfully asks that you oversee the task. He wishes for you to man the post. He would like for you to be the first steward of Stone Castle. He has provided the means." Earl pulled from his vest a large and heavy pouch of coins, dropping it onto the stone wall of the garden. There was a heavy ring of gold coins clinking inside. "This is for you, my friend. The rest will come as needed for repairs."

Dom stood in amazement and pondered what to say as Earl continued. "Think it over. The king suspects that you may want to join the monk faith, yet I have known you quite a long time, Dominick Sebastian. Although you may have gained considerable enlightenment here in these walls, I told the king that I strongly doubted any such thing. Perhaps you may be better suited for the stewardship, rather than a life of celibacy? Am I far off?"

"You are not far off, my friend," said Dom, with a chuckle, "yet I do not know if the restoring of a castle is in my calling, but I will think on it."

"That is all we can ask of you, my sailor friend."

"So…" remarked Dom, "the king is a changed man?"

"I do believe he is trying…yet Rome was not built in a day…"

"Tell me…" joked Dom, "when and where do you expect him to release the pent-up maidens? I should like to be there to console them!"

Earl shook his head and laughed, "Once a pirate … always a pirate!"

17

hile Dominick and Earl were talking in the garden, young Jon and King Lawrence strode along the edge of the Deep Forest and talked. The two seemed an unlikely pair…this stately and colorfully dressed nobleman, and this simply-robed monk of the abbey. And yet, something about them seemed familiar. The more one looked at the two, side-by-side, the more obvious their relationship appeared. Although Jon possessed his mother's deep and compassionate eyes, many of the king's facial features had found their way to him as well. As the two walked along the forest path, their strides and stature were nearly identical.

"I feel awkward calling you Father," said Jon. "I have addressed Mathias in that way for so long that it seems unfitting. And yet, *King* seems so informal."

"Call me what you wish, Jon," said the king, "I have done nothing worthy of being called father. I sometimes wonder if I have done anything worthy of being named King."

"You have been a valiant king. Your city loves you. I hope that maybe together we can make a difference. Maybe together…we can bring a strong community into the future. I think that we can blend spirituality and strength in leadership. I think we can build a greater Cobblestone."

"You speak wisely for someone so young," said the king. "Although I am still coming to terms with it, I am very proud to have a son… especially one of your strength and compassion. Your city loves you, perhaps more than their king."

"I had no intention of that," said Jon. "I have no desire to rule, only to help, to counsel, to teach."

"And that you have done. I have watched it happen, to my amazement."

The two continued their walk and discussed the many facets of the king's leadership within the city. They covered the king's plans for Stone Castle and discussed the many options for its use. They talked of Dominick and Mathias and the many young monks of the abbey, and covered Mathias' plan for Jon to take over the abbey one day. The king listened attentively as Jon spoke and realized how much more there was to his city than he had ever imagined. Within every society, there are many tiny societies working out their problems and doing their best to move forward. It was a rewarding walk for the king, and he was enjoying this time with his son.

Soon, the two came to a small clearing in the forest and paused there as they continued their discussions. When the conversation slowed, Jon became somber. He then said to the king, "There is something else I would like for you to know. It must remain secret, although it pains me to keep it such. This place in the forest is special. We are not far from the city, not far from the abbey, but it is special."

The king looked about and took in his surroundings. It was then that he noticed the row of fieldstones protruding from the ground. It was then that he noticed the one marker stone of this tiny cemetery. He quietly read aloud the words upon it, "*Here lie great men.*" He studied the words upon the stone moment and then looked to Jon. "Tell me why we are here."

"Ten years ago…" started Jon, "there was a great upheaval in the abbey. It concerned the nine Elders of the abbey and another that had been banished from Cobblestone. You knew him as Anté."

The king acknowledged his knowing of Anté with a nod.

"It also concerned the Leaflings and a disgusting troll by the name of Tolokah. In the end, there were no winners in this battle…no victors of this bitter upheaval. There was only death and dismay. It almost eliminated the Leafling colony, and since then, it has nearly taken the abbey. It took the lives of both Anté and Tolokah."

Jon hung his head and struggled to maintain his composure. "It also took the lives of the eight monk Elders. They are here," spoke Jon, tears sliding down his face. "Here lie great men."

"These men died…and no one came forth?" questioned the king.

"There were no victors…no spoils," spoke Jon. "There was only death. Both sides had paid their dues, and it was costly to us all. Nothing could be helped by this knowledge…only more death. I chose to keep this to myself, even though the weight has weathered me beyond my years. It has haunted my soul since the day it happened, and I expect to carry it the rest of my life. I deal with it daily."

As the king absorbed the words of his son, it began to make sense to him. The young man had chosen to end the killing…end the tragedy… end the bitter war while both sides had time to rebuild and move on. It was a touchy call, and Jon had been willing to stand by his decision, be it right or wrong. He took great risk in telling the king, and the king realized that. In a time where honor and obedience played strong roles in all walks of life, Jon stuck to his guns and was prepared to face the consequences.

The king finally broke the silence. "Why have you told me this? Why have you perjured yourself now, after a decade has passed?"

Jon looked into his father's eyes and said, "I needed to tell someone. It has been an awful weight to carry. It has been heavy on my heart. But, most of all, I felt you should know. You are the king. You are my father, and I will stand tall to your decision."

The king looked Jon in the eye and stood motionless for what seemed like an eternity.

The king finally spoke. "It appears that only you know of these proceedings. What good would a trial do? You merely have information. I see no need to concern the city with this. It feels like deception in my heart, yet I can see no better solution to the problem. I see no benefit in the telling of this information. I see no gain for Cobblestone."

The king paused and paced the ground around the graves of the abbey fathers. He finally spoke, "Your secret is safe with me. See to it that it is safe with you. We need no more controversy in Cobblestone. We need no ill feelings. We need faith and leadership. I believe we have it now. If we are to move forward, then we must persevere. We must lead our peoples with all that we have. We must provide strength. And...*Cobblestone hearts will again be freed."*

In the edges of the Deep Forest, a powerful king and a faithful monk set out to renew Faith...to build strong the foundations of their society. They chose to inspire life like the Literati' of old. They chose to take life by the horns and steer it where they would, thus proving that blood is much thicker than water, and that the wheels of justice need not always turn.

Father and son walked away from this visit ready and willing to lead their people. From castle to abbey, Cobblestone would become a different place. It would rejoice more in the laughter of children, the love of life, the colorful sunsets, than those worrisome days of late. This city would turn over new leaves, and ironically...the Leaflings had played a part in it.

18

The cold winter wind did not hinder the towns-folk of Cobblestone on this blustery morning. The sun was still shining and the civilians scampered about in their church attire, trying their best to stay in the sun and avoid the bitter breath of old man winter. The past few months had changed Cobblestone. It had become much more important to the townspeople to visit the abbey and other nearby churches. The king had slacked some on his taxation…not a large amount…but enough that the commoners could eek out their livings and still be the happy members of society here in Cobblestone. Things were on the up-and-up.

In fact, the city of Cobblestone seemed to be living a fairy tale. From the outside looking in, the tell-tale signs of a perfect story were taking place.

For instance, a great Elder of the abbey was about to hand his reins over to a new monk. The monk just happened to be the king's son. And, the entire city was happy with the new transformation of itself, and the hustle and bustle of daily life seemed to perk at twice the velocity. Although the town was as happy as it had been in years, Jon's life was about to take a heartbreaking change, and he knew it.

Father Mathias had begun a process of withdrawal from his church. He had begun a practice, a month or two ago, of letting the younger monks take over the counsel after the usual sermon of the week. It had given the townsfolk a chance to come to know the younger lads of the monastery and seemed to let the old monk back away from his duties a little at a time.

But, the last few sermons had been cut quite short, and then finally, Father Mathias allowed the younger ones to give the sermon and allowed himself to sit in the front row long enough to hear it out and then return to his quarters. It was clearly not his choosing, but also clearly what the old monk was capable of doing.

By now, the entire town realized that Mathias had reached an age older than anyone in the city had ever attained. Some suspected the powers of the ring, and many credited his long life span to his spiritual ways and healthy lifestyle. All of which, of course, had helped in the old monk's longevity. He was a good old fellow, and everyone knew it. But unfortunately, no one lives forever, and that was Jon's major setback. He would have given his own life many times over to help the old monk. Father Mathias was his mentor, his life-guide, his real father. It would be a crushing day when the lad must take the office of High Elder. It would be grand and spiritual and vibrant, yet it would also be a gut-wrenching and sorrowful loss of a special loved one. It would be a day that would certainly tear him down, and hopefully, build him back up again. And, as Jon watched the failing health of his friend and mentor, time ticked along waiting for that horrendous day.

By now, the members of the abbey and the people of town all knew that Jon was to take over and become High Elder. It would be a different ceremony for Jon than any in abbey history. In years past, the remaining Elders would hold an inaugural ceremony to welcome in the new Elder. But, in Jon's case, there were no Elders left to hold the ceremony, and it appeared to Jon that it would seem more like the crowning of a new king than the rise of a monk to High Elder. Jon did not want the ceremony to take place in such a way, but knew of no other avenue. He needed to talk with Mathias about it but could not manage to hold back his emotions. He just could not manage to think of life without Mathias, and it seemed disrespectful to discuss with him what would happen after his death. The old man's health had dwindled to nearly constant bed rest and speaking was as difficult as breathing for him. Thankfully, the old monk had been around Jon long enough to know that something was bothering him and finally did his best to speak through the pain.

Jon was sitting at Mathias' bedside monitoring his condition. The old monk wheezed as he raised his head and asked, "Jon, don't you think it is time to discuss what is bothering you? I have noticed that something is out of place with you lately. Let us bring it into the open."

Jon wriggled uncomfortably in his seat and finally spoke. "We do not need to talk of such things, Father. You are tired. There will be time later."

"There will be no time later, Jon. I am tired…always tired. I wish to discuss what is bothering you, if I am able." The old monk wheezed and cleared his throat.

Jon swallowed hard after the old man's words and finally broke the silence. "I feel uncomfortable obtaining the office of High Elder without the blessing of Elders before me. I feel like I will be being crowned, rather than stepping into your shoes. It does not feel right to me. It feels pious, not humbling."

"It is time you faced something, my son," spoke Mathias. "It does not take a prophet to see that you were destined for this task. You have the blessings of the townspeople. You have the blessings of your Brothers of the abbey. And, you have my blessing. You are destined to be great, Jon. It is time you embrace this fact. It is time you become the man you are destined to be. You need not worry with how I would have things done. Lead your followers as you will. You must use your strengths as you see fit and inspire others to do the same. You have my blessings to run this abbey. You have had since the day you came into this world, and I will leave this world strengthened by having you by my side. There will be great things in store for Jon of Cobblestone Abbey, and I shall look down from Heaven with pride. Do not fear for me, my son. I will be sharing the light with almighty God, and sharing wisdom with the likes of the Literati' of old. This is *your* time, my son. Use it wisely and strongly and boldly. You are not filling my shoes. You are bringing greatness into the halls of this abbey. Embrace the power within you, Jon. You are not filling a position in an abbey. You are leading people into the light. That is so much more important. I am so very proud."

Mathias took Jon's hand and held it tightly. Tears overflowed from Jon's eyes as he tried to maintain his composure. The old monk's hands trembled with pain, and his breaths grew shorter and shorter. He cleared his voice with a faint cough and spoke again, "I love you, my son. You have been a joy." And as he spoke those words, he gently dropped his Amethyst ring into Jon's palm and cupped his fingers around it. "It is time."

Mathias let his head ease back down onto the pillow and pulled his Bible to his chest. Jon grasped the old man's hand for dear life. It still trembled with pain. As the next few hours slowly passed and the grip on Jon's hand lessened, Mathias, High Elder of Cobblestone Abbey, passed the torch…and died.

19

Father Mathias was laid to rest beside the eight missing Fathers. Stones were erected and inscribed with each of their names and dates, and a small garden of wildflowers was planted alongside. A large stone shrine was erected within the little cemetery. It was engraved with vines and leaves and wildlife. It displayed four simple words chiseled deeply into its surface…*Here lie great men.*

Dominick Sebastian moved to Stone Castle and oversaw its restoration, just as the king had wished. He and Good Earl remained great friends, and the two spoke often with Earl's regular visits to the castle to keep the king informed of the project's progress. He spent a good deal of time at the abbey, as well. He still stopped by for a sermon or two and enjoyed his counsels with Jon in the garden. By Jon's orders, Dom began the long and tedious job of recopying books for the library of the Castle. He managed to finish *The Book of Lore* before tiring of the project. He had little time with the restoration of the castle, travel time, and…oh yes, the occasional fair maiden. One maiden eventually tied him down, but that is another story altogether.

The king, too, was ensnared by a maiden. It seemed unlikely after his many years as a bachelor, but stranger things have happened. Maidens have always had a way with that sort of thing. He conducted many visits with his son in the abbey, and had, in fact, become a better man. A close friendship was enjoyed by both he and his son.

Jon stepped into his role as High Elder with ease. He had been unknowingly filling the position for years, he had just never thought of it in that way. Attendance rose in the abbey, and the Faith gained a few more monk Brothers to share in the workload. Jon commissioned a huge mural of Father Mathias to be painted on the wall of the Great Hall, and a marble bust of each Elder Father was carved for the entry hall. Numerous other works of art were brought into the abbey by its many new members, and the old building seemed to enjoy its new colors. Those with a trained eye could see tiny leaves painted here and there that were remarkably lifelike…maybe leaf-like.

Jon made an occasional trip to Tal Kator to visit Kimbli and Kikah and the rest of the Leaflings. Kimbli had become the Elder of the Leafling colony, which had greatly increased in size since the days of the tragedy with Anté and Tolokah, over a decade ago. The Leaflings now occupied a vast section of the forest around the Miraré, and even though they knew that they were welcome in Cobblestone, they chose to stay tucked away in their favorite place in the world. Kimbli would visit Jon occasionally and share news of the forest, but even those visits were quite infrequent. Jon mentioned the Leaflings many times in his sermons and counsels, but the people of Cobblestone seemed to just forget about them, which didn't bother the Leaflings in the slightest. They were quite happy without the footsteps of man, and the colony continued to grow in the middle of the Deep Forest, just as it had done for generations beyond account.

So, as these early days during the leadership of Jon as High Elder unfolded, life flowed with a harmony unsurpassed. Because of the many fascinating and remarkable occurrences that had taken place, Jon began to feel a need to record his own bits and pieces of those stories. Strangely, he also began sensing a change coming. He began having strange thoughts about the future. He wasn't just certain of what his mind was trying to tell him, but he never questioned his intuition. So, high up the winding stairs of the abbey tower, young Jon sat at the table of his mentor with pen in hand. Before him, was a very large (and empty) leather-bound book. "Let's see," he said to himself, "where to start? *The Scribes of Jon...*yeah, that should do it."

And outside this tall and beautiful tower, kings ruled and children played and Leaflings scampered in the woods nearby...and life was grand in Cobblestone.

Leaflngs

Book Three

The Prophesy Rhymes

Of Cobblestone Castle

Excerpt From "The Fall of the House of Romb"

1134 A.D.

Beware the crooked stranger
That walks beneath the trees.
Beware his precious holdings
In basket lined with leaves.

Beware the doctor's poison tongue
And poisons in his hand.
For he may seal the fate of kings
And on castle precipice stand.

Beware to those of Tal Kator,
Beware to Cobblestone!
For he shall bring forgotten sons
And sit upon the throne.

Look to the east…the rising sun
To concur and to save.
There will be roars of battle cries…
Enormous fighting waves.

But the least of all the soldiers…
Simple little souls,
Will see the truth behind the lies…
And turn the key they hold.

…and the Prophesy begins.

The midday sun warmed the canopy of tender young leaves of the Great Forest as a swift shadow glided overhead. A light breeze cooled the dark feathers of a raven as he drifted effortlessly above the waves of greenery below. But this was no mere raven. It was a Tower Raven from Cobblestone Abbey. His name in English (and in Raven) was Cah. His strong wings had carried him over this vast wood hundreds of times in his long life, delivering messages from abbey to castle and back, and he knew the way without thought or bother. He could navigate it in both night and day and considered it his favorite route.

Ordinarily his heart would have been soaring along with his body as he glided from gale to gale, but today Cah carried a load. It was not just his tiny message attached to his leg that burdened him but the enormous weight of grave news. He was unable to read the words on the parchment or fully understand the solemn words spoken as it was tied, but Cah had lived long enough to sense anguish … sense despair. He carried that weight along on this journey.

Cah navigated his way through the dense forest as he closed in on Stone Castle. He took his normal path around the giant hemlock tree and dropped onto the rock ledge of the upper tower. The rock felt cold on his tiny feet as he bounced over to a small bell attached to the wall. He rapped gently against the jingling bell and waited patiently. In a matter of seconds, the tall stature of Dominick Sebastian stepped from inside the castle and out onto the rock balcony.

"Cah!" he called with a beaming smile. "It is good to see you!"

But Cah did not show his usual enthusiasm. He would normally bounce along the precipice ledge chirping "Cah back, Cah back!", looking for a handful of nuts and berries and a playful rub on the head. But there was no bounce in Cah today. He let his head drop and extended his leg to Dominick.

Dominick quickly untied the note from the raven's leg and held it up to the light. And even though he knew the raven would only understand bits and pieces of the news inside, he read it aloud for his benefit.

Dearest Dominick,

I regret that I am the bearer of bad news. I must ask for your immediate return to Cobblestone. I weep as I write, for my father, our king, is gone. The King of Cobblestone is dead. We await your return.

Jon

A tear slid from Dominick's eye and seemed to crash onto the cold stone floor. He picked up the forlorn bird beside him and raised him to his face. He tenderly uttered two words. "King…gone."

Cah gave a quiet coo and nestled his head into Dominick's chest. "Oh, Cah…I will miss him dearly."

Dominick pictured the many hearty handshakes he and the King had exchanged during the restoration of this beautiful castle. He remembered the dozens of fantastic meals the king and queen had shared with him and his wife here in these merry halls. He could nearly hear that strong and cheerful laugh echoing from the rock walls. The king's love of life was like no one Dom had ever known.

Dom glanced around, taking in the beauty of the day and observing this enormous building in which he lived. Could twenty years have passed since the restoration began on this old castle? Had two decades somehow slipped away since he and the King took on this challenge of restoring it? It seemed like such a short time ago when the cleanup began. The time had slipped away much faster than Dom had realized. Now his old friend was gone.

He wondered how Jon was taking this dreadful news. Jon was as close a friend as his father, the king, and Dom felt a pang of remorse for him as well. As he stroked the black feathers of Cah, Dom realized just how precious the days with our friends truly are. And as man and bird sat high above the woodland world, tears fell from the high ledge of Stone Castle and dampened the king's soil.

2

A light frost covered the stones of the Old Road. The sound of galloping hooves clattered in the early morning air as Dominick Sebastian raced through the near darkness. The cold wind was invigorating on his skin, but sorrow burrowed deep in his chest and tugged on his spirit. It was a long three hour ride to Cobblestone at a full gallop, and the poor horse was getting few rests.

At last, Dom slowed his pace and stopped at a small winding creek near the roadside. As he drew water for his flask, he spoke aloud to his horse. "Flag," he said, "I don't know what we will find in Cobblestone. Something is dreadfully awry. Old Lawrence was certainly old enough to die unexpectedly, but I feel odd in some way."

Flagstone, lovingly named for Dom's childhood home in Cobblestone, lapped gently at the water's edge and paid no attention to his master's words. Dom often spoke aloud to the horse as if he understood every word.

"But Jon would have mentioned it if there was truly something out of place. We talked often, through Cah, and kept close, I suppose. Where is that old crow anyway?"

About that time, old Cah flapped up by their side and hopped over to the running water in front of them. After taking a few long sips of the cool water, he hopped onto Dom's lap and began to peck at his vest pocket.

"Oh, alright, old bird," he joked, "here's a fig to keep you content. We have another hour of tough travel before we reach the abbey."

Both animals gazed off into the brightening light of the early morning and paid little attention to the fellow chatting his thoughts into the air. Cah was clearly more interested in his fig than the ramblings of Dom Sebastian and slapped it vigorously against the rocks near the water's edge, pecking at its tough surface.

"One thing for certain, my friends, Sir Lawrence will not extend that familiar handshake upon our arrival…and it will be a blow to my heart. Come, friends…let us move on."

* * *

Meanwhile, Jon of Cobblestone Abbey was struggling with his own sorrows. The father that he had not known during his childhood had somehow miraculously stepped back into his life two decades ago. The old king's less-than-upstanding ways had changed, and his views on life had grown and prospered in ways that surprised even Jon's overzealous expectations. The last twenty plus years of his life had been as rich as any man's…shared with both his unknown son from years ago, and that of his newly found family of wife and young son and daughter. He was a rich king indeed.

But none of this helped Jon now. He struggled with the loss of the only family member he'd ever known. He had been enormously fond of Father Mathias, his monk Elder and father figure of his early youth. He somehow felt sorrow over the loss of the mother he never knew, who died during his birth. But this last death was of his father… real father…flesh and blood. And this was as harsh a blow to his soul as Mathias and his mother combined. The two had gotten incredibly close over the years and shared the many things father and son should. They rode the far reaches of kingship soil on horseback. They had long discussions on religion and astrology, on love and war. Each cherished one another's company and sipped the marrow of those special days. It was a relationship neither had ever expected, yet each relished in it. It was God's good fortune for them both.

But that relationship was now gone. This new mother that Jon had tried to love had been less than receptive to him. She showed compassion when the king was near and shunned Jon's presence in his absence. She was a good woman but held much higher regard for her own flesh and blood than that of a prior woman's son. To her, Jon was the kind monk of the abbey…not a man to take the throne after the fall of the king. And unfortunately for Jon, she remained Queen…and the Queen set many things in order. But before the harsh and troublesome pieces of the puzzle were exposed, there was a death to mourn…a burial to take place. And despite her disregard for her step son, she did love her husband…her king. And all stopped for this ceremony.

* * * * * *

The tender steps of nine year old Gwendolyn timidly wandered the cold stone hall to her brother's room in Cobblestone Castle. It was just after midnight, and the normally inviting rooms of the castle had taken on a much darker feel. She had tossed and turned in her bed, unable to shake the fearful childhood thoughts from her mind. Amid those childhood fears, she was also struggling with the sorrow of losing her father. After a number of hours of quiet sobbing, she chose to find her brother. He had always been a stronghold for her, and even though they often battled with sibling quarrels, she loved him dearly. He would sooth her nerves. She was certain.

She stood quietly at his bedside, watching his chest rise and fall in a deep sleep. Even at nine years of age, she still carried her rather tattered rag doll and special quilt blanket. These last two nights she needed every security she owned just to get through the night.

"Malcolm…Malcolm," she whispered. "I'm scared."

"Huh…what?" In the dim light of the room, Malcolm could make out the silhouette of his sister standing by the bed, tears glistening on her cheeks in the near darkness.

"I'm scared…can I stay here?" she asked, tears flowing faster as she spoke.

"Yeah…climb in," he said. He pulled back the covers for her, and she piled in…dolly, blanket, and all. She still sobbed as she looked to him for comfort. "Why aren't you sleeping?" he asked, knowing the answer to his question.

"I…I…I…" The crying had stifled her voice, and she hyperventilated as she tried to speak. "I…I miss Daddy," she finally uttered.

Malcolm pulled her to him. Her arms squeezed him in tight as tears fell to his shoulders. "I miss Daddy. I miss him so much."

"I know, Sis. I know. So do I."

And high above the darkened streets of Cobblestone, amid the many hundreds of its mourning citizens, a brother and sister also mourned the loss of their father.

3

The morning dew blanketed Cobblestone as Dom's horse slowed its pace. "See how she sparkles, my friends?" he asked his animal companions.

The morning sun was beginning to warm the dark leather on Dominick's back as the trio reached the city's outer limits. The dew glistened with tints of gold over the rooftops of the rock-covered homes and houses of Cobblestone. It was a welcome sight for Dom, and it comforted his heavy heart. He reassured himself with a deep breath and a shrug of his shoulders. His destination was just ahead, and he braced himself for it.

The Abbey was as inviting as ever. Its tile roof was damp with dew, and its clapboard siding shone warmly in the sunshine. Daffodils pushed their heads above the soil and the scent of honeysuckle drifted on the air. Dom climbed the front steps and reached to the large wooden doors to knock. Before his hand reached the heavy iron knocker, the door swung open in front of him. Before him, stood the solemn silhouette of Jon. His eyes were red and swollen, and his shoulders sagged with sorrow.

"Hello, friend," said Dom quietly.

"Thank you for coming," said Jon, extending his hand for a shake. Dom passed the handshake and pulled Jon into a strong hug. The monk's small frame collapsed into Dom's heavy leather vest as he tried to maintain himself.

"I am having trouble with this, Dominick. It's a weight like nothing I have ever felt. I guess I was not prepared."

"There is no preparing for such days, my friend. We deal with them as they come."

Jon lifted his head and motioned Dom inside. Dom's heavy boots echoed down the hall of the abbey. The warm smell of fresh biscuits wafted through the building as Dom stared at the familiar surroundings. He loved this old abbey, and every step inside its simple rooms was a comfort to him.

"I don't suppose you're hungry?" asked Jon.

"I could eat the horse I rode in on if he wasn't such a tough old nag!"

"I'll have Brother Michael fetch something for old Flagstone, while we see what the kitchen has to offer," said Jon. "I do hope Cah made it home with you, also. I miss that old rascal."

"Yes...yes," laughed Dom. "The old crow nearly ate me out of house and home. I had to bring him back. He left us for the tower as soon as we were in sight."

"Then I suspect he has already found ample supply of breakfast for himself!"

The two enjoyed a hearty plateful of breakfast and caught up on the latest comings and goings of Cobblestone. It was determined that the funeral services for the king were to be held the next day. Jon had insisted upon waiting for Dom's arrival before getting underway with arrangements, which angered the queen considerably. With the persuasion of the royal guard, the queen agreed to postpone the ceremony another day, giving ample time for news to travel through Cobblestone and surrounding communities.

"I worry so much for Malcolm and Gwendolyn," said Jon, looking distantly out into the abbey garden. "They are such sweet souls. I love them dearly."

"And as for the queen?" asked Dom.

"Ah yes, the queen," commented Jon. "She is…as always."

"I never understood what your father saw in her," said Dom with a shake of his head. "Elizabeth and I always enjoyed our dinners with the two of them, but she could be a sour sort at times."

"She is a good woman, Dom. She loves and cares for her children. She will try to do what is right for Cobblestone. I believe her heart is right…even…"

"Even, what?" asked Dom.

"…even if she chooses to push me away. I have tried so very hard to be a part of her life. I have offered help and assistance. Even my friendship is unwanted. It's a shame."

"Then it is her loss, my friend," smiled Dom.

"I can deal with life without her," said Jon, "but I would miss the children ever so much. They are such a joy."

"She knows how much you love them…and they you. She would not hurt the children in that way. The old shrew isn't that mean."

"I still worry, Dom. Something just doesn't seem right about it all. I have seen nothing unusual, but I feel strange. I feel uneasy. My thoughts have been dark of late. My mind is not clear. I fear something odd is brewing."

"We will worry about it another time, Jon. We have a king to bury. That is enough weight for us all."

And within the comforting walls of Cobblestone Abbey, two heavy hearts waited for their solemn tomorrow.

4

Far from the streets of Cobblestone, in the serene and comforting fens of the Great Forest, the lazily flowing Falling River cleansed the very soul of the woods. The winding waters above Miraré Falls were home to only a few species of woodland creatures, but the pure waters of this precious stream seemed to beckon life to its pristine shores. Its vibrant currents refreshed this rich woodland setting with minerals and nutrients, and life pulsated through this section of forest, where the water lapped over and around the rugged rock terrain. As one might suspect, the Leaflings loved it here on the river nearly as much as their very own Miraré Falls of Tal Kator just down stream. On a quiet day, the light rustle of Leafing feet could be heard scampering along the rippling waters.

On this day, two young Leaflings were swimming near the water's edge and playfully splashing the bull frogs in the backwaters. They were both fairly important little saps in the Leafling society. Young

Kimbli was a direct descendent of *THE* Kimbli that helped save Tal Kator some thirty years earlier in that awful battle between Anté, Tolokah, and the monks of Cobblestone Abbey. It became known as The War of the Amethyst Stone, and every Leafling knew the story by heart. It was recited time and time again by the young saplings to their elders. That was the Leafling way…history recited from old to young and back again. That was how history was remembered.

The other youngster was a fiery little lad by the name of Tally. He too was a descendent of a veteran of that war. He was a sapling of the Kikah line…war-time best friend of Kimbli. Both had played huge parts in the saving of Tal Kator in the war, and by some strange twist of fate, these two sapling descendents had become great friends just as their ancestors of old.

As the two playful saplings bounced along the river's edge, the late morning sun was warming their leaves and filling their bodies with energy. Nothing stirs the senses of a Leafling like a ray of sunshine. Fresh air and sunshine were as refreshing as any hearty meal.

"Hey, Kim," called Tally in his raspy Leafling voice, "this one looks like a good one."

Tally had been wading the shallow shores of the river, searching for pieces of flint for arrowhead carving. He had stumbled across a particularly nice piece of bluish-gray flint just beneath the surface of the stream and picked it up for inspection. He held it up to the light of the sun and admired its nearly transparent hues. "Hey, Kim," he called again, "this will make a fantastic point!"

Tally's friend, Kimbli, was still downstream doing the same type of hunting. His head perked up with the voice of Tally. "Let me see," he said, wading upstream to get a view.

The two stood waist-deep in the calm currents of the river backwaters examining the flint Tally had found. The common delicate sounds of nature seemed to flow around the two much like the river currents beneath them. The scent of honeysuckle floated on the breeze, and raspberry blossoms almost smiled in the early springtime sun. Mother Nature was showing her wonderful inspiration, and Father Time was awakening from a long winter's nap.

Tally plopped down on a nearby rock ledge and began knapping at the flint in his hand. In a matter of minutes, he had chipped out a beautiful little spear tip arrowhead. He immediately held it up for Kimbli's inspection.

"That's a beauty, Tal. Nice job. You've always been better at knapping than me." He walked over and sat alongside Tally.

Kimbli sat quietly and dangled his long toes in the moving current. The barky surface of his face seemed to wrinkle in thought. He clearly had something on his mind and eventually spoke up. "Tally…there's something I've been meaning to ask you," he said. "Oh, I don't know. It's a strange thing. I wonder …I wonder…have you ever heard a human child sing?"

Tally seemed distracted with his newly knapped stone. "I don't think so," he answered, half-heartedly.

"I mean it. Have you ever heard their voice…its simple, clear tones ringing in the air? There is an innocence woven within it…a pureness stirred into it. I have never heard anything like it. I can't tell you how drawn I am to that wonderful sound. I can't tell you how it touches me. It somehow breaks my heart…and yet heals it too. It's beyond beautiful."

"What child have *you* heard?" asked Tally.

"It doesn't matter. Have you heard such?"

"Evidently not," Tally replied. "I believe I'd remember."

Kimbli gave a compassionate sigh. His mind was drifting back to a special day, and he wanted to share it with his good friend. "I have been to the castle, Tally. I have heard her voice. There is no other like it in the world. It's a simple, yet precious sound. It is breathtaking … simply breathtaking. It *moves* me."

"I think you've been down to the old Apple with the barkies, Kimbo. What are you talking about?"

Kimbli stared out over the forest floor. The distant look in his eye was obvious. It was considered forbidden for young Leaflings to visit mankind without the protection of the tribe, yet young Kimbli had made a number of trips in secret. He felt awkward about his trips and wanted to shed his cloak of secrecy by telling someone. "She is special, Tal. I don't know how, but she is. I can feel it when she sings."

"Alright, I'm lost. Who's special? Let's talk about this."

"I am talking about Gwendolyn. I must confess. We have become the best of friends. She is a wonderful girl."

"Start over, Sap. I'm still lost." Tally shook his leafy head.

"It was early last year, Tal. I was chasing a dragonfly near the Northern reaches of Cobblestone. It was a pretty day, and I paid little attention to how far I'd gotten through the forest. Before I knew it, I had raced out into an open grassland that I thought was a field. It wasn't a field at all. It just happened to be the game yard of Cobblestone Castle. It lies just beyond the high stone wall before the mote. There were no games going on this day, and no horses or dogs scampered about. It was a completely quiet day…except for that sound. Those notes were coming from a castle window. Bless my bark, that sound was almost haunting. It pulled me near, and there I sat completely engulfed in the moment. I was moved…truly *moved.*"

"What did you hear, Kim?"

"Oh…that sound…her voice. It is heart-melting."

"*Gwendolyn's* voice?" asked Tally, still trying to catch up with his friend's story.

"Oh, yes. She could sing souls from the Devil," said Kimbli, shaking his leafy head with a smile. "She had my full attention, and then some."

"Why are you telling me this, Kim?" asked Tally. "There is more to this than the notes on the air, isn't there?"

Kimbli closed his eyes and tilted his head with a look of contentment. "I tell you this ... because ... well ... because it drew me nearer to the humans than I ever wanted to be. It drew me near this young child. I have come to love our friendship. We have become quite close. Gwendolyn is such a sweetheart of a little lady. And it all started with her sweet and gentle notes she sang into the air that day. I can still hear them in my head...still feel them inside me. There is love in her words...love in her heart. There is love all about her, Tal. Cobblestone is so fortunate to have her...so lucky to live in her presence."

"Who is she?"

"Tal...she is the daughter of the king and queen. She is Cobblestone's princess."

"Wow," mumbled Tally. "You sure can pick 'em, Kimbo. How long have you known her?"

"Only about a year...but her friendship is dear to me. I could listen to her sing for hours on end. I am surprised she even accepted me. Most of mankind is scared of us. They feel as if we bite or sting or something. I would not have scared her for anything, but I accidentally stumbled from the ledge of her balcony and fell flat on my face. I should not have been that close, but I simply couldn't help myself. My fall didn't hurt at all, but it startled me, and it definitely caught her eye. In fear, she raced to see if I had been hurt. Imagine that. A little girl was concerned for my safety and not in the least bit frightened. I apologized through and through, but she would have none of it. *Oh no*, she insisted, *you must come in and visit a bit. I've never talked to a Leafling. I am quite curious.* And that's how it started. She is open and caring...a joy to be near. That is where I go when I take my walks. I go to visit...and to hear the wonderful sound of her voice. She is special, Tal."

"So you go to hear a little girl sing. You've got me there, Kimbo. I would never have guessed it. And does your Ori know?"

"No," replied Kimbli with a sigh of guilt. "Ori doesn't know. I'd never hear the end of it."

"Maybe you should tell of your visits. Maybe your Ori would understand." Tally tried to offer hope, yet knew that Kimbli's Ori would fall leafless with such news. "Tell me more," he asked.

"Would you like to meet her?" asked Kimbli with an enthusiastic smile.

"Oh yeah…then we can both be in trouble. That's just what I need."

"Oh," smiled Kimbli, "we could be there in no time. What do you say…want to go?"

"We can't be to the castle in *no time*…you're leafy as a garden hedge."

"Want to bet? Follow me, my sappy friend, and we shall see…and hear." Kimbli's eyes sparkled as he awaited Tally's reply.

A simple bet was all it took to intrigue young Tally. He could not care less for the notes of a singing child, but a bet about forest travel was certainly an enjoyable argument for him. He readily agreed, and the two scampered off into the depths of the forest.

A large portion of the wood had been covered by the Leaflings before Kimbli showed signs of slowing his pace. Leaflings can cover large distances in a short period of time. Their tiny limbs are capable of great speed when they choose. They jump and swing and topple as they run and can maneuver equally well on both hand and foot. They look remarkably like little tumbleweeds spinning furiously over the forest floor, with their limbs flailing about as they speed along.

Kimbli jumped up onto a hollow log and waited patiently for Tally to catch up. He was panting heavily as Tally plopped down beside him.

"Even at this pace, Kimbo," he huffed, "we still won't get there in *no time*."

"Oh, trust me, Tal. Have you no faith? I was just about to prove you wrong!"

"Prove away, Kimbo…I'm tired of running."

Kimbli gave a sly grin and tapped gently on the hollow log on which he stood. To Tally's surprise, a rustling noise came from within. In a matter of seconds, a furry animal hopped out into the light. Tally's eyes widened as he stared in disbelief. He grew excited as he spoke. "That's…that's…a wood hare! I have never seen one! A wood hare… he's fantastic!"

"*She's* fantastic," said Kimbli. "*She* is Molly…and a close friend, at that."

"How do you know this hare?" exclaimed Tally, as the hare silently twitched her nose and yawned. A thump of her back foot startled him to full attention. "How do you know her?"

"It doesn't matter. Time is wasting. We will miss our serenade, if we don't hurry."

The hare hopped over to Kimbli and seemed to smile playfully. "Climb on, Tal…we have a journey to make."

"Climb on?" he asked.

"Yes…how's your grip?"

"My grip?"

Kimbli jumped up onto the hare's back and motioned to Tally to join him. "Come on…I have a bet to win!"

Tally reluctantly stepped closer and climbed onto the hare's back just behind Kimbli. "What about my grip?" he asked.

Kimbli gave an ornery smile, then bent down and whispered into the hare's ear. Instantly, the hare jumped into full speed and raced off into the forest. Tally was hanging limply by one hand, as the hare sped through the forest…his body flailing and pounding up and down with every hop.

"Your grip, Tal…" shouted Kimbli. "This is what I mean by *grip*."

"Thanks for the warning, pal," he shouted back, his voice pounding vigorously.

Tally tugged himself up onto the hare's back and settled himself into a surprisingly comfortable position. With wind flowing through their leaves, the two Leaflings raced through the forest on one of the fastest rides of their lives.

In what Tally later described as *no time*, the three scampered out into the game yard of Cobblestone Castle. The afternoon sun had warmed the spring grasses and dried what little dew had gathered the night before. It was a particularly warm day that felt more like summer than early spring.

Kimbli whispered to Molly, and she began nibbling at the grassy lawn and playing along the forest's edge. He motioned to Tally and made his way over the yard. The two quickly scaled the rock wall surrounding the castle and sat down upon it, taking in their surroundings. "I think we're just in time," commented Kimbli, pointing at one of the higher windows of the castle. "Just sit quietly."

A couple of stories above the castle courtyard, the silhouette of a young lady stepped onto the balcony. As she stared out over the yard and into the forest, a warm breeze gently blew the strands of her golden hair. With a tilt of her head, she began to hum a soft and tender tune. Her notes seemed to blend into the warmth of the day as the light breezes blew. To Tally's amazement, she opened her mouth and sang. Effortlessly her words soared into the valley…rich and wonderful.

Calmly blows the solemn breeze
Warm and sweet so as to please.
Melt my heart in playful tease…
Eternal zephyrs of summer's eve.

Tickling leaves upon the trees
Of joyous yellows, browns, and greens.
Windy words spoke unto me…
Eternal zephyrs of summer's eve.

Hark, the children hard at play
Seize the day, seize the day.
Jump into the swirling leaves...
Eternal zephyrs of summer's eve.

Lift my hair. My skin appease.
Sway the grasses near the stream.
Let me never long to leave...
Eternal zephyrs of summer's eve.

I'll miss your voice in autumn air.
Have no care. Have no care.
When springtime melts the winter freeze,
I'll look for your return to me.

Eternal zephyrs of summer's eve.

Both Leaflings sat motionless on the rock wall, mesmerized by her beautiful tune. It was an old song written long before her time, but now *Eternal Zephyrs* was known far and wide simply as *Gwendolyn's Song*. The citizens of Cobblestone would often make their way to the grassy field behind the castle in the afternoon in hopes of catching a few notes of her song. But today there were no civilians gazing castle high…only two small Leaflings with their vine-like toes dangling over the rock ledge.

Tally was equally moved by the little girl's song and studied his thoughts for quite some time before he was able to utter any words. "That…that was beautiful…"

Kimbli was still staring up at Gwendolyn when she stopped singing. Strands of her golden hair were still blowing gently, but her face was solemn with emotion. A tear slipped quietly from her cheek and fell stories down to the stone courtyard.

"Something is wrong, Tal," murmured Kimbli. "I'm going up."

Within seconds, Kimbli had bounced from the stone wall and splashed into the castle mote. After a few quick stokes through the water, he found himself on the inside shore and scampered up onto the castle wall. Seconds later, he had scaled the wall and was looking into the sullen eyes of Gwendolyn. Tears were still falling from her swollen eyes as she spoke.

"Kimbli…thank you for coming!" she cried and pulled him to her cheek. His leafy arms consoled his young friend as she wept. "I hoped you would come. I needed someone to talk to."

By now, Kimbli was shedding tears of his own, not yet knowing what had befallen the little girl. Tally quietly slid up onto the ledge and listened quietly.

Gwendolyn recited the events of her life over the last few days. She told of her father's passing after his brief but fatal illness and her mother's struggles with the governing of the city. After many minutes of discussion, she noticed Tally sitting on the stone balcony. "Oh, I'm sorry," she gasped. "You've brought company. Please invite him in."

Tally smiled as he shimmied off of the ledge and walked over to them. "I am sorry for your loss, M' Lady…and sorry for our bad timing."

"Your timing was perfect. I needed friends to brighten my day. Thank you both for coming. I am Gwendolyn," she said, looking at Tally. "What is your name?"

"I am Tally," he said with a shake of his head and a raise of his chest, "pleased to meet you."

"The pleasure is all mine," said Gwendolyn with a curtsy and a chuckle. "That's Tally…as in Tal Kator?" she asked.

"Yes…yes…that is correct."

"Let's play hide-and-seek," she suggested. "I want to think about something else for a while. Do you know how to play? I can teach you if you've never played!"

It wasn't long until the cold halls of Cobblestone Castle were filled with merriment worthy of the king himself. The three scampered and played all through the castle and played hide-and-seek in the dusty corners of the lower halls. And upon their departure that afternoon, Tally concluded to Kimbli, "You know, Kimbo…she truly is a joy. She is a precious spirit. I'm glad we came."

As Kimbli called for Molly in the edge of the forest, the two stood listening to the evening sounds near the castle. Gwendolyn's voice could again be heard drifting on the air.

Eternal Zephyrs of Summer's Eve…

Late that evening…

Far below the upper halls of Cobblestone Castle, the eerie darkness was interrupted by the flicker of a torch. The sound of footsteps echoed through the lower halls as a dark figure crept down the stone staircase. After weaving through a maze of dark rooms, the hooded figure stopped near a large wooden door. A small wooden barrel sufficed as a seat as this dark figure waited patiently. Before long, a series of knocks on the door startled him to full attention. With two short return knocks, the figure inserted a large metal key into the lock of the door. With little effort, the mechanisms of the old metal lock clicked within, and the door swung wide, revealing another shadowy silhouette on the other side. It was the shape of a crusty little man, half-hunched over in a filthy robe of dusky brown. His jagged yellow teeth shown in the flickering light of the glowing torch as he spoke.

"I've brought them. They're a right-nice batch, I'd say."

"I'll be the judge of that!" growled the conniving voice of Malus, his hand still firmly grasping the key in the door. "I thought you'd never arrive. What's kept you, fool!"

"I don't take likin' to being called a fool," whimpered the dingy figure. "I've not done nothin' worthy of bein' called such. I've brought them, haven't I? I'm cold and hungry…yet I brought 'em, so I did…I knew you'd be waitin'."

"Yes, yes," spouted Malus. "Let us have a look. Give me that!"

"Alright, alright…got's 'em right 'ere, I do!"

Quickly, Malus tugged a small woven basket from his arm. Its contents were just what he'd been looking for, yet he fiercely slapped the lid shut and again growled a few words. "There's not forty here! I specifically asked for forty! Where's your head, you fool ogre?"

"I'm not an ogre…stop saying that!"

"I'll say what I want…when I want. Where are the rest?"

"They just aren't growing there. You said they would be…yes you did…but noooo, oh no. Not there at all, my Lord…not there at all! Had to find me own, yes I did!"

"Then why so few?" asked Malus…stammering and stewing with each word.

"I can't makes 'em grow on me own, now can I? I've done all I could, and then a bit more, I have. Don't think I haven't…'cause I have. I've done searched high and low, I have. They just aren't there, M' Lord."

"Then find MORE!" shouted Malus. "This is not nearly enough… and I need more. Find them and I shall double your reward."

"But I 'aven't seen a shilling yet, M' Lord."

"I'll show you a shilling, you shriveled little coward. Bring me what I ask and you shall receive. Until then…not a thin sixpence. Nothing. You will be paid on a worthy basis. And I find you quite unworthy!"

"No, no, M' Lord. I works hard…so hard. You'll find me worthy… yes you will. Worthy, indeed. I'll find the remainder. I'll brings 'em right to ya, I will. Don't think I won't! I'll brings 'em right to ya." The scurvy soul wrinkled his nose. "Then I'll be paid, right? I'll gets me dues then, huh?"

"Bring me what I wish, and you will be dutifully served. You have MY word. Now be gone! You turn my stomach, you foul work of nature. Bring me what I wish…"

Malus' words were not accepted well with the loathsome creature that heard them. He turned and stepped out the door, making his way down a long and narrow corridor and away from the lower halls of Cobblestone Castle.

"Disgusting, foul man. Healer? HAH!" He grumbled and growled … snickered and snarled … hobbling his way from far beneath the castle and out into the woods nearby.

His bent and crooked body ached with his steps, and his breathing was labored and raspy. He suffered from a muscle condition considered untreatable by the healers of the time, and it tore at his heart and soul everyday. He was an outcast, shunned and loathed throughout the streets of his home in the city of Blue Haven. Life had taught him to keep to himself to avoid the harsh judgments dished out by those he met in the city. He chose to live in the woods, just trying to avoid personal contact with most of the outside world. He was considered an ogre or warlock by the townspeople, which broke his heart through and through.

He was born Rastus Cubbins, the son of a farming family that lived on the outskirts of the nearby city of Blue Haven. At an early age, his body began to deform. His spine bent with the twisting pain of his disease, and his walking grew labored and unstable. With his shaky actions and grossly bent posture, he very much resembled the rodent vermin that scampered the filthy Blue Haven backstreets. And for obvious reasons, Rastus simply became known as Rat.

By now, Rat had succumbed to the fact that the menacing man that had hired his skills was a most-detestable soul. This "Malus" was a disgusting and conniving individual, yet seemed to possess all the monetary means of attaining what he chose. He had laid the groundwork well. He had set the stage with all the grandeur and becoming nature of a worthy and humble doctor for the family of the king. Yet he was no member of any faculty or membership of any kind within the ranks of the castle guard or any other ranks of servants within Cobblestone Castle. He was merely a medicine man...yet his stature in the castle had become much larger than anyone had ever suspected. His weight had become a cumbersome load to those that worked and served in the king's ranks. Few cared for his demeanor, yet had no means of changing the queen's high regard for him. It was an awkward situation, at best.

So as Rat hobbled his way through the Deep Forest, he grumbled about Malus and the seemingly impossible task the old doctor had put before him. "I'll never find that many...they're just nowhere to be found. No sir, I done found 'em all."

Meanwhile, the heavy wooden door of the dungeon in Cobblestone Castle slammed shut with the anger of Malus. He uttered a few disgustingly quiet words. "Run along, foul errand-runner. Scamper the dark corners of the forest. A few more tiny items for the basket and we will be home-free."

And amid his angry thoughts, his hideous laughter also echoed through the lower halls of Cobblestone Castle.

But unbeknownst to Malus of Bluehaven ... another pair of ears heard his detestable laughter...and all the words before it.

The next morning…

Queen Guinevere sat on the edge of her bed, high above the streets of Cobblestone. The stone floor of the castle was cold on her feet, yet her mind was far from feeling it. Amid the sorrow in her heart, she felt an awkward load to bear in the governing of her city. It seemed a heavy load to carry for a widow within these cold walls. And there were the children to think about. Their precious hearts would be in need of comfort as well. Yet here she sat alone on her once warm bed feeling nearly naked and alone.

A knock upon the door startled her.

"One moment," she called, as she tidied her robe about herself. "I am coming."

Even before she opened the door, she was certain that it was the good doctor paying a call. He had been quite close in the last few weeks with the odd pains and illnesses of the king. She pondered how she would have dealt with the pain of it all without the kind hearted services of the medicine man. His calm temperament and quiet manners soothed her during the solemn hours before her husband's death. He had been a godsend to her in her time of need. It was his kind words that comforted her as the king took his last breaths. He was dear to her.

"My Lady..." he said in his usual comforting voice, "is there something I could get you...something to ease your suffering?"

"No, no...Malus," she replied, "I will be fine." Though even as she spoke, a tear slid gently down her nose.

"My Lady..." he began again, "I would dry every tear for you. But, I am a mere medicine man... unworthy ... unable to help sooth your sorrow. Forgive me...I know not how to help."

"Malus," she wept, "you have already done so much. I don't know how I shall ever repay you."

"Never, My Lady," he gasped, "it is I that owe the debt." His hands fidgeted by his side. "I've brought your medication." He laid down a number of odd herbs and medicines at her bedside.

"Oh, Malus...always the gentle sort," she spoke through the tears. "Thank you for all you have done...all that you always do. You are a dear soul—a dear friend."

"You need your rest, M' Lady. What is it that I might bring for you?"

"Malus...worry not for me. Worry for the children. Worry for Cobblestone. This will be a cold and sad day for us all. We must face it as it comes...be it ever so disheartening."

"I will leave you, My Lady," he replied, "but I shall still worry over your wellbeing. I should be glad to help with the city troubles, should you need counsel. I would help Cobblestone if need be. I would lighten your load if you would so giveth me the chance."

"You will be the first to know, my friend. There may come a time when I shall need just such. Thank you."

Malus nodded respectfully and backed out of the room. Before his body fully reached the door, two clamoring bodies rumbled into the room around him. "Well hello, Lads and Lasses!" he exclaimed.

"Good morning, Malus," said Gwendolyn as she passed. Malcolm continued past without speaking.

"Good morning, Mother," they chirped in unison, surrounding her with hugs.

Guinevere did her best to give the children an encouraging smile. She had not slept any more than the two youngsters in her arms, but she gave her all to be strong for them. "Do you have your clothes all ready for today?" she asked, looking at their shaking heads. "Then run along. Prepare yourselves and let's meet in the dinning hall for some breakfast."

With a playful pinch on their rears, Guinevere shooed the children down the hall and began preparing herself for a long day. She wondered how she would ever stand the exhausting and lengthy funeral about to take place. Aside from the usual pangs of sorrow, she had been feeling a bit sick to her stomach lately. Some of the herbs proscribed by the medicine man had helped her sleep when necessary, but the sickening nausea she had experienced was getting her down. *Just let me get through the day,* she thought, swallowing her distasteful medications.

Yet another gentle rap on the door was heard. "Beggin' your pardon, M' Lady…sorry to bother…"

"It's alright, William. It seems my barrow is a busy place today."

"I'm sorry, M' Lady, but you have visitors."

"I am in no mood for visitors, William."

"But, M' Lady,'tis Jon and Dominick Sebastian."

"Oh, very well then…let them know I shall be down in due time," she said with a wrinkle of her lip.

William scurried along down the long hall, and Gweneviere tidied herself for the visit. It wasn't long before she found herself face to face with her two visitors. "Welcome, Jon…Dom," she said in a courteous, yet cold tone.

The men exchanged pleasantries with Gweneviere, and offered condolences. She accepted them with her usual frigid nature, tolerating their interruption of her day. "If there is nothing more, men…I should like to get on with this long and wretched day."

"Gweneviere…" offered Jon, "…I would love to help in some way, if I may. Perhaps I could keep the children? They could stay with me while you tend to the preparations. Please let me help."

"The children are fine here in the castle. Thank you for your kind offer."

"As you wish…M' Lady," interceded Dom, tugging at Jon's arm as he tried to walk closer. "We only wish to help in your time of need."

"Then you shall run along and let me tend to my own needs."

"Might I see the children?" asked Jon.

At that moment, Malus entered the room and gave comment. "Shall I see these men to the door, M' Lady?"

Jon's normally humble voice was tainted with anger. "The king's son shall see himself to the door…when and how he chooses…Malus of Blue Haven."

"M' Lady?" asked Malus again, shooting a distasteful glare at Jon.

"We were just leaving," commented Dom. "This day will be hard enough without turmoil such as this. We would love to see Gwendolyn and Malcolm later if possible … whenever time allows."

Gweneviere nodded in agreement. She knew the children loved Jon and the always-playful Dominick. In days such as these, comfort of any sort should not be disallowed. "I hope to let you see them after the services, if time permits. Right now, they must have their breakfast and prepare for today. We will see you for the cavalcade at noon."

"That is all we can ask, M' Lady," said Dom, and he turned and motioned for Jon to follow. Jon turned and began to follow, but stopped short, giving one last earnest comment, "I really would like to help. I can tell you don't feel well."

"Thank you, Jon. I appreciate your concern." she said, smiling for the first time in the conversation. With a nod of her head, she turned and left the room, leaving the two men alone with Malus. Even though both were making their way for the gate, Malus still spoke up. "She will be needing no help, men. You may go on your merry way."

It took every ounce of faith Jon had to contain himself. He turned with an uncharacteristic scowl and said, "The queen has a mind of her own, Malus. I will hear her words and not the ramblings of some witch doctor. You have no say in this, and I shall not hear it!" He stepped away from Malus, shaking his head and stomping toward the main gate.

Malus nodded to the gatekeepers, and they allowed the departure of the two men. As the two crossed the mote over the main drawbridge, Jon growled a few words to Dom. "Since when does a medicine man carry out orders in the castle? How do his veins come to be shared amid the royal family? *My merry way...* I'll be on my way alright...and him too. I'll see to his departure myself, one day."

"He has no right to talk to the son of the king with such manners," said Dom. "On other days I might have set him straight. But today is not the day. There will be ample time to set the doctor straight. Let us clear our minds of it and be gone. We will deal with Malus of Blue Haven another day."

As the two men left the premises, Malus began the preparations for the long and necessary funeral cavalcade through the streets of Cobblestone.

Meanwhile, Guinevere and her children were sitting down to breakfast. The servants had the table finely set with the castle's best sterling silver. There were exquisite bowls of fruit set amid various breads and salted meats, and numerous juices had been freshly squeezed and randomly placed down the long table. A tall glass of water sat next to the queen along with various medications along side.

Although none of this group felt like eating, it was considered proper for the royal family to be treated to even finer cuisine than usual on such a devastating occasion. As Gwendolyn picked at a few varieties of fruit, Malcolm stared oddly at his mother. She, too, had picked a few parcels of fruit for her plate and gathered still more medications to take with the glass of water. As she lifted the herbs to her mouth, Malcolm spoke up. "Mother…no!"

"What is it Malcolm?" she asked with a tilt of her head.

"Don't eat that, Mother," he replied quietly.

"Now Malcolm," she said with a hint of distaste. "I need my medicine. I don't feel well, and Malus has suggested I take them. I have to do what he says."

"You don't have to do anything, Mother. You are the Queen. The Queen does as she pleases," he said, as respectfully as he could.

"And what do you know of medicine, Malcolm?" she asked.

"It's not just the medicine I worry about," he said. "I worry about that Malus. I don't trust him."

"Malcolm!" she snapped. "I'll not hear this! What if Malus heard you speak that way? Your father trusted him with his life. We must honor that!"

Malcolm let his head sink. Under his breath he said, "…and where is Father now?"

"That is enough from you, young man!" she growled. "Off to your room immediately. I will come for you later. Now, you think about what you've said! Malus has helped us in our time of need. You owe him your respect!"

Malcolm's shoulders dropped with the weight of his mother's words. He excused himself from the table and quietly climbed the staircase to his room.

Gwendolyn sat quietly, not understanding much of what she'd heard. She watched closely as her mother took the herbs and berries set aside for her.

"What is the medicine for, Mother?" she asked.

"The herbs are for my upset stomach, Honey. The berries are for nutrients. This little mushroom is to help keep me from getting sick like your father. They all taste bad, but they help me feel better. That's what the medicine does."

"Will you be alright, Mother?" she asked, swallowing hard to keep from crying.

"Of course I will, Honey," replied Gweneviere. "Come over here and sit with me. We haven't talked about this much, have we? Let's take time to talk. You have grown up so much lately that I sometimes forget you are my little girl. Maybe you and I need some time together."

In the quiet comfort of the castle dining hall, mother and daughter talked about the awkward tragedy in their life and did their best to move forward. They would each need one another's strength in the next few hours…for soon, all of Cobblestone would be watching.

7

The Royal Guard had mounted their steeds, carrying large banner flags of the city of Cobblestone. Row after row of guards lined up in parade form and stood completely silent. Townspeople lined the streets of Cobblestone for dozens of city blocks. Men stared solemnly up the streets with hats in hand, and women and children wept. The normal bustle of city life had come to a standstill, and complete silence had taken its place. At high noon, the echoing and harmonizing tones of the king's trumpeters filled the air as the huge wooden doors of Cobblestone creaked open. Above the piercing notes of the horns, one voice called aloud, "COMPANY… MARCH".

Immediately, the thunderous and constant sound of marching boots shook the crowd, and the horse-drawn chariot of the king rolled forward. High atop its ornate shell rode the lifeless body of King Lawrence of Cobblestone. Amid the cavalcade that followed was another chariot that carried Queen Gweneviere, Gwendolyn, and Malcolm. Yet another chariot carried Jon, Dominick, and old Earl of Flagstone that had retired from the king's service some five years earlier.

Between these two chariots rode Malus on horseback. After that, numerous men, women, and children walked on foot. Lastly, a number of guards brought up the rear. The entire group marched solemnly on… face-forward and forlorn.

The cavalcade pressed slowly forward. The rows of marching guards led the chariots through city block after city block of mourning citizens. All bowed as the king's body rolled onward. All gave a sigh of sorrow for the queen and her children and the company that followed.

Dominick and Earl both fought back their anguish as they rode forward, while Jon wept openly and quietly. Gentle tears slid down his face and his hands clinched nervously. It was the hardest ride of his life.

Gwendolyn and Malcolm sat at their mother's side, trying to be strong for the citizens of Cobblestone, as their mother had suggested.

The queen sat motionless, holding the children's hands. Her pale forehead was damp with tiny beads of sweat, and she struggled to maintain focus on the waving banners before her. The children could feel the slight twitching in her cold palms.

Citizens fell in file as the Cavalcade became a full-length parade of Cobblestone townspeople. Every home in the city emptied into the parade as it wound through the city streets.

Before long, the cavalcade had completed its journey through Cobblestone and returned toward the castle. It made the sharp turn that led deep into the back grounds of the castle courtyard and stopped at an open hole in a long line of engraved headstones. It was the royal graveyard, vastly decorated with fresh blossoms gathered from near and far for this special occasion.

As the chariot was maneuvered into place, the host of parading citizens filled the back courtyard of Cobblestone Castle, standing at full attention without a word.

The horses and remaining chariots were led away, leaving the royal family standing beside the casket. Each side of the grave was lined with three trumpeters holding their horns high into the air. Behind them stood guards holding the banner flags in the breeze.

The piercing sound of the trumpets shook the silent crowd, as pallbearers carried the casket forward to the hole. As trumpets rang and banners flew, the body of King Lawrence was lowered into the open grave. When the casket reached the bottom of the hole, the trumpets ceased, and all dropped their heads in prayer. Only the sound of the gentle wisps of the banner flags could be heard as all silently prayed.

Then something happened that no one expected. Nothing more appropriate could have graced the king's funeral, yet it came as a complete surprise. In the nearly dead silence of the mourning crowd, Gwendolyn stepped forward to the open grave of her father. And as tears fell from a mesmerized crowd of civilians, she opened her mouth and sang. Her heartbreaking words solemnly filled the air.

I'll miss your voice on autumn air.
Have no care, have no care.
When springtime melts the winter freeze...
I'll look for your return to me.

Eternal zephyrs of summer's eve.

At that exact moment, Queen Gweneviere collapsed to the ground, her face pale and drenched with perspiration.

"Mother!" cried Malcolm, racing to her side. But she did not answer. As the crowd closed in, Malus stepped to her side, feeling her brow and checking her pulse.

"Her pulse is weak," he gasped, holding her hand to his face. "Get her to the castle!"

Dominick quickly stepped forward and lifted Gweneviere's body and carried her onward. Malus turned to Jon, who was consoling the children and gave him a worried glance.

To everyone's surprise, he called aloud, "I'm quarantining the castle. Jon, bring the children. We must stop this dreadful disease before it takes all of Cobblestone."

A hush fell over the astonished crowd, and the silence in Cobblestone grew deafening.

Far over the morning haze of the Deep Forest, the labored steps of Rastus Cubbins trampled the dried leaves and sticks of the forest floor. He winced as he walked and mumbled his usual grumblings to himself under his forced breath.

"There just ain'st no mores of 'em, I tell ya. I can't just grows 'em on me own, now can I? More, more, more…it's all I hears. Stupid doctor always wants more. And do I gets me pay? No Sir…I gets no pay. Not even a bloody thank you. No, no…'course not Rastus. You gets no pay, no thanks…no nothin'. All I gets is an achin' in me back. I gets plenty of that, alright."

By now, Rat had wandered much farther into the forest than usual, searching for the tiny prizes the old doctor so desperately wanted. He had covered every inch of most of the lower farthings of the Deep Forest and knew each painful step of its paths quite well. But now, he was wandering farther into the heart of the forest, following the winding banks of this clear stream.

"Bless my soul…" he said, bending down to the damp soil near the river. "You are a welcome sight!"

It seems that Rat had finally found just what he'd been searching for. Beneath the tiny tussles of fallen leaves, a brilliant yellow mushroom had pushed its way into the light. "Well now, let's have us a look-see at you, little one."

Rat reached down and plucked the little mushroom from the soil. "Yes…you'll do right nice, you will. Got any friends 'round here, do ya?"

Rat continued to scan the forest floor, searching for yet more of these precious little toad stool mushrooms. It wasn't long before he came across a number of others. "Oh yes…you'll make the mean doctor right happy, now. Yes, you will."

Rat was now quite happy with his finds and actually forgot about some of the nagging aches and pains that seamed to plague his every move. "Why, I'll soon have me a basket full! The old doctor will have me pockets full, too! Yes, he will. Right nice, he will."

Then, something happened that shocked Rat into total surprise. Of course, he had thought that he was completely alone in these far depths of the woods. But he was grossly mistaken. Just as he reached down to pick another mushroom, a raspy voice chopped through the forest silence.

"No sense picking those, my friend. Poison, you know."

Rat fell backward onto the ground, clinching his heart and gasping even louder than usual for his draws of air. "Who said that? I can't sees nobody!"

"I said it, my friend. They're no good for pickin'. It'll do you no good. They're not fit, and that's that."

"I don't see nobody!" shouted Rat. "Who's doin' the talkin' already?"

"It's like I keep saying, friend. I'm doing the talking. What's a fellow like you doing, picking mushrooms you know nothing about? It'll put you in the ground, my friend. No sense eating those. They're bloody bad for ya!"

Rat shook from head to toe, gazing frantically out into the forest in search of the source of the voice. "I've done gone crazy, I have. Lost it…yes, I have!"

"You've got to calm yourself, lad. No more mushrooms for you!"

"I don't want no mushrooms! Who's talking?"

"You're never gonna see me looking all up in the air, friend. You nearly picked me instead of the mushroom. I'm right here in front of you. Can't you see?"

Rat gazed down at the forest floor where he had picked the mushroom. To his absolute astonishment, a tiny twig was waving…and somehow smiling at him. "Oh, I've lost it," mumbled Rat. "Lost my last thought, I have!"

"Oh, you men of the city amaze me. Haven't you ever heard of a Leafling? You've got us in all your fancy books in the castles and monasteries. Yet, you still don't believe!" The little Leafling swung from a low-lying branch and bounced up onto Rat's chest with a playful smile, "I…am a Leafling!"

Rat's heart pounded, as he stared at the pleasant little chap standing happily on his chest. The Leafling stood patiently waiting for Rat to come to terms. Beads of sweat dropped from Rat's brow, and his hands fidgeted in the leaves on the ground. "I've got to leave," stammered Rat. "Leave!"

Rat nervously grabbed his basket of mushrooms and scrambled to his feet. The Leafling quickly bounced off to the side and stood watching the frantic fellow in front of him. Rat turned to run, but took one last double-take, as the Leafling stared him in the eye.

"Feel free to come back and visit, my friend…now that you know the way," said the Leafling. "And remember…don't eat those mushrooms."

Rat scampered away as fast as his hurting limbs could carry him.

eanwhile, back at Cobblestone Castle, the world was ablaze with emotion. Workers scrambled to bury the body of King Lawrence. Citizens fretted and frayed about the possible outbreak of some impending disease floating in the air. And the royal family sat nervously at the bedside of the queen, waiting for answers and fearing the worst. Gwendolyn and Malcolm rested in the arms of Jon, as Malus paced the floor in front of them. Dominick stood propped against the far wall of the queen's barrow, accessing the situation and pondering the repercussions of the events that had unfolded. He stood silently watching every move of all within this cold stone room.

Malus finally spoke up. "I've sent away much of the servants and guards of the castle. The gates have been barred of travel, except for only those delivering food and necessities. Now, we have a decision to make. Do we all die here or split up into two groups?"

The whole group stared in wonder.

"What do you mean?" asked Jon.

"I mean this," said Malus. He dropped his head and appeared to be struggling with a harsh decision. "If this disease should take hold…and concur…then are we best to be all together, or should we take a chance and separate?"

"I will not separate from these children!" shouted Jon.

"Hear me out, Jon," said Malus. "We must all be quarantined…. either here or at the monastery. Should we take a chance and separate into two groups? Perhaps we may be safer in separation…perhaps double some of our chances of survival."

Jon quietly pondered the possible outcome of each situation. Some of what the doctor said made sense. Maybe two quarantines could be better than one. After all, communication could be simple via the tower ravens. But Jon had no intension of leaving Gwendolyn and Malcolm. "I will not leave the children," he said again.

"I am not suggesting you leave them, Jon," said Malus. "They could go with you if you choose to go. But should we separate? Should we take chance outside this castle? We must approach this with extreme caution."

"Who will run the castle?" asked Dom.

Malus looked solemnly down at the queen in her bed. "I'd like to think that the queen will be making those decisions. If she…if she…" Malus stammered and appeared to be choking back tears. "If she is too weak, then we can all make those decisions together…either here, or with word from the ravens."

"And what of our guards?" asked Dom.

"As long as they are healthy, we will keep them at their posts. But I suggest we keep them to a minimum at present. We may need many of them later, if this situation worsens."

"I still don't like the thought of splitting up," said Jon. "And I don't feel right about leaving Guinevere alone."

"I will have someone by her side night and day," said Malus. "I will be here as much as time permits. But, there is something else you should know." Malus paused and looked Dominick square in the eye. "Four of the castle guards fell sick this morning. And I fear that I, too, have felt ill. I am alright at present, but I am weak. I would like to see the children elsewhere."

The room grew silent after Malus' words. No one had considered the doctor taking ill. The situation seemed dreadfully hopeless.

Jon looked to Dominick for guidance. Dominick quickly spoke up. "Take the children, Jon. I shall remain at the queen's side as long as need be."

"I don't want to leave Mother!" cried Gwendolyn. Jon pulled her close to his side and consoled her. But Malcolm quickly jumped to his feet. "I'm not leaving her!" he shouted.

"Malcolm!" exclaimed Malus. "Have you not considered the repercussions? You MUST remain safe. You of all people must take caution. You, Malcolm, must take the throne of Cobblestone one day!"

It seemed that the more the old doctor spoke, the more desperate the situation became. Jon had not yet pondered the repercussions of the fall of the queen with Malcolm being so young. Malcolm had always been slated for the throne, since the day of his birth. Even though Jon was the first known son of the King, Royal Decree stated that the first son *born of queen* would take precedence in the line for the throne. Jon's royal lineage ended on the day of Malcolm's birth. Jon had had no desire to rule the city of Cobblestone, even in the early years before King Lawrence had taken Gweneviere to wed. He had always been happy spreading faith and offering counsel to his townspeople in his role as High Elder of the monastery. He would have made a good and just king, yet he had no desire to leave his post at the church.

Dominick again spoke up. "Malus is right. We must separate. The safety of the children is now our priority. Take them immediately, Jon. We will send word each day through the ravens."

Malcolm stood to protest. "I will not leave Mother."

"You must trust me on this, Malcolm," said Dom. "I will do all I can for her. I will be by her side when the doctor is not. We will let you return as soon as possible. I promise."

At that moment, the queen stirred in bed. Although her eyes never opened, her dry voice spoke. "Take the children, Jon. Care for them as you always have." Her breath huffed and puffed into the nearly silent room, her tender heart on her sleeve.

Malcolm and Gwendolyn raced to her side before Dom could catch them. Malcolm took her hand and held it to his face. "Let us stay with you, Mother!"

"I will be fine, Malcolm. But you two must go with Jon. We cannot chance your safety."

"Step away, Malcolm," said Jon, torn between heart and head. "It is time to go." It seemed that biding of time had fallen in seconds. Mal and Gwen needed to go.

Malcolm was certainly struggling with this chain of events and was more than reserved with his feelings of leaving. After many tears and quiet words, the two children reluctantly left with Jon to leave for the monastery. After several instructions from Malus and Dominick, one of the castle guards set out with the three and escorted them to the monastery and set up quarantine in the high tower. He and the three would remain there until further notice from the castle.

Meanwhile, Dom and Malus were making plans for the next few days. "Can you stay with the queen while I check on the guards?" asked Malus. "I am dreadfully tired and weak. If you could watch her while I rest, I will come to relieve you before morning."

Dominick pondered he doctor's words. The poor man was sick and still fighting for the families of Cobblestone.

"I will stay with her," said Dom. "Get your rest. We will all be in need of rest soon, I am afraid."

"I'll give the orders to the guards. There will be no one allowed through the gates. I will keep a head count of the guards and staff. All must report any illness. Heaven help us stop the madness."

"Yes," commented Dom under his breath. "Heaven help us."

And high above the city streets of Cobblestone, the solemn halls of the castle grew dark in many ways.

10

The lower halls of cobblestone Castle creaked with the noises of the large wooden door. Again, in the darkness, Malus had made his way down the long stairwell and awaited the quiet rap of Rat's knuckles on the door. When Rat pounded with his fist, Malus jumped with a start.

"Come in, you rat soul," snapped Malus. "You startled me to high heaven! You'd better have something in that basket of yours tonight. I tire of your petty whining."

"You don't have to be so mean," whimpered Rat. "I has 'em right 'ere." Rat cowered beneath the tall stature of Malus, wondering how to explain the events of his day earlier. His encounter with the Leafling had shaken him to the core. "I…I…" he stammered.

"Oh, spit it out, Rat!"

"I…I…seen sompin' today…"

"I really don't care, Rat. What I want is this basket and its contents."

"But I seen sompin', I did."

"Oh, alright, Rat. I'll play along," mumbled Malus with a sneer. "What ever did you see?"

"I don't rightly know, I don't. Scared me, it did!"

"What scared you?" asked Malus half-heartedly, as he rifled through the basket of mushrooms.

"If I hadn't a seen it with my own eyes, I wouldn't never had a believed it, I wouldn't!" Rat searched his mind for the proper words and crept closer to Malus with every utterance. "It was a little green fella…sort of a leafy little bloke, he was."

Malus' eyes rose from the basket in his hands. He gave Rat an inquisitive glare. "Leafy…you say?"

"Right leafy, he was … yes. A right little stick … strange indeed!"

"Well, now…" uttered Malus with a quiet smile. "…what an interesting turn of events. I hadn't planned on dealing with them just yet…interesting…very interesting."

Rat shuffled back a few paces and tried to raise his voice. "Interesting how?" he asked.

"Never you mind about that, Rastus," said Malus. "It will all come out in the wash."

"Whatever you says," mumbled Rat. "But what abouts me dues, Sir…I could use 'em."

"Oh, very well then…fine," Malus grumbled. "Here, you little worm," he shouted, as he tossed a leather bag of coins toward Rat. Rat quickly caught the parcel and tugged open its draw string at the top.

"No need to count them, Rastus. There are more than we bargained." Malus smiled smugly at Rat pilfering through his bag of coins. "But do tell me more about your story…about the leafy ones in the forest."

"I only saw the one, I did," replied Rat. "But there's more, I'll bet…I would, yes."

"You find them, Rastus…find their home…and you will be rewarded a handsome sum." The wheels were turning in Malus' head.

A crafty smirk replaced his usually dry frown. "I might have a use for that information. And I suppose you could use a few extra coins. Could you not?"

"I could use 'em, I could," worried Rat. "But just how do I find them, do I?"

"You found one, didn't you?" asked Malus. "I suggest you look for more."

"But what if they hurt me?" Rat trembled with the thought of his encounter earlier in the day.

"Run along now, Rastus. Don't you have errands?"

Rat was confused with the sudden change in Malus. His sudden mood swing changed at the mention of that leafy creature. What good could come of these stick animals…or what bad? He made his way for the old door and turned around just beyond the threshold. "Malus?" he asked. "How much is a handsome sum?"

"Run along, Rastus," Malus chided, as he slammed the door shut in Rat's face.

In the cool, dark depths of the castle tunnel, Rastus scratched his head in wonder. On the other side of the door, he could hear the echoes of laughter ringing in the castle's lower chambers.

"Handsome sum, I'll bet," he grumbled. "I don't like that man one bit, I don't…not one bit." Rat fondled the coins in the bag in his pocket. "Now coins…I likes them, I do," he chuckled. And he hobbled his way through the tunnel and into the forest.

11

The morning sun pierced the panes of colored glass of Cobblestone Abbey tower. Only a number of hours had passed since their departure from the castle, yet it seemed more like days.

Jon awakened to the sound of Gwendolyn humming. She was standing near the tower window, gazing out over the cobblestone streets. Her hands caressed the blooming flowers in the window box by her side.

Jon then turned his attention to Malcolm, who was still wrapped in his morning blanket and listening quietly to the notes on the air. He looked to Jon and gave a quiet shush with a finger in front of his lips. Jon gave his usual respectful smile and turned his eyes back to Gwendolyn.

Soon, the humming grew louder, and it somehow blended into a few words strewn together in order.

Malcolm gave a smile of appreciation and did his best to choke back a few heart-felt tears. He had always had an appreciation for

Gwendolyn's singing, but her melodies this morning were mirroring his emotions of worry and sorrow. No one knew where she found her beautiful words, but she always seemed to pull them from deep within and release them like notes strummed upon a harp. Each word harmonized with the next as they fell seamlessly into the streets of Cobblestone…and the city absorbed her music like drops of morning dew.

Like the lovely flowers laid,
How soon the precious petals fade…
And called hence by early doom,
Now those buds no longer bloom.

Pulled from Earth to Heaven's Gate,
Rejoice in love…no longer wait.
For now ye rest in Heaven fair
And may your flowers blossom there.

It wasn't until this moment that Jon realized how much Gwendolyn turned to her singing to lighten her heart. The pure emotion flowing from her lips somehow soothed her hurting heart and provided a sort of therapy for her. It was her release…her way to heal her pain. And the sounds she created with her voice melted everyone. Her songs were rich and wonderful, and beauty seemed to pour out of her soul. Jon sat motionless as he watched and listened … appreciating every ounce of what he was hearing.

When Gwendolyn finished her song, she quietly turned and looked at Malcolm with a few tears still drying on her tender cheek. Malcolm gave her a wide smile and said, "That was beautiful, Gwen…I loved it."

She did her best to smile through the tears and joined Jon at the foot of his bed. He gave her a long hug and consoled her as best he could.

There was little he could say. This little girl's father was gone, and her mother was gravely ill. It was a harsh and terrible situation, and with still no word from the castle, there was worry in all their hearts.

"Have there been any ravens this morning, Gwen?" asked Malcolm.

"I'm afraid not," she mumbled.

Jon stood and walked to the balcony and looked out onto the precipice ledge.

No new ravens.

There were the usual ten ravens resting comfortably in their cages, patiently waiting for their morning feeding. Jon had expected to see one of the Castle Ravens waiting on the ledge. But unfortunately, there was nothing on the ledge but sunshine and pots of herbs growing here and there. The disappointment on Jon's face was obvious. "Shall we feed the birds?" he asked.

All three wandered out onto the stone balcony of the abbey tower. The sun was pleasant and the young ravens cooed and cawed at the three's arrival. While Malcolm placed food into each of their cages, Jon pulled old Cah from his.

Although Cah rarely missed any meal, he certainly enjoyed the attention he was given this morning. Jon always kept a few extra grapes back from his evening meal and saved them for Cah. After a few playful rubs on the head, Jon placed him down on the ledge and tossed him a grape. Cah caught it with ease and pecked away at it on the balcony ledge.

Soon after Cah finished his grape, he bounced over to Gwendolyn and bobbed his head. "Cah good … Cah good!"

"Yes you are, Cah," she chuckled. She immediately picked him up and held him close to her chest. "I love you Cah. Cah good." Cah's head continued to bob, as he received his morning affection from Gwen.

"Can we send Cah to the castle?" asked Malcolm.

"I suppose," said Jon. "I thought we would have heard something from the castle by now. Kroc should have returned, long since. Let's send another note."

Cah could sense he was about to embark on a journey. He still playfully toyed with Gwen while Jon and Malcolm penned a note.

Malus and Dominick,

We three are fine in the tower. We are not suffering any ill effects as of yet. Please send word on Queen Gweneviere as soon as possible. We await your reply.

Jon, Mal, and Gwen

Malcolm quickly folded his note and tied it around Cah's leg. Cah rested patiently as the note was tied and he received his orders.

"Cah…Castle…" said Jon. Cah bobbed his head and chirped a few words. "Cah good. Cah…Castle. Cah good. Cah Castle!" He bounced to the rock ledge of the balcony and looked back at the remaining grapes in Jon's hand.

"Oh yes, my friend," said Jon. "Here you go!"

He tossed the two grapes into the air and Cah caught them both with ease. He swatted them on the stone ledge and gobbled them down in a flash. With a tilt of his head and a flutter, he dropped from the ledge and flew off into the distance.

Gwendolyn sat down on the stone bench along the wall. Her shoulders sagged a little and she spoke. "I wish we were at the castle. I miss mother. I miss my friends."

Jon offered hope. "We will return as soon as possible, Gwen … I promise."

"I know," she said. "I just want to see Mother and play with my friends."

Malcolm had a puzzled look on his face. "What friends do you have at the castle?"

Gwen seemed startled by the question and quickly looked away. "I shouldn't have said anything."

"What do you mean, Gwen?" asked Jon.

Gwen's foot swirled in a circle on the stone floor. Her head turned away yet again.

"It's okay," said Jon. "We all have friends. They help us through hard times … and share the good times. It is perfectly natural to miss your friends."

"My friends are different."

"Different how?" asked Malcolm, still searching his mind for anything that resembled a friend of hers in the castle.

"Well…" she stammered. "Kimbli and Tally are Leaflings."

Jon and Malcolm looked at one another in complete disbelief. Wide eyed and surprised, they both spoke in unison, "You have met a Leafling?" Clearly, there was much more to this little girl than either had ever imagined.

"Yes," she chuckled. "Kimbli is very sweet …Tally is so funny."

"How do you know Leaflings?" asked Jon, still shocked with the little girl's words.

"They come to listen to me sing. They have such kind words to say about my songs. They are such sweet little fellows…things…whatever they are. I just love them. We have great fun in the castle."

"Well, little lass," said Jon. "You never cease to amaze me. Tell me more of your little friends."

"There's not much more to say. We are the best of friends."

"Well," said Jon again. "Would you like to hear more about your friends? They have been great friends to me, too."

"You know them!" exclaimed Gwen.

"Well," said Jon. "I knew their ancestors. And from what I gather… your friends very much resemble those before them!"

Jon pulled an old and yellowed map from his desk and laid it out on the bed. "This is the path I took so many years ago during the War of the Amethyst Stone." He pointed to a clearing in the Deep Woods along the winding stream. "That waterfall is Tal Kator."

The children stared intently at the old map and studied its many paths and roads from city to city and forest to forest. The ancient parchment was partially faded and tattered, but its markings were as accurate as ever. They felt as if they were pirates looking at a treasure map of old. It was a pleasant distraction from their current state of mind.

So as Jon relayed the many experiences he'd shared with the Leaflings over the years, Gwen and Mal learned much of the lore of Tal Kator … and much about themselves. Somehow, a small part of their lives seemed a little bit happier. And high in the abbey tower … three siblings waited for news from Cobblestone Castle.

12

In the far reaches of the Deep Forest, the clumsy steps of Rat thumped and pounded the forest floor. He did his best to tiptoe quietly, but his efforts were useless. His hurting limbs simply could not navigate nimbly in the dense flora of greenery all about him. Each step was labored, and his huffing breaths echoed through the woods. A young elephant could sneak along quieter.

Before long, he found himself near the site of his Leafling encounter. His eyes searched and scoured the leafy ground for signs of life. He was growing impatient with his long search and sat down on a hollow log to rest.

"There must not be no more of 'em," he grumbled. "No more talking sticks, no. Wastin' my time, I am."

To Rat's startled dismay, a tiny voice called aloud. "That's what I tried to tell you last time, my friend. Those mushrooms are a waste of time."

"Who is it?" chattered Rat.

"Oh, come now. We talked before. Don't you remember?"

"Yes…yes, I do. But where are you? I don't see nobody!"

"I am here," commented a young Leafling, as he slid down the branch of a small maple tree and landed at Rat's feet.

With a bow of his head, he spoke again. "My name is Hirah, direct descendant of Ralfalla … the first of the writing Leaflings, you know. Of course, I am merely the triple great sapling of the second house of the third offspring since the War of the Oaks … or perhaps it was the War of the Amethyst Stone. No, wait. I believe my Great Ori served under Kikah … no two greats, I believe."

Rat stood bewildered with the ramblings of the young Leafling at his feet. The little bloke continued to chatter aloud about his lineage, almost forgetting about the man before him.

"Of course, most of my Oris fought in one war or another. Valiant fighters, we were," continued Hirah. "The element of surprise … yes … that was our tactic. Surprise!"

"Maybe you bored them to death, ya did," mumbled Rat.

Hirah was shaken back to the present. "Oh, how rude of me. Do accept my humble apologies. I often get lost in myself. What might I do for you, my friend?"

"I don't rightly know, you see. I just gots curious, that's all. I never met one of you little blokes before. I thought I'd come back and take a look-see for me self. Where do you lads and lasses live?"

"Well now. We are not lads and lasses at all. That's lesson one. We're just Leaflings, and that's that. But where we live, now that's a special place, in deed. Tal Kator it's called. Two words, you know? Tal, being short for *Telesma.* That means a spiritual act, or *rite* we call it. Kator is short for *Kata-strephein,* or catastrophe. Our name means life created from disaster. Tal Kator …life from disaster…yes." Hirah smiled from ear to barky ear.

Rat shook his head with confusion. He had decided that if all Leaflings talked as much as this one, that Tal Kator must be a noisy clatter of rambling voices.

"Ah yes," continued Hirah. "Life from disaster. When the great meteor crashed into the earth, its energy changed the wooded forest around it. It breathed life into the plants near the scorched hole in the ground. The Leaflings awakened. And there you have it! Simple as that!" Hirah jumped into a small back flip and rolled back over to Rat's feet. With a beaming smile, he raised his arms and said, "...and here we are!"

"You say *we*. But I don't sees no more of ya."

"Oh, there's more—many more. Lots of us, really." Hirah seemed amazed by Rat's comment.

"Where is this Tal Kator?" asked Rat.

"Well, it's nearb ... now wait just a minute. You know I can't tell you that!"

"Tell me what?" asked Rat.

"... that Tal Kator is nearby, of course! They won't let me tell folks that."

"Well, now ... your secret is safe with me, lad. I gots no need to know where it is, no I don't. It must be a beautiful place, I'll bet, I would, yes. Pretty, no doubt."

"Pretty is not the half of it. There's no better place in the world, if you ask me. Why...the Great Falls that cloak the Amethyst rings sparkles in the sunlight. The pool of the Miraré glistens like the heavens. Its waters are always cool and refreshing."

By now, even Rat's slow mind was gathering information he knew he shouldn't be receiving. This little Leafling liked to talk.

"Amethyst rings?" asked Rat.

"Why yes. They're behind the falls, of course. Everybody knows th ... Now, you know I can't tell you that!"

"So sorry," offered Rat. "I have no need for such information, I don't. No need at all, really. I was just curious to see a Leafling, that's all. And I've done it. You've been kind, you have. A right nice fella, I'd say, I would."

"You're not leaving are you?" asked Hirah. "You've only just arrived, and I have no one to talk to. I tire of setting idle at post with no one to break the boredom. I'd very much like to talk with you some more. Care to stay and talk a while?"

"I could stay a bit, I could. But I've got to get back to searching soon," said Rat.

"Searching for what?" asked Hirah.

"I'm still looking for mushrooms, I am."

"Those mushrooms are all over near here," said Hirah, "but why in the world would you want such nasty little toadstools?"

"I gets 'em for the doctor, I do. He uses 'em for medicine, or so he says, he does."

"Medicine, you say?" asked Hirah. "Never heard of it. 'Course we Leaflings don't eat like you folks. We wouldn't know, I don't suppose. But my Ori always said they were poison to anything that ate them."

"I just knows I has to finds 'em, that's all." Rat shook his head. "I has no idea, I don't. I just finds 'em, that's all."

"Well, now … I can help you find as many as you want. No one here wants them. You might as well fetch them up!"

"You'd help me?" asked Rat.

The Leafling smiled back at him. "I'm so bored," he said, "I could help you watch them grow. I must remain close to here and keep watch, but we can find many close by, I'm certain."

Rat was nearly beside himself with the Leafling's kindness. Rat had never been around anyone, or anything for that matter, that was so genuinely helpful and pleasantly forward. This Leafling nature was completely foreign to him. "I've never met someone so willing to help."

"That's because you've never met someone so bored as myself. But come now, surely the race of man cannot be so bitter and drab. You must have met some kind-hearted men during your travels."

"I have not," said Rat, looking down at his twisted form of a body. "I have yet to find kindness in the world of man, but they say it is there, somewhere beneath the surface."

Rat turned away as the Leafling studied the bent individual before him. His body was hideous, even if his tender voice seemed passive and timid between the huffings and puffings of his labored breathing.

"My mother was kind…" mumbled Rat. "…but that was a long time ago, it was."

"Well, the race of man is a long way from here," said Hirah. "You are in Tal Kator now. Let us find some mushrooms for you."

"I'd be much obliged, I would," said Rat.

"Good. Come along. There's a patch right over here."

Hirah and Rat wandered through the dense flora of greenery on the forest floor. Just as the Leafling had suggested, numerous mushrooms had pushed their little yellow heads from the soil and dotted the damp soils along the creeks and paths of the forest. Rat was elated with their finds.

"I sure don't know hows I can repay you, I don't," he said, gazing at his basket of mushrooms. "I gots a good batch here, I do."

"Think nothing of it, my friend," said Hirah. "You could come back for a visit now and again. It's lovely here, wouldn't you say?"

"I sure would, I'll say." Rat glanced at his serene surroundings. The midday sun had warmed the forest and the chirpings of woodland creatures filled the air. Life was pleasant here, far from the villages of man. Rat loathed leaving, but knew he'd need to make the long trek back soon.

"I reckon I'd better go," he said. "But I sure don't want to. It's beautiful here. It just seems natural, I'd say."

A wide smile stretched across the barky cheeks of Hirah. "Welcome to Tal Kator, my friend. It doesn't get any better than this."

Rat returned a crooked smile. "I reckon it don't. I sure reckon it don't."

13

The evening sun was setting near Cobblestone Castle. Two full days had passed since the leaving of the children and Jon. Dominick entered the main hall of the castle and found Malus staring out over the city. The old man looked frail, sitting atop the threshold of the windowsill. He turned to Dom with solemn eyes.

"What news do you have, Dominick?"

"Three more guards have taken ill. We now have thirty-two and me."

Malus shook his head. "Have we no more from our forces?"

"There are others in isolation at the old mine, just outside of the city. But as fast as we bring them, they fall ill. We send the ill to the Caverns for quarantine, but know not of how they fair after their arrival. They may be dead, Malus. What do you suggest?"

Dominick held little hope in finding a way to conquer this frightening illness sweeping through Cobblestone.

Malus leaned back against the wall and wiped his brow. His hands trembled slightly as he struggled with his composure. "What are we to do, Dom? It is almost a death sentence bringing a guard within these walls. Are the townspeople suffering the same consequence?"

"I have not had contact with anyone outside the castle."

"What if the guards are bringing this sickness into our halls? How can we be certain?"

Dominick had no reply. Malus had a suggestion. "We could gather guards from another city. Perhaps fresh blood will be strong." The look on his face was strained as if his spoken thoughts were a stab in the dark. Neither appeared to like the idea.

"Who would guard our city's fair castle? We have no allies."

"I have allies, Dominick. I have given medicine near and far. It could be done."

The guards near the door looked as worried as the two men talking. They too felt the dangers of their job.

Dominick was not yet willing to go to extremes. "I fear that such harsh measures may not yet be advisable. Have the troll guards taken ill as well?"

"All five trolls left when the king died. It appears their allegiance lied with him and him alone. If bringing others here worries you, then we shall wait. It is merely an option. We shall discuss it more in due time."

"Have you gotten word from the abbey?" asked Dom.

"No. This troubles me greatly. I've waited in worry at the raven's keep, hoping for news, but alas…none has arrived."

The old man leaned forward on his haunches staring at the floor. "I would go to check on them, but I haven't the strength. And I fear that we could infect them by sending a messenger. I am at a loss, Dominick. I simply don't know what to do." His voice trailed off as he continued to stare into the floor while his body twisted with the pangs of his apparent oncoming illness.

"I will go," said Dom.

The old man raised his head slowly and stared out toward the abbey. "I fear you will endanger them. How will you manage to gather news without jeopardizing yourself or them?"

Dom felt confident. "I can shout from the streets to the high tower. I will find word and return immediately. I will not hinder them. If you will look after the queen for a few hours, I will see to the task."

"It is risky, my valiant friend. You seem to be this castle's only healthy soul. We may need you in this battle. You and I have had our differences over the years, Dominick, but these times are hard. We may both need one another before the end."

"I want to go. I shall return as soon as possible. I will not tarry."

Malus shook his head in worry. "Then so be it. If you must. Travel light and swift."

The old man again raised his eyes to Dom. "And try to offer them hope, Dominick. The queen's condition is grave. But offer hope … for the children."

Dom stepped forward and grasped the old man's hand. "I will offer hope. I shall return. Watch after the queen."

Malus shouted aloud to the guards at the gate. "Allow him through. Let it be known that Dominick Sebastian is departing the castle to find word of the prince."

The giant wooden doors of the main gate creaked open, offering the first drafts of fresh air in days. The darkening sky outside was no more welcoming than the hollow halls of the castle.

Dominick rushed through the gates and raced on to the stables. Finding Flagstone within its stalls, he quickly mounted his steed and galloped with all the speed he could muster, navigating the winding road down from the castle. He would be there within the hour.

Malus shouted aloud. "Bar the gates. Check on the other guards. I shall check the raven tower for news. Eat and rest as you may, men.

Conserve your energies. Food, water, and medicine are our only hope."

As the guards scurried about their commands, Malus shook off his fake illness, and a nasty smile took its place. "Run along, my little puppets. This is almost too easy." And the pieces of a long devised plan continued to fall into place.

14

While Dominick Sebastian and Flagstone ran through the streets of Cobblestone, again the lower halls of the castle were receiving a visit. The familiar bent stature of Rat gave his knock on the tunnel door.

Its mechanisms turned and the door creaked open, revealing a much more congenial Malus of Blue Haven than Rat was accustomed to seeing. His different demeanor was more than a little odd. Rat felt even more uneasy on this visit.

"I assume," said Malus with a smile, "that you have come bearing good news about our enemies in the forest."

"Enemies?" asked Rat.

"Yes, those devious little monsters of the woods."

"I found 'em right nice, I did."

"Yes, of course. You clearly must have only met one. They get testy in numbers."

"I don't reckon I understand, M' Lord."

"Ah, I see the Leaflings have ensnared the heart of Rastus Cubbins. Beware, my friend, of the twisted tales and cunning lies of those fairies of the forest. They are not as they appear."

Rat didn't realize the old doctor knew his full name. It was quite discomforting. He had gone from *Foul Ogre* to *my friend* in one meeting. Something didn't seem right.

"Do you remember the War of Two Cities, Rastus?"

Rat nodded in agreement and continued to listen.

"Of course, the Deep Forest lies between Cobblestone and my fallen city of Blue Haven. Although it was countless years ago, my city remembers well its harsh battle with Cobblestone. The king of Cobblestone and his army conquered Blue Haven and seized our land as their own. We have been under their governing ever since. Our great king—King Romb of Blue Haven—died in that conflict. Those miserable Leaflings were our downfall. We had made great strides in the war to save our own walls. Yet the Leaflings infiltrated our regiments and sent spies among us. They set traps in the forest, and even strangled many of our troops in their sleep. Once those long and twisting fingers wrap around your neck…"

The old man paused and gave a frightening glare into Rat's eyes. He clinched his fingers into the air as if a neck was within them. "… you're done-for. Just ask the monks of the abbey about them—what's left of them."

Rat's simple mind struggled to keep up with the flowing information. "How could those little blokes strangle a fellow? They're tiny, they are."

"Two decades ago, Rastus, a band of rogue Leaflings crept into Cobblestone Abbey. They tiptoed through its halls and into the quarters of the elders of the monastery. One by one, they strangled the life out of the monk fathers and stole their jewels like candy."

Rat's eyes were as wide as saucers.

"Strange, don't you think, that only the high elder and his future replacement lived. They were both sympathizers of those stick fairies of the woods. Young Brother Jon stood by and WATCHED as the Leaflings strangled every ounce of life from the monk Fathers. And now, it seems that only Jon of Cobblestone Abbey retains one of the ancient jewels so taken by the Leaflings. Only he—the enemy's ally—wears an amethyst ring."

Rat's head spun with the information he was being given. "I don't rightly know what this all has to do with me."

"I wanted you to meet one of these creatures—wanted you to see for yourself how enchanting they can be. They are fairies! They will enchant you! They seem so utterly happy and kind. All the while, they will slowly wait for the proper moment—and strangle the life out of you."

Rat was starting to tremble. "I want me life left in me!"

"As do we all, Rastus. That's why Rastus Cubbins will be the one…THE ONE…to end the madness. You, my friend can rid our lives of these wretched little beasts forever!"

"No, no. Not me. Not little old Rat. It's not for me, no."

"But only you know the way, Rastus." Malus quieted his words and crept close to Rat, weaving his intricate web. "It would be so easy, Rastus. Easy. Imagine…"

He paused again and waved his hand into the air for effect. "Instead of Rastus Cubbins being the social outcast of society … you will be the one … the one who rid Cobblestone of the dangers of the fairy world! You would be a hero!"

Rat now felt trapped, but was more than intrigued by the prospect of shaking the scorn he had always endured in the cities of man. His labored breathing was worsening and his hands trembled with nervousness.

"You, Rastus, could walk the streets of town and be proud. Hold your head high. Be someone."

Again he paused and let the information soak in. "In one simple afternoon, you could end the hold the fairies have over us! If you can bring me those rings…those Amethyst rings…I will build you a home worthy of a king!"

By now, Rat had backed himself into the dark corner of the stone room, trying to fight the words being stabbed at him. He shook his head, trying to make sense of it all. Could he really walk proud through the streets of Cobblestone? Could he own a home like a real man? Would the townspeople embrace him as an equal? And those Leaflings—they seemed so docile. They seemed so kind. They seemed enchanting—maybe like fairies. "How'm I supposed to get those rings, I don't know…"

"Think it over, Rastus. We have time. But remember, you don't have to live like a beggar in the forest. You can be a man. You can live life—not just exist in it. There is a way to gain the rings. It's all so very simple."

Malus walked to the door and held it open, knowing that Rat had heard all the information he could hold.

As the pathetic creature limped toward the door, Malus made one last comment. "Become a man, Rastus. It is your destiny." As he spoke, be reached into his pocket and pulled out a beautiful golden coin and placed into Rat's palm.

"Here is a down payment, my friend. You can be one of us." Malus paused and watched Rat's reactions. "You will find what you need at the end of the tunnel tomorrow. Two of my men will travel with you. Show them the way and do as they say, Rastus. You will be rich, my friend. That small coin is but one of many! Become a man, Rastus. Become a man of Cobblestone!"

Rat was beside himself. He had never held more money in his life than that one coin. And it was his! Rastus Cubbins owned GOLD! His mind was awash with a hundred thoughts as he crept down the old tunnel. He barely heard the large door behind him slam shut. Tonight—could change his life.

15

The night air seemed foreboding as Dominick Sebastian raced onward toward the abbey. Flagstone was exhausted from his run from the castle, but kept a steady pace and forced himself to take in deep breaths as he pressed on. Dom could see the dim light of the abbey tower in the distance, giving him inspiration to force forward. He worried over what he might find upon arrival and desperately hoped the three siblings were safe and sound. As he rounded the last street corner, he was elated to find Brother Michael standing watch at the front entry. Keeping his distance, he shouted aloud.

"Brother Michael, it's Dominick!"

Brother Michael stood from his post and peered into the darkness. "You are supposed to be at the castle!"

"I've come for news. We have received no word."

"Nor have we. We have worried so."

Dominick again spoke up, still keeping his distance. “The queen is still alive, but many others have fallen ill. It is bleak at the castle.”

“The abbey is in good health. The children are safe.”

Dom breathed a sigh of relief. “That is good news, Brother. I have been worried sick.” Though as he spoke, a sinking feeling was settling into his mind. *Why no word?* “Brother Michael, why have you not sent ravens?”

“We have sent many.”

With those words, Dominick felt a pang of disbelief. He had been deceived. As many thoughts bounced through his head, one fear came to mind immediately.

The Queen!

At Dom’s command, Flagstone turned on his heals and bolted away into the darkness. *I must get back to the queen!* In his earnest to find information about the children, he had unknowingly jeopardized the queen’s wellbeing. His heart sank in his chest as the two rushed through the night back toward Cobblestone Castle.

Brother Michael stood bewildered at the door, not fully understanding all of what had just occurred. He called to the others inside. Something was dreadfully wrong at the castle—he just didn’t know how dreadful it had become.

* * *

Meanwhile, Malus had made his way upstairs to the raven tower. In a rush, he quickly penned a note and fastened it to one of the ravens. He needed to buy time, keeping the abbey at bay while the rest of his plan fell into place.

Friends of the Abbey,

Our queen still lives. Her condition is grave, but she holds onto life by a thread. Many guards have fallen ill, and we have set many afoot to save themselves. The rest of us wither. My condition worsens, but I too am holding on. Heaven help us.

Malus

He again fell back into his fake illness, and rushed down the stone stairwell. As he stumbled down the stairs, he called aloud. "Guards, guards…"

Two guards who had been manning the front gate raced toward him, jumping steps with great strides. As they met Malus on the stairwell, he collapsed to the steps. "Save yourselves!" he moaned.

The guards were taken back by the words moaned by Malus. Each stared in wonder as they watched the man before them clinch his fists and wheeze in agony. Malus again spoke up. "Four more guards have fallen ill…" His voice trailed off.

The guards trembled with the news, as Malus continued. "Save yourselves…all of you. I am dying. Save yourselves!"

"But, M' Lord…"a guard stammered, "…the queen?"

Malus raised his weary head. "The queen of Cobblestone is DEAD. Save yourselves!"

As more guards raced up the stairs, panic ensued. Never had such chaos shook the halls of the castle. No one had answers, and the future looked dreadfully bleak.

With one last gasp of air, Malus shouted out. "Save yourselves!" He collapsed into a pile as castle guards raced in all directions. Soon, the giant wooden doors of the castle swung open and what few guards the castle possessed raced into the night, fearing for their lives.

As the last frantic guard fled the castle gate, Malus of Blue Haven picked himself up and dusted off. Those large gates creaked shut with a slam, and the castle became dreadfully quiet—except for the three hundred Blue Haven soldiers infiltrating the lower tunnel.

Cobblestone Castle had been taken without a fight, and Malus of Blue Haven could only smile at his own brilliance.

16

ong before Dominick reached the gates of Cobblestone Castle, he had already guessed the outcome of his actions. Rushing guards filled the side streets and alley ways as doors slammed shut in fear. The city was in panic ... and so was Dominick Sebastian.

As Dom and Flagstone raced around the final corner and came into view of the castle, his fears were confirmed. A huge bonfire had been built on each side of the castle doors, illuminating the front entrance, blatantly showing the barred gates. As Flagstone came to a halt, anger and sorrow raced through Dom's mind. Just as he had suspected, the gates were barred—the draw bridge fully in the up position. He slid from Flag's back and stood silent, infuriated not only with Malus, but with his own poor judgment. His eyes were drawn high up to the castle precipice and the scurrying figures above.

Several guards were wrestling with some sort of large tapestries on each side of the barred gates. In seconds, Dom would see and understand the meaning of those actions. Two large cloth crests unfurled, falling into the night sky and settling in against the stone walls. In the bonfire light, their insignias were unmistakable. They were old. They were clear and precise to all who saw them. These were the banners of *The Sons of Romb*. Cobblestone Castle had been taken by the old city of Blue Haven without a battle. Malus had deceived them all.

Amid the cool darkness of the night sky, drops of rain began to fall. Clouds gathered and covered the moon and stars. As rain pelted his face like tears from heaven, Dom raised his fists to the sky and screamed at the top of his lungs.

"MALUS!!!!!!!!"

* * *

Drops of dreary rain fell from the brow of Dominick as he stood disheartened in the stone foyer of Cobblestone Abbey. He had already surmised that the illness within the castle walls was all a hoax. Everyone outside the castle had either remained in good health or had regained their health once out of the castle confines and the diet of food and medicine prescribed by the good doctor. It was a brilliant and elaborate hoax, created in the dreadful heart of Malus of Blue Haven. When Jon approached, his eyes widened as Dom spoke.

"I have failed…"

Jon's head dropped as he looked to the other monks for help. "Gather some towels for him! We must talk."

Two sets of other eyes stood in silence and watched as those two raced to the library. Dom had motioned Jon down the great hall and both darted into the room, lighting candles and oil lamps as they went. Jon continued to shout orders to the other monks while

Malcolm and Gwendolyn stood frightened in the darker corners, hearing their words.

Dom slid into a chair and began wiping his soaked face with a towel and watching Jon arrange the oil lamps and candles upon the heavy table. As he gathered his thoughts, he spoke aloud in bits and pieces.

"It's the Sons of Romb" he chattered, his blue lips shaking with cold.

Jon sat bewildered at the words his dear friend was speaking. *The Sons of Romb are just a myth ... a long ago figment created by those smited by war in Bluehaven—decades and decades ago. How could this be?*

Dom again spoke up. "My mind has been racked with this. Something about that war…it's in that book. I read bits and pieces of it years ago."

Jon looked puzzled. "You speak of *The Fall of the House of Romb?* Written by our father of kings?"

"I tell you…it is in there. I remember."

Jon let his head roll back on his shoulders, pondering the book he read as a young monk. He, too, had thoughts coming back to him. He, too, could remember. It finally hit Jon like a premonition.

"THE PROPHESY QUATRAINS!"

He raced from their seated position and across the darkened floor of the abbey library. His fingers tore away at many volumes before he found the book he sought. He pulled that bound volume from the shelf and scampered back to the table, leafing through as he went.

In a matter of only a few seconds, he found the passages he was seeking. He opened those special pages up into the light of Dom's candle and read the one special list of prophesies, hand-written by a victorious king ages ago.

Beware the crooked stranger
That walks beneath the trees.
Beware his precious holdings
In basket lined with leaves.

Beware the doctor's poison tongue
And poisons in his hand.
For he may seal the fate of kings
And on castle precipice stand.

Beware to those of Tal Kator,
Beware to Cobblestone!
For he shall bring forgotten sons
And sit upon the throne.

Look to the east…the rising sun
To concur and to save.
There will be roars of battle cries…
Enormous fighting waves.

But the least of all the soldiers…
Simple little souls,
Will see the truth behind the lies…
And turn the key they hold.

Dom let out a groan. "*Beware the Doctor's poison tongue and poisons in his hand.* That's it, Jon. It's poison."

Jon, too, had come to that conclusion. One line struck home for him. *He may seal the fate of kings …and on castle precipice stand.* "He's standing on my father's precipice, having sealed his fate."

Both men raced through the other words on the page and those pages that followed. Very little of it made sense in the dark and foreboding room of the library. There was just so many words, so many riddles in the rhymes. *Who's the crooked stranger?* And more importantly, *who will see the truth behind the lies, and turn the key they hold?"*

"What do we do?" asked Jon, thinking, hoping, and praying all at the same time.

Just as Dom was about to speak, a tremendous scuffling noise came rushing down the hallway. In seconds, Brother Michael was dragged in the room by a strangely-dressed soldier clad in blue. Michael's head was held high by the hair of his scalp, and another hand held a razor sharp blade against his throat. The two jostled into the room as fierce stares bounced back and forth. The gruff voice of the captor pounded into the room.

"Nobody move."

At that moment, a dozen other soldiers raced in, taking in their surroundings and rushing toward the two at the table. Surrounded by drawn swords, all stood silent as the first soldier's voice again chopped through the room.

"Hold still, Sir Dominick! Your friends are at risk!"

The soldier tossed Brother Michael off to the side and sauntered forward.

Dom bit his tongue, his fingers twitching at his own sword as all stood in the weight of the moment.

One of the soldiers picked up the candle from the table and shed light into the shadows of the room. It only took a second to see two pairs of eyes staring coldly.

"Well, now…I believe this is just who we are looking for."

"NO!" shouted Dom, pressing himself near the swords. "You will not take them while I still live!"

As the room turned to glance back at the children, now shaking and whimpering alone, Dom did the only thing he could think of.

With one swift sweep of his arm, he knocked two oil lamps from the table and onto the two soldiers in front of him. Fire jumped onto each man as they kicked and screamed on the floor. Drawing his sword, two more soldiers fell at his feet, bleeding mortally wounded.

Jon pulled his chair from the table and flailed it at the man edging toward his siblings. It bounced off the floor and knocked him off guard, but not off track. He was still easing in on the children.

A storm of new soldiers raced into the room, swords drawn and fire in their eyes. Dom raced into them all, sword swinging as he chopped his way through them.

A swift thrust of a soldier's arm toppled Jon to the floor. Grasping at the slippery floor, he frantically tore with his arms and feet to get to the children. Long before he gained his goal, two strong hands ripped him up and slammed him against the wall. Jon's body fell limp with the blow.

Dom still battled. Sword after sword fell to his, blood filling the library floor for the first time in history. Despite the oncoming battle, he could see from the corner of his eye that both children had been hoisted from the floor, tears flowing wildly. Jon, too, had been dragged toward the exit door.

He still battled on, taking on two, and sometimes three soldiers at once. As the forth soldier raced in to help, numerous holes in Dom's skin were oozing blood onto that of the enemy's covering the floor. At a startling yell, a commander's voice shouted above all.

"COME!"

Each soldier battled backward in retreat of Dom, still fighting all with all he could muster. One paused just outside the door, apparently waiting on the proper moment. The last two soldiers thrust forward, knocking Dom back a few feet, then they dashed out of the room. The one remaining soldier stood silently watching as Dom stood to charge him. Dom's words were chilling.

"Not while I'm alive, you don't."

The soldier's evil smiled beamed. "As you wish."

With one fell motion, the soldier hurled a dagger from his fist, sailing it into the burning fire of blood and people within the room. The knife centered its target and Dominick Sebastian fell to the floor—that dagger embedded deeply in his chest. Blood flowed from the wound, his body quivering in the burning mess of death all about the room.

The soldier dodged left and raced away into the night with the rest of the soldiers … along with three precious pieces of cargo—the King and Queen's only blood kin, Jon, Malcolm, and Gwen.

17

The morning sun was beginning to rise over the mountains as Malus stood atop the precipice and stared below. He could see his soldiers returning with the three hostages in tow. Young Malcolm kicked and fought as they all made their way up the drawbridge planks. Malus turned to his men nearby.

"The pieces are falling into place," he said, his arrogant smile filled with self-appreciation. "Prepare your men. Johan, separate—one battalion rides to the old mines. William—you and the others to the caverns. We must reach them before word travels. Summon the trolls."

"Did the trolls not leave into the night?" one asked.

"All five are in the hold below the castle awaiting your call."

"How did you gain their loyalty, M'Lord? Why would they fight?" Each of the nine Blue Haven men looked to Malus for answers.

"Quite simple, really. I promised them Stone Castle, all to themselves. With Dominick Sebastian out of the picture, they can be our western stronghold and reclaim the old castle. They will be quite happy without the likes of us around them, and they will defend our border well enough to keep their home. There, they can live out their lives to extinction, grumbling and growling to the bitter end."

It seemed Malus had thought of all angles. In his mind, it was all perfect. With the descendants of the king held hostage, what few remaining soldiers still willing to fight for Cobblestone would have little choice but to surrender. None would jeopardize the royal family held high in the castle tower. With the king's soldiers caught unaware in the mines and caverns, the Bluehaven warriors would take them by force. With menacing trolls for full back-up, Malus' hand will have reached deep into the city of Cobblestone and have taken it with ease. With the location of Tal Kator also soon within his grasp, he and the final nine Sons of Romb would attain the Amethyst rings and rule this realm for years beyond account. Malus had now secured his own ring ... the one proudly worn by the monk, Jon.

"The hour grows late," Malus warned. "You two must ride to the caverns and caves. You seven, I have plans for you."

"As you wish, Sir." Johan replied.

"That would be *Sire* now, Johan. The new king of Cobblestone has risen!"

The nine men immediately bowed their heads in respect. As the two turned to ready themselves for battle, Malus gave them one last command.

"Take no prisoners."

* * *

Meanwhile, far across the city of Cobblestone, three monks beat at the burning mess on the abbey floor with blankets and towels. Brother

Michael dragged the nearly lifeless body of Dominick out of the burning room and into the hall, now partially lit by the morning sun. He gazed down at the shiny dagger embedded deeply into Dom's chest, just below his shoulder. With each movement, drops of blood ran from the wound, filling the hall floor.

Brother Michael summoned his courage and wrapped his fists around the blade and prepared to tug. As his fingers grasped the dagger, Dom's eyes opened in surprise.

"Wait!" he winced, his voice mirroring the sharp pain in his chest. He whispered two words to Brother Michael and pushed his hands from the blade in his chest.

"Get Cah!"

The monk was puzzled by his strange request but did as he was told, scurrying up the spiral staircase to the abbey tower. In minutes he returned, Raven in hand, and placed it on the floor by Dom's head.

With what little energy still left in his body, Dom whispered a few commands to the bird as its head bobbed up and down with understanding. With one bounce, the old raven fluttered into the air and out into the bright light of sunrise.

Dom then looked back at Brother Michael and gritted his teeth in pain. He closed his eyes and said the words.

"Pull it."

A bloodcurdling scream bounced from the stone walls of the abbey and echoed deep into its smoky halls. As the last few embers of fire were stamped out in the floor of the library, the hopes and prayers of many solemn monks were also extinguished.

* * *

The same rising sun fell upon two Blue Haven soldiers sitting on two, small wooden barrels of liquid somewhere near the lower tunnel entrance to Cobblestone Castle. As they suspected, the grumbling and stumbling figure of Rastus Cubbins jostled into view.

"Are you ready, Rat?" one asked.

"I reckon I is, I is…" he stammered.

"Then let's do it," one stated. "I rather like the safety of the castle over the darkened shadows of the Deep Forest."

The other spoke up. "The sooner we accomplish our task, the sooner we return. Make haste."

Rat grumbled beneath his shaky breath. "Eh, uh, ummm, um, come along then."

With that, one of the last pieces of Malus' well-laid plan was falling into place.

18

The Flagstone mines and the Old Caverns were nestled about a half mile apart, facing one another across a valley plain of pasture land. The jutting cliffs above each towered over their cave-like openings that viewed the open spaces between the two locations. When the illness started sweeping Cobblestone Castle, it was decided to separate many of the king's men. A band of healthy soldiers were to be kept separate and safe for call in the abandoned mines below the city. One of the tower ravens would summon the soldiers in certain amounts as needed.

The sick and dead were quarantined at the ancient caverns that were often considered Cobblestone's stronghold during some of the early wars. These age old caves served as shelter for years beyond account.

Strangely, the sick healed quickly once away from the doctor's "medicines". And oddly, on this day, both locations had a number of their men sitting idle just outside the confines of their cave-like openings in the rock bluffs. They were taking a breakfast of fruit in the early morning sun. All seemed normal on the half-mile plains before the entrances to each.

A lookout for the Blue Haven Army spotted the men outside of both entrances. Both locations could be seen from one section of cover near the grassy field between them. It was time for a storm of action from this new army from Blue Haven. A strong charge would catch them off guard and place them very much in harm's way. Long before the blue stripes of their army apparel could be seen, the mass of two hundred soldiers would separate and take both locations in one fell stride. The element of surprise would kill many, and undoubtedly force the rest to surrender or die, hunted down in the rock tunnels within the mountains. Five large trolls secured and fortified the rear flanks of the army, their heavy armor nearly impenetrable by mere means of men. They carried medieval fighting tools that consisted of large metal-spiked balls on the end of a ten foot chain…and they possessed the brute force to wield them.

These unknowing soldiers in the caves and tunnels were doomed. Upon command, all two hundred Blue Haven soldiers raced on horseback across the plain, trolls taking up the rear on foot. At the halfway point, the band split, each taking aim at separate targets. Johan and his horsemen took aim for the mine.

The bands of men outside the mines and caverns looked puzzled by the approaching horsemen. Each tarried to see what trouble could be arising. As soon as the blue stripes of Blue Haven's Army could be made out, loud battle cries rose and the men fled to the supposed safety of the caves.

"Fools," shouted Johan. "There is no escape!"

A number of Cobblestone men stood outside the cave entrance in a feeble attempt to guard the entrance to Flagstone Mine, their spears dug in and swords drawn. As the horsemen drew near, the Cobblestone men showed no fear, standing their ground without hesitation.

Just before the clash of both armies met, the Cobblestone men ducked to the ground. Simultaneously, dozens of crossbow arrows left the cave, most hitting their mark in the hearts of the horses carrying the soldiers. A dozen horses fell, their riders careening forward onto sharpened spears. Another band of horsemen toppled onto these, meeting much the same fate. Swords were drawn on both sides as battles broke out around the entrance to the mine, all fighters slowly closing in on its opening.

When three trolls caught up to the fight near the cave opening, it seemed all was lost. Those huge spikes flailed in the air, ready to unleash upon the remaining few fighters. All three trolls and six remaining fighters closed in on five frightened Cobblestone soldiers at the entrance to the mine.

Just as all was nearly lost, two tiny lights flickered inside the cave. The five soldiers dashed backward into the cave and onto the ground. Simultaneously, a rustling noise was heard above the cave opening. As the trolls and men gazed up, a huge crock of liquid came crashing down around them. It smelled strongly of lamp oil. A split second later, the two tiny lights from within the tunnel released. Two burning arrows landed at the feet of the trolls and men, erupting into a giant wall of flame. Trolls and men scattered frantically about, burning to their deaths.

As the flames died out enough to make passage, the remaining Cobblestone soldiers within the mine raced out, swords in hand, charging across the open field to help their endangered friends in the Caverns a mile away. When a flash of red flame jumped from the ground across the field at the cavern entrance, battle cries met with cheers. Fifty-seven Cobblestone men fled the cavern in search of opposition. There was none left to fight. Their simple plan had worked on both sides of the field!

A quick head count gave saddening news. Cobblestone had lost seventy-five men in the skirmish. Though Blue Haven had paid dearly, the loss was a sullen indication as to what could soon come to the rest of Cobblestone. This was just the beginning, and most present understood it without question. Cobblestone was at war.

One of the lead soldiers raised his hand to the sky. From high above, a black bird sailed down to meet it. The cackled voice of Cah screeched out. “Cah Good! Cah Good!”

That soldier was once one of King Lawrence’s first in command. Matthew Lohr rubbed the bird’s head with words of thanks. “Once again, my friend, you have proven as valuable as any warrior. Now, you must race to Cobblestone Abbey.”

The bird fluttered away at top speed.

Matthew summoned four of his remaining eighty-six men. “Tend to the wounded and the dead. I will send word as soon as possible. Send all who can fight to Cobblestone Abbey.” He turned to the rest of his companions.

“Men!” he shouted. “Make haste! Gather your things. We ride to Cobblestone Abbey … and to war!”

19

The heavy footsteps of Rastus Cubbins tromped through the leaves of the Deep Forest. A half-mile before reaching their destination, Rat collapsed onto a fallen tree to rest. Panting heavily, he looked to the two soldiers by his side. "I gots to rest, I do. Huff, huff. We only gots a little ways to go, we do. Honest, we do."

Rat continued to huff and puff and point in the direction of their travel. He gave the men a brief overview of where he had met his Leafling friend and where the creature suggested that the confines of Tal Kator would be located. With a quick nod to one another, both men separated, each taking an opposite path into the dense undercover of the forest.

Rat spoke up. "Where you be goin', you two?"

"Just go meet your little buddy and buy some time."

Rat struggled with his many thoughts. He had a terrible feeling that what he was doing might not be the right thing. His mind kept going over that same conversation with Malus. *Become a man, Rastus...a man of Cobblestone...*

Once out of view of Rastus, both soldiers pulled a tiny cork from their wooden barrels as they walked. They looked like simple travelers, merely wandering about through the woods. Even the occasional Leafling lookout took little notice of the passers-by...or the odd liquid trickling into the leaves behind them. Both walked for nearly a mile in parallel, a quarter mile apart.

Rat caught his breath and struggled on, fighting with his aches and pains and struggling with the uneasiness in his mind. *Sompin' don't seem right, it don't. No sir, it don't.*

Soon, Rat found himself in that same location where his little leafy acquaintance was usually standing guard. It only took a few seconds before the little bloke spoke up.

"Well, now. I remember you! Good to see you again, my friend! How are you?"

Rat fought with the *enchanting fairies* comments Malus had plugged in his brain. In his usual timid voice, he whimpered a reply. "I...uh...I'm gettin' by alright, I reckon I am, I am." His quaking limbs twitched as he struggled with his thoughts and fears.

"You know," barked the Leafling, "to be in such a safe part of the Deep Forest, you sure are a bashful sort. We Leaflings are quite friendly, and that's a fact. I suppose it's obvious that we do enjoy a bit of conversation, even with a fellow like yourself—you know, one with so few words. Why, reminds me of that time I talked to that box turtle on the south side...now HE was quite the listener, that old bloke!"

"Oh yes, back to you. What brings you to the wood, my frightened pal?"

"I...I don't rightly know, I don't."

"Still hunting for those nasty mushrooms, are ya?" His playful words were just what Rat needed.

"Uh, why yes it is. Mushrooms, yes. I am, I am."

"Well, just follow me, my now-old friend. We can walk up the stream here. Why, the best mushrooms grow up near the Miraré. You know the Miraré, right? Grand place, if I do say so myself. LOVE it there. Why, I'd be there right now if I didn't have to stand post all day. I'd like a dip in the Miraré, I would. And you could pick mushrooms. Oh gosh, let's do go, shall we?"

By now, Rat was lost in the little one's rampant conversation but discerned enough to hear Miraré and taking a dip in what he assumed was the pool Malus had spoken about. Maybe it was Tal Kator?

"Come along," said Hirah. "We haven't got all day, well, actually we do—but that's beside the point. We *could* take all of today and tomorrow…and maybe even the next…no telling, really. So much time, so little to do, you know."

Ranting and flailing his arms, his raspy voice continued. "Where you from, friend…and what's your name, anyway. Never heard it, not once that I can recall. You look like a Daniel, or maybe even a Stephen. What is it, friend?"

Rat took a deep breath and did his best to answer the many questions tossed his way by the Leafling. His mind kept thinking, *they just don't seem like demons…like the terrible fairies Malus spoke about.* More importantly, he felt something just wasn't right about this whole trip.

"Come along," spouted the Hirah. "You'll be safe with me … they all know me, of course. The Leaflings are splendid folk. We might even let you take a splash in the Miraré along with us. Looks like you could use a good clean up, not that I mean you are filthy dirty or anything. What I mean to say is that a good dip is quite refreshing. The Miraré is magnificent for swimming. It's sparkling clean and wonderful."

Rat was walking forward now, his mind awash with thoughts about a large group of these Leaflings and the fact that perhaps Malus could be right about them. *What if they enchant me?*

As they plodded along up the winding waters of the small river, Hirah continued his incessant rants. The lad never slowed his pace, both in movement and in banter.

"I can't recall the last mankind visitor we've had in Tal Kator. It's been a right-long time, I must say. There was a time when the kingdom of man would stop by … you know—have a short visit and catch up on the news of the forest. Not anymore, though. It seems we've all vanished from the mind of man. Not that that is all bad, of course. We live quite peacefully without those heavy footstep pressed into our soil. Why, I was stepped on once near here. Of course, it didn't hurt all that badly. We Leaflings are quite hardy, we are."

A few more steps and many words from Hirah found the two nearing the pool of the Miraré. The rushing water from over the falls created a wonderful pitter-patter of rippling waves across its surface. A faint chatter of squirrels could also be made out along with chirps of numerous birds and frogs. So many walks of life made this beautiful setting home, and all seemed to blend seamlessly into one another.

As the two stepped into the open terrain of the Miraré pool, the sweeping hush of whispering Leafling voices shushed the area. Russssssssh … and all was silent.

Hirah called out. "It's alright, friends, this is my new pal, Rastus … Rastus Cubbins from Cobblestone and New Haven."

Slowly and cautiously, many bands of Leaflings crept forward, still many with their tiny spears in hand. Not all present were as trusting of their new visitor as Hirah, and each eased up near the edge of the Miraré where the two stood. It had been more than a couple years since the colony had been paid a visit by man, and many had never really gotten the opportunity to see and hear a human in their lifetime. Each curious Leafling closed in, their barky smiles emitting a playful and pleasant vibe.

"Oh, come along, Rastus," chirped Hirah. "The water is perfect today."

Hirah and a group of others had already splashed their way into the Miraré and had begun tossing one another into the air, making their splashes out into the rippling surface of the pool. Their leafy heads would bob under and pounce back out with a fun-loving zest. It was quite hard to imagine that this small, playful colony of Leaflings were the vicious killers portrayed by Malus. *They seem so happy...*

Rastus was actually considering entering the water's edge and cooling his limbs with the healing waters of the Miraré. But as he hobbled closer to the pool, something changed in the Leaflings.

One of the young Leaflings popped his head high from the water. Craning his neck back and forth and looking in all directions, he pushed his nose toward the sky. "What's that smell?" he asked.

Hirah quickly chimed in. "Oh, I don't smell a thing. What ever do you mean? It's always something with you, Keeto ... smelling this or seeing that. Why, if I ..."

Hirah stopped short, his nose now sniffing the air. "I do smell something odd. It's...it's...oily smelling."

Soon, many Leaflings were scampering out of the water and investigating their surroundings. Several approached Rastus suspiciously. Their tiny eyes locked upon his bent stature as he stood trembling along shore.

"Are you alone?" one asked, eyeing him suspiciously.

"I ... I ... I had company, I reckon I did, but they went along ... I ... well, they left me, they did."

Rat's comment was met with disapproval. Each Leafling was growing increasingly uneasy as wafts of strange smelling scents floated in the forest air. Again they pressed Rastus.

"Why are you here?" one asked, pressing his spear closer and closer with each step.

"I ... I ... don't rightly know, I don't. I just came along, you know ... just passing through as people do. I gots no reason for harm."

As several Leaflings closed in on Rat, spears edging closer and closer, Rat's heart sank. Even as they drew near, several other tell-tale signs of disaster were unfolding. A huge rush of raspy voices roared from far into the forest. A deafening whisper thundered across the Miraré as a cloud of gray smoke loomed in the distance. Seconds later, a rumbling roar of fire ripped through the woods on both sides. FOOM, the flames roared past them all on both sides. Chaos ensued immediately. In every direction there was fire and smoke rampaging through the forest around them.

"Oh my God…" whimpered Rastus.

Massive green waves of Leaflings raced into the safety of the water. Raspy roars and cries filled the smoky air. In fear and sorrow, Rastus Cubbins stood in shock as tiny creatures he knew nothing about scampered in panic.

"What have I done?"

20

High atop the castle precipice, the midday sun fell on the colorful hues of Malus' new attire. He had abandoned his doctorly coverings for a much more kingly robe of rich and brilliant colors. His new clothing only fueled his inner fire. His thoughts wrapped around this one day…this one culmination of his lifelong aspirations to concur Cobblestone. It was all coming together so beautifully.

Confident in the fact that Johan would no doubt defeat the scant few warriors in the caverns and mines, his mind now bent to his other Blue Haven Captains setting fire to the realm of Tal Kator. When the crusted remains of that portion of woods smoldered to a bitter end, he would send his armies in and pluck the precious Amethyst rings from their long hiding in the caverns behind the Miraré Falls. It was all too easy. With Dominick Sebastian dead and the scant few Cobblestone warriors left to fight, the meek and pitiful residents of Cobblestone would simply melt into a groveling pile at his feet.

Bow, my puppets!

With Malus' new adornments in place, it was time for the last and most relished part of his new attire. He had waited long to gain the one righteous ring of Father Mathias of Cobblestone Abbey. A life of planning now had that ring nestled in a room high in this very tower. Many stories above the precipice walls, Jon of Cobblestone sat in wait with his siblings and the nearly dead queen of the castle. It was time to gain that powerful ring. It was time to step into the shoes he'd longed to fill. This…this was the day for Malus. His new kingship was borne, and it was time for him to take possession of his prize.

For the first time in many days, Malcolm and Gwen sat by their mother's side. Her condition only seemed to worsen as they each held a hand, offering what little love and hope they possessed. So much sadness and despair had befallen them in recent days. The two clinged to their mother's palm, hoping beyond hope that somehow things could change—that they could somehow reach back in time and regain all that was lost. Death and dismay had taken hold, and even the strong willed nature of Jon was sullen and helplessly lacking in hope. He silently watched the two as his thoughts swirled from the sadness at hand, to the worries of what took place in the abbey only hours ago. He held little hope for his dear friend Dominick, who he last saw bleeding furiously and inches from raging flame. *Poor Dominick ...*

The deadbolt latch of the heavy wooden door clanked with a ratcheting chatter. Its echoes startled the four in the room.

Jon jumped to the bedside, willing and ready to defend his family. The door pushed open and two soldiers preceded Malus into the room. Malus' smug smile struck fear into the hearts of the siblings bedside.

"I've come, Jonathon. It is time."

Jon had no idea what the old doctor was talking about. He stood tall by the bed, trying to protect what he could with his small stature.

"You shall not harm this family, Malus of Blue Haven."

Malus laughed out loud. "I can and will do as I please, Jon of Cobblestone Abbey. And YOU shall address me as YOUR king!"

"NEVER!"

"Such spirit for one hopelessly bound to your fate! You have no choice, my monk friend. I am now King—with that precious heirloom from your hand, I shall rule for a very long time!"

Jon recoiled. "I will do no such thing! This ring was given to me by Father Math—". His words were cut short by Malus' sharp voice.

"DO NOT lecture me with history, Jon! I know precisely what I ask of you!" His words shrank almost to a whisper. "Only this is no request—you have no choice."

Jon's anger turned to sorrow as he gazed down at the ring on his finger. A hundred memories of Father Mathias flashed in his mind as he struggled with his words. His muddled voice cracked, even at a whisper. "I shall never freely offer this ring to anyone … not until it is my time to leave this earth."

An evil grin tugged at Malus' face. "That is precisely what I'd hoped for."

With a nod from Malus, the two guards stormed Jon. Easily conquering his small stature, the two guards held each arm by its shoulder, dragging him closer to Malus.

In the past several seconds, few had been watching young Malcolm at his mother's bedside. In his hands was the large wooden club-like devise used to smooth the surface of the feather-tick bed. It's long handle and heavy flat surface resembled a rowboat paddle with wickedly narrow leading edges and enough length to inflict harm if used more as a weapon than a household bed tool. His fingers twitched as he grasped its handle, waiting for the precise moment.

"I had suspected that you would not be cooperative, dear Jon. It is such a shame that you will not simply give in to the fact that I am now king. It is treason to disobey my wishes. You know this. I WILL have that ring Master Jon."

Malus extended his hand toward Jon, his palm open in wait of his prize. A guard forced Jon's arm forward, exposing the ring shining upon his finger, extending toward Malus. Malus reached further, preparing to tug the ring from its rightful home.

In a flash, young Malcolm dashed from his bedside position, racing forward at Malus. With a roundhouse swing, he wielded his wooden club sword down amid the men before him. The leading edge of his weapon fell squarely on the wrist of Malus, shattering the bones behind the hand. Malus screamed in agony as a swift backhand punch leveled the boy. His body flailed backward into the wall and collapsed into the floor in a pile.

"NO!" cried Jon, but his efforts were in vain. The punch had knocked Malcolm out of consciousness, but not before the damage had been done by his wooden household weapon.

Malus grasped his hand in pain, falling to his knees wincing almost to the point of tears. Jagged edges of bone could be seen beneath the bruised and bloody skin of Malus' forearm. Anger and pain coursed through Malus as he growled his words.

"You will PAY for this, you conniving worm!"

He gazed up at his soldiers, now wrenching Jon's body to the point of dislocating joints. His wrinkled nose and hideous scowl spoke volumes. His voice struck fear.

"Take that ring…finger and all!"

With that, one of the soldiers drew his sword, the deafening ring of its sheath sliced through the air with a sharpness equal only to its honed edge. As Malus watched, Jon's hand was raised high above him, his ring glistening in the light of the room. The heavy sword pressed along side its brilliant surface, edging up against skin and bone. Gwendolyn squealed, seeing a drop of blood falling from the knuckle of Jon's hand as it trembled in the air above him. With one harsh downward thrust and a wailing scream from Jon, the precious heirloom given to him by the very hand of Father Mathias fell to the floor…

…finger and all.

21

Captain Matthew Lohr rode at the head of his small army of men just on the outskirts of Cobblestone. When his scout returned from the city streets, all halted awaiting news.

"Captain!" exclaimed the scout, still saddled upon his steed. Both horse and rider gasped for breath as they panted and sweat from their ride.

"There are no Blue Haven sentinels in Cobblestone. How can we be at war with no army to fight?"

The captain struggled in thought as his fists ground at the graying hairs on his chin. Many things were just not right with this whole ordeal. A few questions were coming to mind.

"The people…the people of Cobblestone…are they sick?"

"None appear sick, but chaos and panic have set in. Our township is petrified."

"Perhaps we still have time," offered Matthew. "Maybe our foes misjudged us. There is still hope men." The Captain's words fell on disheartened ears. There were simply too many questions left unanswered.

Matthew again questioned the scout.

"Have you been to the abbey?"

The simple body gestures of the scout offered little hope. His desperate glance preceded his words.

"Dominick Sebastian has fallen."

Captain Matthew's shoulders fell with the weight of the news. This had clearly not been part of his plans. His friendship with Dominick transcended mere soldier acquaintance. These two were good friends and Matthew had hoped to let Dominick lead the way and decide the proper course of battle. Without Dominick Sebastian, Cobblestone's minor army would have little direction. Matthew could lead that charge, but help from Dominick would have been paramount. Matthew's words to his scout were in earnest.

"He is dead?"

"Sebastian is still alive, Sir. But his condition worsens. Brother Michael is tending his wounds, but his body has bled for hours. There is little hope for him."

Captain Lohr still had many questions.

"Is there no resistance in the city? Are there no Blue Haven soldiers standing guard?"

"None I could find, Sir."

Weighing his options, Captain Lohr made his decision.

"I ride to Cobblestone Abbey! I must see Dominick Sebastian before it's too late."

He gazed back at his men, raising his sword high and shouted, "MEN! You must ride the streets of Cobblestone! You must muster men and boy…anyone who can carry a sword. We have not yet lost this battle! Rally our PEOPLE! It is time for Cobblestone to stand tall! Raise the charge, men! SOON! Soon we will take back our city!"

In seconds, Captain Matthew Lohr and his scout dashed away, racing to Cobblestone Abbey where his dear friend, Dominick, lay nearly lifeless in a pool of his own blood.

22

In the lower halls of Cobblestone Castle, four soldiers held Malus pinned against a heavy cot as he winced in pain. The snap-pop of his arm bones being reset nearly overwhelmed him. Even through the pain, his mind struggled with thoughts about his plan. Much of today's happenings were taking longer than he had expected. He had long since looked to the west in full confidence that Johan and his men would be returning from their assured win in battle. Their late arrival had him worried.

But in his mind, he knew several things had taken place—all of which should insure his plan's success. Dominick Sebastian must be lying dead in the abbey—the kingdom of Tal Kator was most certainly ablaze with no hope of salvation—and at the very least, five of his best men … those known as the Sons of Romb, were by his side and still willing to fight for what they believed was a worthy cause, one justified by decades of being held under the thumb of the city of Cobblestone. As a makeshift wooden cast was bound to his arm, Malus, new King of

Cobblestone, still stood proud of his accomplishments. His plan simply could not fail now. All the pieces were in place. Another day or two and he could make his formal address to both Cobblestone … and to Blue Haven.

23

Hours earlier, in the headwaters above Miraré Falls...

Again on this particular midday, two young Leaflings were swimming near the water's edge and playfully splashing the bull frogs in the backwaters. As the two fun-loving saplings bounced along the river's edge, the afternoon sun was warming their leaves and filling their bodies and hearts with energy.

As Kimbli and Tally scampered about the ripples and waves of the Falling River, the two bantered and played as usual, bouncing from stone to stone and chasing the many dragonflies along the water's edge. Tally finally spoke up.

"When can we go see Gwendolyn again, Kimbo? I miss the little lass, you know?"

But strangely, Kimbli heard little of Tally's question. He jumped high atop a boulder in the stream, his head cocked to one side, his ear taking in the sounds.

"You hear that, Kimbo?"

"Hear what?" asked Tally, still shaking water from his leafy head.

"I don't know ... that something ... that soothing sound."

Tally, too, raised his head, hearing every sound the forest had to offer. "Bless my bark, Kimbo...all I hear is nature."

"No...listen," said Kimbli, closing his eyes and swaying like the river current. "It's more than nature. I hear it. Ahhh...that's wonderful. Don't you hear that, Tal? Close your eyes...listen."

Tally reluctantly closed his eyes and listened as Kimbli suggested. Somehow, amid the quiet barking of the squirrels and the dribbles of falling water ... he did hear something. And yet ... it was nothing at all. It seemed almost as if nature was being amplified, or perhaps enhanced by some outside force. Somehow the confines of the setting they were in seemed to open into song—into some peaceful bliss—into vibrant, sweet harmonizing tones of the world around them. Nature was singing aloud, and it engulfed them both.

"What is that?" asked Kimbli again as a smile tugged at his face.

Tally was too mesmerized to answer. His limbs slowly eased their way to shore and up onto the banks of the river. He, like many of the other woodland creatures, was hopelessly drawn to a farther upstream bend of the river. It seemed that every creature in the forest was also somehow pulled to this spot. Birds began to light in nearby trees. Rabbits nervously crept near the sound. Even the burrowing muskrats tarried from their routines to witness the heavenly tones emitted from this portion of the wood. It was as if life had stopped ... to witness itself.

Yet above it all ... amid harmonies of water, wind, land—amid all sorts of natural euphoria, a voice was heard.

It was a voice ... yet no words could yet be made out. There were lyrics ... yet no true note was sung. There was peace with all the colors of the rainbow ... and with equal beauty. Its delicate, tender, succulent drippings of purity encompassed everything within ear's distance. It was as if the heavens had rained down into the forest, and the forest accepted it with open arms.

Amid the sparkling haze of grandeur, the voice was still heard, whispering love and happiness as it flowed.

The two Leaflings wandered toward the voice, almost oblivious to the world about them. A long stretch of river had been traversed by the two before they had any knowledge of their own movements. They lived a sleepless dream of pleasant sights and sounds … almost floating in glorious slumber. Joy and love melted their hearts as they plodded along, lost in the beauty of the moment.

The two continued on, barely noticing anything other than the beautiful sounds filling their ears. When they reached a wide turn in the river, they stepped high onto a large boulder and stared in wide wonder. Both fell to their knees, humbled atop the stone pedestal.

Before these two Leaflings sat a being like nothing they had ever witnessed. Amid the swirling currents of the water, the form of a woman emerged. Her shape seemed to be formed of water … ever flowing back into the stream. When she wished, her shape would take on color and depth, reflecting the nature around her, and then wash away again into the falling water. She appeared to be part of her surroundings … and yet somehow creating it at the same time. The sounds of water filled their ears. Cool, humid air comforted them both as they wept in the splendor of the being before them.

And behold … the being spoke.

"Welcome, young Leaflings! I have waited long for this day. Come with me and rejoice in my waters. Rejoice in my life—in my love."

Her face flushed with warm hues, and her lips smiled with contentment.

At that moment, the being began to stroke the dripping cords of an enormous golden water harp that also washed up to her beckoning hands, somehow rushing from the depths of the river and filling her wondrous hands. Harmony filled the air … notes blended seamlessly with the sounds of the forest. The two Leaflings were swelled into the currents of voices and notes and the beautiful, quiet whisperings of nature. They were speechless as they stared in wonder.

"All is well, my friends," spoke the voice again. "Join me. Rejoice with me in my waters."

Tally could barely speak. His eyes were hopelessly drawn to the beauty before him. "Not—not in all my teachings … have I heard of such a being. Never have I known such beauty. Who … who are you?"

"I will take that as a complement, young Tally of Miraré Falls." Her face flushed with almost human-like colors when she spoke, and her smile radiated when the Leaflings spoke. "And young Kimbli…has your tongue gone woody?"

Kimbli desperately wanted to ask how she knew their names, but couldn't utter a word. He simply gazed into her eyes, being completely engulfed in the moment and melted by her presence.

Tally finally uttered a few more words. "Who…who are you?"

The woman raised her flowing hands from the harp and reached to the Leaflings. She picked them from the rock ledge and placed them on her lap as the water flowed around them. With her face flushing in wonderful hues, she spoke again.

"Young Leaflings…you do not know my name, but you have always known me. You have swam in my pools … floated in my currents. You have given me great pleasure. I have cradled you in my waters, loving your spirit, embracing your love of life."

She smiled warmly as her face beamed with color and emotion. "Little ones … I am Aquavita! I am the Spirit of Water! I am the driving force—the rejuvenating pureness to the waters of the world. I have come to you now at a turn of tides. I come bearing news for you."

"News…?" mumbled Kimbli, feeling light headed.

"You, little ones, will be famed beyond that of your kin. You…" she smiled, "…will save the fate of Cobblestone…and the fate of the forest."

"Ohhhhh," uttered Kimbli with a gasp. Feeling faint, he toppled backward into the currents of her lap.

Aquavita chuckled softly at the little one's antics, her body flowing in shades of blue and green. She picked him up again; caressing his leaves with a splash of water.

"Wake up, Kimbli of Tal Kator. We have a journey to make."

"What?" he chirped, shaking water from his leaves.

Tally timidly spoke up. "We know nothing of Cobblestone. We know nothing beyond our tiny section of the woods. Our little bodies cannot save a city. We are no warriors."

Aquavita beamed with joyous colors as her voice chuckled in harmonious tones. "Cobblestone does not need you to fight, little ones. It needs your bodies … and your hearts."

With that, Aquavita melted into the stream around them. Her hues disappeared, her presence still very much in the waters about them.

The swirling currents swept them downstream, bouncing along in her frothy waters. With Aquavita holding them high and singing joyously, the two young Leaflings were swept downstream toward their home in Tal Kator … and to a task beyond their imagination.

24

Two lone monks stood guard at the door of Cobblestone Abbey with little more than their fists as weapons. Nonetheless, each stood valiantly at the steps of what was once a peaceful place of worship. They stiffened with the echoes of hooves galloping toward them.

Two horses approached at top speed, rocks and gravel flying as they slid to a halt. Captain Matthew Luhr dismounted, leaving his scout to stand guard in the cobblestone street.

Both monks recognized his stately stature and greeted him.

"Captain Luhr! You are alive!"

"Yes, men, I live, but our numbers are few. I have come to see Dominick Sebastian. Please tell me I have not arrived too late."

The monk brothers gave no attempt at explaining Dom's condition. They simply parted, pushing the door open and allowing the captain's entry.

"You will find him beyond the Library," they called after him.

Captain Lohr's heavy boots rumbled like thunder down the stone hall of the abbey as he raced to his friend's side. Brother Michael met him at the door.

"He is here, my friend," Michael said, grabbing the captain's shoulder. "He is gravely ill."

Matthew pushed past Brother Michael and into the dimly lit room. Dominick lie motionless on a small cot in the center. The captain knelt by his side and placed his hand on Dom's arm.

"Captain Dominick … it is me, Matthew."

Almost no movement was made by Dom. At long last, his eyelids eased open and his gaze pulled toward Matthew. He tried to speak, a low gurgle of sound escaping his blood-filled lung.

"I failed…" he whispered.

Matthew came to his defense. "You have never failed Cobblestone, my friend—my captain."

A tear slid from Dom's eye and trickled into the pillow. His labored breathing shook the bed with labored gyrations.

"Dom," Matthew pleaded, "I know not what to do. Our numbers are few. I fear we cannot storm the castle."

Dom's eyes again met his. "You cannot storm the castle—not with a thousand men. They…" his voice trailed off.

"What Dominick?"

"They took the children … and Jon."

Matthew had not yet heard this piece of information. He had not had time to think of what his enemy had done while he fought in the battle at the mines. An attempt on the castle seemed hopeless even before this news reached his ear.

"What do we do?" he asked, hoping Dom had answers. But Dom had no more answers. His eyes closed and no other words left his tongue. He drifted into unconsciousness.

25

Flames and smoke crept closer as Rastus Cubbins inched into the waters of the Mirarė. Hundreds of Leaflings now floated in the water, watching the fire engulf their homeland. None knew for certain if Rat was a part of this hideous occurrence, and none had time to ponder it in the chaos. The raging fire frightened them all.

Somewhere behind the line of fire were two figures creeping closer to the Mirarė high above the falls. Once the flames above the rocky bluff had dwindled down, the two eased near the edge of the falls, gazing down at the pond of Leaflings floating about and the still blazing forest nearby.

Rat immediately recognized the two men and his heart sank. He knew without question that this raging fire was of their doing. But even worse was what he saw next. The chill running up his spine took his breath. Fear entered his every thought. As he stared at the men through the smoke and haze, he noticed that each had their barrel of liquid held high over their heads. He knew what would come next. Once dumped into the pool below, their oily liquid would soon be ablaze atop the water, too. The Leaflings were doomed, and Rat was right in the midst of it all.

Just as the two men began tugging at their barrel corks, a loud rush of water was heard from behind. The currents of the Falling River increased as all stared in disbelief. To their absolute amazement, the water just above the falls began to rise straight up out of it channel. In that spire of water a shape took form. Tall and formidable, a frighteningly-lifelike shape swirled into the form of a woman—forceful, angry, and strong.

With an enormously powerful backhand swing, the monstrous watery arm of the beast smited each man, smashing their bodies against the smoldering trees, killing them both on impact.

The form again melted into the water and slid into the pool, seeking yet another victim. At the base of Rat's feet, the being again took form, rising like a spire above him. The once tender voice of Aquavita now boomed like thunder as she growled into the sky.

With a giant clap of her hands, water exploded in every direction, scattering rain all about the flames nearby, quenching them immediately. She then turned her attention to the cowering man beneath her. Her piercing eyes burned like hell fire as they peered down upon him.

Rat closed his eyes, knowing full well he would be her next victim. He shivered, waiting for the blow.

But as he trembled beneath her, her voice boomed into the forest.

"RASTUS CUBBINS! WHAT HAVE YOU DONE? YOU KNOW BETTER!"

Rat toppled backward into the water, his face buried in his hands, shaking head to toe.

"ANSWER ME, RASTUS! LOOK INTO MY EYES!" she shouted, her voice rumbling like thunder.

Wind and rain pelted his skin as he tried to lift his eyes to meet hers. His chattering lips could not speak.

"YOU HAVE BEEN DECEIVED! YOU HAVE NOT LISTENED TO YOUR HEART, RASTUS CUBBINS! I SHOULD SMITE YOU DOWN!"

Her fist raised high into the air, ready to thrash down upon him. But she did not. Her watery hand dropped into the pool and snatched him up.

"BUT I HAVE PLANS FOR YOU."

25

Poor Jon knelt on the floor clutching his hand in pain, blood covering his clothing as he squeezed tightly at the severed opening where is finger had once been.

Malcolm was still lying motionless along the wall.

Gwen raced to Jon's side, tugging a blanket from the bed as she came. She began tearing at the cloth in an attempt to create the best makeshift bandage she could manage. Much of the bleeding had subsided, but Jon's pain was still dreadful. She pressed and bound his hand tightly, staving off most of the bleeding.

She turned to her brother lying unconscious on the floor. She pulled a wet cloth from the bedside table and wiped his forehead with its cool water. His eyes opened as he struggled with the painful bruise on his cheek.

It seemed the day could get no worse.

Meanwhile, across town, Captain Matthew Lohr was summoning his ransack army of townspeople. His men had done as they were told and had gathered over one hundred citizens to help in the fight. Unfortunately, the captain still wasn't certain of his strategies and methods. He hoped and prayed the answers would come to him before the castle had time to prepare for strategies of their own. Malus would likely have his plan in place, and it was an unsettling feeling knowing that the king's only blood relatives were held captive against their will and very much in harm's way.

The castle was a fortress virtually impenetrable. With its perimeter river mote and its high walls, only the strongest bows and arrows could reach far enough to be beneficial in battle. Unless Blue Haven's army was willing to storm Cobblestone and battle hand to hand, there would probably be no valid way to take back their castle from the outside—and the waiting game was as frightening as not fighting at all.

He addressed his small army. "My fighters! I had hoped that Dominick Sebastian would help us lead our charge into battle. But alas, no. He is badly wounded, perhaps mortally. Without our Steward of Stone Castle to lead the way, I must take charge of our forces. We will soon go into battle."

As the captain spoke, a strange and shaky voice chopped into the crowd. From a side road nearby a hobbling figure crept forward, speaking as he huffed and puffed and wiggled his way to the head of the crowd.

"I gots a way to help, I do."

Captain Lohr raised an eyebrow. "And how could you be of service, lad? You can barely walk. I commend you for your bravery, but how is it that you could benefit our charge?"

"Because I will get you inside the castle," he grunted.

"Who are you?" asked the captain.

Rat's head dropped in shame as he spoke. "I am Rastus Cubbins, and I am the one who helped that evil doctor take Cobblestone Castle."

Astonished gasps swept through the crowd.

Captain Lohr drew his sword and stomped closer to Rat, pressing its honed point against his neck. "I suggest you start talking, Rastus Cubbins, lest I behead you here in the street."

"It's like this, it is," Rat whimpered. "All is not lost. You have allies, honest you do."

"Why should we trust the likes of a conniving and deceitful soul that has already betrayed us?" Matthew pushed harder against the hilt of his sword, pressing against Rat's bent neck.

"'Cause I met the Water-Goddess … and she let me live."

26

A slow and deliberate drum cadence bounced through later afternoon sunlight as over a hundred villagers marched forward through Cobblestone with twenty soldiers leading the way. The villagers carried any possible weapon they could find within their homes and barns. Many carried axes and still others held machetes as makeshift swords. It was a pathetic display of warriors, but it was the best Cobblestone had to offer. The usually peaceful town of Cobblestone had been transformed into a vigilante mob of angry farmers. Unbeknownst to those in Cobblestone Castle, there were seventy other soldiers marching quietly elsewhere.

The marching crowd rounded the last turn before the castle and began their slow and loud ascent up the long stretch of cobblestone to their destination. The two leading soldiers exchanged worrisome glances. One whispered to the other. “I hope this works.”

Their loud march didn’t fall on deaf ears. Two hours had passed since the setting of Malus’ arm. By now, he stood high atop the castle precipice, his bandaged arm held tightly in a sling. A finger upon his bruised and scabbed hand sported a new fixture—a beautiful Amethyst ring. He smiled in disbelief at the ruff band of pretend soldiers making their way up the road. His confidence soared.

Thumpity-bump, thumpity-bump, thumpity-bump, bump bump. The slow rhythm and cadence of the drum pounded against the castle walls as they marched.

"Fools," chided Malus. "Is this the best army they could conjure? We'll simply just wait them out. It's hard to swim a mote while carrying an ax. And besides, Johan will likely greet them from behind any minute with an army to outnumber them."

Soon, the road came to an abrupt end where the drawbridge usually rested upon the earth. Cobblestones and soil crumbled and fell into the water below where wooden plank boards normally lay. All came to a halt and fanned out along the mote's edge.

One soldier called out. "Malus of Blue Haven! We demand that you surrender the castle and the family of the true king!"

The crowd of soldiers inside the castle roared with laughter. Malus spoke up. "And what will you farmers do when I do not heed your request? What? Cut our trees with your axes?"

More laughter erupted as the castle walls filled with smiling faces watching the outsiders shout their weak commands. They had their complete attention as they continued their threats.

"We demand restitution, Malus. We will not stand for your pious takeover of our kingdom."

"Tell me," shouted Malus, "What is your name, Soldier?"

"My name is of no importance to you."

"Oh really? I would like to know the name of the first one of you we shoot. But since I'm a sport about this all, I will allow you to turn around and march yourselves back to your pathetic little holes before we punch you all full of holes."

"We demand our castle!"

Malus' words to his soldiers were said loud enough for all to hear. "Cock your crossbows, soldiers and prepare to fire."

27

wen lay sobbing at her mother's side while Malcolm paced the floor. Jon was bent over his hand, keeping pressure on the wound. The three sat in misery, locked away in their own little prison tower. It was a seemingly hopeless predicament.

Malcolm still paced, trying to find some semblance of a plan to get out of this mess. All four were getting very hungry as they both waited for their next visit, loathing the many possible and horrible outcomes. As Malcolm paced past the window, his two words only made things worse. "Oh, no."

Jon stood, wincing in pain, and walked to the window. It only took one glance to see the hopeless scene unfolding below. Even from up high, Jon recognized many of the village soldiers lined up near the mote. He turned away from the window, shaking his head. "I can't bear to watch."

Malcolm pushed at the pains of glass in the window frame. The jam eased open, allowing fresh evening air to blow into the room, but it offered little hope. Shouts could be heard from down below, as the bitter scene continued beneath them.

"It's all so hopeless," mourned Jon. "Hopeless."

But even as he spoke the words, the most wondrous thing occurred. From the window's edge, two little Leaflings bounced into the room.

Gwen jumped from the bed and raced toward the two. "Kimbli, Tally!" she squealed.

Kimbli spoke up. "You've gotten yourselves in a bit of a pickle, you have."

"Thank you for coming," cried Gwen.

"No time for talk. We need to open a door ... one that leads to a tunnel leading out into the woods."

Malcolm smiled. "I know that door! Mother always said I'd need that key one day. I keep it in my room."

"Well, what are we waiting for?" asked Kimbli.

Kimbli quickly slid under the wooden door and flipped its outer latches. The door swung open and he and Kimbli raced down the stone hall to the bedroom. Tally gathered Jon and Gwen together. "You two must stay here. We have a plan!"

"What's happening?" asked Gwen.

"We need to buy time. Malus looses patience with our little distraction out front. We need another minute while hopefully Malcolm gets that door open!"

Jon spoke up. "We have soldiers?"

Tally smiled. "Yes, and hundreds of Leaflings!"

Gwen grabbed Tally and pulled him to her chest in a warm hug. "I love you, Tally! Thank you so much!"

"Well now, lass. You have work to do."

28

Dead silence covered the castle and the grounds across the mote. It seemed as if every breath could be heard.

"Men," shouted Malus, "prepare to fire."

Rows of soldiers took aim from the castle wall. Just as Malus was about to give his command, something very strange happened. Amid the silence and tension of pre-battle, something else was heard.

High above them all, from a tiny alcove window, a voice was heard. It was so uncharacteristic and out of place in the moment that all stood in amazement. Soldiers and farmers and all of Malus' men gazed upward at the tender voice filling the void. It was Gwendolyn—and she was singing.

Calmly blows the solemn breeze'
Warm and sweet so as to please.

Melt my heart in playful tease...
Eternal zephyrs of summer's eve.

Tickling leaves upon the trees
Of joyous yellows, browns, and greens.
Windy words spoke unto me...
Eternal zephyrs of summer's eve.

Her beautiful voice was heard by all as she continued to sing into the sky. No one understood why in the heat of battle, a little girl would be singing. And just as Tally had hoped, it was buying a little time.

Malus pulled his gaze from up above and looked to one of his soldiers. "Something isn't right." He looked all around, taking in all he could see. "Everyone, stand guard here."

He looked again to his soldier. "Come with me. Quick. Something isn't right."

The two ran from the precipice and into the castle, listening and looking in all directions.

Meanwhile, hundreds of Leaflings climbed the outer walls in wait for the perfect moment.

Kimbli and Malcolm raced from his bedroom and back down the hall toward the lower rooms of the castle. Malcolm had made the trip many times in his life, playing hide and seek with his sister in the damp and dark corners of what they called "the dungeon". Only now, his mission was much greater. Key in hand, he navigated every step by heart, running top speed down the many flights of steps. Years he had tucked that simple skeleton key away in his bower, never expecting need for it. Now, perhaps more than ever, he needed it far worse than he ever expected. The entire realm of Cobblestone hinged on this one race into the dungeon.

Mal raced from one of the spiral stairwells and out into a vast room. As he did, a voice called out behind him. "Stop, or I'll wring your royal neck!"

One of Malus' soldiers had caught a glimpse of him and nearly cut him off with a mad dash across the room. Thankfully, he had not seen the scampering Leafling shuffling along with Mal. Just as the man was groping for Mal's shirt at a dead run, Kimbli stretched his long fingertips around the soldiers feet, tugging for all he was worth.

The soldier crumbled into a pile on the floor, his head banging the stone floor with one hard blast. He was out cold.

Kimbli continued the chase behind Mal, now descending the long and winding stairs to the dungeon. Unfortunately, so too was Malus, and Kimbli was bringing up the rear.

Step after stone step twisted down into the darkness. Both Mal and Malus were operating in almost total darkness, taking the steps by memory more than sight. Ten steps from the bottom, Mal miscalculated one step. It was a horridly bad turn of his ankle and he immediately toppled down the steps, his head again feeling the pounding pain of a harsh blow. As he rolled out into the dungeon floor, one sound obliterated all others.

Cling….cling, cling.

The key he had held so tightly in his hand flung loose in the fall and bounced into the darkness, ringing its notes on the cold stone floor.

Malus heard the noise, too. At the top of his lungs, he shouted back up the stairs. "GUARDS! Come quick!"

By the time his words resonated up the cold shaft, Malus was standing at the bottom, ready to stomp on the head of Malcolm. In the blackness of the dungeon he waited for any sound the help him determine the exact location of the boy on the floor. Nothing.

Soon, a pale light began to show from up the stairwell. The rustle of soldier feet accompanied it as Malus waited patiently for help and light to arrive. As he peered back up the stairwell, he inched closer to the light, ready to take the torch from the first soldier racing down the shaft.

It was close now. Thirty more steps and he would have what he needed to find Malcolm and more importantly, that key.

The fourth and final soldier racing down the shaft never knew what hit him. A tiny Leafling bound his feet, forcing him flailing down the shaft onto his fellow soldiers. By the time the pile hit bottom, all collapsed onto Malus, snuffing the torch in the process.

"Fools!" he shouted. Raising his voice even higher, he shouted up the shaft again. "Guards!"

Malcolm fought the pain in his head and limbs. As he lie coldly in the dark, he tried desperately to focus in the pitch black air. He had completely lost his sense of direction when he fell. *Where did that key land?*

When the crashing soldiers hit bottom, Malcolm took opportunity to scramble a bit farther away, keeping deathly quiet in the process. He grappled at the stone floor hoping for the faint miracle of him finding that key by mere accident. As he struggled with his balance and his aching head, he began to realize that there were many new noises joining the toppled soldiers. More heavy footsteps were heard on the stone overhead. Two more very important things were making noise, also.

A harsh thumping of hand on wood came echoing into the room from a far wall. As Malcolm stared in the direction, a faint light peered from underneath a door—the tunnel door!

Mal crept ever so quietly toward the light, hoping that some soldier didn't come racing at the new light across the room at that door. A thousand thoughts raced through his head as he still groped at the floor for that key.

It was then that the next odd sound tickled his ear. It sounded like a thousand butterflies had been set loose into the darkness. Wisps of wind and tiny slappings chattered about him. *What was going on?*

It only took a second to realize what was happening. When the raspy voices started chattering, Mal knew who had arrived.

"Malcolm," one Leafling barked into the air.

Malcolm lay petrified on the stone floor, afraid to speak. He slid as quickly away from any path toward the tunnel door and shouted aloud…

"The key is on the floor!"

Immediately, a body pounced in his direction. The dungeon floor was an absolute mess of beings of many varieties. He felt those little butterfly wings flapping about him and a few harsh hands beating at him.

Malcolm had finally gathered enough of his senses to dart on his hands and knees toward the light of the tunnel door. He had no hope of opening it without light or key, but it was the only focal point he had to guage anything by. He was lost in a sea of Leaflings, soldiers, and darkness, all flailing around in a painful mess.

Just as a band of soldiers fled into the room, the light of their torch illuminated a menagerie of strangeness all over the floor. Men and leaves were mopping the floor with themselves in waves of arms and sticks. Just as Mal was gaining his sight with the light of the torch, a raspy voice cried out…

"Malcolm!"

At that moment, two paramount occurrences happened. First, that same raspy voice yelled, "catch" as he peered through the pale light. Slap! The door key hit his palm perfectly and he caught it. He spun on his heels as he groped for the door lock. Just as he mashed the key into the hole and gave it a twist, he also peered over his shoulder.

Where's Malus?

29

Files of Cobblestone warriors and men flowed into the lower halls of the castle. Swords drawn, they hacked their way through the rubble of soldiers and Leaflings of the dungeon, each aiming for the stairwell.

The Leaflings quickly scattered out of the way and let the soldiers fight their way through. One of the soldiers spotted Malcolm, back against the wall, trying to avoid contact in the fighting mess. The soldier was none other than Matthew Luhr. Even Malcolm recognized his father's chief captain.

"Matthew!" he cried.

"Malcolm!"

"We've got to find Malus. We've got to get to the tower!"

The stairwell was a disaster for travel. Blue Haven soldiers from up top were fighting their way into the Cobblestone warriors at the bottom. A stalemate happened about the halfway point, and no soldier made it past that point, up or down.

Its passage was hopeless.

* * *

Malus raced across the large hall before reaching the stone stairwell to the castle tower. Its entry was almost within his grasp. Many noises followed him and he listened closely for those that may still be outside on the precipice. He had no time to gather his men. His only salvation was nestled above in the stone tower.

* * *

Soldiers and men stood helplessly across the mote. All heard screams and chaos from deep within the castle, wishing that somehow they could gain access to help.

The peaceful voice from high in the tower had long since stopped, and all sorts of ugly sounds were echoing into the now-darkened sky. As night fell, darkness seemed to engulf the once beautiful halls of Cobblestone Castle.

One man stood precariously close to the mote's edge. His mannerisms were somehow different from the rest. He was no simple citizen. He was no battle soldier. He was Brother Michael from Cobblestone Abbey. Before all … his presence would be magnificent.

Brother Michael bowed in holy prayer before the waters of the castle mote. His quiet prayer slowly became evident to all as his voice raised in volume and stature.

"God in Heaven … I pray…". The foreboding tone of his voice mirrored the horrific chaos deep inside the castle. "I ask of you … I ask in the name of the Holy Spirit … gain us entry!"

The night sky rolled in thunderous booms. Clouds bellowed against a frightening moonlit sky. Rumbles echoed in the ground.

Something—something—was happening.

The waters of the mote began to shake and shimmer. The pounding echoes of sound seemed to be only a foreboding prelude of what was to come. The crowd of soldiers and Cobblestone citizens stood amazed at the happenings before them.

Something more than human was at work here. God, spirits of a sort, or just plain mystical miracles were happening before their eyes. What happened astounded them all. Shivering lips blanketed chattering teeth as all witnessed an occurrence none had ever seen before.

The waters of the mote began to rise before them. Swirling winds and current erected a towering water-like bridge connecting land to castle, using only water and power. The inspiring awe of it all wasn't lost on a single person there. No one feared. No one worried. All raced out onto the watery trail, rushing into Cobblestone Castle. Every soul stepped onto that special bridge, rushing to aid their queen and three siblings somewhere in this shadowy castle. And by the love of God—or the grace of Aquavita—Cobblestone Castle was infiltrated.

* * *

Winded, Malus reached the top of the staircase. Panting, he turned the latch and found it already unlocked. Pushing, the door wouldn't budge. On the other side of the door, chairs and beds were piled high against its wooden surface.

Malus franticly and angrily searched the bedrooms for a ram. In seconds, he found one. A tall marble candle stand stood just outside Malcolm's room. In a simple ten seconds, it was racing down the hall—top speed with Malus at the helm.

BOOM!

The door knob splintered upon impact. Several strong shoulder slams and the door edged open, pushing the contents of the room a bit farther across the floor.

Malus edged into the room, snarling like rabid dog. His gaze soon found the cowering tears of Gwendolyn by the bed.

"Well, now, Miss Gwen. You are JUST who I'm looking for."

30

alus darted across the room and scooped up young Gwen in his good arm. Before Jon could stand and fight, Malus already had her in his grasp.

"Stand back, Jon. I'll snap her neck right here."

Jon scowled, fighting his urges to retaliate.

Malus began inching his way back to the door. He knew if he could get away from Jon that he could bar himself in one of the other rooms with Gwen, she being his only bargaining chip. He began pushing against the pile of rubble at the door, gaining a little more room for the two to squeeze through.

"Jon!" cried Gwen, wincing in Malus' grasp.

Jon stood paralyzed in his shoes, not knowing whether to fight or heed the doctor's order.

The door wiggled open a few more inches, and Malus backed himself out of the narrow opening, tugging Gwen along with him.

Just as Gwen was inching out of the door, something miraculous happened. With a jarring thump, Malus fell to the floor, dropping his hold on Gwen. She raced back through the door and into Jon's arms, petrified.

Jon raced to the door, expecting to slam it shut, but when he peered into the hall, he was taken back by what he saw.

Standing over the body of Malus was Rastus Cubbins. In his hands was a large wooden club, sharpened to a point. Before Jon could utter a word, that wooden stake slammed downward and into the chest of Malus. Its thrust skewered Malus and jolted the floor beneath him.

Tears in his eyes, Rat towered over Malus for the first time in his life. Many times he had pictured this moment, during those hurtful times when Malus would chide him and call him names, belittling him to the bone. Now, after so much death and destruction, Rat felt justified by his actions, but it didn't help the sorrow in his heart. Nothing he could do would take back the poisons he had unknowingly delivered to these lower halls. Nothing could take back the life of King Lawrence. And nothing could take back the sorrow he had helped create in the royal family and in Tal Kator. He collapsed onto the bloody corpse in tears. Through pressed lips, Rat cried out.

"YOU, Malus! You are the fowl ogre."

* * *

Meanwhile, villagers, Leaflings, and soldiers battled in the hall below. With the storm of new fighters raging in from outside, twenty Blue Haven soldiers surrendered and the battle stopped. The best-laid plans of Malus of Blue Haven came to a bitter end.

31

Soon, the castle tower was full of friends and family. Joyous hugs were shared by Gwen, Mal, and Jon. Matthew's wide grin warmed the room with the first rays of hope the walls had felt in days.

It was only moments before a dozen Leaflings pounced into the room.

"Kimbli! Tally!" Gwen cried, scooping them into her arms in embrace. Her tears of joy dampened their leaves as they smiled their playful grins.

"You know," laughed Tally, "the next time we visit, we simply must play hide-and-seek, rather than these terrible war games."

Gwen kept squeezing for all she was worth. In time, she released her embrace and smiled happily.

Kimbli tugged at a small pouch at his side. From within, he pulled a few small leaves and extended his vine-like fingers toward Gwen. "Take these," he said, glancing over at the queen lying motionless on the bed. "Place these under her tongue. They will help fight the poison of the mushrooms. We had no idea where those mushrooms were going. I wish we could have stopped it when it happened."

The Leafling turned to his fellow friends. "We have a mess at Tal Kator to clean. The forest needs our attention."

With that, the little creatures all gave a silent bow and scurried out the open window and down the walls into the night.

"We will visit soon, Gwen," called Kimbli. "Our next visit will be much more fun."

* * *

As the Leaflings scampered down the walls and into the mote, a voice was heard. The warm and tender words of Aquavita filled the night air.

"Where do you think you're going, little ones?"

Kimbli and Tally looked all about, trying to find the source of the voice. They didn't search long. Soon, the rippling waters around them rushed upward, creating the beautiful woman they remembered. Her dripping shape sparkled in the darkness of the night.

"Aquavita!" chirped Tally, who had taken quite a liking to his new watery friend.

"Yes, Tally, my friend. You and your kind have done well! I'm so very proud of you."

"Ah shucks," whispered Kimbli, his barky coverings blushing bashfully and his leaves rustling like goose-bumps.

"My dear friends," she continued. "You are likely to never see me again … not in these times. But I will still be here, and I will feel you and love you as I always have. You will feel me in the waters. You will see me in the rolling clouds. And you will know I'm here."

A tear slid down Tally's face. "I'll miss you, Aquavita."

"No tears for me, Tally of Miraré Falls. I will always feel your presence … and you shall always feel mine."

Tally gazed longingly into Aquavita's eyes. "We must go back to Tal Kator. Our village is burnt. We must rebuild."

"Yes, you must, Kimbli of Tal Kator, my valiant soldier."

"Oh, shucks…" he mumbled again.

"Why don't I help you get there?" she asked playfully.

In seconds, the currents of the mote and that of the Falling River flowed BACKWARD, carting hundreds of happy Leafings floating like leaves in the stream. Never before or never since has such a display happened in the Deep Woods, and the Leaflings were a part of it!

32

Two weeks had passed in the streets of Cobblestone. The castle halls had been cleaned, and hundreds of holes had been dug and filled in the castle graveyard. Through all the pain and suffering, Cobblestone had regain much of its dignity, and had starting living life much closer to its norm.

As the last few shovels of soil were tamped in the final burials of the cemetery, Matthew Lohr gazed down the path behind him. A tall and familiar figure was walking his way.

"Well, Dominick Sebastian. Aren't you a site for sore eyes!"

"Hello, Matthew. They tell me great praise is in order for you. I missed all the fun."

"Yes, just like you to show up once all the swords have been sheathed and holes dug and filled!"

The two bantered back and forth for quite some time. Their conversation finally turned to the kingship. Dominick spoke up.

"I have been to the queen today. We talked for hours. I remember days when we had no kind words for one another."

Matthew nodded his head, understanding fully as Dom continued talking.

"She wants me to take over the kingdom…until Malcolm is of age."

Matthew raised a brow. "She wants you to become Steward?"

"Yes, yet I ponder if the job may be better suited for you, my friend." He gave Matthew a long stare. "You have earned the right, my Captain."

"Wow. I'll have to think about that. That's a lot of weight for a mere Captain."

"Well," continued Dom, "I could always help advise. I have a Stewardship of my own at Stone Castle that must be maintained. And after all, it is my home. I miss it … and I miss my wife dearly. She awaits my return."

"I suppose the Ravens know the way, should I except the offer."

Dominick smiled. "You'll accept. I already told her you would."

"Always the crafty one, Steward Sebastian."

"Ah yes, Steward Lohr. I think you are up for the challenge. Although I must say, your task tomorrow will be no easy one."

Matthew looked at the ground and took a deep breath. "I had not planned on being the one making the decisions tomorrow. I had only planned on carrying out the royal wishes."

"It now falls completely upon your shoulders, my friend. What you say and do is up to you."

"I don't know what I should do, Dominick. This city needs no more death. A public hanging of twenty men will be ugly."

"Perhaps there will not be a hanging."

Mathew looked troubled. "They helped kill our king, Dominick!"

"Through lies and trickery of another soul," Dom said.

"It is Royal Decree. Treason is punishable by death."

"Punishable," said Dom, "not mandatory."

"We must stand firm and make a precedence of this."

"There are many ways to skin a cat, Captain. Give it thought."

"What do you suggest, Dominick?"

"I suggest you read the book."

"The book?" questioned Matthew.

"All of this stems from the one book, written and bound by our forefather kings. *The Fall of the House of Romb* lies in your quarters, my new Steward, as we speak."

"Will I find answers there?" asked Matthew.

"No. You will find the whole story."

33

A crowd of townspeople gathered in the courtyard the following day. Looming above the yard was a newly erected gallows, formidable in the midday sun.

Soon, the giant doors of the castle creaked open, and a long file of people marched out single file. Twenty-one men in black hoods were led, hands bound, down the drawbridge and out into the yard. Twenty Blue Haven soldiers walked solemnly toward the gallows, sharing their demise with one more prisoner of war—the bent and hobbling stature of Rastus Cubbins. Numerous soldiers followed along, as well as the queen and royal family. Leading them all was Cobblestone's new Steward, Matthew Lohr. Word had gotten out through the streets of town about the change of leadership. All stood at attention to hear his words.

When the group reached their destination, the steward addressed the crowd.

"My people! I, Steward of Cobblestone, stand humbled by our queen's generosity, offering me opportunity to serve as temporary leader of our fair city. Rest assured, I do not carry this oath lightly. I stand tall to its challenges."

Matthew continued to talk as he paced in front of his listening crowd.

"Today, fellow citizens, it pains me to deliver my first order of business as Steward of Cobblestone." He cast a glance over his shoulder at the twenty-one hooded men, chained and tied.

"As you all know, treason is an offense punishable by death. These twenty-one men infiltrated our castle walls and helped the evil of Malus of Blue Haven manifest itself within our walls!"

The crowd roared in anger. "Death to them!" many shouted.

"I have pondered their demise in these past two weeks. I have laid awake at night, struggling to find proper judgment to impose. Last night …"

He paused, waiting for total and complete attention from the crowd.

"Last night, people—I read the book written by our forefathers—kings of old. The book is called *The Fall of the House of Romb*. Within its pages I have read words describing why and how Cobblestone took Blue Haven by force, so many, many years ago. I fear that few who now hear my words have studied this scripture. I worry that few will understand my reasoning today. I will do my best to convey my thoughts as I stand before you."

By now, the crowd was exchanging puzzled glances, and Dominick Sebastian stood along side the queen, hearing every word.

Matthew turned to the hooded men, then to his captains. "Remove their hoods!" he shouted.

"Making a decision such as mine today has been a terrible burden. I feel it is a curse—this judging the fate of another. In my doing so, I consulted yet another book."

From within his pocket, he pulled a tiny leather-bound book. It was his personal Bible.

Tiny murmurs hummed through the crowd as Matthew continued his speech.

"Prisoners of war—I ask you to look me in the eye. I hold the power to end your life, right here and now. Yet, somehow I feel compassion for your souls. You were all deceived. I have read the passages … I now know why Cobblestone took Blue Haven by force. It is all right here."

The Steward was approached by one of his captains who held a large leather volume in his hands. Matthew took the book and held it out before his audience of townspeople and prisoners.

"Decades ago, our forefathers took Blue Haven by force, conquering its army by hand combat. There was a reason few now remember."

He held the book high for all to see. "These pages tell of the Red Devil Ships sailing into the harbors of Blue Haven. These greedy pirates were taking over that city by the hundreds. Untold crimes were being committed in the streets of Blue Haven, unchallenged by the city's fearing army. Its failing Kingship was joining forces with Red Devil Pirates, allowing hideous pillaging to take place as far west as Cobblestone and far sections of the Deep Forest."

The crowd was astonished with the story being told in the courtyard. Even the queen listened intently.

"I shall not tell the whole story here, but it is paramount to me that you twenty men of Blue Haven know that we took your city out of the greater good. Whether you believe it or not is your decision. But my decision is what counts today, men of Blue Haven."

He paused, looking each on in the eye. "Men, I ask you this. Has your city not been allowed to live freely and happily? I ask you, have your halls not been protected by both your army and ours? Has life in Blue Haven not been safe and sound with our watchful leadership? We have left you to live your lives as Blue Haven citizens, not some belittled beggars in a land of filth."

With each passing word, his temper seemed to rise. Matthew paced eye to eye with each man, now petrified with each new word unleashed by the steward.

"It is we, the realm of Cobblestone, that has given you freedom!"

Another roar of enthusiasm boomed from the crowd.

"But alas," Matthew calmed his words. "I shall not bow down with the likes of Malus of Blue Haven. I shall not take part in the hypocrisy of dealing death and judgment like that foul soul that shared our halls. *This* book has taught me that."

Matthew pulled his Bible close to his face, eyes closed, kissing its cover. He looked to his Cobblestone soldiers.

"Unchain these twenty men."

Gasps ripped through the crowd.

Rastus Cubbins stood, still chained and bound, his black hood laying at his feet.

Matthew walked deliberately to one of the Blue Haven men and handed him his copy of *The Fall of the House of Romb.*

Dumbfounded, the man accepted the offering.

Matthew shouted aloud. "I, Steward of Cobblestone, release you from our bond."

A wave of relief passed through the Blue Haven men, as the citizens of Cobblestone stood aghast. *What was happening here?*

"Men," continued Matthew, "for your freedom, I present a request. Go back to your city. Tell of our deeds here today. Study this book. Soon, I will arrange a meeting with those in your command. We will discuss the contents of this book, and create a new goal for us all. We will restore a raven path and communicate as we did in days of old. Soon, we will hold the most important council we have ever held. It will be the Council of Three Cities, and all will join in and take part."

Confusion still stirred in the minds of all present. *Three Cities? What was the third?*

Matthew could tell that he had the full attention of all present. "Yes, three cities, my friends. We cannot forget our dear friends in Tal Kator. To them, we owe a debt of gratitude."

It was all starting to come together.

"We three cities can all live together in harmony. It only takes communication and compassion. We all possess those qualities."

As Matthews words settled in, a string of horses were led into the courtyard and offered to the freed New Haven men.

"Ride, men. Ride on to your freedom. Share our words with the city of Blue Haven."

The row of twenty men stood bewildered. They had come inches from certain death and been handed the keys to a better life for three different cities. With a bow of their head in thanks, twenty horses galloped away into the forest.

With those twenty gone from view, one more soul stood helplessly before the gallows, trembling, now in tears.

"Rastus Cubbins!" Matthew shouted. "You stand charged with treason, as well. How do you plead?" His words stabbed at Rat like needles.

"I … uh … I don't rightly know, I don't."

"That is no answer, Rastus of Blue Haven. You perhaps have created more havoc than any soul still left living in the wake of this disaster. How do you plead?"

"I…I'm sorry, I am," Rat cried, tears falling like rain. "I didn't know, I didn't."

"And yet you killed a man in the halls of our castle."

Rat's head sank even farther. When he looked up into Matthew's eyes, he spoke. "For that—I am guilty. And I reckon I'd do it again, I would. I am guilty."

Matthew spoke again, "I, too, find you guilty, Rastus Cubbins, of both treason and of murder."

The crowd gasped yet again, feeling sorry for the bent little man standing alone by the gallows. Most had heard the story of what had happened in the halls of the castle and in the fens of the Deep Forest. Most knew of his plight.

"I, Steward of Cobblestone, now sentence you."

Rat nodded, understanding the weight of his words. He stood up straight, bending himself painfully, and steadied himself for the steward's next sentence. Tears of sorrow dripped from his face.

"I sentence Rastus Cubbins to a life of incarceration in Cobblestone Castle."

Rat's posture crumpled back to its original form, bent and saddened. But Matthew's next words were quite unexpected.

"You will be under my watchful eye, and you will be sentenced to work within the castle walls. You, Rastus, will be my personal assistant. You will not be jailed. You have merely gained a new home. You are now a man of Cobblestone."

Rastus collapsed to his knees in prayer.

34

year after the occurrences in the courtyard, the Council of Three Cities took place. A vast array of men from Blue Haven and Cobblestone gathered inside Cobblestone Castle. A number of their leafy friends were on hand as well.

The Raven Routes were reinstalled and all three cities continued to communicate for decades to come. Little by little, though, the cities of man slowly forgot about their dear leafy friends of the forest. The Leaflings rather liked the confines of the woods, the city families preferred the townships over the woodland realm. When necessary, the two would join forces to protect their borders, but by and large, both species lived out their merry lives as they would, leaving the other to do the same.

For many years, though, two special Leaflings made the journey to Cobblestone Castle to play with their dear friend. Molly, the rabbit, made many trips to and from the castle courtyard with her two little buddies in tow. Many days and many songs were enjoyed during their long friendship with Gwen. Kimbli and Tally spent many nights listening to Gwen's lovely songs drifting out across the castle courtyard meadow. No better version of Gwendolyn's song was ever sung than by her graceful lips, high in the castle overlooking Cobblestone's graveyard where her father was buried. *Eternal Zephyrs of Summers Eve…*

Less than a decade after the horrendous ordeal with Malus, young Malcolm came of age. On the eve of his eighteenth birthday, he was crowned King in front of hundreds of townspeople. Unbeknown to most, hundreds of little Leafling eyes saw it take place as well—a proud reminder of days long gone. His days as King were peaceful and caring. He was a fair and just king.

Queen Guinevere lived the rest of her life spending more time with family and friends than governing the city. Her near-death experience had drawn her closer to her family than ever before, and even Jon became dear to her. She led a rich life to the end of her days.

Father Jon maintained his post as High Elder of Cobblestone Abbey. In a selfless act of kindness, he relinquished his ring back to Tal Kator. Those rings had caused so much death and destruction during their time in the abbey that their rejuvenating source of life just didn't seem worthy of their paid price of lives lost. Jon happily gave his ring back to the Leaflings to hang with the rest of the Amethyst rings in the mighty caverns behind the Miraré Falls of Tal Kator. And after all, he had no finger on which to wear it.

Dominick Sebastian returned to his post as Steward of Stone Castle. He and his wife cared for the glorious castle once restored by their close friend, King Lawrence. He and Steward Matthew Lohr remained close friends as long as they lived, ever fighting for what was right for Cobblestone.

Rastus Cubbins lived happier in the halls of Cobblestone Castle than ever before. His incarceration was more a formality than an actual sentence. His work in the halls of the castle brought him confidence and a sense of pride he had never experienced. In his elder days, he retired to a humble home on the outskirts of town, where he truly became a man of Cobblestone.

And old Cah…

Well, he lived to be a right jolly old bird. His jet black feathers grew gray with age, and his chubby old body still carried a few messages until his dying days. Traces of his royal lineage linger to this day in the ravens of the world who were once much, much prouder in those glory years as Tower Ravens of Cobblestone Castle.

In those days of the House of Lawrence, King of Cobblestone, life carried on with a harmony unsurpassed. Perhaps some place in this world there are still weathered cobblestone streets that once carried hooves and feet, leaves and limbs, and special people lived special lives.

And in that special place, Eternal Zephyrs still blow.

www.ingramcontent.com/pod-product-compliance
Lightning Source LLC
Chambersburg PA
CBHW020530310726
48979CB00014B/2275/J

* 9 7 8 1 6 0 4 1 4 2 1 9 8 *